STALKED BY TERROR

The mist I had noticed from my bedroom window, rising in wisps from the river gorge, had thickened, partly obscuring my way as I headed down toward the River Walk.

Where was I going? And why? I hardly knew. It was almost as if my feet had a life of their own. I had no choice, it seemed, and yet I felt no fear — until I reached the bend of the track close to the cliff edge where Harriet had almost met her end and Miss Inglewood and Ishbel had most certainly met theirs.

From out of the murkiness, muffled voices emerged. It was impossible to tell where they came from, or what they were saying, but it was clear to me that they spoke in anger. There was danger here, and it loomed ever closer.

In the damp iciness, I pulled the edges of my cloak about me. I turned around, ready to escape back to the house, but the fog had come in full force and I did not know which way to go.

Keenly aware that one step in the wrong direction might send me over the cliff edge into the swirling pool below, I took slow, careful steps, advancing inch by inch, only to catch my foot on a sharply projecting root. I fell forward, toppling down into a dark void, unable even to scream. . . .

A Memorable Collection of Regency Romances

BY ANTHEA MALCOLM AND VALERIE KING

VIVIEN FISKE WAKE

THE SECRET SHADOWS OF RAVENSFALL

ZEBRA BOOKS
KENSINGTON PUBLISHING CORP.

For all my friends and colleagues at
D. Russell Parks Junior High School
in Fullerton, California and
Wanganui High School in
Wanganui, New Zealand.

ZEBRA BOOKS

are published by

Kensington Publishing Corp.
475 Park Avenue South
New York, NY 10016

First printing: August, 1992

Printed in the United States of America

Prologue

Ravensfall
May 1904

I am dreadfully afraid. I have crouched here all day, waiting desperately for help; nursing my injured foot, gazing through my window at driving rain over the flooded river.

Will they reach me in time?

No canoe, no craft of any kind can make its way on such a river. They will have to struggle through miles of rain-drenched bush.

Dear God!

From over the river the women wail; wave on wave of shivering sound, sifting through sodden, tangled ferns and trees.

The men will have taken up their burden, bearing it on their shoulders, garlands of green leaves entwined about their heads, hiding their faces, concealing their thoughts.

On the bank opposite, across the chasm containing the swollen waters, a shadow flits between giant tree ferns. A trick of the fading light, I suppose, until the blur emerges and focuses into sharp outline — and there he stands, a malevolent old man; my enemy, my accuser.

He is looking toward my window; I know it — I can almost feel the shafts of his hatred vibrating through the pounding rain.

Is this a deathwatch?

I shudder, thinking of his warning of just the other dawn.

"You are accursed, you and your family . . ." He had whis-

5

pered the words, his ancient tattooed face hovering disembodied through the wreathing mist. ". . . I warned you I warned you . . . and now it is too late. . . ."

Too late. Why did I not pay heed?

Over the river, the women's voices waft upward, echo upon echo. Is it my imagination, but does the still figure opposite stiffen slightly?

What are they doing now, I wonder, with that poor creature they dragged from the river, whose death they blame on me?

Pain shoots through my ankle as I glance behind me at my barricaded door. If only I could escape, but it is impossible and the old man opposite knows it. Is that why, I wonder, he is standing there? Is he waiting for vengeance, payment — *utu*, as these Maoris call it — my life in return for the one who died trying to save me?

Is he waiting, as I am waiting, for the one I fear most to come for me as he has threatened; creeping out of the bush, entering the empty halls, sidling up the stairs to my isolated chamber? Has the old man with his terrible sight already seen my end?

I force myself to take a deep breath and clasp my elbows to control my shivers. Malvina Raven, I tell myself in my mind, you are twenty-four years old and it is time you learned to see things as they are, not as they might be. Have courage! Perhaps help will arrive in time.

What if it does not?

What shall I do?

Outside, the rain dies and the women's voices sound no more. There is a terrible silence.

Beyond my door, floorboards creak in the hall and there is a soft scuffling.

I take another deep breath and seize a pen. I will occupy the hours, I think — and steady my nerves — by writing down all that has happened to me.

I look out my window.

In the dimming light, the old man still waits.

One

"Ma'am, I believe you dropped this?"

He towered over me, clearing my five feet ten by at least six inches; broad shouldered, too, his gray worsted waistcoat stretching across a gigantic chest.

A little dizzy, I peered up through my pince-nez at a wonderfully ugly face topped by grizzled copper-brown hair.

"Your handkerchief, ma'am; you dropped it by the receptionist's desk." The voice was deep — almost a bass — and slow, with broad, flat vowels and soft, unclipped consonants.

"You are an American!"

With a crooked grin, he asked, "That's an accusation?"

"Of course not!" In my agitation, my pince-nez, as usual, slipped down my nose and I found myself gazing shortsightedly up into a pair of sleepy, hazel eyes spaced by a crooked, once-broken nose.

"It's just . . ." I cast about for something to say, covering my confusion by accepting my errant handkerchief from strong, brown fingers. "It's just that New Zealand is so isolated; I hardly thought. . ."

"To meet one of our rare breed?" A soft laugh; the broad chest quivering with the rumblings of a distant volcano. "I assure you, ma'am, that this little country is well traveled by some of my richer countrymen; especially those in search of solitude amid beauty. But from your accent, you are no New Zealander, yourself?"

"No. I'm from England, although . . ."

"Papa!"

The word pronounced American fashion, with no stress on

7

the second syllable, issued from a young girl of fourteen or so, standing in the stairwell above us. Slender and mercurial, all gangling arms and legs, her relationship to the man beside me displayed itself in her rich copper hair that tumbled over the ruched shoulders of her dark-blue woolen overcoat.

"Papa, you promised." A narrow, booted foot tapped impatiently at the stair. "You know you did!" A pale triangular face turned from the huge American to glance disapprovingly at me, the slanting eyes—more amber than hazel—to my surprise, were filled with animosity.

Her father was unperturbed. "I was just coming to fetch you, honey!" A rueful smile at me. "She is in need, or so she tells me, of some feminine fripperies. . . ."

"Not fripperies, Papa!" The pointed chin was raised imperiously; the amber eyes flashed. "Slippers—dancing slippers—for Betsy Turner's birthday party!"

"Of course, sweetheart!" A hint of a smile before the huge man turned again to me. "I'm afraid you will have to excuse me—Miss . . . ?" He glanced down at the monogrammed handkerchief still dangling from my fingers. "Miss H.?"

I opened my mouth to explain but before I could voice the words, he grinned and turned away. "Come, Miranda!"

The young girl glanced at me slyly as she passed by and I was again aware of the enmity in her amber eyes.

Upstairs in my room, I crossed to the open window and looked down into a street busy with carts and horses and late-afternoon shoppers scurrying along under corrugated iron canopies arching out from cream-painted, wooden colonial buildings.

Wanganui, again, I thought, and then murmured the soft syllables aloud—Wang-a-nu-ee; the home of my girlhood. Had I been wise to return?

I glanced down at the handkerchief I still held and gently touched the embroidered H, remembering the occasion when Harriet, my stepmother, had given it to me, just five days before I had left England.

She had stood in my bedroom doorway, shaking her head

8

over the pile of handkerchiefs she held. "The seamstress completely misunderstood my order, I'm afraid, Malvina, but there's not enough time to embroider more!"

She crossed to the steamer trunk I was packing and placing the handkerchiefs on a pile of freshly laundered linen, turned toward me with a sigh. "How I am going to miss you—I swear if it were not for the twins, I would insist on accompanying you!"

Pausing a moment, she gazed out my window at our rugged Yorkshire moors. "Malvina, I love this place and have done ever since we came back to England . . . but, it's as your father once said to me—that there is something about New Zealand, that once seen, sends out a call . . ."

She grinned up at me, her elfin grin. "How ridiculous that sounds, especially from your practical father! But it is true. Sometimes, in my dreams, I find myself sailing again up the river, wandering through the bush, exploring the old house—why, sweetheart, whatever is the matter?"

Too late I tried to repress a shudder and rearrange my features.

"What is it, Malvina? Come . . ." she sank onto my bed and with one small hand, pulled me down beside her.

"Nothing, Etta. Really, nothing!"

Desperately, I tried to banish from my mind the pictures she had conjured up—the misty river, the thick, tangled forest . . . bush, they call it in New Zealand . . . and the house—That house—with its dark hallways and haunted, silent rooms, where in my nightmares, I still saw . . .

"Malvina!" Worried hazel eyes peered up at me. "You are hiding something. . . ."

I made myself smile. "Of course not, whatever would I want to hide from you! It's just the jim-jams, nothing more—mere nerves, I assure you, at the thought of being on my own . . . and the homesickness I know I shall feel, when I am away from all of you!"

This last, at least was true, I told myself, looking fondly at my little stepmother. How brave she had been, taking on my father—and in such circumstances—with my brother, Reginald and me! And now with her own brood to cope with . . .

9

My ears were firmly seized and my head pulled down.

"Shame on you, Malvina! Stop trying to bamboozle me!"

"Really, Etta, it's nothing!"

I tried to laugh. How could I tell her the real reason behind my journey to New Zealand? She and Papa would never have let me go.

I was no match for my tiny stepmother. "It's Ishbel, isn't it? Your nightmares about her and Callum have returned? Yes—I can see it in your face! Oh, my dear, I blame myself—but with all the worry over the twins, not to mention Mark's breaking his leg and Ariadne's measles . . . and . . ."

"My brother Reggie's high jinks at Oxford!" I finished for her, clasping her hands and sighing with relief; she had not, after all, divined the whole truth. "Please, you must not distress yourself so, overburdened as you are with all of our problems. And really, dearest Stepmama, at twenty-four years old I am a woman grown; in fact, if poor, dear Edward had not been killed at Mafeking, I should be a married woman by now and off your hands altogether!"

"Oh, Malvina, really . . ."

What my stepmother would have said, was interrupted by the abrupt appearance of the twins' nanny to report that they had caught Ariadne's measles.

What would have happened, I wonder now, if Harriet had managed to pry the truth out of me? Certainly, she would never have let me leave for New Zealand—and if I had not gone to New Zealand, at least one life might have been saved.

Perhaps I felt a forewarning on that April afternoon as I looked down from my hotel window, for I remember shivering at the thought that for the first time in my life, I was completely alone and it was only then, I think, that I realized the enormity of the task I had undertaken.

From the hall outside my room the hotel gong clamored, announcing high tea. Quickly I splashed some water on my face at the marble-topped washstand and taking out a comb, attempted to tidy my straight fair hair that I had plaited into a chignon at the back of my head. As usual, fine wisps had escaped and I thought again how marvelous it would be to have thick, curly hair like Harriet's. But I had taken after my mother — in more ways than one, I thought, as I glanced at her photograph on the dressing table. Although I had inherited my father's height, having sprung up "like an ash tree," Harriet had once said, between my twelfth and fourteenth years, I had my mother's long, narrow bones and oval face. I also had her large blue eyes, but she had not been shortsighted.

Adjusting my pince-nez upon my nose, I picked up the photograph for a moment. Although I could not imagine my life without my clever, loving little stepmother, there were still times when I looked at my mother's likeness with a wild longing. She had died when I was ten, yet I still remembered the cool touch of her long fingers checking my forehead for a fever, her bright smile as she tucked me down for the night, and her gentle voice bidding me to sleep well.

I still remembered her and I resented bitterly the tragic circumstances of her death — and the horror that had happened afterward from which Harriet had rescued us.

I thought of Harriet now, how when I was younger, she had held me in her arms after one of my nightmares.

"Come now, sweetheart, it's all over. Your mother has gone to a better place where there is no sorrow and Ishbel. . . ."

"Ishbel!"

"And Ishbel, too; for she was insane and Callum also, I expect . . . they were mad and mad people are not responsible for their actions, you know."

"They were evil!"

Harriet looked at me for a long moment. "Perhaps. How can we tell? But it's all over; you must let them go. Ishbel is dead — you saw her drown, didn't you, from the cliff above the river? And Callum is dead, too. You remember the letter we received from the police in New Zealand — that he had fallen in the Wanganui River when he was trying to escape and that his body must have been swept out to sea? It's all over, Malvina, they can no longer hurt you. You must get them out of your mind, my dear — you must let them go; now promise me!"

The gong sounded again outside my door, recalling me to the present.

Hurriedly, I repinned the cameo at my throat, Harriet's last words still resounding in my mind — "You must let them go!" And of course, I had promised her that I should. "Let them go, let them go," I told myself fiercely, as in my mind I saw Ishbel's long, red hair entangled in the reeds and Callum's blue-green eyes glinting from the bushes at the water's edge. . . . Truly, I had tried, but I had reckoned without those tangled, horribly real nightmares that had invaded my sleep, causing me to wake up screaming.

Finally, unwilling to let Harriet or my father know that my problem still existed — somehow, this became a matter of pride to me — I told them that I had been invited to a house party in the Lake District and instead, sneaked off to a specialist in London's prestigious Harley Street.

He was an older man, with a circlet of silver hair around a marble dome, a walrus mustache, and a full spade beard.

"Miss Raven," sleepy, pale blue eyes regarded me from behind gold, wire-rimmed spectacles. Pudgy fingers entwined themselves across a Harris tweed waistcoat. "You must be more specific. You have nightmares — yes? And Ishbel and . . . er . . . Callum? . . . figure prominently? Ishbel was your half-sister, I collect, but was she your father's or your mother's child? And who exactly was Callum?"

The pale blue eyes, suddenly no longer sleepy, twinkled at me. "Miss Raven, please feel free to talk with me; I am not your judge, after all, just the person you have selected to hear your problems!"

I took a deep breath and tried to organize my thoughts.

"Relax, Miss Raven. Whatever my appearance, I am not an old ogre! Let us start with your half-sister. . . ."

I began hesitantly, trying to keep to the straight facts. "Ishbel — baptized Isobel, but because she was born in the Scottish Hebrides, she was always called by her highland name — was my mother's child by her first marriage to James McCleod. Unfortunately, my mother did not know that Mister McCleod was . . . was insane. And afterward — after he had killed himself in a mental asylum to which she had had him committed — she did not realize that Ishbel had inherited the malady. . . ."

12

I found my fingers twisting my handkerchief and took another deep breath.

He coughed politely. "Did not realize or did not want to recognize?" his words were soft and his pale blue eyes gentle.

"I . . . I don't know . . . it's just that when I was small — Ishbel was always . . . always what she called playing tricks on me and Reggie — my younger brother, you understand?"

"I understand. And your mother? What did she say when Ishbel 'played her tricks'?"

"Well, usually she did not know, because Ishbel would tell us that if we told . . . But sometimes Mama would gather us to her and explain that poor Ishbel was very sensitive because her papa was dead and her mama (our mama) had married again. . . ."

"Ishbel was jealous, then — of you, of your brother, of the happiness you enjoyed with your mother?"

I looked at him in surprise. "Yes . . . yes, I suppose she was . . . but there was more than that. I overheard Mama talking to my father once and it seems that Ishbel had resented Mama committing James McCleod to a mental asylum and blamed Mama for his death. . . ."

I paused a moment, hardly knowing how to continue.

He coughed delicately. "And so, Ishbel put an overdose of laudanum into your mother's medicine — and your father was accused of her murder?"

"Yes — but, that is . . ."

"Your father was not convicted for lack of evidence and to avoid gossip, he took you all to" — he paused as he glanced down at my letter — "Ravensfall. Your family property in New Zealand?"

I gazed up at him, distraught. "Yes . . . but . . . but . . . Miss Inglewood. . . ."

"Ah, the governess your father engaged to go with the family to New Zealand and whom Ishbel pushed into the Wanganui River?"

"Yes, she looked very much like my mother, you see and Ishbel thought that Miss Inglewood and Papa . . . would . . ."

"Hmm — I see. And Callum, who was he?"

"Oh, Ishbel's half-brother. Mr. McCleod, you see, before he

married my mother had . . . that is to say . . ."

His eyes held a faint twinkle. "Callum was illegitimate? Of course, I see. And even though your father took him in, he remained the support of Ishbel—for, of course, they—both Ishbel and Callum—had inherited James McCleod's malady. . . ."

All of a sudden, his pale eyes lost their smile and looked toward me thoughtfully. "Miss Raven, both Ishbel and Callum are dead long since. Why do you allow them to haunt you?"

"But I don't! It's just that in my sleep . . ."

"Precisely, Miss Raven; in this life, there are the hunters and the hunted—and it's our choice whether we be of one or the other. . . ."

"Sir, I don't understand!"

"Do you not?"

The pudgy fingers disentwined themselves to adjust to the gold, wire-rimmed spectacles. Behind the spectacles, his pale blue eyes gazed at me, enlarged, unblinking. "Miss Raven, you feel guilty, do you not, for your mother's death—for the death of your governess?"

"No, of course not . . . I could not help it . . . I really could not help it. . . . It was Ishbel—I tried to warn them—I really did. . . ."

To my horror, I felt hot tears coursing down my cheeks.

"But your warnings were ineffective, weren't they? Why did you not say 'Ishbel did this and that. . . .' Why did you not cling onto their skirts, cry, scream, shriek—anything—until they listened to you?"

"I . . . I . . . did the best I could—I was only ten years old!"

Through the spectacles, his eyes beamed at me, pale, cold.

"It was my kitten . . . in its death throws and hanging only by its tail . . . and Reggie's little dog . . . poor little Rogue . . . and . . . other things. . . ."

Through the thick lenses, his eyes appeared huge, cold, utterly relentless.

"So, Miss Raven, you have become one of 'the hunted.' "

"No . . . no. . . ."

In your nightmare, are you always running from Ishbel, from Callum? Do they pop out at you from odd corners, their maniacal faces screaming silently from behind skeletal fingers?"

"Please . . . oh, please!"

"And what do you do, Miss Raven? Do you stand and face them or do you retreat . . . backward, perhaps to the edge of a sharp cliff, a black chasm yawning below?"

I tried to pull my wits together. "Yes . . . sometimes . . . but how do you know?"

"How do I know?" For the first time, the pale eyes softened. "The phenomenon is common enough."

There was a short silence. Under that considering gaze, I began to feel like a pinned butterfly.

"And yet you do not lack courage or initiative — as evidence, this visit to me, without it would seem, the knowledge of those most concerned about you. . . ."

He held up a pudgy hand. "No, do not speak. You have allowed yourself to become one of the hunted, Miss Raven!"

"No . . . yes . . . that is . . ."

"In effect, Miss Raven, there is hope!"

"Hope?"

"Indeed, yes. Your stepmother was right. Ishbel and Callum no longer exist, save only in your mind — and it is your mind, as you well know, my dear, over which only you have control. But the mind is strange — it accepts ideas readily, but does not as easily reject them, especially if there is great emotion, such as fear involved.

He again adjusted the spectacles and his blue eyes gazed at me magnified. "Your mind, Miss Raven, needs to be reeducated. Consciously, you know that Ishbel and Callum are no more but you are still in such a state of tense anxiety that your mind refuses to accept the reality. Miss Raven, to prove to your conscious self and therefore to your mind that Ishbel and Callum no longer exist, you must return to Ravensfall.

"Return to Ravensfall?"

"Yes, my dear. You must return there to prove to your mind that your unfortunate half-sister and her scheming companion, have truly gone. You need to pace the halls, to traverse the rooms to . . . to . . . explore the attics, to prove to your subcon-

15

scious — that lively imagination of yours that brings about your nightmares — that Ravensfall is truly empty, that Ishbel and Callum have gone forever and have no business interrupting your dreams!"

"But . . ."

He had smiled at me and patted my hand. "It is time, Miss Raven, that you became one of the hunters! Go back to Ravensfall, my dear. Have courage!"

Have courage, I thought, my soul shriveling, wishing for the thousandth time that I were more like Harriet, who at an age younger that I, had sailed off to fend her way as governess in a distant, unknown land and had ended up successfully battling my murderous half-sister Ishbel on the banks of a wildly flooding river.

Oh, to be like Harriet! But I was not. I was Malvina Raven, afraid of shadows. Always afraid of that which seemed to flicker beyond the peripheral vision of my eyes. Sometimes, indeed, I wondered, if like Ishbel, I were going . . ."

"Miss Raven!"

I looked up with a start, into now earnest blue eyes. "Your half-sister, Ishbel McCleod, was insane, but you are not. It was from her father Ishbel inherited her malady, but you, my dear, and your brother, Reginald, are quite safe; please believe me!"

Under that intense gaze, what could I do but nod my head?

And so, my dear, you will go to your Ravensfall, will you not — and look your nightmares in the face and let your mind see them for what they are . . . mere fantasies?"

I found myself nodding in agreement.

There was a slight pause, and then he frowned thoughtfully. "You will not, of course, be going alone? Your stepmother? A relative? A companion of some sort? You should, you know, have someone in whom you can confide your thoughts — share your anxieties, as it were. . . ."

"Not my stepmother — not Harriet — she has had enough to do, sorting out our family problems!"

"But surely she will want to know why you wish to return to New Zealand?"

"Oh, I shall tell her — and it's the truth, after all! — that for some time, I've longed to go back . . . to see again — oh, I don't know — it's just . . . well, not all my memories are awful ones, you know!"

I thought for a moment of snowcapped mountains, wild, tangled bush and the haunting call of birds never heard in England.

"In any event, I am sure my friend Julia Hall will go with me — she's been at me for ages to go back and take her with me. And Harriet will be easy about us going, for Ravensfall is not empty. Some of my father's Canadian cousins are staying there for a few months. . . ."

He nodded approvingly. "In that case, my dear young lady, I shall entertain no anxieties regarding you!"

Reaching across his desk, he picked up his pen. "I shall, however, prescribe a soothing draught that you must take in warm milk at bedtime every evening until you arrive at . . . let me see . . . Wanganui?"

He smiled as he peered at me over the tops of his spectacles but his eyes were serious. "Please note, my dear young lady, that I say until your arrival. The draught which is strong, will for a time numb your mind and chase away the nightmares, but eventually, it will lose its efficacy and you will dream again. . . ."

There was another pause while he dipped his pen into the inkwell before writing the prescription. He looked up at long last. "In any event, I should not want you to become dependent on the medicine."

He studied me in silence for a long moment and then smiled slightly as if satisfied with what he saw. "You have strength, my dear, perhaps more strength than you know. I have the greatest confidence that you will track down your nightmares and dispose of them for once and for all."

He blotted the paper, folded it, and handed it to me decisively. "And after all, you will have another young lady with you, will you not? I suspect, that in the end, you will both enjoy a pleasant holiday!"

Faced with such confidence, I found myself smiling in agreement.

But in the end, of course, at the last possible moment before sailing, poor Julia had fallen off her hunter and fractured her leg, leaving me to face New Zealand — and Ravensfall — alone.

Giving a final twitch to my long black poplin skirt and pulling at the cuffs on my white grosgrain blouse, I took a deep breath and sailed at last out of my room.

The heavy plush curtains were already drawn against the evening and the hall was dark, lit only with the flickering gas bulbs in their sconces at the turn of the corridor.

Perhaps, because of this, the late afternoon sunlight seeping through an opening door, seemed bright to my weak eyes and the rangy, masculine figure looming in the opening appeared no more than a silhouette with no distinguishing features.

"Excuse me, madame!"

The voice, a pleasant tenor, was redolent with a foreign accent. French, perhaps?"

In my confusion, my pince-nez slipped as usual from my nose, leaving my face bare to the setting rays of the sun beaming from the window in the room behind.

Conversely, the features of the man facing me were totally obscure, a dark enigma with the rays of the setting sun shining in a sort of nimbus playing about his head.

"But we have met before, have we not?"

The voice was gentle, playful even; a tremor of laughter in it somewhere.

"Have we, sir?" That voice, I wondered, where had I heard it before? I looked up at him doubtfully, shielding my eyes against the glare. "I don't believe we've met . . . that is to say, I have just arrived from England and . . ."

He laughed brusquely. "Forgive me, a trick of the light, I suppose." The sun was eclipsed as the door shut, leaving me blinking in the sudden darkness.

I readjusted my pince-nez. How odd that the gentleman had closed his door so firmly, for surely he had opened it to venture out . . . What was it, I wondered, that had made him shut his door? Surely not my innocuous self?

Two

"One lump or two?"

Sugar tongs poised, my high tea companion simpered at me from across the table.

"No sugar, please. I prefer my tea without!"

"How sensible, my dear Miss Raven! How I wish that I could . . ." One plump hand waved resignation while the other with unerring ease directed an amber stream from a tilted teapot spout into my waiting cup. "But I am pleased that you accepted my invitation . . . there is nothing so dull as to sit all alone in the dining room of a strange hotel!"

"Thank you, Mrs. Trillingham-Bean. I really appreciate . . ."

Not at all, my dear!" From under heavily folded lids, small brown eyes glinted up at me. "After all, as dear Gervase . . . my son, don't you know . . . says, 'One should not keep entirely within one's shell, one should . . .'"

What one should do was lost suddenly as Mrs. Trillingham-Bean glanced toward the dining room door, where in the aperture loomed the enormous American I had met earlier.

For a moment he looked about the room, pausing suddenly as his gaze came to rest where I was sitting. At first I thought he had recognized me, but then I realized that his eyes were directed at my companion. The pause was so brief as to be scarcely noticeable: the next moment his attention had switched to me and half inclining his head in recognition, he made his way to a table in a far corner, where he was soon joined by his daughter.

19

A titter erupted from Mrs. Trillingham-Bean. "I must say, what a huge man—a walking mountain, one might say." Another titter spilled from behind a plump hand, but the eyes above were watchful. "You are acquainted with him, my dear?"

The tone was abrupt, not so much a polite question as a command to tell all. I had a ridiculous urge to tell her a wild story of secret meetings, but restrained myself in time.

"Not to say, acquainted with him, Mrs. Trillingham-Bean. We just met this afternoon by the reception desk when he was kind enough to return a handkerchief I had dropped."

She smiled wickedly. "Indeed!"

It was quite evident that she did not believe a word.

What was it Harriet always said? 'The best line of defense is to attack' or some such words? "And you, Mrs. Trillingham-Bean? Are you acquainted with the gentleman?"

She raised an eyebrow. "I, Miss Raven?" Then with a considering look, she said, "Of course, dear Gervase and I are well known in society—perhaps the gentleman may have . . . although, I really don't remember. One goes to so many functions, don't you know. And then, of course, dear Gervase and I travel so extensively, perhaps on one of our expeditions . . . Why, only last month we were in Fiji for Gervase's health, you understand. Our specialist in Harley Street insisted that dear Gervase should leave the social whirl and try the quieter clime of the antipodes."

"I . . . I see. . . ."

"But, how I do rattle on, as poor dear Mister Trillingham-Bean—my late husband, don't you know—used to say. Now, how about you, my dear Miss Raven? You are here to visit your childhood home—Ravensfall, was it? What an intriguing name!—where you will stay with some Canadian relatives you have never met? How exciting . . . but here, my dear, is our cottage pie, at last. . . ."

It was only afterward, on leaving the dining room, that I realized that Mrs. Trillingham-Bean had revealed scarcely anything about herself. What, for instance, was she doing, after all her travels, staying in a hotel in Wanganui, New Zealand? And where was dear Gervase?

Three

The hall was dim: the only light now that the evening had drawn in came from flickering gas sconces and an occasional glow from a street lamp through ineptly drawn portieres.

After the coziness of the dining room with its roaring fire and softly tinkling glasses, all seemed dark and dank. I shivered, clutching my arms close, wishing I had brought down a shawl. Yorkshire seemed suddenly very far away and before I could stop myself, I started to think of Harriet, Papa, and the children, wondering what they were all doing and if they missed me as much as I missed them.

"We're going to miss you, sweetheart," Harriet had murmured, drawing me close. "Don't you think that with Julia not being able to go . . ."

To my surprise, it was my father who had backed me up. "Let her go, Harriet. We all have our path to follow and Malvina must follow hers . . . and after all" — he smiled at Harriet, the special smile he always reserved for her — "she will not be alone. Lucy and Clinton will be there and I am sure they will look after her. . . ."

Follow my own path, I thought now, in the darkness of the hall. I shivered — how solitary that sounded — but I knew Papa was right: Here I was, twenty-four years old, and yet I had never broken out of my chrysalis, never really made my own decisions. Even after all the horror with Ishbel and Callum was well and truly over, I had never really felt free. First, there was Papa to please — and Harriet, of course — and as for my engagement to Edward, what had that been really but an agreement to exchange one form of protection for another?

"Ravensfall. . . ." The word, a merest whisper, sifted so subtly through the shadows that for a moment I wondered if I were dreaming.

"Ravensfall." The word again emerged from a sea of whispers issuing, it seemed to me, from a partly opened doorway down the corridor to my right.

Almost without thinking I began drifting down the corridor, eventually finding myself standing outside the door, my ear straining to hear I knew not what.

I heard masculine voices and through the crack in the partially opened door, I glimpsed hands and papers scattered over a green baize-covered table.

Masculine voices and the whiff of a pungent cigar.

"Ravensfall," I heard again, and then, "but the Maoris . . ." and a rumble of laughter.

"Not to worry, we have young . . ."

There was a clink, as of a glass overturning, and a muffled curse. Then a shuffling of feet and a shifting of chairs.

The door opened further and I fled up the passage straight into what seemed to be a huge feather bolster.

A pair of arms encased me. A finger tilted up my chin.

"Ah . . . Miss H.?"

I pried myself loose.

"The same, sir . . . that is, I am not of course Miss H.," I stammered.

"Of course not. That much I realized!"

The American's tone was light, joking even, but his words were like daggers. "Now, don't tell me, if you are not Miss H., then you must be Miss Malvina Raven!"

"Yes, of course—but, how did you . . . ?"

With a quirked eyebrow and a turned-down mouth, he exclaimed, "How indeed, but your trunk, my dear Miss Raven, the luggage label plain for all to see when it arrived late this afternoon and the hall porter asking the receptionist for the whereabouts of your room—very clever!"

"I don't understand. . . ."

"Oh, do you not?" Above me the face loomed granite-hard, as the eyes, narrowed to mere slits, peered past me down the hall to the doorway I had just left. The door, now fully open, let out a flood of light into which was stepping the tall, rangy figure of the man I had earlier seen upstairs.

"Ah, so that's the way of it, is it?"

All of a sudden, my temper snapped. "Enough of these innuendoes! I assure you, I have absolutely no idea what you mean — nor do I wish to! I find you, your words, and your tone of voice all utterly offensive. Good day, sir!"

Holding my head high, I stepped swiftly around him and walked, my knees trembling, back up the passage to the stairs.

From behind me came a rumble of laughter. "Oh, bravo! Encore! Encore!"

At the stairs I could not resist turning my head. There, just outside the closed dining-room door across the hall, her head tilted toward the passage I had just left, stood Mrs. Trillingham-Bean.

Upstairs a small fire had been lit in my grate. I drew near it, rubbing my hands. I had forgotten how cold New Zealand could be in winter. It was strange to think that in Yorkshire now, it was spring, the daffodils nodding on the lawn, the snowdrops pushing their tiny, delicate heads through the winter's remaining mold.

My knees were still trembling but I did not want to sit down. Instead, I found myself pacing up and down my room as I had always done when I was upset. What had come over me, I wondered, to have talked in such a way to an unknown gentleman. Although, I allowed with an inner giggle, that knowing or not knowing the gentleman scarcely made things better or worse! Gentleman? I asked myself scornfully. Surely, no gentleman would have talked to me as he had done?

But what had come over me? Me, Malvina Raven, the peacemaker among her brothers and sisters. Malvina the protectress, who never lost her temper — not that I had not wanted to, of course. I remembered, blushing a little, a pummeled pillow or two in the privacy of my room, and once a book thrown at the door after a departing nuisance. Also, I admitted to myself, I sometimes said things in my head that were not . . . well not exactly "ladylike!"

But to say such things out loud! Not that he had not deserved them!

Suddenly I was filled with exhilaration, total euphoria at the realization that I, Malvina Raven — "Mallie the Mouse" as my brother Reggie had once called me — had called the bluff of a . . . a . . . what had Mrs. Trillingham-Bean called him? . . . "a walking mountain"?

Is this what "following my own path" meant? I wondered. The pain of being away from all I loved and yet the freedom of being my true self?

I crossed to the window and pulled the curtain aside, gazing up into a blue-black darkness too early yet to be lit by stars.

"What are you doing here, Malvina Raven?" I whispered at last to myself.

Letting the curtain fall, I drifted back to the fireplace, sinking at last into the low, chintz-covered chair nearby. Why was I there? I asked myself again. To solve the problem of my nightmares — or was there some other deeper reason? Was I without consciously willing it, engaged perhaps on a journey of self-discovery?

"You think too much, Malvina Raven!" The words were so sharp in my head, it was as if they had just been spoken and in my mind, I saw again, Jemima Pruitt, my last governess. "Remember, Malvina, that gentlemen do not appreciate females who think!" She had tossed her pretty blond curls as she spoke and her shrewd, blue eyes — always instantly vapid at the approach of our local curate — had regarded me sharply. "Even with your fortune" — the curls were tossed again as the blue eyes contemptuously studied my long, skinny form — "it will be hard for your parents to find you a husband! Remember, Malvina, you must always be agreeable, refined . . . and *never* venture an opinion!"

As if to prove her point, she had married her curate shortly afterward: he, poor man, becoming vicar of an up-and-coming London parish within the next year.

"Never venture an opinion!" I couldn't help grinning at my recent escapade. What would Miss Pruitt have thought of that? I wondered.

What, indeed, would she have thought of this whole situation? My being approached by a strange man — an American — and then being accused by him of . . . ?

Of what?

I reviewed the afternoon's events and then sat back in my chair, completely mystified.

He had accused me of claiming to be someone I was not!

I shook my head in disbelief. No, no, that was not it! He had accused me of being myself!

But, I was myself. Wasn't I?

Although, after this evening's events, I had certain . . . well . . . questions. . . .

And then, Mrs. Trillingham-Bean? What was her part in all of this?

That she had a part, I had no doubt: her reaction when the American had entered the dining room and then afterward, when I had spied her at the dining room door as I was making my angry way up the stairs.

In the midst of all this, I suddenly realized that I had no clue at all as to the identity of the man she had dubbed "the walking mountain."

Even more intriguing, why should it be so important to him that I should — or should not be — who I was?

Four

Midmorning and heavy clouds clinging desperately to an unruly sky. Stepping out of Foster's Hotel onto Victoria Avenue. I was met by sneaking icy-cold winds and a flurry of raindrops biting into my upturned face.

A southerly, I thought with delight. A true New Zealand southerly, with winds whipping and rain squalling and in the icy-freshness of it all, the cobwebs dashed out of my head.

My gloved hand closed over the letter of introduction, deep within the pocket of my ulster. It was addressed to Messrs. Blankenship, Blankenship, Ogden, and Glenby, the law firm that took care of our family affairs in New Zealand.

Fighting my way against the wind, I arrived finally at the tall, narrow, cream-painted building in its cul-de-sac off Victoria Avenue.

It should have been quiet but was not, the cul-de-sac acting as receptacle rather than hideaway from the tearing maniacal wind that, once caught, fought its way around the little square trying to find an exit.

I pummeled at a blue-painted door with the usual brass plaque announcing the qualifications of those within and — in the tumult, hearing no answer — twisted the brass doorknob and plummeted down two steps, landing in an untidy heap on a rattan mat below.

Above me loomed a shadowy, spindle-legged figure, that struggling with the door, finally pushed it shut.

Total silence.

Then a helpful hand and an inquiring, bewhiskered, elderly face.

I struggled to my feet, abysmally aware of my disordered appearance: my ulster flying open, my windblown hair hanging in a tangled, inglorious mess about my shoulders.

"Miss?"

I asked myself what Harriet would have done, and then, forcing myself not to fuss with my hair or my ulster, I raised my pince-nez, balanced them firmly on my nose, and squinted down into the elderly face.

"Miss Raven," I announced, "to call upon Mister Ogden."

With my free hand, I fished out my card case from my ulster pocket, but before I could pick out a calling card, the dry, old voice asserted itself again.

"Miss Raven, yes? And Miss *Malvina* Raven, no doubt!"

Doubt, in fact, gleamed up at me from the little eyes in the cobweb-lined face; six inches below my own. Doubt and something suspiciously like arrogance.

I delved into my pocket. "I have here a letter to Mister Ogden."

"A letter, yes! And to Mister Ogden! The thin lips parted in a smile of smug triumph. "Well, he's in Fiji, isn't he? Has been for the last three weeks."

To my astonishment, a rheumy eye half winked at me.

"Mister Blankenshhip, then!"

"Ah, well, the elder Mister Blankenship has gone to his reward, hasn't he? These ten years and more. And young Mister Blankenship, he's being tended by his granddaughter, isn't he — after his heart attack?"

I tried to maintain a steely stare. "Mister . . . er . . ." — I glanced at the envelope — ". . . Glenby?"

The old face below me dissolved into a knowing smile. "So, you don't remember Mister Glenby? The gentleman who defended Miss Newcombe, got her off from a murder charge after she'd pushed Miss McCleod into the river?"

Miss Newcombe? Miss McCleod? I thought, my mind racing. Of course, he must mean Harriet, who in those far-off days, before she had married our father, had indeed been Miss Newcombe to Reggie and me. And as for Miss McCleod, he meant, of course, Ishbel, who . . . for an appalled moment, I suddenly remembered with startling clarity. I was twelve years old, entrapped behind an upstairs window, while forced to watch the death struggle between my half-sister and governess on the riverbank below.

"So," the dry, sarcastic voice cut into my thoughts. "You don't remember Mister Jeremy Glenby?"

With an effort, I pulled myself together. "Mister Jeremy Glenby? No . . . no, I . . . that is, my brother, Reginald and I . . . when . . . when it happened, were sent to stay with some of Papa's friends until it was all over. So, of course, I don't remember any of the details. . . ."

"None of the details. No, of course not!" There was another half wink and the thin lips quirked knowingly. "Well, you wouldn't would you — remember any of the details — *because you weren't there, were you?*"

"But, of course I wasn't there — I just told you! That is, I would have been there, but I was sent away. . . ."

"Yes, miss. Exactly!"

I gritted my teeth. "Look, I don't know what this is all about, but I am Malvina Raven and this is a letter from my father, addressed to Mister Ogden."

"But, he isn't here. I told you, miss."

"I — know — that. So, give it to Mister Glenby!"

"He isn't here, either."

A long pause. I took a deep breath. I smiled pleasantly. "No doubt, he is in Outer Mongolia?"

"Beg pardon, miss?"

"Never mind. Perhaps you could give it to him on his return?"

"But, you say the letter is addressed to Mister Ogden."

"Why, so it is! I had quite forgot! But, Mister Ogden, Mister Glenby, the young Mister Blankenship — if, of course, he survives — are all welcome to read the letter; it is, after all, only a letter of introduction. My father addressed it to Mister Ogden, purely because he, in particular, handles our family affairs. . . ."

Out the corner of my eye, the merest flutter, as if of a skirt, as a door — half ajar — started to close.

"So, miss?"

My eye was still on the almost shut door. Someone had been listening to our conversation. Who? Why?

"So? So please give my letter to Mister Ogden upon his return. When does he return, by the way?"

Who can say, miss?" The old eyes gleamed wickedly. "Perhaps one month, perhaps two . . . he is settling the estate of a late client of ours, isn't he?"

"I see. So, please keep this letter until . . ."

The door I was watching closed with a soft click.

Following the direction of my gaze, the old gentleman turned his head. "That'll be young Thomas, won't it? Attending to young Mister Blankenship's papers?" His face, when he turned back to me, was completely expressionless, as closed as the door behind him.

Thomas? I thought, but surely that had been a skirt I had seen? And why had this up-to-now, uncooperative old gentleman, suddenly seen fit to provide me with an explanation?

"Your letter, miss!"

I glanced at the hand held out demandingly and then at the closed door and back again at the expressionless face.

"I believe I shall keep it for the moment."

The expressionless features relapsed into a leer. "Just as you like, miss!" The tone of his voice clearly implied that there was something havey-cavey about my decision.

"What is your name, please?"

"My name! Well, it's Simms, miss — with two m's — Jeremiah. But you wouldn't know, miss, would you, because you've never met me, have you?"

Back at Foster's Hotel, tidying myself for lunch, I tried to untangle the events of the morning.

There had been something particularly insinuating about Simm's last remark, the sarcastic tone of voice implying that if I were indeed who I said I was, that I should certainly know him. And, then again, from the beginning of our strange interview, he had clearly expressed his doubt regarding my identity. On looking back, it was almost as if he had been expecting me — or rather someone claiming to be me. Why, for instance, had he immediately addressed me as Malvina Raven, although I had introduced myself only as Miss Raven?

Frowning, I dragged a wet comb through my impossible hair, in an effort to tame the windblown, flyaway wisps. The huge American, I remembered, had made similar accusations about my identity.

What on earth was going on?

Was the whole thing a coincidence . . . or had the American visited the law offices to reveal his doubts to Jeremiah Simms? But why should he — and how would he know beforehand what I had intended to do?

And then there were those whispers I had overheard about Ravensfall — but surely that must have been a coincidence? Perhaps they were referring to another place of the same name? On the other hand, the American had seemed to be on his way to that room.

I grabbed my hair and started to rebraid it into its usual chignon.

Jeremiah Simms.

It would seem that I should remember him.

I didn't.

It was, after all, at least ten years since we had left New Zealand. So many things had happened since that time and Papa and Harriet had always encouraged Reggie and me to "bury the past" — not realizing, it would seem, that there might be ghosts.

Jeremiah Simms?

A small memory niggled: trees, a misty river, a tall, shadowy shape and through the mist, sunlight glinting . . . sunlight glinting . . . sunlight glinting on of all things . . . "Gig lamps," Reggie had said. . . .

Outside my room, the gong clamored for lunch.

I slipped in my last hairpin. For a change, my chignon looked reasonably secure.

Gig lamps.

The memory tugged. I looked about the room, picking up my abandoned ulster and rescuing Papa's letter of introduction from its pocket.

Gig lamps.

If only I could remember! Remember what — and why was it important? We had kept a gig, of course, for our use at our town house in Wanganui — and I supposed it had lamps, as most gigs did. . . . Shrugging my shoulders over the elusive memory, I gave up, telling myself that if it were really important, then I should recollect whatever it was, later!

Taking Papa's letter, I placed it in my valise with his other letter to his cousins at Ravensfall. Patting down the papers and pressing down the lid, I remembered his voice as he had handed me the envelopes just before I had left. "If you must travel on such short notice, my dear, the best I can manage will be letters of introduction: the journey to New Zealand taking so long . . . approximately three months, as I recall . . . you may as well take the letters with you. That way, both you and the letters should at least arrive at the same time." He had smiled at me then and patted me on the shoulder. "In any event, Malvina, there should be no problems. . . ."

No problems!

Thinking of Jeremiah Simms, I choked back a laugh.

The gong sounded again and I set the valise down on a side table.

At least, Clinton and Lucy — Papa's cousins — would not accuse me of pretending to be myself!

On Papa's advice I had sent a letter to Ravensfall as soon as my ship had docked in Wellington, advising of my arrival. I had explained that I would be spending a few days in Wellington and Wanganui regaining my "land legs" before braving the steamer that would take me up the Wanganui River.

Clinton and Lucy, I thought. How comfortable the names sounded! Especially now, when I felt so very much alone. Of course, Papa and they had never actually met — they were the children of Papa's youngest uncle who in the tradition of younger sons, had left England a generation before to seek his fortune in the colonies. But duty cards were exchanged at Christmas with the usual encapsulated family news; or an infrequent letter detailing some sad event.

It was one of these that Papa had received several months before. Apparently Cousin Lucy, having lost her husband in a train accident and having been greatly injured herself, needed rest and repose in some quiet, remote spot that would hold no painful memories.

Where better than our New Zealand Ravensfall, standing tenantless at the moment?

The request was made and permission granted.

Clinton—who had retired from banking—had, my father told me, agreed to accompany his sister and look after her during her convalescence.

"I must say, my dear," Papa had told me on our last evening together, "that I am glad that Clinton and Lucy will be there. I really could not have countenanced you going alone to an empty Ravensfall." He looked down again at the letter which he had been rereading. "You will be well looked after, I am sure; Cousin Clinton seems a capital sort of fellow. He says here that he is all the more willing to accompany his sister because he likes to paint and that he's heard there is magnificent scenery along our famous river valley—so he's not entirely an old fogy!" Papa looked up again and smiled. "And no doubt, by the time you arrive, Cousin Lucy will be on the mend and able to act as your chaperone . . . so you will have no excuse, my dear, to hide yourself away as usual. . . ."

I looked about my hotel room. Though it was furnished well enough, it seemed bare and impersonal.

Instead of waiting till Friday, I suddenly decided I would take the river steamer the next day. Perhaps my new cousins could help sort out the mystery that seemed to have overtaken me!

It was only later, on the edge of sleep—after sipping my doctor's soothing draught—that I recalled my fugitive memory.

Gig lamps! Of course! Lying there in bed, I stiffened at the recollection: myself and Reggie standing on the misty river landing at Ravensfall, waiting for the steamer to dock and watching two passengers apparently ready to disembark, a shaft of sunlight sifting through the haze and catching the round spectacles of one of the passengers, turning the lenses to disks of flaring gold.

"Gig lamps," Reggie had whispered, giggling. We had been

32

reading Louisa M. Alcott at the time — *The Eight Cousins* — and one of the characters had been nicknamed Gig lamps because of his spectacles.

I had a hazy memory of the man with the spectacles descending the gangplank first, the other, much shorter — and surely wearing an old-fashioned top hat? — following behind. And there had been lollipops, produced surreptitiously from beneath floating coattails.

I almost laughed with relief.

I had no recollection who the man with the spectacles was — one of the elusive Messrs. Blankenship, Blankenship, Ogden or Glenby, no doubt! But the clerk with the lollipops could only have been — unlikely though it seemed after our deadlocked interview — the now irascible Jeremiah Simms.

I wanted to laugh again. I wanted to find Jeremiah Simms to tell him that he could not pretend to be such an old curmudgeon, when I — Malvina Raven — remembered him giving us lollipops!

It was a pity in a way, I thought to myself, turning over sleepily, that there would not be time to see him before I left for Ravensfall in the morning. I would have loved to have seen his face as I imparted the news that I really was who I said I was!

It was only as I was finally drifting into sleep that it occurred to me with a shock that woke me up again, that the mystery of Mr. Simms's attitude and the large — and somewhat unpleasant — American's doubts about me had not been solved. Why should Jeremiah Simms doubt my identity in the first place and what possible interest could the American have in my affairs?

Five

Dawn and a hansom cab—sent for specially by the hotel—from the stand around the corner on Ridgway Street.

Then Hatrick's Wharf and a flood of memories.

So often Reggie and I had stood there, in the half darkness, clasping hands, giving each other courage at the thought of returning to the isolation of Ravensfall . . . and Ishbel. . . .

Ishbel.

Over ten years, and yet standing there by the riverside, nothing seemed to have changed: the motley crowd waiting in the vagrant light; Moutara Gardens sloping up behind, its trees spreading dark shadows, the monument to those fallen at the Battle of Moutoa in the Maori Wars a darker blur and cresting the hill, its outlines scarcely visible, the old courthouse.

Even the sounds were similar, the crowd's quiet murmur, the baaing of sheep waiting to board the steamer docked at the riverside and from upriver a distant chant from the Maori canoes bringing fresh fruit and vegetables down to the market. Any moment now, I thought, I would hear Ishbel's bell-like laugh and see her tall figure, graceful as ever, gliding toward me. . . .

"Stop it!" I told myself sharply. "Stop it at once!"

"Excuse me?"

Embarrassed, I looked down into a rosy face topped by a brown, beribboned hat. "Sorry . . . er . . . just talking to myself!"

The face creased into a smile. "Oh, well, we all do that, don't we?" The voice with its colonial twang was kind. The ribbons nodded toward the river and the side-paddle steamer being

34

loaded at the dock. "She's a good, old girl, the *Waiwere* — always been my favorite. Not that the *Manowai* isn't all right; lovely for excursions and that, but she's so big, a body feels lost on her! Now I always feel at home on the *Waiwere* — perhaps because she's smaller and more . . . more . . ."

"Cozy?"

An answering smile. "Yes, that's it. Cozy — and the lounge they fitted out for us ladies . . . very elegant!"

"Yes, I remember."

"Oh, so you come from around here? I thought — from your accent — you'd just come from 'home'."

I took a deep breath. Harriet had warned me about this. Even after ten years, she had told me, there were bound to be those who would remember bits and pieces of the old scandal and by now, no doubt, the stories would have become exaggerated. "Better to be direct," Harriet had said, "and the less they will have to talk about . . . and if there are any who do not wish to associate with you, my dear, then you are better off without their company!"

I forced myself to smile calmly down into the expectant face. "You are right on both counts. I have just arrived from England and yet I also used to live here; upriver — at Ravensfall."

She frowned faintly. "Ravensfall?" The brow cleared. "Oh, yes, of course, old Josiah Raven's place — your grandad was he? Quite a character he was; I remember my dad talking about his whiskey still in the bush and his deal with Bully Hayes . . . . gunrunning, was it? Whatever it was, my dad told us that the Maoris said there was a curse on the place and that no Pakeha — would ever . . ."

She stopped abruptly, her rosy face turning an even deeper shade of pink. "Please excuse me — I don't know what's come over me, repeating such nonsense and talking like that about your grandfather!"

I couldn't help grinning. "But it's true! Except, of course, Josiah was not my grandfather, but my father's uncle. Papa inherited Ravensfall from him."

The brown ribbons quivered as the head nodded in sudden comprehension. "Oh, yes, I remember now . . . that poor child . . . your sister, was it? I saw her once in Wanganui — such a

35

pretty, young lady, a real beauty! Such a shame that . . . that . . ."

I came to the rescue. "Ishbel was my half-sister. Unfortunately her mind was . . . disturbed. She inherited her malady from her father."

"She flashed a comforting smile. "Oh, well, that was a long time ago, wasn't it? So the old place is to be opened up again?"

"It already has been, really. Some cousins of ours are there. I'm on my way to join them — I'm Malvina Raven."

A gloved hand was held out. "And I'm Nellie Possett; my husband Sam and I live downriver from you — I hope you'll drop by and see us; we like a bit of company. Oh, it looks as if they're ready to board!"

As she spoke, the steamer whistle sounded and the crowd surged forward.

As we passed Hatrick's Wharf with its shadowy tangle of ships, dawn gradually seeped down over the eastern bank, tinting with a roseate glow the shining river waters and cream-painted wooden houses in dwindling rows on the outskirts of town.

Perhaps it was the clear sky and the first rays of the sun — the southerly from the day before having reduced itself to a gusty breeze — but for the first time since my arrival, I began to feel true joy at the sights I recognized from my childhood: the slender, carved Maori canoes skimming downriver, their crews chanting as they slipped under the railway bridge at Aramoho; the shady fronds of tall ponga ferns reaching out from patches of native bush left on the riverbanks, and all along the edges of the banks, the weeping willows planted by the early missionaries, bending gracefully over the flowing water.

"A cup of tea, dear?"

"Why, thank you, Mrs. Possett, that's very kind of you. And now I come to think of it, this is just what I need!"

I gratefully accepted the steaming cup and saucer held out to me, but waved aside the sugar bowl.

The bright eyes twinkled. "I thought you might, but you seemed so lost in a dream, I didn't have the heart to call you away from the rail when morning tea was served. I don't expect you've seen many changes—they tell me that Wanganui stays pretty much the same?"

"Pretty much, except for those wooden blocks they've laid down in Victoria Avenue—what an improvement on the old ruts and potholes; I couldn't get over it yesterday when I got back to my hotel with no mud on my shoes! But as for the river . . ." I glanced back over the rail; the native bush, no longer in patches, now lined the banks with clumps of tall, yellow-white toe-toe grass waving feathery plumes in the breeze. I sipped my tea. ". . . as for the river, nothing seems to have changed—in fact, it's almost as if . . ." Hurriedly, I stopped myself from what I had been going to say . . . "that I felt almost as if I were traveling back in time." What would this practical farmer's wife have thought of such a sentiment? I took another sip of tea, while trying to think of other words to finish my sentence.

I need not have worried; Nellie Possett herself seemed lost in thought, her hat ribbons fluttering in the breeze as she glanced down over the ship's rail at the rippling water. She turned at last to me, her eyes for once without their twinkle. "I'll be getting off any minute now, my dear, so I just thought I'd repeat my invitation—do come and visit us, whenever you have a fancy; it will be lonely for you in the bush. From what you've said, it's your father's cousins, so they'll likely be at least middle-aged—and one of them, an invalid?"

"That's really very kind of you; thank you, Mrs. Possett!"

For a moment, the twinkle returned. "Oh, no it isn't, I really meant it when I said we like a bit of company!" The eyes turned serious again. "But I've been thinking since we came aboard and I just don't like the idea of you away from all your family and friends, all by yourself in that great place in the middle of the bush. Ravensfall is very isolated, you know . . . and . . . and . . . well . . ."

It was obvious that she wanted to warn me about something, but before I could press her, the call came that the steamer was about to heave to and in the ensuing activities, the moment was lost.

On the wooden landing jutting out into the river, Nellie Posset was greeted by a squat, broad-shouldered man, hardly taller than herself. She said something to him and he waved in my direction, raising a broad-brimmed hat to reveal a wide, big-boned face, decorated with a bristling mustache. Sam Possett, I thought to myself; somehow, the name seemed to suit him.

As the steamer drew away offshore, the breeze turned icy and clouds started to gather, dulling the deep greens of the wild tangle of trees and ferns now hemming us in on each side. I knew I ought to seek the comfort of the ladies' lounge, but could not bring myself to face a barrage of politely inquiring eyes. Instead, I stayed at the rail, but my earlier joy was muted. What was the matter with me? I wondered. Was it what Mrs. Possett had said — or rather, what she had not said? Why had she looked so serious? What had she almost told me?

Six

"There we are, miss!"

My cabin trunk was deposited on the wooden landing beside me, followed immediately by my carpetbag, valise, and hat-box.

"Someone meeting you then, miss?"

One of the crewmen a big, wide-shouldered man, turning back from the gangway, looked doubtfully at the dark throng of trees and bushes crowding down to the water's edge.

"No—I'm not expected till Monday. But I'll be all right, thank you; I'll walk up to the house and they'll send someone down for my things."

There was a concerned look on his broad-featured face. "Best if you stay where you are, miss; you don't want to get lost in the bush. The captain will blow the whistle as we pass under the bluff to warn them someone is on the landing—you can't see the house from here: it's at the top of the bluff behind the trees."

I shivered; was it from a sudden cold gust bursting down through the trees—or was it the thought of the house up there on the bluff, in its stark isolation, waiting for me? Another gust buffeted my hat and the thick ship's cloak I used for traveling. The sky, I noted, was now almost completely covered in cloud and my earlier joy seemed to have dissipated with the sunlight. I found myself looking longingly at the steamer. Even now, I thought, it was not too late; I could still reboard. There was a tourist hotel, I remembered, farther up river; perhaps I could stay the night there and return the next day to Wanganui? And then . . . and then . . . what?

All of a sudden my doctor's words flashed into my head and in my mind I saw his pale eyes behind the gold-wired spectacles. "So, Miss Raven, you have become one of the hunted. . . ."

Clasping my cloak firmly about me I raised my head and turned to the patiently waiting crewman. "It's all right. I've been to Ravensfall before. There's a path up through the trees; it starts behind that tree over there." I pointed to a tall, gray-trunked pukatea whose thick, spreading roots had often provided seats for Reggie and me as we waited for the steamer to take us down to Wanganui.

"That's all right then, miss; if you say so . . . look after yourself, then!"

Clearly reluctant to leave me by myself, the burly man trudged back up the gangway, turning to wave as he disappeared under the awning.

Gradually the steamer drew away from the landing and back into midstream. I had been on her decks only a few hours, but I felt as if I were losing a friend. Raising a hand in farewell, I looked almost with envy at the remaining passengers scattered in small groups along the rails. Where were they going? I wondered. To isolated farms or — Wanganui having become famous as the "Rhine of New Zealand" — perhaps some of them were foreign tourists, on a weekend's excursion to the hotel, another three hours' journey upriver? In any event, talking and laughing together as they were, none of them seemed to be as lonely as I felt at that moment.

I was turning away, when my attention was caught by a young girl trying to steady a wobbling cup and saucer as she made her way along the deck. Sure enough, as I watched, she tripped and a nearby group of women backed away to avoid the splattering drops.

I blinked. In the gap momentarily left by the long skirts whirling out of the way of the spilled tea, appeared a familiar, short, stout figure: Mrs. Trillingham-Bean.

It seemed to me that she looked right at me, and yet she gave no hint of recognition. The next moment she turned, and in the confusion of the group of ladies reconvening, disappeared altogether.

I almost rubbed my eyes; I could not believe it — and yet I was sure I had not been mistaken. There was, of course, absolutely no reason why Mrs. Trillingham-Bean should not have been traveling on the *Waiwere* — but how was it that I had not seen her? True, over a hundred passengers had boarded the steamer in Wanganui, but in the hours I had been aboard I had circled the decks so many times, I must surely have seen her — or even more likely, she me, if only because I was so tall! And if she had missed me on deck, she must surely have seen me disembark.

I thought over the incident again; though the glimpse I had had of her had been momentary, it had been obvious from the quick turning away of her head and her prompt scuttling behind the other passengers that she had not wanted to be seen.

Why was she hiding from me? I asked myself in bewilderment. For that matter, I wondered, thinking of her unexpected appearance outside the hotel dining room door two nights before, after my argument with the huge American, why was she apparently trailing my footsteps? What nonsense, I tried to reassure myself! The whole thing was almost certainly just a series of coincidences! I tried to quell my uneasiness as the steamer, reaching the bend in the river, gradually disappeared from view, leaving me alone on the solitary landing.

I had forgotten the silence. Except for the water's gentle lapping and an occasional rustle of leaves from the wild, thick tangle of trees, bushes, and giant feathery ferns scrambling up the steep hillsides, all was quiet.

It suddenly occurred to me that no one who cared about me knew where I was. I listened again to the silence. Anything, I thought, could happen to me and no one would know. Unwelcome memories tugging at my reluctant mind, I glanced unwillingly beyond the landing to the lee of the cliff. There the water was deep and when the river flooded, the current twisted itself into a small whirlpool. It was there, Ishbel used to tell Reggie and me that a taniwha — that mythical, man-eating monster of Maori folklore — used to lie waiting for succulent human flesh. And it was from the cliff top above the pool, when the river had been at the height of its flood, that she had pushed

Miss Inglewood our governess and later had attempted to push Harriet. I started to shiver. For the first time in my life, I felt utterly alone.

A scattering of icy raindrops across my face recalled me to my senses. The clouds, now pewter-colored, were welded in a dark mass overhead, dimming the midafternoon light.

I clasped my cloak around me and looked at my luggage. No doubt someone would come down from the house to fetch it, but in the meantime, I didn't want it to get wet. The cabin trunk would be all right, I knew — Papa had insisted that it be water-proof — but I couldn't possibly move it by myself; I did, however, carry my hatbox and valise over to the shelter of the puketea tree where they would keep reasonably dry under the spreading branches.

Pulling down my hat to shield my face from the now increasing rain, I glanced back one more time at the river and the dark waters of the pool beneath the cliff; then squaring my shoulders, I took up my carpetbag and set off up the steep path to the top of the bluff.

I traveled along the River Walk, as we had called it, trying to avoid mud on my hems by hitching up my skirts in an unlady-like bundle. On one side rose the bush, now dark in the slanting rain, and on the other, all along the edge of the steeply sloping cliff, marched a line of huge tree ferns, planted, so Papa had told us, by Great Uncle Josiah when he had first built the house after his whaling days were over.

Sometimes the edge of the cliff could be seen through the ferns, but I kept my eyes on the path ahead, trying not to stumble on occasional slippery stones or damp exposed roots.

I stopped a moment. Ahead was a slight bend and I knew that beyond it, I would catch my first glimpse of the house. There would be smiles of welcome, I told myself firmly, and on a day like this cheerful lamps and tea with scones and cakes on a tray by the cozy drawing room fire.

I rounded the bend.

They say that childhood haunts revisited appear smaller, lacking the luster often bestowed by memory. This was not so with my reacquaintance of Ravensfall. Above the trees, the gabled roof, a shadowy line against an uncertain sky, rambled, it seemed to me, as much as it ever did; the cupola — Josiah's Folly, as it was known — a scarcely tangible shape in the metallic light.

As on the steamer, I had a moment's wild fantasy of traveling back in time. Soon, I knew, the third and second floor windows would appear and then gradually the side of the house, the verandas of the first and ground floors and the French doors opening out onto the lawn.

The big pohutakawa tree would be there, spreading its enormous branches outside the study windows and around the edges of the lawn where the bush had not encroached, would be the descendants of those British spring flowers planted so long ago, flowering again, despite the New Zealand winter, in this sheltered valley.

My feet moved almost on their own volition and I found myself gliding forward like a ghost in one of my own dreams.

Seven

Ravensfall. I gazed up at the wooden façade of the house, experiencing a sense of déjà vu as details — forgotten till now — met recognition in my memory: the pair of ivy-bedecked urns guarding the shallow stone steps leading onto the ground floor veranda; the tall, narrow, stained-glass windows flanking the huge front door; the row of ravens carved into the wooden lintel above.

Though heavy gray clouds promised more, the rain had stopped for a moment, its presence remembered in a lingering damp and earthy scent from lawn and encroaching bush. The breeze had died down and somewhere in the still trees a bird sang, the melody floating in counterpoint to a motionless quiet. The three stories of the house stared down at me in silence.

I braced my shoulders to keep myself from shivering and shifted the weight of my carpetbag. Tea, I reminded myself firmly, with finger sandwiches and fairy cakes and buttered scones dripping with strawberry jam and whipped cream beside a cozy fire. Of course, I thought with relief, that's where they all must be at this time in the afternoon — in the drawing room. No wonder I had spied no movement from behind the study and library windows as I had passed by the side of the house.

"Courage, Malvina," I whispered to myself as I mounted the steps. I put forth a hand and firmly rang the bell.

There was no reply.

I waited and rang again, hearing the bell's dim echo reverberating in the hall behind.

No footsteps. Nothing.

I remembered the green baize doors at the back of the stairs, separating the kitchens from the front part of the house. Perhaps the bell was not sounding down in the servants' quarters — and of course, those in the drawing room would not realize this?

I had better announce myself.

Tentatively I stretched out a hand and turned the etched copper doorknob.

The door swung open . . . onto silence.

Before me, the staircase swept up into darkness past the closed dining room doors to the left and the passage leading to the rooms at the side of the house. At the back of the hall, beyond the stairs, scarcely visible in the muted glow filtering through the stained-glass windows — St. George on his rearing steed to one side of the front door and the rope-bound maiden cowering from her dragon on the other — loomed the green baize doors. To my right, through the partly open double doors to the drawing room, gleamed a faint light, but there was no murmur of voices, no creaking of chairs, no muted clink of teacups.

I stepped over the threshold and stood listening.

Still, no sound.

Clutching my carpetbag, I made my way to the drawing room and pushed open the doors. The portieres were not fully drawn, allowing the faint light I had seen to diffuse itself about the room, illuminating a chair here, a gate-legged table there, a brass ornament on the mantelpiece, the glass doors of a curio cabinet. On the arm of one chair lay an open book, facedown; a half-open knitting bag was propped against another, sharp needles sticking out like exclamation points.

Had my new cousins gone out for a walk? I wondered. Or, considering their years, perhaps they napped in the afternoon?

Wandering over to one of the windows, I pulled aside the portieres and at once drew a sharp breath. Though the light now allowed in was dull, it was sufficient to illuminate the pink and mauve Aubusson carpet I remembered from my childhood, the plum-colored, Louis Quinze chairs and sofas and the high ceiling with its ornate chandeliers.

45

Again, my sense of déjà vu was overwhelming; I began to feel awash in the past. Soon, I thought, it will be as if I have never been away. I looked toward the small dais at the back of the long room, almost expecting to hear a soft sonata from its half-curtained off piano. Ishbel, I remembered, used to practice there for hours. . . .

I forced my eyes away from the piano and crossed the room to ring the bell set into the wall by the huge stone fireplace. The fire, I noted while I waited for a servant to arrive, was all set to light, its kindling and small coals piled in readiness. However, there was a scattering of dust on the wood and on the wads of paper inserted between the coals, as if the fire had been laid for some time.

I looked up at the ormolu clock, softly ticking away on the mantelpiece. Almost four-thirty; why, I wondered on such a damp winter's day, had the fire not been lit? Had Lucy and Clinton gone off somewhere — but if so, where and for how long?

Setting down my carpetbag, I draped my damp hat and cloak over the back of a chair. Where were the servants? Or were all the bells not working? Still no one came in answer to my summons and giving up at last, I decided there was nothing to do but to look for the servants myself.

Out in the hall the remaining late afternoon light barely struggled through the stained glass, scarcely revealing St. George's pale features or the twisting coils of the dragon in the companion window. Soon, I knew, it would be totally dark and I looked hopefully toward the rosewood table at the foot of the stairs, where traditionally we used to set out lamps and candles to light our way upstairs in the evenings.

The table was bare.

Never mind, I thought to myself, trying to ignore the silence and increasing dark, I should soon find the servants. I walked down the hall and opened the baize doors.

Beyond stretched the passage, dark and empty.

The kitchen, I remembered, was at the end, to the right of the backdoor. Reluctantly I made my way down the passage, past closed storeroom doors and the dark opening to the back-stairs leading up to the attics and the servants' bedrooms.

As I had come to expect, the kitchen was empty. The big oil-cloth-covered table was set for a meal and—as in the drawing room—kindling and coals were laid ready in the cold fireplace. On the battered, old settle along one wall reposed a raffia mending basket accompanied by a pile of socks and left hanging from the back of a wooden chair half turned from the table, a white linen apron fluttered in the cool draft from the door. Beside the fireplace, a pair of threadbare carpet slippers lay face-down and crooked, as if kicked off in a hurry.

Had the boarding party, I wondered, of the *Marie Celeste,* felt as I did at that moment?

I took a deep breath and told myself not to be ridiculous. Doubtless, there was some perfectly simple explanation! For some reason, they had all left, but quite evidently—with the fires all set ready to light—they meant to return before too long.

Not that night, though, I realized with a sinking heart. The light now filtering through the kitchen windows was dim indeed—and it was highly unlikely that anyone would travel through the bush at night.

I thought of the huge empty house around me and shivered at the idea of spending the night there alone.

Taking a deep breath, I tried to steady my nerves. Think of Harriet, I told myself; what would she do?

Light, I thought; my practical stepmother would first provide herself with a candle—or, better still, a lamp. I looked about the kitchen and heaved a sigh of relief at the sight of a candle in its holder on the ancient dresser by the door. And the means to light it? Thank goodness, in the drawer beneath was a box of Lucifers.

Though my hands shook as I lit the candle, I began to feel more confident. Harriet had not brought us up to be helpless . . . "You never know what life will bring," she used to say, as she taught us all—even the boys—to light a kitchen range and cook a simple meal.

I would light the range later, I thought, and explore the larder for the provisions I was sure would be there—but first, I would look for a lamp; I seemed to remember a cupboard near the baize doors where lamps and candles were stored.

Seizing the candlestick, I reentered the passage and made my way to the cupboard at the end. Sure enough, the candle's uncertain glow lit up a number of lamps on one of the shelves. I took two of them to the rosewood table in the hall; I would leave one of them in the hall, I decided, and take the other with me back to the kitchen. Luckily, they seemed to have been recently filled with oil. After lighting the wicks with the Lucifers I had placed in my pocket, and steadying the long, tapering glass funnels, I adjusted the light.

It was then, as I was rejoicing in the golden glow and stretching out my hand to take up one of the lamps, that the silence was shattered with a jangling bell.

The noise was so sudden that for a moment, I stood frozen, unable to breathe.

Taking a deep breath at last, I turned toward the baize doors I had left open behind me. The bell had sounded from the end of the passage and I suddenly remembered the row of bells — one for each major room in the house — on a wooden panel above the kitchen door.

A bell had rung.

I was therefore not alone in the house.

In that case, why was the house so dark and silent?

And where was the person who had rung the bell?

I told myself not to be an idiot. Obviously, one of my cousins must have come back before the others and gone into one of the other rooms, perhaps even up the stairs, while I had been in the kitchen. Perhaps he or she did not realize that the servants — wherever *they* had gone — had not yet returned and had rung for assistance.

In any event, I told myself, taking up one of the lamps and turning back down the passage, I should be able to tell which room was occupied by the swaying bell.

I returned to the kitchen and looked at the triple row of bells above the door.

They were all still.

There was nothing to do but to explore the house until I found the occupied room.

* * *

Returning to the hall I took up the remaining lamp from the rosewood table. Still no light in the drawing room and no light in the dining room, as far as I could see as I opened the doors a crack, just to make sure. The passage behind the dining room leading to the study and library was also dark as pitch.

Returning to the foot of the stairs, I stood for a moment, listening; the glow from my lamp highlighted the carved raven on the newel post, its wooden wings outstretched, as with one hooked talon, it clutched the small, lifelike mouse that was its prey.

The badge of our house, Harriet had once called it jokingly, but I had never liked it — Ishbel used to terrorize Reggie and me with stories of it coming alive at night and sweeping down on us in our beds. I made myself look away and peered up into the darkness.

I coughed. "Anyone there?"

Despite all my efforts, my voice came out in a high-pitched squeak. I tried again. "Anyone there?"

Silence.

Suddenly — shockingly, it seemed to my overburdened nerves — from far off, down the kitchen passage, another jangle of a bell.

I resisted a temptation to turn tail and bolt straight out of the house.

Telling myself not to be ridiculous, I caught up my skirts in one hand and holding the lamp high with the other, I climbed up the thickly carpeted stairs to the third-floor landing.

A bearded face peered down at me from the gloom, its light brown eyes questioning — accusing, almost.

Our Great Uncle Josiah, of course — I had forgotten all about his old portrait in the well of the first-floor landing — well placed, as Papa had once said, to observe the comings and goings of those inhabiting his former domain.

Papa, of course, had been joking, but Ishbel with her stories of old Josiah's hauntings, gleaned from our superstitious servants, had been perfectly serious.

I still remember the clutch of her fingers as she had forced me to look up at the thin, narrow features in the portrait. "Look, Malvina," she had told me in her musical tones, how his eyes follow you, no matter which way you turn . . . he still 'walks' you know—old Moana has seen him in the library and the other night, she saw him coming down the cupola stairs. . . ."

Old Moana; the great grandmother of Ngaire, our Maori parlor maid. . . . It was she who had told Ishbel about the *taniwha,* and had spent hours with Reggie and me, telling us about the myths and ancient stories of her people—and yet she had hated all of us. I looked about me at the shadows and shivered—the old woman had had a disturbing habit of following us around and appearing suddenly, when we least expected it.

My hand trembled and among the fluid, dark shapes created by the lamp's wavering glow, Great Uncle Josiah seemed to shift slightly in his frame. What nonsense, I thought sharply; as Harriet had told us once, the only ghosts were those in our heads! If I were not careful, I thought I would be hearing voices next!

"Stay where you are!" I adjured Great Uncle Josiah, aloud.

From along the corridor to my left, I heard a giggle, soft and musical.

I froze.

No ghosts except in my head, I reminded myself—with difficulty.

"Who's there?" Despite myself, my voice trembled.

I need not have worried; there was no reply. I took a deep breath and forced myself to move from the landing into the hallway. On either side stretched a row of doors, each apparently shut—and no gleam of light.

Had the giggle been a mere figment of my fevered imagination? The carpet was so soft it was impossible to hear footsteps, but was that slight noise the clicking of a door or part of the creaking of the old timbers?

I restrained a cowardly impulse to rush downstairs and lock myself in the kitchen.

No ghosts, I reminded myself. In that case, someone—who?—was playing a trick on me. Why? Perhaps because of my frazzled nerves, I began to feel angry. With anger came a kind of courage. I walked down the corridor and thrust open the first door I came to.

In the glow from the lamp, I recognized the furniture of what had been Papa's sitting room. The partly open door in the opposite wall led to the rest of the apartment. Could the owner of that soft laugh be hiding in the dressing room or bedroom? To my dismay, as I made my way across the room, my skirts brushed against the side of a small writing desk, dislodging a cigar box and disturbing a set of papers, the topmost one of which drifted down to the floor. I couldn't help noticing the crabbed handwriting on the paper as I picked it up and hoped that the Mr. Aaron Blunt the letter seemed to be addressed to, would be able to read it! Perhaps my cousin had arthritis in his fingers, I was thinking, as I straightened the cigar box, when a slight noise behind me caught my attention.

I whirled around at once but could discern nothing in the darkness beyond the door.

The back of my neck pricking, I seized the lamp where I had placed it on the writing table — unfortunately, in my haste, sending most of the papers drifting to the floor again — and cautiously returned to the corridor.

Silence.

Except . . . what was that soft tapping behind me? I looked back toward the yet uncurtained window and found myself laughing with relief. It was raining again; the drops starting to pound with increasing vigor against the dark, wet glass.

Slightly hysterical, I turned toward the door again and stepped out into the hall.

To my right, where the darkness of the first floor landing should have been, was a delicate golden glow that softly but surely grew in intensity.

I gathered my courage together. "Who's there?"

My voice, trembling despite my resolve, was drowned by an increased strumming of the rain.

There was no reply.

Who was coming up the stairs?

Why had I not heard any sound of arrival?

All the frights I had experienced that evening seemed to come together in one overwhelming wave of fear, making me realize anew my aloneness, my isolation in the middle of the bush.

I thought of the bells jangling from empty rooms and the

mocking disembodied laugh. Was there a lunatic in the house? What should I do?

The light on the landing grew brighter. Soon, I knew, whoever was carrying the lamp would reach the top stair. Almost without thinking, I found myself turning off my own lamp and backing into the room I had just left. I would hide behind the open door, I thought, placing my unlit lamp safely out of the way on the floor. Anyone on first entering the room would not see me and with luck, I would be able to slip out unobserved. Surely, in the vast darkness of the house, I should find somewhere to hide until morning.

Unfortunately, luck was not with me that night.

I waited behind the door as the light first paused on the landing and then grew brighter as it turned toward the room where I was hiding. Would it pass by?

It didn't.

I held my breath as the light from a lamp held in the doorway flowed past me, swept around the room and then paused on the papers I had knocked off the writing table.

A soft exclamation and then a short pause, before the light flared brighter as the lamp was carried into the room.

It was a man holding the lamp; that much I could see, a man who cast gigantic, shifting shadows that waltzed crazily about the walls, as if participating in a hellish dance.

NOW, I thought, while he's looking at the letters!

I grabbed up my skirts and slipped around the door.

A huge hand shot out and seized my upper arm, jerking me back with such strength that I would have fallen if the same hand with lightning suddenness had not twisted me about and shifted its hold onto my other arm, thereby imprisoning me in what felt like an iron clamp.

I found myself looking up into the granite-featured face of the enormous American.

The thin lips twisted into a smile. "Why, the estimable Miss H.!"

Throughout these maneuvers, he had managed to hold onto the lamp without setting either of us alight. He now force-led me over to the table with the apparent intention of setting the lamp down. As he leaned over, I seized my opportunity by stamping him firmly on the instep.

His arm slackened as he used a word I had never heard before and I was able to twist myself free and run out the door. As I rushed along the corridor to the stairs, I heard a crash. Evidently, he must have lost his balance. . . . I did not stop to wonder if he had spilled the lamp and set the house alight.

The landing, of course, was almost pitch-black, but I managed to feel my way with one hand on the wall until I found the banisters leading down to the ground floor. Stumbling down the stairs and panting for breath, all I was concerned about was escaping from the house. . . . I believe I had some idea of finding a hiding place in the bush. However, halfway down the stairs, I gradually became aware of a glow slowly seeping through the stained-glass windows down in the hall. Hurriedly, I jammed on my pince-nez, fallen off in the struggle. The haze focused onto one source of light: someone with a lantern was apparently approaching from outside.

Friend or foe?

As I reached the last stair, the front door swung open. Framed in the entrance stood a tall gentleman wrapped about by a dripping riding cloak. The bowler hat he wore cast a shadow over his features but from the way he stood, and from what little could be seen in the inadequate glow from the lantern he held, he appeared to be somewhere in his late thirties or early forties.

As he stepped over the threshold, he caught sight of me at the foot of the stairs. Raising his hat, he paused a moment, regarding my somewhat tousled appearance inquiringly. I found myself looking up at a pair of pale, very clear gray eyes.

Above the eyes, dark brows quirked. "Good evening," a well-timbered voice greeted me, its accent curiously reminiscent of that of the American I had just left. "I am Clinton Raven. Who the devil are you?"

Eight

A breeze, bringing with it a scattering of raindrops and a heady scent of drenched ferns and trees, burst through the open doorway, stirring the folds of Clinton Raven's cloak and shifting the lantern hanging from his hand.

"Who the devil are *you?*" he had asked me, his Canadian-accented voice sharp with surprise. And now he waited for my answer, dark brows frowning above clear, gray eyes.

And who the devil *was* I? I thought for a moment with grim humor, recalling all the apparent doubts of Jeremiah Simms and the huge American. Indeed, the whole situation seemed so unreal, that for a moment, in that chill, drafty hall—so redolent with memories—I felt as tenuous as one of the shadows fluttering in the swaying lantern's light.

I opened my mouth to reply but before I could do so, a deep voice rumbled down the stairs behind me. "Your cousin Malvina, my dear Raven—fresh from England—surely you were expecting her!"

Halfway down the stairs loomed the American, completely unruffled, a glowing lamp in one upraised hand, my unlit lamp in the other. "We met in Wanganui . . ." he continued, "and again, just now—but allow me to introduce myself properly, Miss . . . er . . . *Raven;* you British are so formal!"

He smiled urbanely at my look of outrage. "Devlin Fordyke at your service, ma'am! My daughter and I rent one of the cottages on the Ravensfall property. . . ."

"This g-g-gentleman . . ." Humiliated, I found myself stuttering to my newfound cousin and tried again. "This *gentleman. . . .*"

He chuckled softly before I could continue. "Please accept my apologies, my dear Miss . . . Raven. I fear I mistook you for an intruder!"

Another urbane smile, this time directed down the stair to Clinton Raven. "I came across to see Mister Lucas—I understood you to say he was going to be here—but when there was no response to my ring and yet I saw a light moving about inside when all was darkness elsewhere, I grew suspicious . . . I'm afraid I gave your cousin a fright. . . ."

"Cousin." Clinton Raven raised his lantern a little higher. "Ah, Cousin Malvina! From England!" His tone was not so much welcoming as inquiring.

My heart sank. Not another misunderstanding . . . oh, please, God! "You did not receive my letter?"

"From England?"

"No . . . from Wellington: I wrote it when I first arrived, to warn you that I was coming. Papa said that I had better . . . though, of course, he wrote letters of introduction to bring with me . . ."

The gray eyes looked at me thoughtfully and then brightened. "Of course, you must be Cousin Marcus's eldest daughter! How unwelcoming you must think me! No doubt, your letter will be waiting for me . . . I am afraid we have all been away these past few days—except for Paul, of course. But what am I thinking of, to keep you standing here in the cold . . . you must come into the drawing room—and I shall ring for Mrs. Hodges to bring us some tea. You'll stay, of course, Fordyke?" he added to the American still standing behind me.

The ugly face creased into a sardonic grin. "If Miss Raven does not object!"

Without waiting for an answer, Clinton Raven turned, lifting his lantern high to light our way across the hall to the drawing room doors. These, I now noticed, had been shut.

I followed him, puzzled: "Mrs. Hodges? But when I arrived, there was no one . . . oh!"

My newfound cousin had opened the drawing room doors to reveal soft, welcoming lamplight and a glowing fire within the grate.

"Please go in and warm yourself—I'm glad Hodges managed

to get the fire going!"

Followed by Devlin Fordyke, I made my way over to the fire. Sinking gratefully into a fireside chair, I noted as I did so, that my hat and cloak had disappeared but that my carpetbag had been placed beside the door.

"Ah, that's better!" Rubbing his hands together, Clinton Raven reappeared, minus his lantern and divested of his cloak. He was wearing dark gray riding breeches topped by a black wool jacket and a silk cravat, damp from the rain, of a rich, deep crimson hue. His dark hair, tousled and worn somewhat longer than the current fashion, had curled softly from the rain — just like Papa's, I thought nostalgically.

His brows wrinkled as he sat down in the chair beside mine. "There was no one here, when you first arrived? How awkward for you! I suppose that Paul must have given the Hodges the afternoon off to visit Mrs. Hodges's sister-in-law over the river — she's cook-housekeeper to the Turners . . . and of course, the rest of us have been at the housewarming."

"Housewarming?"

At my startled astonishment, he threw back his head and laughed, but before he could explain, the doors opened to reveal a short woman in her midfifties, her stout body clad in house-keeper's correct, black bombazine, her gray curls surmounted by a starched snowy cap.

"Ah, Mrs. Hodges! We have a guest: my . . . that is *our* cousin, Miss Malvina Raven from England — who arrived when you were out — but perhaps you two have met? You used to live here as a child, did you not, Cousin?"

"Yes, but I don't believe that Mrs. Hodges and I . . . of course, it's been so long since . . ."

Mrs. Hodges shook her head, the white ribbons of her cap twitching briskly. "No, we can't have met, miss — I only came here when I married Hodges."

From Clinton Raven's expression when he had asked the question, he had meant nothing more than polite inquiry. However, after all the doubt I had encountered, I had to stop myself from sighing with relief.

I was very much aware, however, of Devlin Fordyke. He had seated himself on one of the sofas, taking up enough room for two

56

people, and now was lounging back, his massive arms folded, a faintly amused look on his out-of-kilter features.

"I'll be glad to bring some tea and finger sandwiches, miss, and now that Hodges has got the fires going, there should be hot water soon and I daresay you would like to change for dinner — which will be at eight — unless, of course, after your long journey and all, you'd prefer to take a light supper in your room?"

Mrs. Hodges paused a moment, looking down at my carpetbag. "I must say that this was a surprise; I thought the cloak and hat must have belonged to Mrs. Wilkinson or Miss Hackett, so I placed those in the cloakroom to dry. I told myself that they must have come back early, but this was quite a puzzle! I'll take them with me, miss, and prepare a room for you. . . ."

"Perhaps you would like your old room?" Clinton Raven turned toward me politely.

My old room. I thought of the small room isolated at the top of the house, where I had shed so many frightened tears. With difficulty, I repressed a shudder.

"Perhaps you don't remember it?" My cousin's narrowed eyes seemed intent upon my face.

Had I taken too long to answer? Before I could reply, Devlin Fordyke spoke up from his sofa. "So many years," he remarked. "How many, Miss Raven? Nine? Ten?" His eyes seemed half shut as he gazed into the fire; his American tones almost sleepy.

I knew better. "Twelve years, to be precise!"

I resisted a childish temptation to stick out my tongue and turned instead to Clinton Raven and smiled. "My room was on the nursery floor — perhaps a room could be provided more befitting to my advanced years? I believe I'm a little too old now to have a governess?"

I found myself blushing as he momentarily gazed at me appreciatively, one dark eyebrow raised in devilish flight.

"Quite right!" Smiling a little, Cousin Clinton turned questioningly toward Mrs. Hodges.

"The second floor, sir, with a nice view of the river!"

She gave me a cozy smile. "Most of the superior rooms on the first floor have been taken up, miss; but I'm sure you'll be quite comfortable with what I have in mind!"

"Thank you, Mrs. Hodges. I'm sure I shall!"

"Well then, miss, I daresay the rest of your luggage is down by the river?"

"Yes. I had to leave my trunk out on the landing, of course, but I managed to put my valise and hatbox under the puketea tree to be out of the rain. . . . I'm sorry for the bother!"

"No bother, miss! The trunk will be safe enough until the men get back in the morning — but Hodges can bring up the rest as soon as he's got himself straight!"

She looked inquiringly toward Clinton Raven. "Will that be all, sir?"

"Thank you, Mrs. Hodges. Would you please tell Mister Lucas that Mister Fordyke is here and would like to see him. . . ."

Devlin Fordyke looked up from his contemplation of the fire. "Please don't disturb Mister Lucas; it's not urgent. I had merely wanted to ask him something about the gold mining towns down in the South Island. . . . I believe he mentioned he had been to Greymouth?"

"Come now, Fordyke, Paul wouldn't mind, I'm sure! If he is in and I see no reason why he should not be — you would not, of course, have seen the studio light from the front of the house — although, what he is doing working at this time of night . . ."

My cousin shook his head and turned toward me, his brow flying up again in amusement at my bewilderment. "You are wondering, naturally, who Paul Lucas is — and have other questions, also?"

"Yes, no, that is . . ."

"No mystery about Paul, I assure you. Simply a fellow artist who decided to come with us when he heard about the beauties of New Zealand."

"Oh, I see. An artist." My mind suddenly cleared. "Yes, of course, in your letter that Papa read to me, you said you liked to paint . . . it's just . . . well, I thought it was just a hobby!"

With new eyes I looked at the tousled hair, the carelessly tied cravat. "In fact, I had expected you to be somewhat older. If you'll excuse my saying so, you don't look in the least like a retired banker!"

The gray eyes gleamed. "Thank you for that! I'm sorry to have disappointed you, Cousin, if you were expecting an old fogy!"

"No. No, of course not! That is . . ."

He laughed gently. "What do you know of my father?"

"Your father? Nothing much." I wracked my brains, thinking of the Christmas cards over the years and the little Papa had told about his uncle. "Except, your father was a banker also, wasn't he?"

He drew a deep breath. "Yes. In fact, he died of a heart attack at the bank before he could retire."

"I'm sorry."

A hand waved away my condolences and the clear eyes darkened. "My father and I did not . . . did not rub well together, shall we say? He thought only of banking; lived and breathed banking. Art, yes, he *collected;* but only collected — for the prestige, the power it brought — but that his son should follow such a profession . . ."

He paused and shook his head. "You must forgive me for talking with such passion and on such short acquaintance!" He gave me a brief, apologetic smile. "Suffice it to say, that after my father's death, when all restrictions were removed, I turned at last to my avocation!"

He paused, looking into space, his eyes reflecting for a moment the firelight beyond me.

The tensions of the evening had upstaged the rain. Now, in the sudden silence, I was aware again of the continued pounding against the windows and of an infrequent hiss as errant raindrops slipping down the chimney alighted in the flames below, sending acrid wisps of smoke twisting about the hearth.

A strangled cough — more like a hiccup, really — was followed by another, this one quickly smothered from the direction of the sofa. An enormous pocket handkerchief was produced and Devlin Fordyke's muffled voice issued shakily from behind it. "Excuse me . . ." He coughed again. "The smoke from the chimney, no doubt!"

It seemed to me that for a such a small amount of smoke, the immense shoulders seemed to heave unnecessarily, but before I could comment there was a knock at the doors and Mrs. Hodges entered with her tea and sandwiches.

"And Cousin Lucy?" I asked Clinton Raven, as Mrs. Hodges bustled about setting up cups and saucers on a small table by the fire. "She is completely over the accident, then?"

"The accident?" My cousin looked toward me, politely inquiring. "Oh, yes, of course, the accident. My poor sister! She's been very brave, but it has taken a long time for her to recover—in fact, that is why Norah Hackett is with us; as friend, companion, nurse . . . and indeed, even governess in a way to poor Bertram; though of course, Paul helps us with him as much as he can."

"Bertram?"

"My sister's son—poor little creature!"

"I'm sorry, I had not realized . . . that is to say, in your letter to Papa, you told about the accident and the demise of poor Lucy's husband . . . but . . ."

"But not about Bertram?"

There was a pause as the gray eyes studied me hesitantly. "Poor Bertram—though in some ways he is extraordinarily gifted, he has suffered from birth, from a . . . a . . . physical debility that has led to various mental . . . anxieties. Lucy and Silas did their best to care for him; however, after the accident . . . when Lucy was all alone and suffering, I suggested that Bertram be placed in a foster home while she recuperated in New Zealand—hence my letter to your father, not mentioning Bertram."

"I see; but Lucy would not . . ."

A rueful smile. "I'm afraid that Bertram is still with us; I suppose that all we can do is try . . ."

I had a sudden mental vision of a sad, pale-faced, little boy all by himself in some dark and distant region of the house. "Poor little soul! Where is he now?"

"In the cellar; chained to the wall . . . but not to worry, bread and water are within easy reach!"

A laugh spluttered from the sofa and Mrs. Hodges setting out a plate of buttered scones permitted herself a small smile.

"Forgive me!" Alight with laughter, the gray eyes were clear and light again. "But for a moment, you looked so serious!"

I could not help smiling in reply. "It's the effect of all this rain—and the circumstances of my arrival. I begin to feel that I'm a heroine in a gothic novel!"

"No gothic terrors for you here, I assure you! When I left this afternoon, young Bertram was hiding from Norah Hackett—who was after him with his medicine—while my sister played whist with James and Honoria Langton. They are new neighbors who have been celebrating their purchase of the property on the other side of the bluff with a week-long house party! You will remember the old owners, of course — I'm afraid their name escapes me!"

He looked at me inquiringly and though the question had been asked casually, to my tired mind there seemed to be a watchfulness about him as he waited for my answer.

For the life of me, though the name was on the tip of my tongue, I could not think of it. The silence — surely no more than a few seconds — seemed to stretch to a yawning gulf. From the sofa, Devlin Fordyke regarded me with a sardonic smile.

I was rescued by Mrs. Hodges, putting the finishing touch to her tea things. "That would be the old DuPrès place, I expect?"

"Oh, yes, the vineyard! I had forgotten all about it!" With difficulty, I restrained myself from letting out a relieved sigh.

"That's right, miss." Mrs. Hodges slipped a linen napkin over my lap and nodded toward the silver teapot. "Perhaps you would like to do the honors, miss? And I'll pop up and prepare your room. I've had Hodges light a fire so it should be nice and cozy for you."

She stood back and looked down at me a moment, her plump features concerned. "If you don't mind my saying so, miss, but you look tired out. I'll have Hodges take up some hot water for you and later, when you've had time to find yourself, I'd be glad to send up a light supper, as I suggested before. . . . After all the traveling you've done, seems to me you need an early night!"

Until Mrs. Hodges spoke, I had not known quite how tired I was; but now I realized that my long journey, the weather, and most of all, the tensions of the evening, had all conspired to drive me to the point of exhaustion. I had hardly, I thought to myself, even the strength to lift the teapot!

Paul Lucas. Who was he? I thought. And Norah Hackett. And Bertram. And as for my cousin, Lucy: Was she as different as her brother Clinton had turned out to be? My tired mind could take no more. Avoiding all but the barest civilities of polite small talk, I poured the tea, passed the sandwiches — and then made my escape.

Nine

As Mrs. Hodges had promised, my room turned out to be cozy and well lit; a small lamp on the bedside table reflected its pink glow over the colorful patchwork quilt spread upon the four-poster feather bed and a freshly lit fire twinkled in the grate.

By the marble washstand stood two tall copper jugs filled with steaming hot water and on a cedar chest at the foot of the bed sat my now unpacked carpetbag — my nightdress, shawl, slippers, and toilet articles laid out temptingly beside it. My spare blouse hung in the huge oak wardrobe and my change of underwear was stored neatly in the top drawer of the oak chest.

Mrs. Hodges stood back after ushering me into the room. "Hodges had gone to fetch your valise and hatbox, miss. If you'll give me a ring when you're ready, he'll bring them right up. I'd be glad to help you unpack!"

"Oh, no, please . . . I have everything I need. Perhaps, in the morning?"

She smiled kindly. "That's what I thought. In that case, I'll tell Hodges to take care of your valise until tomorrow and when the maids come back, I'll send one of them up to help you.

"That's very kind of you!"

"Not at all, miss — I'm just sorry there was no one here to give you a proper welcome! Mister Lucas, of course . . ." — she raised her eyes toward the ceiling in humorous despair — ". . . would never hear you, up there in the attics. That's where they have their studio; they say they need the light or something!"

She shook her head, smiling indulgently.

I thought suddenly of the jangling bells that had so unnerved me on my arrival — my later confrontation with Devlin Fordyke and subsequent events having driven the memory from my head. Perhaps, here then was an explanation? Maybe Mr. Lucas had rung for afternoon tea? But then, of course, the attics would not be connected to the bell system — and even if they were, Paul Lucas had given the Hodges the afternoon off and so would know they would not be available!

"Something is bothering you, Miss Raven?"

"Nothing, really; it's just that you said the house was empty . . . and yet . . ."

"Yes, miss?" Suddenly Mrs. Hodges's kindly face was still.

"It's just . . . well . . . the bells rang in the kitchen and yet there did not seem to be anyone there. . . ." I found myself laughing self-consciously. "I'm afraid I did find that a bit unnerving!"

"Well you would, miss, wouldn't you? Anyone would . . . especially on a dark, rainy afternoon in a strange house! Not to worry — I expect it was a hiccup in the system!"

"Yes . . . but, well . . ." I stopped, all of a sudden feeling tremendously silly. Somehow the lamp's comforting glow and the attitude of the matter-of-fact little person now before me, distanced me from my earlier nerve-racking experiences.

"It's just," I tried again, "that I heard . . . thought I heard? . . . a laugh — well, a giggle, really."

For a moment Mrs. Hodges looked up at me, her face expressionless. "A giggle, miss? Oh, you mean a gurgle! It's surprising what sounds an old house like this makes, especially after a heavy rain. I expect it was the pipes."

She smiled at me brightly. "Now then, I'll leave you to relax. Please ring when you're ready and I'll bring you up a light supper . . . perhaps some poached eggs on toast and a good, hot pot of tea?"

Alone at last.

Though I looked with longing at the steam rising from the hot water in the copper jugs, I headed straight for the window.

63

Thrusting aside the thick, red plush curtains, I knelt on a window seat and throwing up the heavy sash, peered out into the night.

Outside, all was dark and dank.

The rain had slowed to a sporadic patter and the air wafting upward from the river far below, was heavy with scents familiar to me from childhood — acrid fern and damp, rotting leaves in sudden undergrowth and most of all, the wild fragrance of water running fresh after a downfall.

With all these sights and sounds assaulting me, I remembered what my father had once told Harriet . . . that once visited, New Zealand sent out a call.

Had I answered that call, I wondered, or had I in spirit, ever really left?

A sodden breeze swelled out the curtains behind me. Closing the window to within its last inch, I retreated back into the room. A sponge bath, I told myself, then supper, after which — at long last — bed!

True to her word, at my ring, Mrs. Hodges brought up her promised poached eggs on toast, accompanied by a large slice of her special apple pie, a pot of tea, and a small glass of port.

"Not a lady's drink, miss; but my grandfather always swore by it . . . 'relaxes and restores,' he always said. And it seems to me, miss, that after such a day, you need to be restored!"

"Thank you, that's awfully good of you, Mrs. Hodges."

"Not at all; you just sip that as I said and then into bed with you and sweet dreams!"

She moved toward the door and then, pausing, turned back to me, her features half in shadow.

"There is something the matter, Mrs. Hodges?"

"Oh, no, Miss. Nothing *wrong!*" Though I could not clearly see her face, her voice issued reassuringly from the shadows. "Nothing wrong at all. . . ."

"Then?"

"Oh, nothing, as I said. It's just . . . do not be disturbed if you should hear footsteps in the hall at night. . . ."

"Footsteps? At night?"

"Your cousin, miss, or Mister Lucas or sometimes Miss Hackett or Mrs. Wilkinson. . . ."

"Cousin Lucy?"

"Yes, miss. Up and down to the studios in the attics. But they're all artists, miss, aren't they? All entitled to their 'poetic license'?"

"I see."

She smiled wanly. "Well, there you are, miss. But not to worry, as I said . . ." She cast an encouraging look toward my port. "Drink up and you'll be right as rain!"

I had eaten up my eggs and apple pie and was just about to sip at the port, when from beyond the door I heard the same musical laugh that had followed the earlier mysterious clanging of the kitchen bells.

So much for Mrs. Hodges and her comfortable theories, I told myself. Without thinking, I thrust my feet into my slippers, twisted my shawl about my nightgown and dashed out into the corridor.

Behind me, the lamp in my bedroom softly illumined the corridor leading back to the stairs.

Beyond the stairs, all was in darkness.

I thought of Harriet. "There are *no* ghosts!" I reassured myself aloud. Someone out there, I told myself, was teasing me. Who? Why?

Forcing one foot in front of the other, I gradually made my way down the silent hall to the second-floor landing.

Far behind me my bedroom light still glowed faintly like a forgotten lighthouse in an unknown sea. Below me, beyond the stairs leading down, yawned a dark, bottomless pit.

From the pit echoed the laugh I had come to recognize: light, bell-like.

Ishbel's laugh.

I thought of Harriet again. There are *no* ghosts, I reminded myself sternly.

Pulling my shawl firmly about my shoulders, I gazed down into the darkness.

All was still; silent.

I resisted an impulse to rush back to my room and bury my head under the bedclothes.

It would be useless, I assured myself, to go down the stairs, as in the pitch darkness I should distinguish nothing. Instead, I made my way back to my room and taking up my lamp, forced myself to return to the landing.

In the wavering light, the turkey-carpeted steps seemed to leap out at me, to twist and turn. I took a deep breath and steadied my lamp, shining it down into the stairwell.

From out of the shadows, beyond, a soft giggle.

I took another deep breath and tried to keep my voice calm and steady. "So, you're still there? Why do you always seek the shadows? Why do you want my attention?"

Silence.

Slowly I descended the stairs until I found myself on the first-floor landing. On my left, Great Uncle Josiah smirked at me from the perimeters of my light and to my right in yawning blackness stretched the corridor I had visited earlier.

From the darkness, a soft scuffle, the swish as of a skirt.

"Who's there?"

Despite my determined courage, my voice sounded weak, uncertain.

No reply.

Nothing for it, I thought to myself, and grasping my lamp firmly, plunged into the dark passage on my right.

Before me, there was nothing but darkness.

Gradually my lamp lit up all the closed doorways on both sides of the passage.

All closed but one.

The door leading into what I now knew was Clinton Raven's sitting room, was still standing open. Did I hear the slight rustle of a retreating skirt?

I hesitated a moment in the doorway, my lamp casting its glow on the dark enshrouded furniture. The upturned table had been set up again, I noticed . . . and the once scattered papers piled neatly on its top.

All at once I remembered Devlin Fordyke coming down the stairs to greet my cousin, Clinton Raven, his glowing lamp held high in his hand.

Had *he* set up the table again? Had *he* straightened the disturbed papers and put everything to rights?

If so, why had he done this?

I thought back over the evening; my skirmish with Devlin

Fordyke, my meeting with Clinton Raven, and then Devlin Fordyke slowly descending the stairs behind me and his introduction of me to Clinton Raven and vice versa.

Devlin Fordyke had implied he thought I was an intruder. Why then — instead of immediately chasing after me — had he taken time to tidy Clinton's room, shifting the table back into position, replacing the papers?

Perhaps someone else had done this?

Who? Why?

Perhaps Mrs. Hodges or her husband had set things to rights as they had made their rounds?

I found myself shaking my head in answer to my own question. In the short time since they had arrived, the Hodges had spent their time setting up the fires in the kitchen and drawing room, preparing a supper, and seeing to my comfort.

I looked around Clinton's dark sitting room; at the unlit lamps and the fire, ready set — but unlighted — in the grate. If Hodges had visited this room, I thought, he would surely have lit the lamps?

The lamps.

I thought again of Devlin Fordyke descending the stairs, his own lamp held high — but mine, held unlit, unobtrusively to his side.

Why had he done this?

Out of the darkness, but this time behind me, another sound — the merest stir — of movement.

Too late, I whirled around.

Nothing.

Not the slightest breeze: except along the corridor and to the right from the stairwell, an elusive waver of light.

Someone was mounting the stairs — probably Clinton Raven.

What was I to do?

How on earth could I explain my nightdress-clad presence on the floor below my bedchamber?

Quickly I dimmed my lamp and running across the hallway, I pulled open the door opposite and thankfully enveloped myself in the oblivion beyond.

As I did so, another soft laugh floated tenuously after me.

Ten

Maniacal laughter, the more terrible because it was silent—Ishbel, her hair streaming like a red banner, twisting her long, white fingers and Callum following close behind.

Callum, his auburn curls in disarray, his blue-green eyes always with that disturbing gleam, looking straight through me as if . . . as if . . .

"Miss Raven . . . Miss Raven. . . ."

I struggled to rouse myself from sleep, to focus my gaze.

"You were screaming, my dear."

Above me, hovered anxiously—though still slightly out of focus—the worried features of Mrs. Hodges.

"You were screaming, my dear—really screaming—as if . . . well, never mind. . . . I'm just glad I managed to disturb your dream—or, should I say, nightmare? Here you are then—I thought you might like a cup of tea before you go down to breakfast."

She helped me up, handing me my spare pair of spectacles I always keep on my bedside table, talking to me soothingly, fluffing my pillows as if I were an invalid and banking them behind me. At last, a breakfast tray was set up before me; a small pot of tea, milk jug, sugar bowl, hot water jug, and two vanilla creams and—horror upon horrors!—a small vase with a nosegay of violets.

"From the north side of the house, miss; where it's warmer and sheltered from the wind. Very English—I thought they might remind you of 'home'?"

I clutched at the tray. "Why, thank you, Mrs. Hodges! How thoughtful of you!"

"There's nothing wrong? You are all right?"

"I'm fine, thank you; it's just . . . it's just" — I cast about wildly for a creditable excuse — "that I'm still half asleep and the nightmare you caught me in the middle of hasn't quite gone."

"Of course!" She put out a hand and for one mad moment, I thought she would ruffle my hair.

Instead, she smiled at me; a plump, motherly smile.

"That's all right, then!"

I watched as she made her way back to my door.

Violets.

I repressed a shudder as I looked down at the delicate little blooms — and thought of Ishbel, who had tended them.

Ishbel.

I could see her now in her mauve and white striped gown, her violets freshly culled, in the straw basket over her arm. "Come along, Malvina, Reginald;" she would say, her voice low and sweet as always. "We must honor dear Mama — we must never forget her, you know!"

"Poor Mama," she would add, as under the cool gaze of her aqua eyes, we entered the dining-room, "what a pity she had to die so young!"

Pausing a moment, she would gaze up at Mama's portrait above the head of the long dining-room table, before directing us to fill with violets, the small vases beneath.

On Sundays, though — whether it blew fair weather or foul — she would take us to the top of the bluff to our family graveyard where a small cairn had been built as a memorial to our governess, Miss Inglewood. Here she would stand, her cloak billowing about her, looking down at the plaque set in the rough stone of the lonely, windswept monument.

She did not need to read the words aloud; we all knew them by heart:

Sacred
To the memory of
Mary Inglewood
Drowned in the Great Flood

of the
Wanganui River
February 11, 1892
Loved governess of the Raven family
At peace

"Poor Miss Inglewood," Ishbel would murmur at last. "You will notice, children, that the plaque does not give her date or place of birth? That is because no one knew them. You see, she was a mysterious person; she never told where she was born nor who she was. She came apparently out of nowhere. . . ."

Here, Ishbel would pause, looking down from the bluff to the glimpse of the river wending its way through the tree-lined gorge far below. She would smile then and Reggie and I would shiver, knowing what she would say next.

"Mary Inglewood came from nowhere," Ishbel would tell us gently, "and she went nowhere—for her body was never found, was it?"

Dumbly, we would shake our heads.

"Because," Ishbel would continue in the same gentle voice, "she was eaten up by the *taniwha*, wasn't she? As are all deceitful people—people we can't trust—people who spy on others. . . ."

Beyond my door a shuffle in the hallway recalled me to reality.

A furtive knock, followed by an apologetic cough.

"Who's there?"

Even to my own ears, my voice sounded sharp.

Another cough; this time followed by a thumping sound.

A hoarse voice rasped."Not to worry, miss! Just Hodges."

I heard a series of coughs and mumbles. "Daresay . . ." Mumble, mumble. "I'm too early?" More mumbles.

I pushed aside the tray, sprang out of bed, and grabbed my shawl. "Not at all, Mister Hodges—do pray, come in . . . you've brought my valise, I expect?"

My door opened a fraction. A marble dome appeared, surrounded by a mousy fringe of hair. "Yiss . . . and this . . . this. . . ."

"My hatbox?"

"Ah!" The dome was raised briefly to reveal a pair of shy brown eyes, a drooping brown mustache, and a large, pink-veined nose.

A fleeting glance at me, then the eyes were discreetly withdrawn to gaze uncertainly at a pair of copper-toed workboots.

"Thank you, Mister Hodges. If you would . . . er . . . please place my things over there, by the wardrobe. . . ."

Mumble, mumble. Thump, thump.

"Thank you. I'm sorry to be such a nuisance!"

Mumble. "No nuisance!"

For a moment the brown eyes met mine before flying to a spot beyond my left shoulder.

So intent was their gaze, I turned to look.

Nothing, as far as I could ascertain, was wrong with the curtain rail.

Mumble, mumble. "No trouble, miss." Mumble. "No trouble at all. . . ." The eyes shifted to the mat under the washstand and then addressed a corner of the ceiling. "Left your bags by the stairs last night . . . brought them up this morning . . . no trouble!"

"Well, that's all right, then."

"Yiss." A quick glance at the mantelpiece. "G'day, then, miss."

Surprisingly, the copper-tipped boots made hardly a sound as they tiptoed around the door.

I glanced at the small clock above the mantel, noting it still lacked five minutes to seven. Hadn't Mrs. Hodges said something about breakfast at seven-thirty? My valise, I thought, could wait. Though I was a little nervous about meeting my cousin Clinton again—and more especially, his fellow artist, Paul Lucas—I was hungry!

The dining room was just as I remembered it, long and narrow with dark paneled walls; the only light note provided by gold-tinted, heavy plush curtains now drawn back to reveal a misty morning.

On the wall at the head of the table, where my mother's portrait had once rested, hung a landscape—all deep, rich greens,

71

sun-stroked russet browns and murky blues — of sharp-edged hills and a deep wooded valley, the bend of a river glinting among the trees.

I was prepared, of course, for Mama's portrait not being there. "We shall take her back to Yorkshire, where she belongs," I remember Papa telling us before we had left Ravensfall — but somehow, I had expected the space left vacant by the portrait to be empty.

Instead hung this landscape; a New Zealand scene — here and there, tree ferns raising their feathery fronds — puzzlingly, hauntingly familiar. Where had I seen this picture before? Stored in some back room, perhaps, until Papa had had it moved down to the dining room. Or, was it the scene itself that I recognized? If so, where and when had I seen it?

"Miss Raven?" uttered a deep, warm baritone.

Startled, I turned. Off the dining room another door had opened, leading as I remembered to the library.

"Paul Lucas. I'm sorry if I startled you!"

A man of my own height, but square, big-muscled, almost squat in build, stood in the doorway. He stepped into the light, revealing a wild mane of waving, red-gold hair and a beard to match.

"Miss Raven?"

I recovered myself. I stood my ground.

"How d'you do, Mister Lucas? I'm sorry, I'm afraid my mind was elsewhere."

Paul Lucas smiled genially as he looked toward the picture I had been studying. "So, you enjoy Clinton's painting?"

"Cousin Clinton? You mean, he . . . ?"

"Painted this picture?" A small smile and a shrug of the broad shoulders. "Your cousin, Miss Raven, is a man of many talents; however, in this case, he discovered this painting quite by chance, in Mrs. Smythe's attic."

"I . . . see. . . ."

He looked amused. "Do you? Are you acquainted with Mrs. Smythe and her attic?"

"Well, no, I don't think . . . that is to say . . . it's been a long time since . . ."

"Exactly!"

In the early morning light filtering uncertainly through the gold velvet, enshrouding curtains, I found myself regarded by a pair of very pale blue eyes. "You don't remember Mrs. Smythe and you don't remember her attic—*but you do remember this painting, don't you!*"

"Yes—that is . . ."

"Yes, of course you do! I read it in your face as I came into the dining room just now." Another blaze from the pale blue eyes. "It's a Heaphy, of course—one of his early paintings of the upper reaches of the Wanganui River. . . ."

"Oh, of course, *now,* I remember! Papa, and sometimes Ca—Callum, a family relative, would take Reggie and me up-river in the Ravensfall canoe . . . and there was one place in particular, where we would stop to have a picnic. I recognize the shape of the hills!"

"The shape of the hills. Of course!"

Was there an underlying note of sarcasm in the otherwise warm baritone? And if so, why?"

Before I could analyze my thoughts, my elbow was gently seized and I was guided toward the sideboard.

Silver covers were lifted. "Scrambled eggs, Miss Raven? Deviled kidneys? Kedgeree? Braised sausages—perhaps a rasher of bacon? Please allow me. . . ."

"Thank you; just a piece of toast at the moment, I think, and a little of the stewed apple—and a cup of tea."

"A cup of tea. Naturally! Where would you British be without it?" The pale blue eyes lit up as the sarcasm dissipated into pure joy.

We sat down and eyed each other over a snowy expanse of tablecloth.

What was it about this man that I found so disturbing?

From over the table my new acquaintance regarded me thoughtfully, bushy, red-gold brows quirking. "So . . . Clinton tells me you used to live here at Ravensfall? Have you returned to revive old memories, then?"

Strange, I thought, the one question Clinton had not asked me last night. The most obvious of all. Briefly, I wondered why he had not done so.

I attempted a light laugh. "In a way, I suppose. . . ."

Behind me the door to the hall opened.

"Cousin Malvina, I see you have met my friend and fellow artist, Paul Lucas. Please forgive the lack of formality . . . I really ought to have been here to introduce you."

I turned to meet the cool gray eyes of my cousin Clinton, his left brow, as usual, flying devilishly. He was dressed in formal dark gray — but with a magenta cravat spilling out from under the points of his starched shirt collar over a dun-colored embroidered waistcoat

"Yes, of course, Cousin; Mister Lucas and I were just discussing the Heaphy. . . ." I nodded toward the painting at the head of the table.

He glanced quickly, with a suspicion of a smile. "Ah, yes, the Heaphy! I discovered it in Mrs Smythe's attic."

"So Mister Lucas told me."

A glance was exchanged between my cousin and Paul Lucas and then both dissolved into silent laughter.

"You see," Clinton Raven said grinning at last, "Paul and I had a wager. *He* said that Mrs. Smythe, despite all her pretensions, would have nothing at all worth a second glance in her attic and I said she would!"

"Second glance? In her attic?"

Another glint of laughter. "Have you not noticed, Cousin, how those who say the most, have the least to show?"

I could not but help an answering smile.

He grinned in response. "But in this case, the reverse is true — because in a dusty corner of Mrs. Smythe's attic, its face turned undeservedly toward the wall was the picture you now see before you!"

"You mean — but how?"

"How did the picture arrive in its present location above the dining room table?"

"Well . . . yes!"

Both men shared another laughing glance. It was as though — like a seesaw — one constantly activated the other.

It was Paul Lucas who answered. *"Quid pro quo,* Miss Raven. Mrs. Smythe was delighted with Clinton's discovery and insisted that he should have it. If it had remained undiscovered, it would in any case have rotted, or so she said. . . ."

Clinton laughed pleasantly. "Hardly *rotted!* But perhaps been buried for another generation, its merits unappreciated!"

I glanced between the painting and my cousin's dark face. "Ah . . . so she gave you the painting . . . What an elegant gesture. . . ."

He smiled slightly, with an almost imperceptible shrug of the shoulders. "Yes, indeed. An elegant gesture and one which, of course, I could not accept!"

I looked again at the painting. "Excuse me, but I thought that . . ."

"Nothing to excuse, Malvina — I may call you Malvina, may I not? And you shall call me Clinton . . . and Paul, here — my best friend — will be Paul to you also?"

"Yes, yes, of course but . . ."

"But? Ah, yes, the Heaphy." Another slight shrug. "But I could not accept it as a gift, of course. It is on loan, only while I stay here, in exchange — on Mrs. Smythe's insistence — for one of my own landscapes."

There was a humorous quirk about the long, curving mouth but at the back of the gray eyes was an emotion I could not place.

It was not until much later that I realized what it meant — but then, of course, it was too late.

Eleven

Back in my room after breakfast, I was pleased to find my trunk deposited at the foot of my bed. The servants, whom Mrs. Hodges had talked about the night before, had obviously arrived back from the house party. Though I had been promised the help of a maid, I couldn't wait to delve into my things. My hat box and valise, I decided, could be unpacked later but the gowns in my trunk, folded away for so long, needed to be brought out and aired. I fished out my trunk key from my reticule and was about to plunge it into the lock when, from outside the partly opened door of my room, I was interrupted by a slithering sound punctuated by a series of soft bumps and squeaks.

By then the mist had vanished and a weak sunlight streamed through my windows; otherwise, I suppose, I might have felt those same fearful chills I had experienced the night before.

Laughing to myself for my former idiocy, I called out, asking who was there.

There was no reply.

I fixed my key in the trunk lock, turned it, and raised the box lid, revealing the shallow top drawer that contained all Harriet's ideas of what a young lady should possess in the way of scarves, gloves, handkerchieves, sachets, ribbons, and trinkets, wrapped safely in tissue paper.

"Dear Harriet," I half whispered to myself, gently rubbing my cheek against a pair of delicately crocheted white cotton gloves, "how I wish you were here!"

As if in answer, from out in the hallway came another set of slithers and squeaks.

Exasperated, I threw down the gloves and rushed for the door. "I have had enough!" I cried. "Quite enough. Now then, whoever you are, reveal yourself!"

An abrupt silence.

Then from out of the dimness of the corridor, a final squeak as if of limbs disjointed on the rack followed by a voice peculiarly sweet. "But there is no need to be afraid, Miss Raven, I am only Bertram, after all!"

The sun chose to come up again that moment and in the corridor illuminated from the stained glass of the red and yellow diamond-paned windows at each end as well as from the light streaming from my open bedroom door, I was able to see quite clearly the strange figure balanced before me.

A little old man leaning on crutches, I thought at first. Then remembering my conversation with Clinton the night before, I suddenly realized that this must be Lucy Wilkinson's son, Clinton's nephew. Clinton had said he had a physical disability . . . and some mental anxieties?

". . . of course . . . er . . . Cousin Bertram? You must come in."

I stood back to let the diminutive figure hobble past me; crutches wedged under armpits, supportive "irons" weighing down skeletally thin, knickerbockered legs.

I wanted to offer an assisting arm but one look at the arrogant profile of the head somehow kept upright between hunched shoulders and I refrained.

Instead, I sank down in one fireside chair and motioned to the other.

"How clever of you, Cousin Bertram, to discover my whereabouts . . . I had not thought . . ."

I stopped my babble, finding myself under the scrutiny of a pair of velvet brown eyes gazing at me shrewdly through the thick lenses of wire-rimmed spectacles.

Quietly, considering all the nuts and joints of his supporting equipment, my small cousin let himself down into the chair opposite and waved one attenuated hand toward my steamer trunk.

"Not really clever of me — er — Cousin. It's just that one thing followed upon another, don't you know? I saw the men leaving

77

and I'm friends with Tamati and he knows how I feel . . . and so he arranged it. . . .

He paused before continuing. "But you won't tell, will you, about Tamati?"

I gave him my sternest look. "What makes you think I won't tell?"

He looked at me a long moment, his velvet brown eyes thoughtful, considering. "Because you don't have a 'telling' face."

"Do I not, indeed?" I inquired.

A sudden smile gleamed like sunlight for a moment, transforming him from a little old man to a mischievous boy of scarcely ten. "No, you don't!"

"But what about your mama and Cousin Clinton? Will they not want to know how you got here?"

"Cousin Clinton?" The smile vanished and the little old man was back. "Oh, of course, you must mean my . . . my *uncle*, my Uncle Clint. Well, he leaves everything to Mama, so if he doesn't see me, he won't question, will he? And as for Mama— well, you'll understand when you see her!"

"Shall I?"

"Oh, yes."

The tone was quite definite. The face looking at me was old and inscrutable, the eyes veiled.

I gave up and turned the subject. "But how *did* you get here and when will your mama arrive?"

"Well, I got here in the Ravensfall canoe, of course, when the men left early this morning and I daresay that Mama—and Norah Hackett, also—will arrive sometime this afternoon. They're coming down with the maids and the luggage on the *Waiwere*."

"Oh, yes, of course, I'd forgotten!"

"Forgotten?"

"That the steamer spends the night at the hotel in Pipiriki and then calls again at all the river landings on its way down again to Wanganui."

There was a brief silence while the brown eyes widened.

"So, you really do remember. . . ."

"Yes, I really do. I was what . . . scarcely older than you . . .

78

no more than twelve, certainly . . . when . . ." I paused a moment, remembering that nightmare time. "When I . . ."

"You had to leave?"

I looked at him, disconcerted. "Yes, but how did you know? How did you know that I . . . we . . . had to leave? What do you know of Ishbel? Callum? The . . . the *taniwha?*"

There was a glint of humor before the velvet eyes, suddenly lacking their former luster, became as dull pebbles.

"Why, Tamati told me all that!"

"Tamati. Again. Just who *is* Tamati?"

"Old Moana's grandson, of course. You remember her, don't you? Tamati says that she was always about the place in the old days . . .

"Yes. Yes, of course, I do remember her." And I did: the old Maori woman with her clay pipe and tattooed chin who had made it her business — it seemed to me now — to scare Reggie and me half to death with her tales of the man-eating *taniwha* and the redheaded fairy-folk, the *patupaiarehe.*

And more than this, her insinuations — never, never outright, but always in "so many words" that our Great Uncle Josiah still "walked" and with him . . . I pulled myself together sharply. "Yes, of course I remember Moana, always about the house and gardens when we least expected her! Although, now I come to think of it, I never really understood her position . . ."

"Her position?"

"Yes: her position in our household. I mean, she was never a servant; I never saw her fetch and carry for anyone in my life! And although she was always full of stories for Reggie and me, she was never anything remotely near a nursery maid."

"But she was allowed the run of the house?"

"Yes . . . that is; not allowed nor disallowed. No one ever told Moana what to do nor what not to do . . . it was as if . . . as if . . .

"She owned the house?"

I looked down at the ancient eyes in the ten-year-old face and admitted some surprise to myself. "Yes. Yes, I suppose you're right. It was almost as if Moana had been at Ravensfall since the beginning of time — and felt some sort of responsibility for

79

the place. She hated us all, you know. Her son was killed in the Maori Wars and she always said that we Pakeha would one day be driven back into the sea. But, at the same time, at least as far as Reggie and I were concerned, she seemed to hold no personal animosity; she was forever telling us stories — Maori legends and myths — as if . . . as if, she were leaving us a legacy. Reggie, in particular, she seemed always to be after; she said he reminded her of our Great Uncle Josiah . . ."

Bertram stirred in his chair a little, the nuts and bolts of his harness squeaking in protest. "And your sister, Ishbel? How did Moana regard *her?* And what about Callum?"

I resisted a shudder. Moana had reacted to Ishbel like a moth about a flame — as if at once attracted and repelled; and as for Callum . . . But how could I explain any of this to anyone, let alone a ten-year-old, long-lost relative?

As if in answer to my thoughts, Bertram's dark eyes gleamed understandingly. "But of course, all of that — even though it was a long time ago — must be extremely painful for you. I'm sorry. Paul is always telling me that I pester people too much, ask too many questions.

"Paul?"

"Yes, of course. Paul Lucas; my — that is — Uncle Clint's partner, I guess you could call him. Have you not met him yet?"

"Why yes, so I did; at breakfast. I believe from something your uncle said last night that Mister Lucas acts as your tutor?"

There was the merest of twinkles deep in the brown eyes "So he does . . . when he's not . . . er . . . *painting,* or even, for that matter, when he isn't!"

I could make neither head nor tail of these extraordinary remarks but before I could question him, Bertram had somehow or other raised himself on his crutches and was now hobbling toward the door. "You will excuse me, Cousin Malvina, but I must make my way to my room to prepare for the descent of Mama and" — an expression of distaste crossed the delicate features — "Norah Hackett!"

Norah Hackett, I asked myself, Norah Hackett? Of course, I eventually remembered, the woman engaged by Clinton to be a nurse-companion to his sister Lucy and a sort of governess to her son.

Twelve

By the time I had unpacked the top drawer of my trunk, carefully stowing away the contents in the huge oak tallboy, the sun had come out in full force. I threw up my window and leaned out, taking deep breaths of the pure, soft air.

One or two sheep's wool clouds still lingered along the eastern horizon but the sun sparkled down from a sky otherwise a clear, calm blue. Outside my window the balcony that formed the roof of the first-floor veranda still gleamed, moist from the rain; with here and there, shallow puddles rippling from a gentle breeze. Beyond the narrow balustrade, the feathery tops of the tree ferns stirred in the same breeze, while lingering wisps of mist floated up from the river chasm far below.

In the bush over the river, native wood pigeons wafted their wings and to my delight, from somewhere in the trees below the balcony, clanged a tui's deep, bell-like tones. Yorkshire seemed suddenly very far away, but though I wished my family had been with me, somehow I seemed to have lost my homesickness. It was as if the tui's song had been a signal that *here* — at Ravensfall — was my spirit's true home.

The tui sounded again and I looked down, trying to find him among the tree-fern tops. As I did so, a flight of tiny wax-eyes rose chittering in a bevy. Here and there below the wide-spanning fronds of the ferns, I glimpsed stretches of the River Walk as it wound itself up from the landing and past the house on its way up to the bluff. Sure enough, a long shadow slowly detached itself from the side of one huge fern trunk and then slipped silently behind another. I did not see it again.

Though the sun still shone, I shivered, crossing my arms protectively. Who was it down there who had needed to move so secretly? Had I been under observation — and if so, why?

The rest of my unpacking could wait, I decided; I needed to leave my room — to get out of the house, in fact. A walk in the garden, in *front* of the house, would do me good, I decided; perhaps I might visit the stables and see if any changes had been made; or even — although reluctant but having to do so sometime — visit Miss Inglewood's memorial.

Before I could change my mind, I snatched up my shawl and left my room to make my way down the stairs.

I paused on the first-floor landing, as I had often done in the past, to admire the glorious rainbows of color created by the sunlight streaming into the hall through the stained-glass portraits of St. George and the Damsel in Distress. Not for the first time I wondered about my Great Uncle Josiah who had brought such beauty about. He may have consorted with pirates and have made illegal whiskey, but surely he had the soul of an artist? I wondered if it was from him that Clinton had inherited his talent.

On an impulse I turned about to peer up through my pince-nez at the bearded, lean features of the portrait in the recesses of the landing. Was there any physical likeness, I wondered, between my cousin and my uncle?

In the diffused light from the hall, it was hard to tell. True, they both seemed to have long, narrow features, though the spade beard billowing beneath my uncle's hawk nose disguised his lower face. However, perhaps in coloring they were similar? Though Great Uncle Josiah's mane was snowy white, his heavy brows — like Cousin Clinton's — were quite dark and as far as I could tell, there were also dark streaks in his beard. The eyes of both men were, however, completely dissimilar; my cousin's being large and of a cool, clear gray, while my uncle's eyes were long and narrow and light brown, just like Reggie's and my father's — topaz eyes, I remember Harriet once describing them romantically.

Below me, down in the hall, there was a swish of the baize door opening and shutting. Thinking it might be Mrs. Hodges, I rushed to the banisters and peered down shortsightedly. It was half-past eleven, already — as I had checked before I had left my room. If I were going for a walk, I decided, I needed to know at what time luncheon was usually served.

It was not Mrs. Hodges, however, who crossed the hall beneath me, but what appeared to be a long, lean youth carrying a box of some kind. As he crossed in front of the stairs — apparently on his way to the passage leading to the library — he looked up, as if he also were suddenly aware of another presence.

Looking down into the well of the hall, against the light streaming through the windows, he appeared no more to me than a dark silhouette and as far as he was concerned, I was probably a mere shapeless blur.

We looked toward each other for what seemed an endless amount of time before he, bowing slightly, departed.

Slightly shaken, though I could not imagine why, I continued down the stairs and out into the front garden.

There all my worries were forgotten with the sight of daffodils and starlit narcissus interspersed with the delicate mauves and pale primrose, yellows of clumps of polyanthus scattered in apparent careless profusion about the edges of the lawn.

I had to remind myself sharply that this was not an English spring but a New Zealand autumn going on for winter.

Great Uncle Josiah; I recognized his hand again. Who else could have planted the ancestoral bulbs of these purely English flowers, taking advantage of the milder upriver climate and this sheltered spot in the bush? I looked behind me at the wooden façade of the house, a colonial replica of early Victorian Gothic architecture — and dubbed Ravensfall after our family seat in Yorkshire.

What had Great Uncle Josiah been about? I wondered. Crusty old whaler, owner of an illegal whiskey still and associate of the gunrunning pirate, Bully Hayes, he had certainly been — and yet, there seemed to have been another side to his character, one that had yearned always for his homeland. I thought of the house behind me, of the row of ravens carved into the wooden lintel above the door and of the carved raven of the newel post, huge wings perpetually swooping down onto its helpless prey.

"The badge of our house, my dear," my father had once explained to me ruefully. "We are descended from the Vikings that once harried this part of the Yorkshire coast, coming into the kill with our raven banners flying; black ravens on a red ground. And according to legend, the forbears of our particular family foraged inland on the moors until they came upon a mountain spring with ravens circling above. That, in fact, is why our lands are called Ravensfall."

Had Josiah Raven tried to emulate his ancestors? I wondered now. Had he, in his turn, set out to tame a wild land in the hopes of founding his own dynasty? In that case, I thought suddenly, why had he never married—or had he? All at once I realized that apart from the family stories—surely exaggerated?—that I actually knew very little about my great uncle. What had he really been like? I wondered. What manner of man lurked behind the legend?

So immersed had I become in my thoughts, that without my realizing it my feet had taken their own way across the lawn and into the stretch of bush left standing between the house and the stable area. I came to my senses at the sound of a low-toned, musical voice apparently chanting nonsense.

"Chush, chush, chush! Now then, now then! Naughty! Chush! Naughty! Leave the birds alone! Chush, chush—you horrible animal, come down at once!"

Intrigued, I stepped around the slender gray trunk of a manuka tree to find myself in a small clearing. The clearing, I saw at once, had been created by the fallen trunk of a large rimu. Perched precariously on the mossy back of the trunk, gazing up into the drooping branches of a young rimu close by, was the daughter of Devlin Fordyke. With her slender form arrayed in a calf-length frock of dark green serge and with a shaft of sunlight burnishing her long copper tresses, she looked like nothing so much as a forest maenad.

Not wanting to upset her precarious balance with the surprise of my arrival, I did not speak; however, on following her gaze up into the thick, olive-green leaves I spied a familiar, never-to-be forgotten, furry white face topped with a gray-striped "cap" and dark gray ears. "Squeak!" I exclaimed with delight before I could help myself.

Two things happened in quick succession: the girl fell off the log and the cat, after a startled glance at me, clawed its way down the tree.

"Oh, I'm so sorry!" I rushed toward the boots kicking from out the green froth of skirts and petticoats. "I do hope you haven't hurt yourself!"

"No thanks to you, if I haven't!"

My helping hand was pushed aside as the boots established a foothold and their owner scrambled upright. "And anyway, that's a stupid name for a cat!"

"Yes. Yes, I suppose it is! But you see, Harriet gave us two cats and Reggie thought it would be fun to have names that would go together. . . . You're sure you're not hurt?"

She had sat down on the log and was rubbing the back of her head. "No, nothing broken; I bumped my head, that's all."

The slanting hazel eyes, tawny in the sunlight, regarded me with all the hostility I remembered from our first meeting. What was the problem here? I wondered. Smiling hesitantly, I sat down beside her. "Miranda, isn't it? I am Malvina Raven; I hope you'll call me Malvina?"

A look of contempt. "If you want!"

Somehow, I maintained my smile. Luckily, at that moment, Squeak, with a yowl of delight, decided he recognized me. Launching his considerable weight onto my lap, he contrived to dislodge my pince-nez and knock me sideways into Miranda who, losing her balance, ended up again on the ground, myself entwined about her and a crazy cat cavorting around us both.

"Stupid animal!" Miranda, the first to extricate herself, brushed down her skirts and sat herself again on the log. A small smile, however, played about her mouth, lighting up her small elfin face and giving her an altogether different look. "But why 'Squeak'? And if you wanted names to go together, what on earth did you call the other cat?"

"Why, Bubble, of course!"

A look of total mystification.

I gave her an understanding grin. "Oh, well, you're an American, so you wouldn't understand. Bubble 'n' Squeak is the name given to leftover cabbage and mashed potatoes that are fried up for breakfast or supper. Mainly, it's a dish for poor

85

people but Harriet — my stepmother — always says that even the rich should remember 'Waste not, want not', and in any event; though it sounds horrible, it's really very tasty!"

I was rewarded with a look of utter disgust, lightened somewhat by an entrancing, throaty giggle. "Papa is right — you British really are crazy!" A long, thoughtful look, shot obliquely from under long bronze lashes. "Harriet is your stepmother?"

There was something about her tone of voice that put me on my guard. "Yes."

"I expect you hate her — especially her making you eat that stuff!"

"But I told you, Bubble 'n' Squeak is really quite tasty, and even if it wasn't, Harriet would certainly not make me eat it!"

She gave me a considering look, taking me in from my disheveled hair and the pince-nez balanced unevenly on the bridge of my nose to the toes of my muddy boots. "Well of course, she wouldn't, would she, because you're old!"

I nodded my head gravely. "Yes, indeed; I am twenty-four. But, even if I were younger, Harriet would still not force me to eat anything I really hated — and in any event, I love her!"

"Love her! You love your *stepmother!*"

Squeak who had sneaked back onto my lap, now shot off it again in fright.

"Yes, I do. I suppose," I explained apologetically, "I don't really think of her as my stepmother, but rather as a great friend . . ."

The slanting eyes shot me a look of total disbelief. "A friend?"

"Yes. That is — well — Harriet is only ten years older than I am."

She sighed, almost with relief. "That explains it!"

Explains what? I thought. An idea occurred to me. "So you . . . you have a stepmother?"

"Did have!"

The dark brows frowned and the copper lashes hid the tawny eyes.

"Did have?"

"She died."

"I see."

"No, you don't!" With a sudden lithe twist, she leaped off the log and stood gazing down at me, her hazel eyes steady and furious. "You don't 'see' at all! She didn't just die, darling Malvina. She died because I wanted her to—I killed her!"

She stood silent a moment, enjoying my shock, before, with a toss of her long copper locks, she hared off through the bush.

I stood up quickly, meaning to go after her, but she was too quick for me, weaving from tree to tree, until with one last wicked glance over her shoulder, she finally disappeared.

She could not possibly have been serious, I told myself; but then I remembered my half-sister. Ishbel had been younger than Miranda, when she had administered those fatal laudanum drops to our mother. But then again, as I reassured myself, Ishbel, though she was perfectly aware that Reggie and I suspected the truth—which is why she terrorized us—had always kept her secret to herself

No, I thought to myself, the tempestuous young woman who had just left me, was surely not capable of such a deed. Why then had she felt the need to make such a statement—and to make such a statement to me?

Thirteen

A mee-aow and an urgent tugging at my skirts, brought me back to the present. Squeak, standing on his hind legs and diligently kneading his sharp, front claws into my black bombazine, indicated his wish to be picked up and petted.

"Wretched cat," I addressed him sternly, doing as he wished. "You must be all of twelve years old; surely, you must have learned *some* manners by now!"

A loud, vibrant purring was my reward. At least I had been recognized in one quarter, I told myself, and then felt an insane urge to giggle. "I mustn't get hysterical," I told the cat firmly, as to his indignation, I put him down again.

I gathered up my shawl from where it had drifted down by the fallen rimu trunk and leaving the little clearing, rejoined the track through the bush.

Five minutes later, I came out into the stable yard. A huge bay, a black, two chestnuts, and a roan peered at me inquisitively over the half doors of their stalls. Otherwise there was no sign of life, except for a spiral of smoke rising from the chimney of a whare, set off to one side in its own little garden. Traditionally, it was inhabited by the manager of the estate; my heart gave a little lurch as I remembered that the last occupant before we had left New Zealand, had been Callum Douglas. Who was living in it now? I wondered.

As if in answer to my unspoken question, the door opened. A tall, lean young man stepped out into the sunlight and for a moment stood on the step scanning the stables. Where had I seen that hawk-nosed profile before? I wondered.

At that moment, there was a sudden "Prrree" at my side and Squeak, who had foraged to and fro on my way through the bush, headed toward the whare, joined on his mad dash by a smaller shape—gray dappled with amber. "Bubble," I said to myself happily. So she, too, had survived, and this young man was evidently in charge of them for as I watched, he put down bowls of food.

As I walked over to the whare to make myself known, the young man turned toward me with a sudden swift movement that jogged my memory. Of course, I remembered, he was the youth I had seen earlier crossing the hall—except, now that I was closer with my pince-nez more firmly balanced on my nose, I could see that he was older than I had thought; in his early twenties, perhaps?

He watched as I approached, it seemed to me, somewhat warily.

"Malvina Raven," I introduced myself, putting out my hand.

There was the slightest hesitation as he took my hand in his own firm grip.

In any other country he would have been taken for a Spaniard, I thought. The face on a level slightly above my own, was flat-planed, high cheekboned, with great dark brows that swept upward from a chiseled, high-bridged nose. His complexion was olive, rather than the brown or bronze of the local Maori people. A Maori with Pakeha blood or a Pakeha with Maori blood? I asked myself bemusedly. Which?

"Miss Raven?" a youthful baritone asked as he again wrung my hand. "How d'you do? I am Tamati.

Tamati. "Yes, of course. Tamati—Bertram's friend."

A deep chuckle. "So, you found us out?"

"Yes, but I promise you, I shan't give you away!"

I was rewarded with another laugh. "Poor little chap, won't leave him alone, will they? Do this, do that! Take your medicine! Brush your teeth! Behave yourself! Get out of my sight!"

"Get out of my sight? They say *that?*"

He grinned broadly; but the eyes behind it were sad, watchful. "No, not in words."

In my mind's eye, I had a sudden appalling vision of Bertram's small, hunchbacked figure, his head somehow held proudly upright, his brown eyes, quick with intelligence behind the thick-lensed spectacles, realizing that he was not wanted.

"It's as bad as that?"

"Yes."

"But I don't understand."

He shrugged his shoulders. "Well, you wouldn't, would you?"

"I wish you would explain yourself," I was beginning in high umbrage, when, from an inner room behind Tamati, there was a rasping sound as if of a reluctant drawer being pulled out of a chest.

Tamati's face was suddenly expressionless. "I'm sorry, I can't talk with you now — perhaps later?"

Without waiting for a reply, he vanished into the whare, closing the door behind him.

In front of the closed door, Bubble and Squeak, replete from the contents of their bowls, sat calmly washing their faces, as if nothing had happened.

But what *had* happened? I asked myself.

There had been a sudden noise and an apparently polite young man had brusquely closed a door in my face.

This did seem rather abrupt; but not enough, I thought, to warrant a certain cold clamminess between my shoulder blades.

What was going on?

In front of me, the front door of the whare remained firmly closed.

You are far too imaginative, Malvina Raven, I told myself sternly. Why should Tamati not withdraw to deal with some domestic crisis — no doubt there was some perfectly good reason for his sudden retreat; and if he had been somewhat brusque, he had also been perfectly polite.

It was none of my business, I decided.

Turning from the whare door — still uncompromisingly shut — I looked out over the stables. As I recalled, beyond them twisted two other paths through the bush: one led to a small clearing down near the River Walk, where there was a spring and some workmen's cottages; the other led upward to the

90

windswept bluff and Miss Inglewood's memorial set in the midst of our small family graveyard.

I thought of the memorial and the memories it brought to me of Ishbel and shuddered. I did not want to go there, I told myself; but I knew, of course, that I had to. It was another memory that must be laid to rest.

Taking a deep breath and wrapping my shawl firmly about my shoulders, I set off past the stables.

Fourteen

To my surprise, the track, though steep, was relatively easy-going. Though not wide, it seemed clear of any straying branches from the tangled undergrowth, thickets, and trees on either side. Briefly I wondered why the branches had been cut back, then looking down at the narrow pathway with the horse-shoe marks implanted in the mud from the recent rains, I understood; the track had become a means of exercise for the horses.

At last I made it to the top, breaking out of the bush onto the cleared headland of the bluff.

I stood for a moment, looking about me, recalling long-lost memories: the decaying wooden fence dividing the burial ground from the bush, Miss Inglewood's memorial on a rise by itself, the grave near the cliff that Reggie and I had always assumed to be that of Great Uncle Josiah. It was hard to discern the words on the wooden cross because they had been obliterated by the weather. Close by were the grassy humps of two small — very small — graves and the plain square gravestone alongside, marked simply "Ihaira."

To my surprise, all the graves had been tended to, the grass cut short, the stones cleared of moss and — except for Miss Inglewood's memorial — provided with small jars of flowers; mainly daffodils, I noted. Were they from the main house — and who had brought them?

Who was Ihaira? I asked myself again. Reggie and I had often made up stories about her and the two pitifully small graves nearby. Had she been the mother? we wondered. Had they all died in one of those awful cholera epidemics that used to happen so frequently among the Maori, years ago? And if so, why were they not all buried with their own people — although, of course, Ihaira may have been a Pakeha; many Europeans gave their children Maori names, though usually associated with flowers, trees, or birds. . . . However, I had never come across the name Ihaira before.

In any event, in what way was Ihaira connected with Josiah Raven? Had she been his wife? In that case, why the one name only? And why had we never heard of her before?

The rising wind stirred the daffodils in their jars as I stood thinking and I remembered how Reggie and I had approached old Moana with the mystery. Who was Ihaira? we had asked her. Had she been our great uncle's wife?

We had rarely seen Moana laugh but when she did, she cackled. She cackled then, the purple-blue lines of her *moko* writhing about her lips. At the last, still without saying a word, she had pushed her smelly clay pipe back between her teeth and wandered off again into the shadows.

A snort and a rush of sweet-smelling, warm breath down the back of my neck brought me to my senses.

Behind me, at the cross-bar gate I had carefully closed, trampled and snuffled the enormous bay I had seen in the stables; and very much at home on his back, sat Devlin Fordyke, a veritable human mountain of tweed, corduroy, and leather.

He was hatless and the short, curling locks of his russet hair stirred in the strengthening breeze.

"Miss Raven, what a surprise!"

"Is it?"

He engagingly grinned. "No, but I had to make some sort of an opening!" He swung in leisurely fashion, down from the bay, looping the reins over one of the bars of the fence.

"Beau Brummell, here, needed exercise and seeing you leave the stable yard provided further excuse!"

"Excuse?"

He flashed mock-guilty grin. "An excuse not to return to my desk."

"You mean, the sight of me dragged you away from your accounts?"

93

"Not precisely."

I gazed at him askance, while he smiled back at me, apparently enjoying my puzzlement. "Not my accounts—no—but rather my current article."

"You are a writer?" Somehow, I could not envisage this huge personage sitting, hour after weary hour, with pen in hand.

His eyes gleamed with laughter at my surprise. "I don't believe I can dignify myself with such a title—journalist, perhaps? I write mainly travel articles. At the moment, I am employed by the *New York Times* for a series of articles about New Zealand—which, of course, eventually I hope to turn into a book."

"Really?" Trying to keep the sarcasm out of my voice, I thought of the three times I had met this man—first, in the foyer of Foster's Hotel when—I had to admit it—he had seemed relatively civilized; second, "below stairs" in that same hotel, when he had accused me of not being myself and then last night when we had danced our hellish dance and then, astonishingly, he had explained to my cousin that he had treated me so, only because he had thought I was an intruder!

I looked at him now, his solid hulk steadfast against the billowing wind. Just how much could I believe of what he told me?

As if guessing my thoughts, he stared back at me, an amused and—to me, highly irritating—smile playing about his features.

"Come now, Miss Raven, let us be friends! I agree that the circumstances last night were to say the least, highly unusual but I assure you I meant no harm—and if I had had the least idea as to your identity, I should never have manhandled you so. However, you took me entirely by surprise and in any event"—he looked ruefully down as he put forward his right foot—"I believe I paid for my audacity!"

To my annoyance, I felt myself blushing at the memory of my well-aimed kick. Why, I wondered, longing to hide my embarrassment by taking the offensive, had he last night, when he had supposedly—in his words—interrupted an intruder, taken the opportunity to examine Clinton's letters? And why, I asked myself, had he acted toward me in such a cavalier fashion the other night at Foster's Hotel? And what was his connection with that strange woman, Mrs. Trillingham-Bean? That there was a connection, I was quite sure. She had quite evidently recognized him in the dining room and had reappeared later, as I had made my ignominious retreat up the stairs.

Most of all, I wondered as I gazed up at the face smiling down at me, what had all this to do with my cousin? I thought again of him peering through Clinton's letters. Did he mean Clinton harm? — and yet my cousin appeared to trust him.

"Come, Miss Raven, why do you hesitate? If at the moment we cannot be friends, at least let us not be enemies!"

Quite obviously, the man was a rogue but it would serve no purpose, I decided, to accuse him then and there. My word against his, after all, and he had quite evidently worked himself into Clinton's good graces. I had obviously better bide my time. Perhaps, if I pretended to be friendly, I could find out what was going on and then take the evidence to Clinton.

I forced myself to look up graciously at the ugly face above me. Was that the bland smile of the consummate liar? I wondered. If so, I could do just as well!

I smiled brilliantly. "Thank you, Mister Fordyke. I accept your apology!"

"Do you, indeed?"

To my surprise, the hazel eyes — so much like his daughter's — expressed amusement, rather than the humble gratitude I had expected.

"Then, by all means, let us shake hands upon it, Miss Raven!"

Before I could prevent it, my right hand was seized in both of his great paws and pumped vigorously up and down.

Somehow, I rescued my tingling fingers. "I believe," I said, with consummate dignity, "that you told me that seeing me leave the stable yard had provided you with an excuse for not writing your present article — I don't understand. Why should seeing me provide you with such an excuse?"

"Only that I want you to do some of my work for me!" he said, grinning mischievously.

"Excuse me?"

A wide, expansive gesture over Miss Inglewood's memorial and the accompanying graves. "These people — who were they?

95

As a member of the family, you must know all kinds of stories about them."

I frowned in irritation. Here we go again, I thought, testing me, finding out whether or not I really am Malvina Raven; and really and truly, why should it matter to him? What was behind all this?

I found myself regarded by an amused grin. Had he guessed my thoughts? "We have family graveyards like this in rural parts of America—I thought a comparison might be interesting; might add 'human interest,' perhaps?"

"Oh. I see." If he were a confidence man, he was certainly a good one, I thought!

"Of course I know Josiah Raven was buried up here somewhere—Tamati told me—an old whaler and something of a pirate, I understand."

"Tamati told you?"

He looked surprised. "Yes, why not?"

"Oh, no reason, really; it's just that I didn't realize that he knew anything about my family—which is stupid of me as apparently he was another grandson of old Moana's, or so my cousin Bertram told me this morning."

"Who was old Moana?"

"Old Moana?" I paused for a moment—who *was* old Moana? "An old Maori woman," I told him at last, "who used to wander in and out of Ravensfall when we lived here. It was as if she owned the place; she used to tell us how much she hated us all and how all of us Pakeha would one day be driven back into the sea."

I was rewarded with a look of amused interest. "Driven back into the sea? Why should the old woman have said such a thing?"

"Oh, because of the Maori land wars. Moana's favorite grandson, Rangi, you see, was a Hau-hau and that was what they believed, that the *Pakeha*—that is, we Europeans—would one day be defeated and totally driven from the country."

He gave me another interested look: this time, lacking amusement. "These . . ." A comical look as he tried to reproduce the Maori word. "These *How-Hows?* Is that how you pronounce it?"

96

I couldn't help smiling. "More or less — they got their name from their battle cry during the wars."

"I see. Well, they must have been somewhat akin to our Native American Indians."

"Yes; you're right."

"So, Rangi was killed?"

"Yes, but how did you know?"

The hazel eyes were surprisingly gentle. "Your face, your tone of voice when you were talking about him — and the fact that Moana seemed to be so embittered."

"Embittered? Yes, I suppose she was. Although she was constantly threatening that we should all be driven back into the sea, she never seemed to mean it when she spoke to Reggie and me. In fact, she really seemed to be rather fond of Reggie, as if for some secret reason of her own she was keeping a special watch over him; when she told us all her favorite old Maori myths and legends, she always seemed to be talking directly to Reggie. I used to feel quite jealous!"

"What happened to her?"

"I don't know, really, but she must be dead by now: she was very old when we knew her."

"She must have known your great uncle; perhaps that was why she had the run of the house."

I looked at him in surprise. "Yes, you could be right. I suppose because we were so young, Reggie and I never really questioned Moana's presence. To us, she was just a part of the house and gardens and had always been there."

He looked thoughtful. "Sometimes, it takes a stranger to see the obvious . . . or to see behind what others take for granted."

What a mountain of surprises my huge companion was, I thought. Somehow, I had not expected such sensitivity. I looked up at him as he gazed slowly about the graveyard; he reminded me of a picture I had seen once, of an enormous grizzly bear rearing on its hind legs while scenting the atmosphere for danger. But what danger could possibly be here in an old family cemetery?

My thoughts were abruptly interrupted. "You talk about her

grandson Rangi . . . but she must have had other grand-children?"

"Of course, but her husband and most of her children died in one of the cholera epidemics. As far as I know, only her son, Hemi, survived. In fact, Hemi and his granddaughter Ngaire, Rangi's daughter, used to work for us. That's why it's strange that I don't remember Tamati. . . I suppose Moana—or Hemi, for that matter—might have had another son or daughter who survived the epidemic but one I don't remember coming near Ravensfall. It doesn't surprise me really, considering that . . . well . . ." I broke off, hesitant to continue.

"Considering what?" Devlin Fordyke glanced down at me, the lines of his ugly face drawn together in a puzzled frown.

I attempted a light laugh. "Considering the ghosts."

"The *ghosts?*"

"You'll find it very amusing, I'm sure, but most Maori people believe that Ravensfall is haunted and won't come near the place."

To my surprise, Devlin Fordyke did not laugh. "Haunted by whom?"

"By Great Uncle Josiah; who else?" I looked toward Miss Inglewood's memorial and the edge of the cliff jutting out over the river below and could not prevent a sigh. "And others."

He followed the line of my eyes. "Ah, yes, your governess— she *was* your governess, wasn't she; that date on the plaque makes it about right? And, of course, as soon as my daughter and I moved in here, we were told all about that other business with Miss McCleod . . . told, I might say, whether we wanted to hear or not!"

"Yes, of course. Harriet warned me that there might still be gossip even after all these years—and then, yesterday there was Nellie Possett. . . ."

He displayed a look of amused but complete befuddlement. "Harriet is, of course, your stepmother . . . but *Nellie Possett?*"

I thought with affection of the little farmer's wife, the brown ribbons of her hat blowing in the breeze as she had looked up at me earnestly from the deck of the *Waiwere,* yesterday. Was it really only yesterday that she had tried to talk to me one last time? But the steamer had docked before she could tell me what she wanted to say and she had been obliged to wave to her patient Sam as he had waited for her on the landing. She had tried to warn me, but warn me of what? At the time, I had thought it was the possible gossip she was concerned about but now I was not so sure.

By this time, Devlin Fordyke had ventured farther into the little burial ground after carefully closing — I was pleased to see — the gate behind him.

He looked down at me genially. "So there are ghosts at Ravensfall?"

It was more of a statement than a question.

"So the Maoris say." I shrugged my shoulders and attempted an amused smile.

"And you; what do you think?"

All of a sudden, for a few horrible moments I had a mental vision of Ishbel and Callum on their wild, manic chase in my nightmare of the night before. "Of course, there are no ghosts," I managed at last, forcing myself to look up at him, steadily meeting his gaze.

He stood for what seemed a long minute, saying nothing. "Except in our own minds, Miss Raven? Would you not agree? Surely there, in those dark recesses, there are ghosts a-plenty!"

As he spoke, the wind gathered in force and small clouds scudded across the sky.

There are no ghosts, I wanted to shout at him. *There are no ghosts!* Instead, I hugged myself in the sudden cold, silently preventing the words from escaping.

By my side, the American's large bulk seemed to settle like the bulwark of a huge, menacing mountain and his eyes as he gazed down at me, seemed uncomfortably penetrating as if he knew very well what was going on in my mind.

I attempted a light laugh. "You speak from experience, Mister Fordyke?"

There was no answering smile; the craggy face was still as carved granite, the eyes somber. "You are, of course, quite right; I have my own ghosts to lay to rest."

I remembered then my meeting with his daughter and her peculiar assertion about her stepmother's death. Just what *had* happened to the late Mrs. Fordyke? I wondered?

As if he guessed my thoughts, he turned away, surveying again the grassy mounds. "So, which is Josiah Raven's grave?" he asked at last.

I nodded toward the weatherworn wooden cross with the remains of its time-obliterated inscription. "Reggie and I always thought it must be that one."

"Yes, I daresay you must be right; it seems to be the only one suitable."

As he spoke, he walked over the grass to the grave, offering me his arm over the uneven ground. We paused a moment, looking down at the long mound surrounded by its well-weathered, low wooden fence.

"And the two little graves and this one . . . this is a Maori name, I suppose? How do you pronounce it?"

"The letter 'i' in Maori is pronounced like 'ee' as in 'see,' " I explained, "and 'ai' together sound something like 'i' as in 'tie.' "

"I see. So this name is — Ee-hie-ra? What does it mean?"

"I don't know. I'm afraid I don't know much Maori but Maori names usually refer to a quality like *aroha* which means love, or something in nature like *whetu* which means star. Or sometimes, a European name is made to sound like Maori."

"How do you mean?"

"Well, Tamati, for instance, is Maori for Thomas . . . there being no 's' sound in Maori: and because Maori doesn't have a 'g' or a 'j,' Joseph becomes Hohepa and George becomes Hori . . ." I paused, embarrassed. "I'm sorry, I didn't mean to give you a lecture!"

"He grinned pleasantly. "Not at all. So, let's see — James would be?" The craggy features wrinkled in thought. "Haym?"

I couldn't repress a giggle. "Well, you're almost right! I should have told you that Maori names always end with a vowel sound. James, therefore, becomes Hemi which is pronounced something like Haymee except that the 'e' sound is more like . . . Look, I've got to stop this, I'm doing what Reggie calls my schoolmistress act!"

"I wish all schoolmistresses could be as . . . pleasant as well as instructive!"

The hazel eyes smiled down in a way that made me blush.

His intonation of the word, pleasant, had also hinted at a meaning more intimate.

Hurriedly I gathered my wits together. "In any event," I chatted on briskly, in an attempt to disguise my embarrassment, "I can't tell you who Ihaira was . . . though Reggie and I always assumed that she must have been the mother of the children in the little graves."

The wind having strengthened considerably while we talked, now blew hard against my back, pressing against my skirts and tearing at the loose ends of my shawl. I could not help shivering as the cold seeped through to my shoulders.

"I'm sorry," my companion apologized. "I can see you are cold. I really should not have kept you talking!" Tugging at a handsome gold chain, he withdrew his watch from his waistcoat pocket and flicked back the lid. "As I thought, it is almost one o'clock. I believe they serve luncheon round about now at the big house. Perhaps I could escort you back down the trail?"

I looked toward the memorial standing bleak and lonely on its isolated rise. "Thank you, no. There is still something I have to do."

He looked from me to the memorial. "Ah, yes, I see: Miss Inglewood. But you are cold — could you not come back later; tomorrow, perhaps? I should be glad to accompany you."

I was tempted; not so much for his company, which, though I hated to admit it, had become . . . disturbing . . . to me but because I simply wanted to delay what I knew had to be done.

Telling myself not to be such a coward, I made myself shake my head firmly. "No — thank you — but I must go now."

He flashed a shrewd look of understanding. "And you wish to be alone?"

"Yes."

"Very well, then, Miss Raven. I shall leave you now. I expect we shall meet again soon enough."

He bowed slightly before leaving the enclosure to go to Beau Brummell. I stood waiting while he unhitched the great horse and swinging aboard, raised a hand in farewell. As I made my way up to the memorial, I felt his eyes on my back but when I turned, he was already disappearing into the bush.

* * *

From the top of the rise, I could see the darkly shining gash of the river winding below and mile after mile of dark green, thick native bush. In the distance on an absolutely clear day, I knew I would also have seen the snowcapped peaks of Mount Ruapehu, far off to the north in the center of the island with perhaps a white wisp of smoke wafting up from its ancient volcanic cone; while far over to the west would slope the graceful, almost symmetrical sides of the volcano, Mount Egmont, called Taranaki by the Maoris.

That afternoon, however, the clouds, gathered together again by the wind, now tore overhead in a great, pulsating gray mass. Behind me, the cairn raised its rugged top against the sky; it was an illusion, I knew, but gazing up at the surmounting iron crucifix sharp against the clouds, I felt that it, the cairn and I were all whirling in one last mad race through space.

With my skirts buffeting about my ankles and the ends of my shawl flapping in the breeze, I read again the inscription on the metal plaque. "At peace," I murmured to myself aloud, quoting the last line; but the wind whipped away the words as soon as they were uttered. Was Miss Inglewood really at peace? I wondered.

I tried to say a prayer, but couldn't. Instead, I tried to think of her as I had known her; a small-boned, fair-haired, blue-eyed woman in her early thirties. She had been very like my mother and, therefore, of course, like me. In fact, when we were together, strangers always assumed that she and I were related—as we were, of course, for it all came out at Harriet's trial.

But before the trial, no one except Harriet—and Ishbel— had realized that the woman calling herself Mary Inglewood, was really Mama's cousin and childhood friend. Newly widowed, she had returned from India after the scandal of Mama's death and being one of the few people aware of the mental problems of Ishbel's father and having subsequent suspicions about Ishbel and her part in Mama's death, she had, without revealing her true identity, applied for the advertised post of governess to our family and on acceptance, had traveled with us to New Zealand.

Poor Miss Inglewood, I thought—whatever her true name,

this was the one I should ever remember — after such a well-intentioned beginning, to end in such a manner!

I thought of her now; her many kindnesses to Reggie and me — and yet, on reflection, I realized now that we had never felt completely at home with her. Though she had fussed over us like another mother, there was always something that we didn't quite trust. Perhaps it was the questions she perpetually pestered us with — though now, of course, I well understood the reason — and the way, that just like Moana, she would suddenly appear, when we were least expecting her. As someone once told us, she crept like a little mouse from room to room.

Perhaps it had been this last habit that had given rise to the rumors after her tragic — and at the time mysterious — death, that like Great Uncle Josiah, she still "walked"?

I shivered in the biting wind.

Certainly after that time, no Maoris would work at Ravensfall. Only Hemi and Ngaire stayed — because of old Moana, I supposed: though why she, with all her Maori superstitions and respect for the supernatural, dared to face the spirit world at Ravensfall, was another mystery in itself.

But she had stayed, I thought now, even after Ishbel's drowning — although Hemi and Ngaire had absolutely refused to come back. It was almost, I thought, as if Moana had been a spirit herself and so tied to the place.

I looked down at the graves; so many tragedies and so many mysteries. What would Great Uncle Josiah have thought of it all, I asked myself, looking toward the little enclosure with its weather-beaten cross?

Would he have approved of sharing his family burial ground with the memorial to Miss Inglewood? I wondered. And what would have been his feelings toward Ishbel?

Ishbel?

I suddenly realized that there was no grave for Ishbel. Before I could ponder the strangeness of this, my eye was taken by something white fluttering through the trees beyond the graveyard gate.

As I watched, a plump, pink-faced young woman in a maid's white cap and apron, stumbled out of the bush. As she rested, out of breath, against a tree, I walked down to the gate.

"Beg pardon, miss, I'm sure! But I'm not much used to 'ills and I h'ought to 'ave walked slower. But that there Mrs. 'odges, she were right worried. . . ."

She paused for breath and I seized the opportunity to speak. "Oh, dear me, I fear it must be very late — I'm afraid I hadn't realized . . . no doubt, I'm late for luncheon!"

"Not to worry about luncheon, miss. Mrs. 'odges said as 'ow she'd save you some — she's serving it later h'anyways because of Mrs. Wilkinson and Miss 'ackett. We all just h'arrived on the steamer."

"Oh, I see! As long as I haven't caused any extra bother for Mrs. Hodges. . . ."

"Lor' love you, no, miss; she were just worried about you. She wondered where you got to!"

"Well, I suppose we'd better go back at once and relieve her anxieties, although I can't imagine what harm could possibly come to me!"

To my surprise, there was no answering smile to my jibe. Instead, the young maid, all of sixteen or seventeen, I thought, shivered as she looked about her; her brown eyes wide as she noticed the graves behind me.

"That's as may be, miss: but this place 'as got a reputation!"

Without further ado, she turned back to the bush path, clearly indicating that the quicker I did as I was told, the better!

Fifteen

The maid's name was Betty, she told me, on our way back to the house and she was just out from England — the London area, she informed me.

"Do you like it, here, Betty?"

She sniffed. "Can't say h'as I do, miss — too quiet."

"Perhaps, if you had a position in a town — Wanganui, for instance?"

She snorted. "Wanganui? Call that a town?"

I tried not to laugh and did not succeed. "Come now, how long were you in Wanganui, before you came upriver?"

"Day n'arf!"

"What, a whole day and a half! Well, then; you didn't give the place much of a chance, did you? There are lots of things going on in Wanganui. I expect that if you stayed long enough, you'd find yourself going out every evening in the week!"

A look of total disbelief. "H'if you say so, miss!"

A sudden thought occurred to me. "But tell me, if you dislike quiet so much, why did you accept a position at Ravensfall? If I remember rightly, trained servants are in very short supply in the town: it's a wonder you weren't snapped up!"

"Well, I ain't trained — well, not really. And then again, it were the wages she offered."

"She?"

"The old duck . . . beggin' your pardon, Mrs. 'odges, I should say!"

"I should say so, indeed!" I tried to look severe.

"I know I shouldn't call 'er that; but she do take on so! Always, eat this, don't eat that! I 'ope you're wearing your flannels!

105

Keep yer feet dry!' Bloomin' heck, she thinks she's me mam!"

I remembered Mrs. Hodges fussing over me that morning and could not help laughing at the flushed countenance before me. "Yes; well . . . I suppose it's because she cares. And that's nice, isn't it — after all, you are a long way from home."

She grinnned reluctantly. "I suppose she don't mean no 'arm; it's just, I could kill 'er sometimes, that's all!"

We reached a bend in the track and paused before going on.

I thought for a moment. "You say you were offered better wages to work here at Ravensfall? I suppose that's because we're in the country?"

"That's right — and though it's dull as ditchwater, here, I figured I could stick it out for a while; me mam's still got five of us to feed and I try to send 'ome as much as I can".

The explanation certainly sounded plausible enough, I thought; but the plump face watching me had grown very still. There was something I was not being told, I decided; but what was it?

The wide brown eyes looking me over shrewdly, suddenly crinkled mischievously. "Oh, what the 'eck! I told the old d . . . that is Mrs. 'odges, that I wouldn't tell nobody, because she didn't want no more rumors. See — it's 'ard enough for 'er to get workers 'ere; but you're different, aren't you, because you live 'ere?"

"That's true," I agreed, a little dizzy after trying to follow the convolutions of her speech. "But what rumors are you talking about?"

"Oh, only that the place is 'aunted."

"Oh, really? Is that all?"

"Yes. There was murders done, see; so there's bound to be a few ghosts. Stands to reason, don't it?"

"Yes. Yes, I suppose it does!" I looked at her in awe. "So you believe in ghosts?"

"Oh, yes. Well I 'ave to, really, don't I; me Auntie Edna being a psychic."

"I . . . I see. So, you're not afraid?"

A frank look and a shrug of the plump shoulders. "I am and I ain't! As me mam says, it's the living you got to be worried h'about, not the dead, but . . ."

106

"But?"

We had started back down the track again and she threw me a considering glance over her shoulder. "Well, as me auntie says, "There's ghosts and then there's ghosts!"

I kept my voice casual, amused. "And have you seen any ghosts at Ravensfall?"

We reached the stables and she paused awhile before she answered. "Well, not so much seen as 'eard."

I took a deep breath. Beau Brummell, back in his stall, I noticed, nickered softly in greeting. "And what have you heard?"

"Oh, bells ringing and such. Bells ringing and footsteps when there h'aint no one there."

"But you haven't seen . . . anything?"

The smoke no longer twisted from the whare chimney, I observed, but the door was now open.

"That's not what I said, is it? I said, 'not so much seen as 'eard, because I only saw the once . . . and it were in moonlight."

"What did you think you saw?"

Though she grinned up at me saucily, clearly appreciating the joy of keeping me in suspense, there was a fear at the back of her eyes; a fear that somehow rang true. "I didn't *think* I saw; I really did see. It were after the dishes were done. The old duck sent me to the libery to fetch a book — she thinks I ought to better meself. . . ." She paused, her eyes darkening.

"So you were in the library?"

"No, in the passage — you know, the one leading to the side door onto the lawn?"

I did know. It was the passage I had seen Tamati about to enter that morning: it led to the cloakroom and study, as well as the library.

"Well, h'anyways, I 'eard this noise — like skirts swishing — and there h'it was, a shape against the moonlight coming in through the glass in the side door . . . and then the moon passed behind a cloud and the . . . the . . . *thing* . . . sort of dissolved into nothing. . . ."

In her distress, she stopped a moment, covering her face with her small hands. "I shouldn't be telling you this, miss; I really shouldn't . . . but I didn't tell nobody before. I suppose it were all sort of banked up inside me . . . I feel a real fool—but I seen it, I know I did!"

I slipped an arm about her shoulders and hugged her gently. "It's all right, Betty. It's all right! I know exactly how you feel. . . ."

She drew away stiffly. "H'ain't no need to patronize me, miss, I'm sure. I may be in a bit of a dither now but I know which way's up! Soon's I got over the shock, I checked in the drawing room and both Mrs. Wilkinson and that there Miss 'ackett were still sitting there gossiping over their coffee cups and t'weren't no other female in the house, unless"—she paused, giving a naughty grin—"you count the old duck! And she were still in the kitchen that's for sure!"

All I had experienced the night before, flashed through my mind. I felt ice-cold and it wasn't the wind, I decided. "I'm sorry, Betty: I didn't mean to offend you."

"No offense taken! I just 'opes that you won't . . . that is . . ."

"Don't worry, I shan't tell anyone . . . but if you have such an experience again, you will tell me, won't you? You see . . ."

I was about to tell her of my previous night's experiences, when we were hailed from the whare.

Tamati appeared in the doorway. He smiled politely. "So, Betty found you, Miss Raven? She was worried about you!"

"I don't see why . . . what could possibly happen to me in the bush?"

His smile vanished as he gazed at me consideringly. "People have been lost before . . . especially people who don't . . . know their way about."

He had been about to say something else, I realized: something not so polite. What, I wondered, and why?

"But I do know my way about—at least up to the bluff: that much, I do remember!"

I turned to Betty. "So Tamati told you where to find me?"

"Yes, Mister . . . Mister . . . you know, that big man— the American gentleman?—sent 'im with a message down to the big house. Said if we was worried, you was h'up in the old graveyard. Mrs. 'odges didn't arf 'ave a fit. Sent me straight away, she did!"

108

"Mister Fordyke took it upon himself to send you a message!"
Try as I might, I could not keep the irritation from my voice.

Betty looked surprised. "Why, yes, miss. He were just doing
the neighborly, weren't he? Mrs. 'odges were h'ever so grateful,
I can tell you . . . she were that worried you'd got yourself lost!"

I gritted my teeth and made myself speak politely. "I'm sure
I'm grateful for Mrs. Hodges's concern. But there was no need
for her to worry — I really do know my way about. And as for
Mister Fordyke, the next time I see him, I shall certainly . . ." I
broke off as I had a sudden thought. "But aren't he and his
daughter renting a cottage around here, somewhere?"

"That's right; they're staying in one of the old workmen's
whares by the spring." Tamati added to my irritation by smiling
at me as if he were amused. He had come down off the whare
steps and now was strolling toward us. "But you won't catch
him, now," he added, his smile deepening. "He told me he was
going to take Miranda down to the landing: the Turners are
having a birthday party for their youngest and they're sending
over their dinghy."

"The Turners? Oh, yes, of course — they farm over the river,
don't they — farther down from Ravensfall?"

I did not mention it to Tamati, but I remembered that Jonathan, one of the Turner sons and at that time a rising young law-
yer in Wanganui, had been in love — not that it had done him
much good! — with Ishbel. What had happened to Jonathan? I
wondered now.

". . . before it rains."

"Excuse me?" I came back from my memories to find Tamati
had been talking to me.

"You were woolgathering! I said I hoped they'd get Miranda
over the river before it rains."

"Rains!" I could not help exclaiming. "What, again?"

Tamati looked up at the sky — he was my own height, I noticed, but more broadly built. "Yes, again, and quite soon. The
wind's dropped and look at those clouds, they mean business!"

He was right; the clouds had welded themselves into a dark,
threatening mass and already we could feel the first few sporadic drops ice-cold on our faces.

I turned to the young maid. "I'm sorry, Betty; I should not

have spent so long talking — we had better go home as quickly as possible. At least, it's not far to go now and the trees will afford us some shelter."

Betty started off toward the path back through the bush. "Yes, miss; but we'd better 'urry, or we'll get a proper soaking!"

"Home?" Tamati's light baritone was not so much questioning as challenging. "You call Ravensfall your home?"

"Well . . ."

I cast about for what to say: surprised more at my own reaction than to his.

"But you weren't even born here!"

His tone of voice was now definitely contemptuous; on the verge, even, of anger.

Why should he be so upset? I wondered. I thought of ways to placate him. I could say, for instance, that I had been talking casually; that the term home, here, meant no more to me than any place where I was staying at the moment; but then, to my surprise I found myself realizing, that would not have been the truth.

I remembered leaning out my window just that morning, listening to the tui's call and the overwhelming feeling I had experienced of being so completely at home.

I looked now at Tamati and answered him as best I could. "You don't have to be born in a place to call it home."

The rain started in earnest and slipping my shawl over my head, I hurried toward the track. As I plunged in among the trees, I looked back to see him still standing there, stiff and straight, looking after me.

Sixteen

By the time we reached the house again, the rain had stopped and we ran laughing across the lawn.

The front door was opened before we had climbed the stone steps and a disapproving Mrs. Hodges watched our ascent in silent reprimand.

"There's cold meats and pickles and bread and butter that I saved for you in the dining room, miss: and afterward, you're wanted in the drawing room! But you'd better give me that wet shawl—and what about your feet? They'll be soaked through, I'll be bound!"

Silently, I lifted my skirts a fraction to reveal my sturdy walking boots.

"Hmph! Well, you've *some* sense, I suppose!"

"Thank you, Mrs. Hodges. I'm sorry . . ." I began humbly, but she had already turned away.

She looked sternly at Betty. "You, girl! Come with me!"

I wanted to protest that our lateness was not Betty's fault but before I could do so, Betty had looked back at me, brown eyes laughing and one finger pressed against her twitching lips.

As Mrs. Hodges marched purposefully toward the green baize door, Betty dutifully followed—imitating the housekeeper's martial gait in such an exaggerated fashion that I could scarcely keep from laughing out loud.

What punitive rations had Mrs. Hodges allocated to me in the dining room? I wondered.

I need not have worried!

Cold meats she had threatened; and cold meats there were: pressed mutton, brawn, and slices of cold roast beef displayed

111

on the sideboard with appropriate greens, potato salad, pickled onions, chutney, piccalilli, cheeses and, of course, the requisite bread and butter. Just in case all this did not satisfy my aching void, a bowl of apples and a plate of macaroons were also presented.

"A cup of tea, miss?"

The voice was soft, hesitant. It belonged to a tiny parlor maid balancing a silver service on a large tray.

"Oh, yes, please! That's what I should like most of all! Just a drop of milk and no sugar, thank you."

I sipped the hot, steaming tea appreciatively while eyeing my newest acquaintance. "And your name is?"

"Helena, miss!"

Her voice was so low as to be scarcely heard and the small hands twisted together in front of the starched white apron. She looked hardly old enough to have left school.

"How long have you been here, at Ravensfall?"

"A month, miss."

"And do you like it?"

A flutter of dark lashes and from under them, a nervous glance from dove-gray eyes. "I like Mrs. Hodges, miss. Matron said as how she would look after us, and she has."

"Matron?"

"At the orphanage, miss. In Wanganui." She said this last in such low tones that I could scarcely hear her.

I put down my cup. How was I to deal with this? "You did not like the orphanage?"

The small chin rose. "What's to like or dislike, miss? We were treated well enough. . . ."

"There is no disgrace, you know, to living in an orphanage!"

"No, miss. That's what Pa said when he left us there."

My curiosity aroused, I wanted to ask about "Pa" but could tell from the closed little face that it would be better not to. I took another sip of tea. "You said 'us'? You have a brother or sister here?"

"Yes, miss. Alfred. We all promised Pa we'd take care of Alfred. So when it was my turn to go, I couldn't go without Alfred, could I?"

"No. No, I suppose you couldn't!"

"And I explained this to Mrs. Hodges. And she was very agreeable: she said as long as I did my work, that Alfred would be welcome here."

"And is Alfred happy?"

The gray eyes were suffused with light. "Oh, yes, miss! Sometimes, he blacks the wrong boots and the other day, he pulled up the radishes by mistake when he was set to weeding the vegetable garden, but he hasn't had a fit since we've been here."

"That's . . . that's wonderful! But what about your other brothers and sisters? Didn't you say you had all promised your father to take care of Alfred?"

"Yes, miss. But Victoria has to have her chance — she's the pretty one, you know — but I daresay, she'll send for us when she's settled; and then Eddie — he took off for Australia to find Pa . . . and as for Alice: she does the best she can, I suppose . . . but . . . so there's only me to look out for Alfred and the little 'uns."

"Little 'uns?"

"Louise and Arthur, miss. They're still at the orphanage, but Mrs. Hodges says that if Pa or Victoria hasn't sent for us by then, that they can come here when they're big enough."

"What a kind person Mrs. Hodges is!"

"Yes. Yes, she is, miss. . . ."

"But?"

"It's this . . . this *place*, miss! It gives me the shivers! And then . . . well . . ."

"Yes?"

"The people who are staying here; there's something . . . I don't know how to put it, miss, and anyway I shouldn't be talking like this; Mrs. Hodges said we shouldn't gossip. Please forgive me, miss — and if you're sure you've finished, I'll take your plate!"

The little face was so hot with embarrassment at her indiscretion, I did not have the heart to question her further. Assuring her that I had indeed finished, I stuffed an apple in my pocket for later and after tidying my windblown hair at the mirror over the sideboard, I made my way out to the drawing room, intent on following Mrs. Hodges's orders!

* * *

If only, I tell myself now, I had ignored Helena's discomfort and pressed her for more details, or had at least paid some serious attention to her remarks, both she and I might have been spared considerable distress — but such is hindsight! As it was, I crossed the hall to the drawing room that afternoon, with nothing more on my mind than a mild curiosity.

The drawing room door was partly open and as I approached, the plaintive melody of an ancient Scottish folksong floated out into the hall. I stood for a moment, fascinated; who was playing the piano, I wondered, and with such skill? The melody, I finally recognized was "Caller Herrin," but as I listened, the pianist launched into a series of variations of such depth that the original tune was completely transposed into the realms of magnificence.

"Wonderful, is it not, Malvina?"

I could not prevent a start. Behind me stood Clinton Raven

He smiled down at me penitently. "I'm sorry, I did not mean to startle you!"

"Apology accepted. I'm afraid I was so deep in the music that I did not hear you approach. Tell me — who is it who plays so well; and who is the composer of the piece? I don't believe I've heard it before."

The left eyebrow flew up devilishly as the dark face dissolved into a piratical grin. "No, I don't suppose you have! Please come into the drawing room and I shall introduce you to both the pianist and the composer — who are, of course, one and the same!"

He pushed open the door with a flourish and stood back smiling, as completely mystified, I entered.

Although I glanced immediately toward the piano, the curtain on the dais where it was situated at the end of the room, was partly drawn, thus obscuring the pianist.

Two other persons turned to me, however, as I entered. One, a big-boned, fair-haired woman with a high color, sat rigidly in a bucket chair, while the other, majestically plump, dark haired, brown-eyed and white of skin — her paleness accentuated by her flowing black robes — leaned languidly back against

114

a sofa, her feet propped upon a footstool. Both women appeared to be in their midthirties.

Cousin Clinton ushered me to a chair nearby. He seated himself next to the sofa, signifying with a nod to the women and a finger to his lips that we were not to speak until the music came to a close.

Thus we sat in silence but I was keenly aware of being under scrutiny; the blond woman throwing me little glances from under her colorless lashes. The dark-haired woman, however, gazed at me openly, in between selecting chocolates from an open box beside her on the sofa. After a while, with a slow gesture of one long-fingered white hand, she indicated to Clinton Raven that he was to offer the box to me.

I selected a chocolate for politeness' sake and she nodded at me approvingly.

At length, with a last few plaintive notes, the piano was finally silent.

"Bravo!" Clinton clapped his hands.

The fair-haired woman yawned a little and said nothing.

The dark-haired woman, pausing between chocolates, sighed deeply, her magnificent bosom rising and falling. "Very nice, dear, I'm sure."

"Malvina, allow me to introduce my sister, Mrs. Lucy Wilkinson and her companion, Miss Norah Hackett. However, as I mentioned this morning, we don't stand on ceremony here; we Canadians are very informal, are we not, my dear?"

He looked toward the lady of the chocolates who nodded at me agreeably if somewhat sleepily. "Yes, indeed; do call me Lucy — and this shall be Norah."

Still wordless, her fair-haired companion nodded in apparent agreement. It was impossible to tell her thoughts from her facial expression — or rather lack of it — her eyebrows being flaxen to the point of invisibility.

"And now, let me introduce you to our pianist and composer — I believe you met him this morning." Clinton looked amused at my befuddled expression. "Come on out, sir," he called toward the dais. "Come and make your bow!"

There was a familiar creaking and a small figure finally rose and stood before us on the dais.

"Bertram!"

My cousin grinned at my astonishment. "You did not realize that we harbored a genius under our roof?"

"No, I did not! That was . . . was . . . tremendous, Bertram!" I looked at him in awe. Wherever did you learn to play like like that?"

To my surprise, Bertram answered me hesitantly, quite without his usual aplomb. "Why . . . in — um — Canada, Cousin Malvina."

He looked toward his uncle.

"And in Paris!" exclaimed Clinton, as if coming in on cue. "Wherever we have traveled, Bertram has always had the very best of teachers."

For some reason I could not understand, Bertram looked greatly relieved. Slowly, he manipulated his crutches down the steps of the dais and made his way toward me, eventually sinking down onto one of the Louis Quinze chairs. "I have been very fortunate with my music teachers, Cousin."

Was there the slightest emphasis on the word music? I wondered. And was it my overdeveloped sensitivity that made me feel that the room's atmosphere had become highly charged? Don't be nonsensical, I told myself sternly. Fixing my pincenez more firmly on my nose, I addressed myself again to Bertram. "But I understand you composed that piece yourself? That takes more than good teaching — you have a great natural talent, there!"

Quite without conceit but as if recognizing an obvious fact, Bertram, his little-old-man expression again taking over his features, nodded his head in agreement. "Yes, I am very fortunate."

I was puzzled. With such great talent, Bertram should surely be at school — or if his health did not permit this, he should certainly be in a place where world class music tutors were available.

"Bertram's health is too uncertain, of course, for him to go away to school." Lucy Wilkinson's husky tones interrupted my thoughts and in the depths of her lethargic, deep brown eyes glowed a spark of amusement, as if she had guessed my thoughts and enjoyed catching me out in them. "And as for a

116

tutor, we could find no one willing . . ." She paused to yawn, raising politely — but with apparent effort — one hand to cover her mouth.

"Willing to come all this way!" Clinton concluded smoothly.

Too smoothly, I thought. I found myself the focus of four pairs of eyes — those of Norah Hackett, I noticed, were as colorless as glass. Was there the slightest breath of relief, when I nodded in agreement with Lucy? Why should they worry about my acceptance of what seemed perfectly sound reasoning?

"So you travel a great deal?" I asked no one in particular; more for the sake of making conversation, than out of idle curiosity.

It was Clinton who replied. "Since my retirement from banking, certainly . . . and of course, Silas knowing my wish to study art, was always more than willing to have me along."

"Silas? Oh, of course, your late husband, Cousin Lucy! I am so sorry, I ought to have offered my condolences at once!"

A languid hand waved away my embarrassed apology. "The accident was tragic. Tragic," the low tones informed me. "But we must live in the present, not the past. God's Will Be Done! No doubt, my dear . . . Silas . . . has gone to his Just Reward. . . ."

I could think of no possible reply to this but Clinton, I noted, was looking at his sister with something akin to admiration. "So brave," he explained when he saw me watching him. "So very brave!" He reached forward and patted Lucy's hand. "Silas was a keen collector of antiques," he explained to me, "which is why he traveled so frequently."

Again I had the impression that all four of them were waiting for my reaction.

"How very interesting!"

A slight relaxation in the atmosphere — did I imagine it? — seemed to indicate that this was the correct reply.

"And you, Malvina? Do you travel a great deal?" I found myself under Lucy's scrutiny.

"About Britain certainly: to London for the Season — though, Harriet, my stepmother, doesn't like it much; she goes purely out of duty! And, of course, north to my father's estates in Scotland for the grouse shooting."

"But out of England?"

Here it comes, I thought. "Oh, sometimes, we cross over to France or occasionally to Majorca; the twins—my youngest sisters—seem to benefit from the sun, or so their doctor says!"

"But you, yourself?" Lucy paused between chocolates, regarding me thoughtfully. "Do you often go off alone, without your family?"

"No, not often."

She smiled prettily, displaying small, even teeth. "How I admire your fortitude, Malvina! To think that you traveled all this way, all by yourself—it is most unusual in a young woman and much to be admired!"

She made it sound as if I were the most foolhardy creature she had ever encountered.

I bared my own teeth in return. "But I am not so young, Cousin Lucy: I am twenty-four years old—and my stepmother brought us up to be independent!"

A sly look from the sultry brown eyes. "Twenty-four and still unmarried? Perhaps you came all this way to find a husband!"

I gave her what my papa has described as my beatific smile, secretly congratulating myself on her mistake. "Perhaps, I did, dear Lucy!"

I looked suitably coy and was rewarded by what can only be described as a rude snort from Clinton, still ensconced on the chair nearby. "Fudge, dearest Malvina! Absolute fudge! You are really doing it too brown—do you really expect us to believe that you have never been bespoken?"

For a few nostalgic moments, I remembered Edward. As I had assured Harriet before I had left England, if it had not been for his being killed at the siege of Mafeking, I would have been well off her hands.

"So, there was someone?"

"Excuse me?" I came back to myself to find Clinton observing me closely.

I wanted to answer, "not really"; Edward being a suitable choice decided upon by my papa (Harriet refusing to take part) and Edward's father (only too delighted that his second son had made connection with an heiress—if only a minor one) had dutifully proposed to me on my nineteenth birthday.

118

I well remembered his proposal: with obviously, careful planning, he had come across me in the rose garden. "I say, old thing, not to worry that you're taller than I am . . . I can cope; and anyway, you sit a hunter pretty jolly well. What say, we get hitched?"

I restrained a guilty giggle: I had liked Edward, even if I had never loved him.

"Yes," I admitted to Clinton, waiting now for an answer. "I was engaged to be married once—but he was killed during the Boer War."

"I'm sorry. . . ."

"That's all right, you were not to know!"

Lucy and Norah made appropriate murmurings and Lucy, in apparent sympathy, urged Clinton to offer me again, the box of chocolates.

"Thank you!" Selecting a large caramel cream, I felt distinctly uncomfortable as I glanced about the watching faces. What was it about me that they did not trust? "I'm afraid that my arrival must have come as a considerable surprise; I hope that I haven't inconvenienced you in any way?"

To my astonishment there was a distinct hiccup from Norah, quickly disguised behind a bony hand, while Lucy and Clinton exchanged glances of amused irony.

"What in this place—in the middle of nowhere, as it were—" Lucy murmured smoothly as if in explanation of their odd behavior, "could we possibly be engaged in that you would inconvenience?"

"I just thought . . ."

"Although of course," Lucy continued, as if I had not interrupted, "we did find your sudden arrival somewhat shall we say, unusual? I did wonder why perhaps you, or more properly, your father had not written to us from Lancashire?"

"Yorkshire."

"Sorry?"

"Our family seat is in Yorkshire, Cousin Lucy."

"Oh, so it is . . . well one English county is very like another, I suppose!"

She helped herself to another chocolate. Had she been testing me out? I tried to keep my irritation at bay by answering her

119

question. "By the time I had definitely made up my mind to come, it was too late to send a letter in advance — and Papa decided that sending the letter under separate cover would be pointless as it and I would in any case arrive on the same ship."

I was aware of a sudden tension.

"Indeed! Then you *do* have a letter from your father?"

"Yes — and a letter of introduction for our solicitor also, but unfortunately, he was not available when I arrived at his office the other day."

Clinton stirred in his chair. "A letter from Cousin Marcus! How good it will be to hear from him — perhaps, you might like to bring it down later, Malvina? I hope he has included some family details — we are always most interested to hear his news. When he wrote giving us his kind permission to stay here, he talked about the possibilities of setting up a racing stud on his Yorkshire estate; does he mention it in this letter, do you think?"

"I don't know, Clinton, but I shall be glad to bring the letter down to you. . . ."

"*Time!*"

I nearly jumped out of my skin.

It was not so much the loudness of the word, shrieked in a peculiarly grating and unmelodious voice, as the fact that it was the heretofore silent Norah Hackett who had uttered it.

"Time!" she croaked again, rising from her chair. "Time for your medicine, Bertram, and your rest!"

Bertram, crouched on his chair, glared up at her, hatred oozing out of every pore.

"Come along, Bertram. Do!"

Lucy, I noticed, paid absolutely no attention; and, in fact, after yawning yet again and settling her head back against the sofa cushions, appeared to be drifting off into a gentle doze. Clinton, however, turned a steel-gray stare toward the boy.

"Go!"

Though it was only one word, it was spoken with such coldness that Bertram crumpled as if physically hit; then seizing his crutches, heaved himself off his chair to follow a smugly smiling Norah Hackett.

Clinton looked toward me, his gray eyes warm again. "I'm afraid Bertram is a little spoiled . . . and we must not let his genius go to his head, must we?"

I was fascinated; if I had not just seen the little episode for myself, I would not have believed that I was dealing with the same man.

With sudden perception, I realized that the Clinton I had just witnessed was the Clinton I had glimpsed upon the moment of my arrival the night before. All at once, I felt cold and could hardly keep myself from shivering.

As usual, my cousin second-guessed me. "Come closer to the fire, Malvina: I see you are feeling the chill. In some ways, this country seems colder than Canada — I suppose it's the damp!"

Rising, he walked over to the fireplace and picking up the poker, expertly stoked up the glowing coals before adding more logs.

Accepting his invitation, I joined him at the fireside, holding out my hands to the rejuvenated flames. "So you have been to Paris often, Clinton? I suppose you have also been to the south of France?"

His face lit up. "Oh, yes, Paul and I . . . that is, we . . . had a studio there for a time at . . . Avignon."

"Avignon? Really? My stepmother took my little sisters there last summer and I joined them for a few weeks. Just think, we may have been there at the same time!"

"Yes, that's a possibility."

"What a pity you did not let Papa know of your whereabouts. You could have met — let me see — at least a third of us!"

He smiled teasingly. "What a thought!"

"Thank you!"

We looked at each other in friendly rapport until a puzzling thought occurred to me. "But if you have traveled so frequently to France, why not to England — and why did you not write to us that you were so near? I am sure that Papa would have been delighted to have invited you to Yorkshire."

A log fell from the fire at that moment and Clinton bent to reinstate it. His head was still turned from me as he answered. "That's just it, don't you see — Georges Duvall. . . ." He had to fumble with the log as it fell again, this time rolling perilously

121

close to the fender.

"What?" I thought I hadn't heard properly.

"Georges Duvall." He straightened up slowly. "He's our agent." He smiled at my puzzled face. "You have a lot to learn, Cousin. Many artists—and writers, too—have people who handle their work for them."

"I don't understand."

He shook his head and gave me a kindly smile. "Of course not, you've never been hungry!"

"What has that to do with it?"

"Everything, when you are depending on your work to support you and you do not know where to sell it!" He stopped a moment, looking rueful. "Or how to make sure your buyer actually pays . . ."

"But . . . but . . ."

"You thought I was a rich banker?"

"Well, yes!"

"I'm afraid not; my father saw to that. He always realized, I think, that I should leave banking as soon as the opportunity presented itself. So before he died, he made sure that most of his assets were tied up in trust for my descendants."

"But . . . but that's not fair?"

"Isn't it? So what is fair? After all, it was my father's money! And he did not leave me poverty-stricken. On the contrary, he left me a reasonable competence! Believe me, it is entirely my own fault that I find myself in my present straits—you see, Paul and I made some rather unfortunate investments. Georges Duvall was kind enough to 'bail us out' as it were—but we now owe *him* and the only way we have of repaying him is through our work. So it is he who determines where we should go and what we should do! And to go to England just to renew family ties is, according to him, out of the question!"

"But that is monstrous!"

A light laugh. "Is it? Think a moment! If Georges had not come to our rescue, we really should have been in dire straits! In any event, the man is not such a monster—as you will see for yourself; he will soon be here at Ravensfall."

"At Ravensfall?"

He laughed at my surprise. "Why not? Because of the early

122

settlers, there are some excellent sources for antiques and art here—and Georges represents buyers for both. He followed us from Canada and has been on a buying trip around the North Island. He should be back again by this weekend, I suppose; he uses Ravensfall as his base."

Something puzzled me. "You said Mister Duvall followed you from Canada? Is he not French?"

"French Canadian."

"Oh, of course! But isn't Ravensfall a little off the beaten track to serve as his base?"

"A little, perhaps, but the amount of storage space—and naturally, we don't charge fees!—makes it all worthwhile. Georges is amassing quite a collection, I assure you!"

"So, how . . . pray excuse me! This is none of my business and I really did not mean to pry!"

The gray eyes studied my face a long moment and then, smiled. "No. No, you didn't. I can see that. . . ."

Incredibly, one of his strong fingers gently stroked the side of my cheek before tweeking back a lock of my flyaway, unmanageable hair and tucking it tidily behind my ear. "Your hair, Miss Raven—you really should be more careful of it!"

His tones were chiding; his eyes full of fun.

He shook his head reprovingly. "And your pince-nez, are you not aware they're about to fall from your nose?"

Gently, my pince-nez were straightened

Across from us, against the sofa cushions, Lucy still slept fitfully, her full lips puckering gently in and out with small, soft, elegant snores.

"I should like to paint you, Malvina, one day, if I may."

I tried not to laugh; but despite myself, a decidedly unladylike splutter erupted.

The eyes gazing down into mine were serious. "Why do you laugh?"

"At the idea of anyone wanting to paint *my* portrait! Tell me, will you include my pince-nez?"

"If you wish! However . . ." Before I could protest, with one hand he removed my pince-nez, while with the other, he tipped up my chin, gently turning my face this way and that. "You should take yourself more seriously, Malvina. Don't you real-

123

ize how classically sculptured your features are . . . those high cheekbones, that graceful nose . . . ?"

With one finger, he touched the tip of my nose and then, before I knew what he was about, leaned forward and lightly kissed it.

From the doorway came a cough.

Clinton's fingers tightened about my chin. "I believe, Cousin, that I have it now!" In his other hand, a handkerchief appeared — as if by magic — which he now used to dab at my eye. "That's the only problem with these coal fires . . . perhaps you had better rinse your eye, just in case!"

I was gently released.

"Ah, there you are, Fordyke! And just in time, too. I was about to ring for afternoon tea."

To add to my humiliation, I could feel my face burning as I hastily crammed on my pince-nez.

I made myself face the door. There, sure enough, stood the large American, his craggy face politely expressionless.

He walked forward into the room and bowed slightly in my direction. "Miss Raven!"

He allowed himself a small smile before turning to my cousin. "Yes, you did say four o'clock, did you not; or rather Mrs. Wilkinson did. . . ."

Lucy, I thought to myself!

I turned to the sofa. There, sure enough, Lucy still lounged — with her eyes wide open. How long had she been awake?

Her dark eyes gleaming with what appeared to be satiric amusement, she reached into her box for the one remaining chocolate.

Seventeen

Somehow or other, I gave my excuses and made my escape. Once in the hall, with the drawing room doors safely closed behind me, I paused to peer out the windows, resting my hot forehead a moment against the cool stained glass.

"Why, Malvina! Whatever is the matter?"

To my chagrin, I found myself addressed in a stentorian baritone from the staircase.

I looked up to find myself inspected by the pale blue gaze of Paul Lucas as he descended.

Quickly I raised my handkerchief and pretended to dab at my eye. "Oh, nothing. Really, nothing! I got something in my eye, that's all. . . ."

"Let me take a look at it!" With long strides, he bounded down the remaining stairs.

"No thank you! There is no need—it was only a smut; from the smoke from the coals, you know! And Cousin Clinton removed it for me."

A raised eyebrow and an amused look. "Did he indeed?"

In the late afternoon light streaming through the stained-glass portrait of St. George, the red-gold of Paul Lucas's hair and full beard was transposed to a burnished, gleaming bronze.

Unlike the attenuated St. George, however, there was a warmth, a vitality about this man that was overpowering. Perhaps it was his clothes, I thought fascinated, politely doing my best not to gaze at them outright.

Although his suit of pearl-gray superfine was cut along conventional lines, his mustard-colored waistcoat was outrageously embroidered with silver swans and other birds of more obscure origins. Beneath his waistcoat, he sported a shirt of an astounding spring green complemented by a flowing cravat, the stripes of which alternated between forest green and gold. Despite all odds, the whole ensemble meshed together in that successful concatenation of colors most beloved by Renaissance princes.

"You find my waistcoat interesting, Malvina?"

"I beg your pardon! I didn't mean . . ."

"Please! I am flattered, rather, that you should like it!" Turning toward the light, he parted his jacket still further over his broad chest the better to reveal his waistcoat in all its glory. "It was embroidered by a . . . a . . . *lady friend* of mine.

He allowed the jacket to swing back into place as he stepped closer to me; his eyes, almost on a level with mine, lively with a wicked sparkle. "Tell me, Malvina, do you like to embroider?"

With difficulty, I forced myself to move away, sidestepping around him to make my way toward the stairs. I must . . . go and bathe my eye," I explained, feeling infinitely foolish.

A rumbling laugh followed me. "I did not think you were lacking in courage, Miss Raven!"

I reached the foot of the stairs but before I could fully effect my escape, there was a crash as the green baize door opened followed by a clatter of wheels, as Mrs. Hodges emerged with a laden tea trolley.

"Where are you off to, Miss Raven?" demanded this being severely, the white ribbons on her cap nodding briskly. "It's time for afternoon tea! Come along, Helena, do!" she tossed over her shoulder into the passage behind her from which was emerging the little maid burdened again with the silver tea tray.

"Thank you, Mrs. Hodges; but I'm really not hungry; as I am sure you remember, I had a late lunch."

She cast a look of distinct disapproval. "That was sometime ago, miss, and only cold meats — and dinner is not until eight. You had better come back into the drawing room and have some of my nice date scones — just freshly baked; and a piece of my iced walnut chocolate cake or a slice of one of my fresh cream sponges."

The expression on her face indicated that if I did not do as I was told forthwith, she would be mortally offended.

I gathered up my courage. "I'd love to but I'm afraid that . . ."

Help came from an unexpected source.

"I believe Miss Raven was about to go to her room to bathe her eye."

Paul Lucas's voice was studiously level but the glance he cast me across the hall, held a subtly mischievous gleam. Astoundingly, he winked at me.

Hastily, I turned my face away.

"Oh, Mister Lucas, I didn't see you standing there! Mister Fordyke will be pleased to see you, I'm sure . . . having come especially . . . but you, miss! Your eye, whyever did you not say so? What happened? A piece of grit . . . a smut? Oh, those coal fires! But go up to your room at once, miss, and I'll send up some of my special eye salve!"

Before he disappeared into the drawing room, Paul Lucas raised a hand in a humorous farewell.

So eager was I to reach my room, that once out of sight of the hall, I lifted my skirts and tore up the stairs as indecorous as a schoolgirl. Pausing on the second-floor landing to regain my breath after my wild flight, I gradually became aware of a dark shape gliding silently toward me down the corridor leading to my room.

Needless to say, Betty's tale of what she had seen in the library corridor immediately came to mind. I tried to steady myself by taking a deep breath; the problem — as I told myself — was the light from the hall windows, which coming from behind obscured the features of the person in front. I made myself stand still and was eventually rewarded by my recognition of Norah Hackett.

Her footsteps muffled by the thick turkey carpet, she passed by in her usual silence acknowledging my presence with only a nod and a brief smile which to me, in my sensitive state, seemed to hold a hint of triumph — as if she had sensed my discomfort and enjoyed it. I took another deep breath, my nerves were getting the better of me. I decided I would settle them down by finishing the unpacking of my trunk and valise. Briskly, I entered the corridor, determined to keep all ghosts—and thoughts of ghosts—well at bay!

Though the fire was not yet lit in my room, the last rays of the setting sun gave an illusion of warmth as they streamed through the window. My hatbox and trunk, I noted at once, had disappeared. One of the maids must have unpacked them. Sure enough, in the wardrobe I found most of my belongings neatly stored: my hats on the top shelf, my boots, shoes, and evening slippers on the shoe rack at the bottom and my skirts and jackets dangling from wooden coat hangers. Most of my gowns and blouses were missing—taken away to be ironed, I guessed.

My valise, however, was still there, though it had been shifted onto a low table. I was just about to open it, when there was knock on the door. I groaned; surely not Mrs. Hodges again—I did not think I could stand it!

To my relief, it was Betty who entered, carrying a tray bearing a small china bowl—steam escaping from under its linen cover—some small flannel cloths, tea things, and two or three napkin-covered plates of what appeared to be food.

I groaned again. "Not food! I'm really not hungry, Betty, and I told Mrs. Hodges so!"

A saucy grin. "Now, now, miss! Mrs. 'odges knows best! And anyway, you wait and see what she sent h'up . . . but before I set up your table, let's 'ave a look at that eye!"

She set down the tray on top of the cedar wood chest and picked up the china bowl and one of the flannel cloths. "Now, you just sit yourself down, miss, and relax and let me bathe your h'eye. Mrs. 'odges sent up her special h'eye salve."

I decided it would be better to be honest! "There's nothing wrong with my eye, Betty. Truly!"

"Yes, I can see that, miss. But let me give it just one wipe and when Mrs. 'odges h'asks me if I done it—*which* she will—I can say I 'ave! Or, right as rain, she'll be up 'ere to see for 'erself; and you don't want that, miss!"

She was right: I gave in gracefully and submitted to her expert ministering.

128

"Was it you, Betty, who unpacked my trunk? If so, thank you! And thanks for putting away my things."

She nodded, putting down the china bowl and wringing out the cloth. "It were no trouble, miss. As you've probably noticed, I've taken some of your dresses and such downstairs for a bit of an h'iron. I didn't touch your valise, though, I thought you might 'ave personal things in it, papers and that. But now that you're 'ere, I'll h'empty it for you while you 'ave your cup of tea! And you can tell me where you want things put — and afterward I can take it up to the box room."

As she spoke, she lit the ready-made fire and brought up one of the low tables which she set up with the tea things from the tray.

"Now then, miss, what do you think about that!"she exclaimed, lifting the covers.

The plates revealed a mixture of finger sandwiches — some cucumber, some ham and egg — three buttered date scones, a slice of the walnut chocolate cake, and a cream sponge decorated with passion fruit icing.

I gazed at the repast and my resolution faded. "I didn't think I was hungry but I must admit . . ."

Betty giggled. " 'opeless, isn't it? She does that to us in the kitchen, too!"

"Well," I thought for a moment, "why don't you just empty my valise onto the chest and I'll decide what to do with my things later. That way, you can take it up to the box room and then go down for your cup of tea."

"That's very good of you, miss!"

"Not at all; one good turn deserves another."

Betty was right, my valise did hold most of my personal papers. Nibbling on a cucumber sandwich, I sifted through some of the things where they rested on the cedar wood chest: my journal that I had not written in since my arrival in Wanganui — shame on me, I told myself, perhaps I could get caught up this evening — my writing case and spare writing paper, some ornaments from my room at home, photographs of the family, and Edward's likeness in the form of a miniature painted in watercolors.

I took the little portrait and the stand that went with it and carried it over to the writing desk by the window. Poor Edmund, I thought, as—bravely attired in his regimentals—he gazed up at me. What would my life have been like, if he had lived? A round of huntin', shootin' and fishin', I suspected, interspersed with a dutiful church fair or two, and if I were lucky, perhaps a month during the season at Harrogate.

The prominent blue eyes—a little too protuberant—looked up at me questioningly and in my mind, I could hear his light-timbered voice, asking as he had asked me so often, "Now, now, Mallie, what's this all about? Daydreaming again?" He had been a kindly man but completely without imagination. I had tried to tell him about my nightmares once. I smiled now, remembering his response—"Nightmares? Never have 'em myself! You think too much, m'dear . . . you need to get out and about more!"

I placed the miniature gently on my desk and turned back for my other papers. I would sort through everything now, and decide what to put in which drawer.

I finished my task more quickly than I had expected. Pleased with myself, I lit the lamp against the encroaching darkness. Perhaps I would sit by the fire and sort through my correspondence and decide whom to write to first. It was then that I remembered Papa's letters to the solicitor and my cousins.

I thought for a moment. Surely, I had placed them on the top of my things? I distinctly remembered placing them there that evening at the hotel and having to cram down the lid afterward. Of course, with Betty's unpacking, my things had ended up out of order. Still, it was strange that I did not remember noticing the letters.

To put my mind at rest, I went over to the writing desk and checked through my papers again. The letters were not there.

I began to feel uneasy; what could have happened to them? Could someone have taken them? I made myself sit down by the fire. It would have been easy enough to have taken the letters. I thought of all the times my valise had been left unguarded: the evening at the hotel when I had gone down to dinner, last night where Hodges had deposited it at the foot of the stairs, and all of this afternoon in my room.

I took a deep breath. There had to be some simple explanation! Who on earth would want to take my letters and why?

Of course, I thought, with relief, perhaps Betty in her hurry to go down for her cup of tea, had not properly emptied my valise — the letters might have slipped beneath the lining or perhaps they had somehow fallen into one of the inner pockets.

How embarrassing it was going to be, if I could not produce Papa's letter when Clinton had especially asked for it.

I should have rung down to the kitchen, but I knew that preparations for dinner were probably under way and I had no wish to cause more bother. I did not remember visiting the box room in the past, but Betty had said it was somewhere in the attics. Not giving myself time for proper thought, I selected a warm wool jacket from the wardrobe and seizing up my lamp, prepared, once more, to brave the darkness of the corridors.

Eighteen

Despite the warmth of my jacket, the damp cold struck chill through to the bone. I was tempted to return to my room for mittens and scarf but knew that once back in the cheery warmth, I should find it difficult to leave. I raised my lamp, instead, and started off down the corridor to the landing.

Once darkness begins to fall in New Zealand, it does so quickly. Only the light cast by my lamp relieved the blackness of the hall and that only in a limited, swaying circle about me. I looked back through the shadows at the vague outlines of doors opening onto the corridor and wondered who else shared the second floor with me. Norah Hackett evidently, as she had been leaving the corridor when I had come up. I supposed most of the others were accommodated on the first floor, Mrs. Hodges having said something about the superior rooms being taken up. I wondered about Bertram, poor little creature; had he been relegated to the nursery floor?

I reached the landing and looked up at the stairs disappearing into the darkness of the third floor. I well remembered what was up there: to the left, the housekeeper's bedchamber and sitting room with a baize door opposite opening onto the backstairs leading from the kitchens far below to the servants' tiny rooms in the attics. To the right, the rooms once belonging to Reggie and me with the schoolroom and governess's room in between. There were other rooms, of course—one, which was long with barred windows apparently intended for a nursery—but in our day, it had been empty and kept locked.

These were the main rooms and then there was the entrance to the cupola.

The cupola or Josiah's Folly, as some of the local people named it at the time, not realizing until after the event that the old man had used it as a lookout in the days of his collaboration with Bully Hayes, was situated at the top of the house, but its only means of access was a spiral stair winding directly up from the entrance on the third floor.

The cupola: even now, I shivered to think of it, up there waiting for me.

Great Uncle Josiah still "walked," Ishbel and Callum had assured Reggie and me and that breeze we heard whistling down the cupola stairs and under the door, as we went past, was our great uncle's restless spirit come back to prey on us.

I gave myself a little shake, the light from my lamp quivering as I did so. That is all in the past, I told myself sternly, when you were young and vulnerable. Ishbel and Callum made up those stories simply to frighten you into doing what they wanted.

I took a deep breath, caught up my skirts with one hand and with the other holding the lamp high, climbed up the stairs.

The shut cupola door gradually emerged into my lamplight as I reached the top steps.

There now, I thought; a perfectly ordinary brown wooden door, no different in appearance from all the other doors in the house; furthermore, as far as I could tell, no breeze whistled from under it!

On reaching the top stair, I shone my lamp to the right and left. The nursery wing was entirely dark but to my left where I remembered were placed the housekeeper's rooms, light gleamed from under a door.

Chiding myself for being a coward, I could not prevent a deep sigh of pure relief. If—given the hour about six o'clock—Mrs. Hodges was down in the kitchen, supervising the preparations for dinner, then at least her unpretentious spouse was safely behind that door. Somehow the thought of another person close by made me feel less alone.

Almost confidently I walked down the hall and threw open the baize door. Beyond a small, wooden landing were the steep, uncarpeted stairs to the attics.

Once, long ago, Reggie and I greatly daring—and having escaped Miss Inglewood—had braved the attics. At the top of the

133

stairs would be another small landing and a door letting out onto the floor directly under the rafters of the roof. It was divided all along the front of the house into the small bedchambers—lit by dormer windows or skylights—used by the servants and into storage areas for discarded furniture where the box room must be. At the end had been a large space completely unpartitioned, which Reggie and I had guessed to be directly over our half of the nursery wing.

It was as I remembered it—almost. As I emerged from the attic landing, I saw indeed the doors to the partitions of the maids' bedchambers and storage rooms; but over to my left where there should have been free space, was a floor-to-ceiling wall broken only by a closed door.

Intrigued, I wandered over. I was puzzled to find the door locked; however, a key was lying on the floor nearby, as if it had fallen from the lock—but then, I asked myself, why lock the door in the first place? I picked up the key and placed it in the lock.

If only then I had realized what would be the dreadful consequences of my action: the series of events that would culminate in a tragic death!

Heedlessly, with no intimation of what was to come, I turned the key and opened the door.

In the wavering light cast from my lamp, a huge room was gradually revealed: a room which in daylight would have been well lit from the dormer windows running down the riverside of the house. Now, of course, it was totally dark, my lamplight hardly reaching the distant, shadowy corners.

Nearby was a large deal table which, from the various untidy piles of papers scattered about its uncovered surface, appeared to act as a desk. I put down my lamp and chafed my freezing fingers. By the look of the papers, many of them appeared to be bills or accounts of some sort. Hastily, I turned my eyes away, not wishing to intrude upon another's privacy.

To one side of the room stood a large japanned screen and a straight-backed chair with a blue and gold wrapper draped carelessly over its back. Across from the screen, in the middle of the room, sat a chaise longue upholstered in dark blue velvet and arrayed with many large cushions varying in hue from orange to gold to fuschia to purple. On either side of the chaise longue were

134

two small, low tables, one of which held a dish of sweetmeats.

Under the chaise longue and small tables lay what appeared to be the only carpet in the room — a rose pink affair, with garlands of intertwining roses and carnations. Everywhere else, the wooden boards were bare.

Puzzled, I shifted the lamp to throw its light along the sides of the room. Out of the shadows loomed two artists' easels on one of which was a picture of some kind and standing propped against the wall, most with their backs turned toward the room, was what seemed to be a row of canvasses.

There were two other large tables nearby. On one of them, centered around an unlit lamp, was a pile of tissue paper, a large china bowl with accompanying pitcher, and what appeared to be a heavy wooden frame of some sort. On the other table close by was an artist's cardboard portfolio, out of which had spilled a profusion of large sheets of paper, though of what nature, I could not at that distance discern.

Obviously, I had come upon Paul's and Clinton's studio. I took up my lamp again and walked over to the easels. On one of them was a half-finished portrait in oils; a dark-haired woman — surely of Lucy? — clad or perhaps I should say, half clad? — in the blue and gold wrap I had just seen thrown over the straight-backed chair. In the portrait, she was seated in that same chair with the japanned screen behind her. The wrap, apparently about to fall off her shoulders, almost but not quite revealed her bosom. An odd portrait, I thought, for a brother to paint of his sister — but no doubt, professional artists held a different view of the world!

I turned away, playing my lamp's light over the canvasses lined against the wall. Those few turned toward me displayed mainly storm-swept landscapes or occasional interiors with one or two still lifes.

However, the papers I had noticed, spilling from the portfolio on the other table nearby, proved to be a collection of watercolors, many of them, it seemed, of New Zealand scenes — all lush and green, with mitred peaks and tumbling waterfalls gushing down rugged, bush-covered slopes with groups of blanketed Maoris standing somewhere in the foreground.

One painting in particular caught my attention. For a moment, I could not understand why it was so familiar and then I realized that it was very similar to the Heaphy, which Clinton had hung in the dining room.

Puzzled, I set down my lamp and picked up the picture, the more easily to examine it. It was the same scene, I soon realized, but painted from a different angle — and sure enough, there on the lower left-hand corner was Heaphy's signature.

A slight noise from behind almost startled me into dropping the painting. There, leaning negligently against the doorway, his hands thrust into his trouser pockets, lounged my cousin Clinton. A slight glow from the hallway to one side of him, suggested that he had turned down his lamp before setting it on the floor out of sight.

Why had he done that, I wondered, and how long had he been there?

"So you have discovered our collection, Malvina?"

The words were conversational; the tone, glacial.

"I'm sorry, I didn't mean . . ."

"Didn't you?"

The hands were withdrawn from the pockets and the long, lithe limbs launched across the space between us before I could draw breath to answer.

"*Didn't you?*"

I looked up into coldly furious gray eyes and wished desperately that I were in any place other than the attics of Ravensfall.

"I'm sorry — truly sorry I really didn't intend to pry . . . it was just that — I was looking for the box room, you see, but this room was such a total surprise! I'm afraid that once I came in, one thing led to another, the screen, the chaise longue . . . I wondered what they were all about . . . and then . . ."

The dark face peering down into mine was suddenly still, the left eyebrow paused in midflight. "When you came in? Tell me dear . . . *cousin?* . . . just how did you get in — the key, after all, is kept in my sitting room!"

I began to feel annoyed. "The key, sir, was on the floor, I thought it had fallen out of the lock!"

"Did you, indeed?"

"Yes! I told you, I was looking for —".

"The box room. Yes, of course. And having entered and finding this was not the box room . . . ?"

His eyes glinted dangerously.

"It was just that . . ." I gulped, blushing with embarrassment. "That I was intrigued . . . I really did not mean to . . ."

A harsh laugh. "So you were intrigued!"

Without further ado, my wrist was seized and I was dragged back in front of the easel holding Lucy's portrait.

"How dare you! Let me go . . ."

The steel grip on my wrist did not relax. "So what was so intriguing about this? What do you see?" His other arm pinioned me to his side. "Look at the portrait . . . look at my dear . . . *sister*. Look, I tell you, look. . . ."

And I did indeed look—but not at first at Lucy's portrait, but rather at him.

His cravat was askew and dark tendrils of his hair curled damply against his forehead. Held so tightly against his chest, I was very much aware of the rapid beating of his heart.

There was something terribly wrong here, I decided. Even if the whiff of whiskey I thought I detected on his breath, indicated that he may have been drinking, why should he be in such a troubled state?

I turned my eyes again to the portrait: Lucy sitting on her chair, her blue and gold wrap half slipping from her shoulders.

I decided to humor him—actually, I had little choice!

"What do I see, you ask? What an odd question! Your sister Lucy, of course, and a very good likeness it is, too!"

I was released as suddenly as I had been seized and stood for a moment, rubbing my wrist.

"A good likeness, you say?"

His voice though polite, held a barely restrained tremor; his eyes when I looked at him questioningly, turned away from mine.

"Yes; a very good likeness!"

"Really, a *very* good likeness, you say!" His tone was savage and before I knew what he was about, he had turned and was sorting through the canvasses leaning against the wall.

"Well then, what do you think of this?"

An oil painting was thrown up onto the other easel.

I caught my breath. It was a portrait also of a young, dark-haired woman. Not Lucy, but that was immaterial. What mattered was the composition of the painting, the thrusts and combinations of color, the play of light and shade—all of which

137

combined to produce in some strange alchemical way, the *essence* of the woman portrayed.

I was overwhelmed; I knew not what to say without resorting to clichés.

"You have no comment, Malvina?"

"No . . . I . . ."

"I gather you are speechless? Allow me to help you! Would you say that this portrait is a good likeness?"

"I can hardly say, I don't know the woman and I don't believe I have ever seen her before . . . but . . ."

"But?"

"Well . . . it's just that even though not every detail of her countenance has been recorded, I should know her if, at this moment, she entered this studio . . . and not only that, I can tell somehow from the painting — and I really don't know how — what kind of a person she must be."

"And what kind of a person is she?"

I looked again for a few moments, at the woman seated, like Lucy, in a chair. "Gentle, kind, suppliant — but underneath it all, strong, unyielding in her pursuit of happiness for her loved ones."

A deep sigh rewarded my response. "And this portrait of Lucy? What do you see, here?"

The room was utterly still: no rain pounding on the roof, no wind whistling through the rafters, even the shadows beyond the lamp's glow seemed to have settled into a motionless, amorphous mass.

Beside me, my companion gazed fixedly at Lucy's portrait, only the light tapping of his foot against the bare boards indicating the coiled tension within him.

I took a deep breath. "It's a fine likeness, as I said, and I love your use of color. For instance, the clever way you have counterbalanced the bronzed highlights of the screen with those hints of dull gold in the leaf pattern of her wrapper. . . ."

"But Lucy, herself? Supposing you had not met her this afternoon — from the portrait, what could you tell about her?"

I looked at the Lucy in the portrait and she stared back at me, her brown eyes, flat, expressionless — the irony, the lassitude that already I associated with her, were missing.

I looked up at the brooding profile beside me and knew I had to be honest. "I can't really tell much about Lucy from the portrait so far—but it's not nearly finished yet, is it?"

I paused, glancing for a moment at the glowing composition on the accompanying easel. "When it is, I suppose it will be the equal of this other painting of yours."

"This other painting of mine?"

The tone was light, as if deliberately so, but there was a haunting note that should have warned me.

"Why yes. . . ." I felt my voice faltering. Why did I feel so nervous, I asked myself.

A laugh was attempted. "The trouble is, you see, that Lucy's portrait is my own but this one—this masterpiece, this glowing work of art that you have so admired—is not."

I stood silent, not knowing what to say.

A long fingered hand reached out, taking the canvas gently by one corner and lifting it from its easel. "This is a copy, Malvina—an excellent copy, if I say so myself—of an early Bonnard; of his mistress, actually."

He smiled down at my puzzled face. "A French painter," he explained. His works will one day I am sure, be valuable. In the meantime, he is greatly admired by those in the know and amateurs such as myself copy him as a learning exercise."

He turned from me, bending to replace the canvas among its fellows against the wall. "An excellent copyist, am I not?"

Though I could not see his face and his voice was muffled, there was something about the droop of his shoulders that suggested complete dejection.

Before I could respond, he had swung up again and stood for a moment looking at Lucy as he had portrayed her. Without the Bonnard beside it for comparison, Lucy's picture appeared colorful, true to life; as I had told him.

I looked at his despairing eyes, his small, bitter smile and wanted to reach out to him but, of course, could not. "Cousin Clinton, this portrait is really very fine—I think that . . ."

I was not given a chance to finish my sentence.

The gray eyes scowled down into mine. "Don't patronize me, Malvina. Never patronize me!"

"But—"

Before I could say another word, Lucy's portrait also was

whipped off the easel and deposited with the other canvasses leaning against the attic wall.

"Now, let me see: what else could possibly have intrigued you? Ah yes, of course — the portfolio with our collection of watercolors that I found you examining when I came in, just now!"

"Clinton, I assure you!"

The look cast at me was savage. "Pray offer me no apologies, dearest *cousin!* Why should you not be intrigued?"

The portfolio was seized and its contents disgorged again over the tabletop.

"Here we have the Heaphy, you were examining — the partner to the one in the dining room — and this is a Kinder. You are familiar, I do suppose, with the works of the Reverend Doctor John Kinder: the foremost watercolorist of New Zealand subjects in his time?"

"Well, no . . . I don't believe . . ."

I found myself examining a rugged coastline of some sort, a rhythmic treatment in misty beiges, dim sunlit, sage greens and in the background, phantasmal blues.

"That's beautiful . . . where is it? Oh, I see!" My eyes discovered the line of straight up and down, no-nonsense writing along the bottom left of the painting. "On Mercury Island, 1857."

"Yes. One of his better-known works — although all his work is good. He died just this past year, you know, and we believe that like Heaphy, one of these days his paintings will be valuable . . . in fact, Georges already has an American collector interested in early colonial paintings, reaching out for a Kinder or a Heaphy — or preferably both, of course!"

"Oh!" I looked again at the painting. "You mean to say, this is an original? Oh, yes of course it is, how silly of me — the signature is right there!"

He laughed lightly as the watercolor was replaced in the portfolio. "And now you know why we keep these paintings under lock and key! And why I was so concerned to find the key missing from my sitting room." He glanced ruefully. "I'm afraid I reacted rather strongly just now. . . ."

I rubbed my wrist again and watched as he carefully slipped the other paintings back into the portfolio. "Yes, you did, rather! Though, I suppose, your anxiety was understandable, considering . . . However, I did find the key on the floor outside the door; and your immediate assumption that I had taken it from your sitting room, I find somewhat insulting!"

"I'm sorry!" His words were apologetic, his tone was not. "The heat of the moment, I'm afraid, and the shock of seeing you there with the watercolors."

My embarrassment returned and I felt my cheeks flushing again. "You're quite right, I really had no business looking at the paintings; however, they were not in the portfolio, you know, but spilling across the table and I'm afraid the Heaphy caught my eye. Naturally, I should not have opened the portfolio, if it had been closed — but then, of course, you were not to know that, I suppose . . . After all, you don't really know me, do you?"

"No, I do not." Both the tone and the glance given me were cool. The portfolio was closed and placed back on the table. "And now, Malvina; the box room!"

"The box room?"

"I believe that was the reason you gave for being up here?"

Again, that hint of suspicion.

"Yes. My valise . . . When Betty unpacked it, I believe she may have missed some letters — my papa's letters, in fact, to you and to our solicitors." Because I was nervous, I found myself talking rapidly to fill in the silence. "I thought perhaps that they might somehow have fallen into one of the pockets."

"I see."

"Of course, I really should have rung for one of the maids, but . . ."

"But?"

I quelled under that stern gaze. "I really did not want to interrupt their afternoon tea!" Even to my own ears, my words sounded ridiculous.

To my relieved surprise, a glint of humor gleamed in my companion's gray eyes as his flyaway, left eyebrow quirked upward.

"Malvina, you never fall to amaze me! Come then, let us find this valise of yours!"

My arm was taken, my lamp was picked up, and I was escorted back onto the landing.

I watched as Clinton, after turning up the glow of his own lamp, left it sitting on the floor at the head of the stairs, apparently

141

against our return, before closing and locking the door and carefully storing the key in his jacket pocket.

"This room was a total surprise to me," I informed him. "As I remember, there used to be nothing here but space—perhaps Papa decided we needed another storeroom; though, I must admit, I do not recall his saying anything about it."

Clinton shook his head. "No, you wouldn't. It was Georges who arranged this—with permission from Cousin Marcus's solicitors, of course. We needed a large studio, you see, with plenty of light—and privacy as well. Naturally, if your father wishes it, we shall take down the partition before we leave."

"I shouldn't think that will be necessary. Oh, excuse me!"

In the half darkness I had stumbled over an uneven board and bumped into my companion, forcing him to steady himself by resting one hand against the jamb of a door we were passing. The door was half open and the light from the lamp now flooded in, revealing a small room with a sloping ceiling. On either side of a dormer window were two narrow stripped beds and a few pieces of sheet-enshrouded furniture. The next room and the one after that, also appeared to be unoccupied.

I turned in surprise to Clinton. "Do the maids no longer sleep in the attic, then?"

A slight hesitation. "No, Mrs. Hodges has arranged quarters for them on the third floor—the nursery floor, I believe you call it. With the house so empty, there seemed no need for them to go all the way to the attics . . . ah, here we are, at last."

He stopped a moment, shining his light on another partially opened door. "The box room, I do believe!"

To my relief, in front of a dusty pile of ancient boxes and steamer trunks, I saw my own trunk straight away, with my weathered valise resting on top.

I hurried over to it at once and flinging back the lid, searched through the pockets—and then, in desperation, under the lining . . . all the time horribly aware of a sarcastic Clinton Raven watching my every movement from the doorway.

The letters were not there.

Nineteen

Back in my room, I found an anxious Helena laying out my beautifully pressed olive-green velvet with its puffed sleeves and ruchings of gold lace.

"We thought, miss — Betty and I — that this would be suitable for your first dinner here. I hope that this meets with your approval?"

"Yes, of course. . . ."

My reassurements were cut short by an exasperated sigh. "Oh, Lor', miss; just look at the time — almost five minutes past seven and dinner at eight with sherry beforehand in the drawing room!"

Despite all my troubles, I could not help smiling.

"It's all right, Helena — with your help, I shall manage! In any event, if I'm a minute or two late, I'm sure it won't matter: after all, this is not a boarding school — I'm scarcely likely to be given a detention!"

"No, miss."

To my amusement, her tone was distinctly doubtful.

Mrs. Hodges, I thought; her influence was everywhere!

Quickly, I stripped down to my chemise, stays, and petticoats, refusing Helena's anxious offers of help. Under Harriet's guidance, I had come to find the assistance of a lady's maid an unnecessary irritation, but I didn't have the heart to send her away. What would Mrs. Hodges say, I wondered with an inner giggle, if poor Helena, under stern cross-questioning, told her that she had not assisted me one wit!

As it was, I had enough to think about: Clinton's look of disbelief at the discovery that the letters I had told him I sought were not in my valise; his stern expression as he had escorted me back down the stairs.

What was this all about? I asked myself for the thousandth time. Why was I so clearly suspect — and of what? What was it I was supposed to be spying on . . . and what were they apparently hiding?

I looked with longing at the still-steaming water in the two shining copper jugs all ready by the washstand. If only, I thought, I had enough time for a proper sponge bath and then, instead of going down to dinner and facing an evening's polite conversation with, no doubt, accompanying innuendo, wouldn't it be truly marvelous simply to slip into my comfortable nightclothes and spend a quiet time beside the glowing fire savoring a tasty supper tray, before climbing up into my cozy, feather-mattressed four-poster?

Enough, I told myself sternly, advancing toward the washstand.

After my wash, I allowed Helena to hook me into my dinner dress and attend to my hair.

"So, your rooms are on the nursery floor? You don't have to go all the way to the attics?"

"Attics, miss?"

In the mirror, I watched as Helena pulled back a lock of my hair before deciding what to with it.

"The attics, yes." I paused, considering my words. "When I lived here before, the maids usually had their quarters up there. . . . I used to feel sorry for them, climbing all those stairs."

"Well, that's it, miss. Mrs. Wilkinson felt sorry for us, too. So she spoke to Mrs. Hodges. Betty told me all about it. Mrs. Wilkinson said that seeing as how the house was so empty, we might as well have the nursery wing for ourselves."

"And Mrs. Hodges agreed?"

"Oh, yes, miss . . . the nursery wing being just down the hall from her rooms, she said she could keep more of an eye on us!"

"That's my Mrs. Hodges!"

"Beg pardon, miss?"

"Never mind!"

As Helena put the finishing touches to my coiffure, I considered what she had just told me. A picture rose in my mind of Lucy, lounging back on her sofa, her attention given more to her chocolates than to her own son. If Lucy thought for one moment of the comfort of others, I should be greatly surprised! Then why had she been apparently so concerned about the maids? Obviously, there must be some reason why the maids should be kept out of the attics—but what could it be? Of course, there was the watercolor collection but the door to the studio was kept locked . . . and in any event, it was highly unlikely that the maids would know anything about . . .

". . . Miss Raven?"

"I'm sorry; I'm afraid I was in a dream?"

I came to myself, to find Helena holding up a hand mirror behind me so that I could see the back of my head.

"Why, Helena! You've worked marvels!"

It was true. My hair, so straight and fine and hard to manage had been elegantly arranged in a great coil at the nape of my neck. A fine, hardly discernible net restrained the inevitable stray wisps and a large bow of green taffeta to compliment the green velvet of my dress, had been pinned on top.

"Yes, miss." Helena's pale little face was for once suffused with color. "If you don't mind my saying so, miss, though your hair is fine, there's a lot of it and you shouldn't wear it on top—that's why it's always tumbling down! And as for the front . . . well, with your kind of hair, it's no use trying to pin it back. Of course, for this evening, I've managed to smooth it back and I expect it will stay in place until at least after dinner but . . ."

She shook her head as she laid the hand mirror on the dressing table and stood back a little to survey her handiwork. "Perhaps, miss, tomorrow sometime, you'll let me take my scissors . . ."

"Scissors!"

A shy smile and a giggle. "That's what Victoria said but . . ."

"Victoria? Oh, yes of course, your eldest sister—'the pretty one'? So you arranged her hair, also?"

"Yes, and a treat she looked, too! And now, she has this wonderful situation: companion to Mrs. Smythe in Wanganui. She meets all kinds of people there . . . and there's one person in particular . . . Oh, excuse me, miss, I shouldn't be rattling on like this! It's just that I know I can help you with your hair; you see, if I snipped some of the front strands, they'd make a softer frame for your face — and being shorter, they'd be easier to manage: I thought perhaps a fringe over your forehead . . . ?"

I looked at myself in the mirror. "Yes, perhaps you are right. You have certainly done wonders with the back — I believe for the first time in my life, I actually look elegant!"

I smiled down at her appreciatively as I rose from the dressing table stool but all the time, my mind was questioning. Who was Mrs. Smythe? I wondered. Why was the name so familiar?

As Helena handed me my evening reticule, I remembered at last; of course, I told myself, Mrs. Smythe — just supposing it was the same Mrs. Smythe — was the lady whose cluttered attic had contained that long-lost Heaphy, which Clinton had found.

I paused a moment on the first-floor landing looking down into the hall. On the rosewood table, a lighted lamp had been left, its soft glow illuminating the paneled walls and outlining the carved raven on the newel post in its perpetual swoop over its helpless, writhing prey. Not for the first time, I wondered about the badge of our house. Were we such a fierce breed, we Ravens, that we should employ such an emblem?

Evidently, Great Uncle Josiah had certainly thought so.

But Josiah Raven, I told myself, from all I had ever *heard* about him had always been a suspect before the law; at the best a distiller of illegal whiskey, at the worst, a pirate and gunrunner to the warring, native tribes.

I thought of Reggie and myself and of our half-brother and sisters. Were we of such stuff? I wondered. Underneath the veneer of polite civilization, at the core of our being, were we — just like our Viking forebears — actually creatures of prey?

From beyond the doors of the drawing room floated sounds of chatter and soft laughter. No piano music, I noted, but probably Bertram had been banished to his bedchamber. Again I wondered which room was his and how with his crutches, he managed the stairs.

Catching up my long skirts with one hand and holding up my own lamp with the other, I started down the remaining steps into the hall. As I did so, there was a ring at the front door. The baize door opened and a hurried Betty crossed the hall just as the bell rang again.

"Good h'evening, sir; please to come h'in! You are h'expected in the drawing room!"

Devlin Fordyke filled up the doorway, his enormous figure looking surprisingly elegant in well-cut, dark evening clothes. "Good evening — Betty, isn't it?"

He smiled down at the maid and then catching sight of me on the bottom stair, nodded toward me. "Good evening, Miss Raven. I have been invited to dinner as you can see . . . in honor of your arrival, I believe!"

Perhaps it was my extrasensitive state, no doubt brought on by all the trials and tribulations of the day, but his nod, it seemed to me, appeared to be one of gracious condescension and his tone of voice infinitely patronizing — unctuous, even!

Well, no wonder, I thought; after all, each time we had met, I had appeared at a considerable disadvantage — usually with my pince-nez dangling and my hair falling down! Well, we would see about that! Very conscious of the sophisticated changes Helena had wrought with my coiffure, I stepped forward with great dignity.

"Good evening, Mister Fordyke," I enunciated clearly, accompanying my greeting with an affable glance. "How kind of you to come!"

His eyes narrowed as he apparently took in my altered appearance. "Not at all, Miss Raven; it is a pleasure . . . but may I say how very charming you look this evening!"

I told myself that he had meant to pay me a compliment, but there was a tremor to his voice — of amusement, I wondered? — and this, combined with a slight emphasis on the word, evening, managed to imply that generally I looked like a hoyden!

I resisted a strong temptation to rush forward and slap his face. Instead, I raised my head proudly as, in a dignified manner, I stepped down the final stair into the hall. Unfortunately, the effect was spoiled as I caught the heel of my evening slipper on the edge of the stair and would have plunged forward, if I had not had the presence of mind to fling my arm about the swooping raven.

"Your lamp, Miss Raven—pray, allow me!"

For a man so large, he moved forward with astonishing speed. Dexterously, my lamp was removed from my shaking hold and I found a strong, supporting hand under my elbow. Whether I liked it or not, I was steadied and calmed.

I felt like a mettlesome horse.

I gritted my teeth and forced my lips into an appreciative smile. "Thank you, Mister Fordyke. Without your help, Ravensfall would doubtless have been set well ablaze! I am truly grateful!"

There was a rumbling guffaw from the depths of the wide chest as the huge shoulders shook. "No, you're not!"

"Excuse me?"

"No, you're not. You're not in the least grateful—you hate the sight of me! At the moment, you would probably like to strangle me or, at the very least, slap my face!"

"I *beg* your pardon!"

He guffawed again, this time gentler, as I felt myself propelled, willy-nilly, toward the drawing room, where a fascinated Betty stood ready to open the doors.

"Mister Fordyke, if you please!"

"Ah, but what if I don't please! What then, Miss Raven?"

"Mister Fordyke!"

There was a brief silence as my lamp was safely deposited on the rosewood table and then a lopsided smile was directed toward Betty. "It's all right, Betty—we Americans know how to open doors—and I'm quite sure Mrs. Hodges is wondering where you are?"

"Yes, sir!"

Betty grinned wickedly at me; then, before I could respond, with a flip of her skirts she retreated down the hall and disappeared behind the baize door.

"And now, Miss Raven, I believe we have a few things to say to each other!"

"I was not aware, sir. . . ."

"No—that, I gathered! Aware, you certainly are not!"

I glared up at him in irritation. "Aware of what?"

The hazel eyes blazing down into mine softened suddenly. "You really are not aware, are you?"

"If you would only tell me what this is all about!"

My hands were seized and then released immediately. "Please, excuse me—but what is this?" My left wrist was taken up again, but gently. "This bruise? How came you by it?"

I was about to reply that it was nobody's business but my own, when the baize doors opened to reveal Hodges, improbably clad as a butler.

He was followed by Betty holding a laden tray and by Helena wheeling a trolley loaded with dining room items including a huge tureen of a delectable mulligatawny soup.

A wooden spoon-wielding Mrs. Hodges appeared behind them in the doorway. "And make sure you put it over the spirit lamp on the sideboard, for to keep it warm—and then after that, when you've made *sure* that all is right in the dining room, *then* you go to the drawing room and announce that . . ."

"Dinner is served! Yes, dear, I know! Now give over, Imogen, do!"

This last was commanded in a gentle, absolutely expressionless voice, apparently—from the direction of the gaze—an admonition to the front doorknob.

A great sigh followed and the little procession recommenced its triumphal progress across the hall to the dining room.

Then a gurgle of laughter erupted as Devlin Fordyke drew me into the shadow of the drawing room doors.

Not for long.

Mrs. Hodges, recovered from her temporary silence, descended upon us—luckily, her wooden spoon in abeyance.

"So, there you are, Miss Raven! I do hope that Helena has done right by you . . . I wasn't sure that I ought to have let . . . oh, but now I see that I was right! Yes, indeed! Just what I should have wished . . . and you, Mister Fordyke, I'm so pleased that you were able to honor us . . ."

A swift glance encompassed Devlin Fordyke's attire.

"I do hope, Mrs. Hodges, that I meet with your approval—

I should really hate to discommode your arrangements!"

"Oh, yes, sir—that is, no, sir!"

"And now, I suppose, you would like us to go into the drawing room, engage momentarily in polite conversation and then proceed to dinner after, of course, we have been summoned thence in an official capacity by your estimable husband in his role as butler?"

"Yes . . . oh, sir, you're funning me!"

The ugly face beamed down at her. "Not, really, no; but that's what you really want—isn't it?"

"Yes, but . . ."

A sturdy elbow was presented to me. "Please allow me, Miss Raven, to escort you into the drawing room!"

What could I do but accept!

The drawing room, softly roseate in the glow from the lamps and close with the warmth from the roaring inferno in the rough stone fireplace, welcomed us in after the bleak chill of the hall.

Lucy was lounging back against the same sofa cushions on which I had last seen her; had she been there all evening? I wondered. However, her black woolen robes had been exchanged for ones of velvet, I noted, while on her dark head reposed the ruffles and long streamers of a widow's cap.

Beside her, Norah, a symphony in sky-blue poplin, crouched in a nearby, chintz-covered bucket chair, her large, bony hands entwined on her lap. So involved were they with their earnest discussion, that neither noticed my entrance.

Not so, however, with Clinton and Paul, both of whom were standing before the fireplace, looking over what appeared to be a sheaf of sketches.

They both looked up as Devlin and I entered the room, but—after we had been duly seated and provided with glasses of sherry—it was Paul who spoke to me first.

"Malvina, I can't tell you how sorry I am! It was Alfred, you see. . . ."

"Alfred? I'm afraid I don't understand!"

"Nor should you! But, it was Alfred—our boot boy, I guess,

150

you'd call him . . . or general messenger boy? You see I gave him the key to our studio with instructions to bring out these sketches and then to lock the door and bring the sketches down to me . . . but I'm afraid that Alfred isn't — that is to say — he did follow my instructions: he brought out the sketches and did indeed lock the door but, unfortunately, he left the key in the lock and according to Clinton, here, it fell on the mat and so you found it!"

"Alfred? Oh, yes, of course!"

I thought of Helena pouring me only that morning, a breakfast cup of tea and entertaining me with descriptions of her numerous brothers and sisters, who had all faithfully promised their father to look after Alfred. According to his sister, Alfred had pulled up the radishes by mistake and blacked the wrong boots.

Paul grinned at me, his smile expansive, his light blue eyes twinkling under their red-gold bushy brows. "So you have heard of Alfred?"

"Yes, of course, Helena's brother — she told me all about him at breakfast; I understand he has some special problems that . . ."

Before I could reply, Clinton spoke at last. "Please accept my apologies, Malvina. I'm . . . I'm afraid I got a little carried away when I met you just now up in the attics. All I can plead is the unexpectedness of finding you up there in the studio. At first, I hardly realized it was you; all I was aware of was a dim figure moving in the shadows. In fact, for one crazy moment, I wondered if I had come across one of the Ravensfall ghosts! But, of course, that is no excuse for my crass . . . my unforgivable behavior!"

Beside me, Devlin stirred; his eyes, I noticed, seeking my wrist where from under the long sleeve of my dinner dress, the bruise Clinton had inflicted on me earlier, was still partly revealed.

Hurriedly, I tugged my sleeve back down over my wrist.

"Apology accepted, Cousin Clinton — and after all, as I said to you before, if I had been thinking properly, I should never have entered your studio in the first place! As I told you, it was just that I was looking for the box room and . . ." My voice

151

trailed off into embarrassed silence as I remembered the miserable outcome of our visit to the box room. How on the earth, I wondered, was I going to explain the absence of the letters?

"The Ravensfall ghosts, you say, my dear Raven?"

The words, comfortably filling in the silence, came from Devlin, seated beside me on the loveseat adjacent to Lucy's sofa.

He turned toward me with a mock-serious frown. "Ah, yes, of course; your wicked, Great Uncle Josiah, Miss Raven, whose burial plot we saw this afternoon in the family graveyard. I remember now, you said something about the local belief that he still 'walks'—but surely your cousin did not mistake you for him!"

An answering chuckle from my cousin and an amused lift of his flyaway left eyebrow. "I should say not! However, I believe there are supposed to be female ghosts, are there not, Malvina?"

Before I could answer, Lucy's languid tones joined the conversation. "At least two, are there not, dearest Malvina? Your governess, Miss . . . Ingleside?"

"Miss Inglewood."

"Ah, yes, of course! And your sister . . . Ishmene? . . . I believe."

"My half-sister, Isobel, actually; though she was known by her highland name of Ishbel."

I had steadied myself by taking a deep breath and to my relief, my voice did not quiver. It was now or never, I realized, if I were to dissociate myself from the dark tales of gossip. "Ishbel, I'm afraid, had a malady she inherited from her father, James McCleod, which led her into . . . doing . . . the things she did. . . ."

"And Callum?" It was Clinton who asked the question, his face half turned away as he bent to throw another log onto the fire.

"Callum?"

"Yes, Callum Douglas, as I collect; Ishbel's illegitimate half-brother by the same James McCleod. Did he suffer from the same malady?" He used the poker to shift the log into place and then stood up.

For a moment, I recalled my nightmare of the previous night of a silently screaming Ishbel — red hair flying — chasing after me, closely followed by Callum, who looked through me as if . . .

I found myself shaking and desperately tried to stop.

"What another ghost?" Beside me — crammed together, as it were, in the loveseat — I could feel Devlin's huge body quivering with laughter. "When will you Ravens let up?"

Clinton shrugged sheepishly and grinned. "You're right, it must appear that way; but you wouldn't believe the number — and variety — of stories we've been told about this place! I was just wondering if there were some story we had not as yet heard . . . which is why I was quizzing Malvina."

He frowned suddenly and turned toward me with an apologetic smile. "But my dear Malvina, how insensitive of me! I was forgetting that you must have been in the thick of it all. Whatever made you want to come back — and alone?"

I was aware of four pairs of eyes gazing at me disconcertingly: Lucy, in the act of popping an inevitable chocolate into her mouth, Norah, slyly from under her flaxen lashes, Paul, consideringly over a glass of sherry, and Clinton, his gray eyes, it seemed to me, chill and questioning.

Only Mr. Fordyke seemed to pay me no particular attention. I heard him yawn and felt him shifting his weight slightly, as if settling as best he could in the cramped space allowed us. In another minute, I thought, he would fall asleep! Sure enough, a sideways glance from me revealed his rugged head sunk upon his gently heaving chest, his eyelids apparently closed.

Pulling myself together, I made myself face the united gaze of my other companions. "You ask why I have come back here? Oh, well . . . New Zealand, of course, and Ravensfall itself; the beauties of the river and the native bush . . . and . . ."

I felt myself prattling on and stopped for a moment. The reasons I had given seemed impossibly puerile, even to me.

"And?" Paul studied me from over his glass, his pale blue gaze thoughtful. "You have other reasons, of course, Malvina."

I found myself stammering. "No. No, not really, I just . . . wanted to . . . explore the house again . . . revisit favorite places . . . catch up upon old memories. . . ."

The bright blue eyes studied me thoughtfully. "So you have some ghosts to lay?"

Beside me, Devlin stirred slightly but made no comment.

I forced myself to breathe slowly and deeply and then to give a light laugh. "Yes, of course!" Solemnly, I ticked off the names on my fingers. "Now, let's see — Great Uncle Josiah, Miss Inglewood . . . Ishbel . . . Old Moana, probably and . . . and . . ."

"Callum." It was Clinton who spoke. "Callum, you've forgotten Callum."

I had not — I just hoped that *he* had. I arranged a bright smile upon my face. "To be sure, and Callum, too, of course!"

"So Callum Douglas was just as . . . as . . . insane as . . . Ishbel?"

"Yes . . . well, no! That is, as far as I know, he did not actually cause anyone any bodily harm . . . it was just that . . ."

I stopped to prevent my voice from faltering. It was true, I thought — I had never actually heard of Callum physically hurting anyone. Yet, it seemed to me, he had always been there, a subtle support to Ishbel, sometimes even egging her on. It was almost as if he had been some kind of alter ego to her — perhaps, a behind-the-scenes puppet master; that he made the plans and that she, without truly realizing what was happening — indeed, believing herself to be fully in control — had carried them out.

Someone coughed and I returned from my world of nightmare thoughts to find myself again the focus of four pairs of eyes. However, there was now an intensity about the gaze that bewildered me. Why should they be so concerned about Callum Douglas? I wondered.

The tension was eased to some extent by Paul.

Empty glass in hand, he had wandered over to the sherry decanter situated on a low table nearby. "Another glass of sherry, anyone? I must say, Malvina, that this house and all the stories about it — perhaps, I should say, rumors? — certainly intrigues us! One never knows quite what to expect in its dark, Gothic corridors or on its gloomy stairs late at night!"

A titter followed his remark; surprisingly from Lucy. "Yes, indeed, dearest Malvina: I swear that when I mount the stairs at night to my chamber, I never go without a companion. One never knows quite what to expect! In fact, one night . . . but no matter; I really have no wish to make you feel uncomfortable. . . . I'm sure, after all, that it's all a lot of non-sense!"

In contradiction to her last statement, she hunched her shoulders and shuddered.

Norah, of course, said nothing at all but looked at me without expression, her wide, pale blue eyes unwinking in the lamp-light.

"Enough of this!" Paul returned to the fireplace. "Malvina will wonder what she has come to!"

Another titter from Lucy. "So, she well may! Or so, she might, if indeed we were so uncaring as to leave her to her own devices."

Paul frowned. "You mean?"

"What could I mean?" Lucy lay back again among her cushions; the soft smile she cast over us, thoughtful—motherly, even. "Obviously, we must have a house party here, both to fulfill our social obligations to Mrs. Smythe and to our other acquaintances who have so kindly entertained us—but also to introduce our newfound cousin into Wanganui society."

For a moment there was silence, then Paul clapping a hand to his thigh, gave his booming laugh. "By Jove, Lucy, that's capital! Don't you think so, Clinton, old fellow? Do the proper for your cousin and at the same time—if Lucy has in mind, what I think she has—we shall be able to hold an exhibition!"

"Very admirable." Clinton's response, I thought, came a second or two too late for great enthusiasm. He looked thoughtfully between his sister and Paul and then at me—it seemed to me, a little sadly—at length nodding his head in agreement. "I expect Georges will agree that it is a good idea."

Paul coughed. "Excuse me, the smoke from the fire—Georges?"

"Yes." Clinton smiled toward me and then turned back to Paul. "Georges is a hard taskmaster, as I have already explained to Malvina. But he is our agent after all and we do owe him a considerable amount of money, do we not?"

Another cough. "This wretched smoke. Yes. Yes; I suppose we do!"

The words were perfectly agreeable but they were accompanied by an ironic, questioning glance.

Paul, I guessed, like Clinton, disliked being under the hold of Georges Duvall. Before I could think further, Lucy stirred on her sofa.

"So it's settled, then? Norah can start writing out the invitations tomorrow morning?"

Though her voice questioned, it was obvious that she considered the matter decided. Beneath her languorous ways, I began to realize, was a will of iron.

Clinton shrugged his shoulders. "I suppose so, if you wish it. . . ." He looked toward me. "Malvina, you must be wondering where my sister finds her strength after her ordeal?"

Ordeal? I wondered. Oh, yes, of course, the train crash; the reason why these Canadian cousins of mine were originally at Ravensfall.

"Not at all; it is obvious that Cousin Lucy must be very brave—I am glad that she seems to be recovering so well."

"Seems!" Clinton pounced upon the word as if I were a mouse and he a cat. "Ah, yes, *seems!*" He looked toward his sister. "I do hope, dearest Lucy, that you are not overdoing things. As Malvina says, you are very brave, but you are after all an invalid! Don't you think that a house party might be a little beyond your present strength?"

Lucy, one long-fingered hand spread across her ample bosom, issued a long, fluttering sigh. "I daresay, Clinton, that you are quite right—but I do not, of course, intend to undertake the arrangements myself. Mrs. Hodges, I imagine, is very capable."

"Mrs. Hodges! Of course!"

As if in answer to a summons, the drawing room doors opened with a magnificent flourish.

"Dinner is served!" Hodges announced to the chandeliers.

Twenty

Dinner was praised as one of Mrs. Hodges's finest; from the mulligatawny soup, through the baked sole with dill sauce of the fish course, the steamed fricassee of chicken as the entrée, and then for the main course, Mrs. Hodges's special roast hogget with mint sauce, accompanied by roast pumkin, kumara, potatoes and cabbage, followed by her famous, sherried trifle with custard and lashings of freshly whipped cream.

Everything was delicious, but after the cheese and biscuits and the requisite hour or so of chitchat over Columbian coffee ("contributed by Mister Fordyke," related Mrs. Hodges, "who, my dear Miss Raven, brought it all the way from America — just fancy!") in the drawing room afterward, I was only too ready to seek the comfort of my room.

To this day, I cannot explain my actions of that evening.

I arrived in my room replete from Mrs. Hodges's splendid dinner, but because of this, or perhaps because of Devlin Fordyke's rich Colombian coffee, I could not settle — even after managing to unhook myself from my green velvet evening dress (having firmly sent Helena upon her way) and after a long-awaited sponge bath, donning my flannel nightgown and wrapping myself in the woolen shawl, the fancy edge of which crocheted as a parting gift by my sister Ariadne.

"Ten minutes of rest before the fire," I told myself firmly, "and then, bed — and no nightmares!"

It was this last, of course, which kept me from my bed.

No nightmares?

Oh, how I wished!

157

I was frightened. I had followed my doctor's orders precisely, leaving off his pills as soon as I had arrived at Ravensfall . . . hoping desperately that the treatment had perhaps cured me. But he was right, of course, the pills—as witness my horrible nightmare of the night before—had acted as a buffer only. Once without their protecting panacea, the terrifying creatures of my nightmares had taken firm hold of my dreaming mind and I was victim yet again to the original problem, that as yet remained unsolved.

What was I to do?

I wandered over to the window seat and sat looking out into darkness.

On an impulse, I drew close the long curtains cutting off the alcove from the rest of the room and raised the window, letting in the cool, damp night air.

The moon had risen and its beams cast into relief the fronds of the giant ferns guarding the River Walk far below. From the river, deep in its gorge, mist was rising.

The wind and rain of the earlier evening were a mere memory.

Down there was the River Walk, where Miss Inglewood had met her end and Harriet—except for her fantastic courage—had almost met hers.

And here I was, Malvina Raven, so scared of my own shadow that I did not have courage enough even to allow myself to fall sleep!

Almost without thinking, I rose and making my way to the wardrobe, dragged open the door and pulled out my heavy boat cloak. "You have ghosts to lay, Malvina Raven," I informed myself severely. I twisted a warm scarf about my head and neck, kicked off my bedroom slippers, and shoved my woolen bed-socked-clad feet into sturdier gear.

I damped down the fire within my grate, fixing the fire screen in front of it and looked with longing at my comfortable four-poster; the patchwork quilt in the rosy glow from the lamp, turned down and welcoming. Under the covers, I knew would be resting, the flannel-wrapped earthenware hot water bottle that Mrs. Hodges and all others of her ilk, felt was indispensable when welcoming a guest.

At that moment, I almost shed my cloak and I barely prevented myself from quenching my lamp before climbing tiredly into bed. Instead, hardly allowing myself to think, I seized up my lamp and leaving my door slightly ajar to let the glow from my fire illumine the corridor without, I marched out into the passage.

I had no misadventures on my way downstairs. It was not until I found myself placing my softly glowing lamp on the hall table that I realized the enormity of what I was about to do.

There were no sounds from the drawing room now, I noted, no light but my own. The rosewood table, which traditionally held the lamps of the household before the residents went up to bed, was left with one lamp only.

I almost jumped out of my skin when the tall clock in its position beside the stairs, chimed midnight.

So much for the witching hour, I told myself! Gathering myself together, I advanced toward the huge bolts of the front door only to find that the door was not bolted. I was surprised at first until I remembered that in New Zealand no one bothered to bolt their doors — especially in the country.

The door swung open and I stepped out.

Where to, now? I wondered:

Despite a nervous trembling, I felt strangely exhilarated: as if I had just shed chains.

It was bright moonlight and from where I stood at the top of the stone steps leading down from the wooden veranda, the lawn was touched with silver. There was a scent of damp grass and moist leaves and from the depths of the dark bush the edges of which crowded upon the lawn, echoed the wild, lonely shriek of a morepork.

Immediately I was transported back in time.

I was standing with Harriet in front of the house, on a sun-drenched morning — Harriet instructing Reggie and me in the calls of the birds.

"And at night," Harriet had told us, "you will hear the cry that sounds like more pork or mo'pork, and that, of course, is the New Zealand owl."

159

Before Harriet could explain, old Moana had appeared—suddenly and silently, as she often did.

"Not morepork, not owl—he is *ruru*."

She had sucked at her gums a moment, her rheumy old eyes glistening with malice. "You want to change everything, but one day, one day . . ."

Harriet had put her arm about my shoulders to comfort me; but her arm had trembled.

The morepork's cry rang again throughout the night and I was recalled to the present.

In the bush, across from the steps, something stirred and a small creature scurried across the lawn to disappear in the darkness of the thicket on the other side. What had disturbed it? I wondered; perhaps a cat out hunting? I wondered if Bubble and Squeak were out there in the undergrowth.

Experimentally, I whispered "Kitty, kitty, kitty!" as loud as I dared. To my delight, one pale shape, closely followed by a darker shadow, darted out into the moonlight, cavorting across the lawn to entwine themselves, loudly purring, about my skirts.

I picked them up and petted them, one after the other. There was nothing quite so comforting, I thought, on such a night, as a warm, furry, purry body!

Perhaps it was the arrival of the cats—fellow living beings playing about me—that gave me the confidence I needed. Almost before I knew what I was doing, I had descended the stone steps onto the lawn and had headed to the right, around the side of the house down toward the River Walk.

The mist I had noticed from my bedroom window, rising in wisps from the river gorge, had thickened, even surging here and there across the track in clouds diaphanous in the moonlight, partly obscuring the tree ferns and my way downward.

Where was I going? And why? I hardly knew. It was almost as if my feet had a life of their own. I had no choice, it seemed and yet I felt no fear, just a tremendous outburst of exhilaration—until I reached the bend of the track close to the cliff edge where Harriet had almost met her end and Miss Inglewood and Ishbel had most certainly met theirs.

Here, perhaps because the mist had coagulated into what

seemed to be a solid wall of fog, I found myself coming to a stop.

In the damp iciness, I pulled the edges of my cloak close about me and looked around. In front of me, behind me: all about me, it seemed, stretched this damp wall of clinging nothingness.

Behind me, there was a muffled crack — as of a twig snapping and Bubble and Squeak disappeared into the undergrowth, refusing — despite all my urgent, whispered summons — to come back. It was this last, that finally unnerved me.

I turned about, ready to effect my escape back up the River Walk, but from out of the murkiness somewhere around me, muffled voices emerged. It was hard to tell in the closeness of the fog, from what direction the voices issued, or even what was being muttered; but it seemed to me that it was not English that was spoken — but though I did not understand what was being said, I could tell from the intensity of the utterances that what was said was said in anger.

Sure enough, as I waited, wondering which direction to take to avoid the speakers, the voices after rising in an intense crescendo, ceased abruptly. Shortly afterward, there was a crashing about as if someone was trying to find a way through the trees. The fog cleared a little at that moment and in the moonlight, through the shining gauze of a suddenly thinning mist, I was able to glimpse a dark shape struggling through the thick undergrowth beneath the tall, shadowy outlines of the tree ferns, back out onto the River Walk.

It was Tamati.

His shoulders were hunched and his head was bent. As he passed by, his face glistened in the moonlight. With my short sight, I could not be sure, but it seemed to me that tears streaked down his cheeks.

I stood for a moment, not knowing what to do; at length, I decided to turn about and return to the house. Easier said than done! The fog had returned full force and totally disoriented, I did not know which way to turn. Not only that, but I was keenly aware that one step in the wrong direction might send me over the cliff edge down into the swirling *taniwha* pool below.

Tentatively reaching out with my hands, I took slow, careful steps, advancing gradually, inch by inch, only to catch my foot on a sharply projecting root. I fell forward, wrenching my ankle in the process and ending up with my fingers connecting momentarily with what seemed to be the rough trunk of a tree — but the tree moved and I found myself reaching out into nothing and toppling down into a void.

Before I could even think about screaming, I felt myself seized and set back into my place.

Above me, through the moonlit, misty haze, loomed a tattooed face; lean and ancient.

I fought down hysteria. This was not a nightmare, I assured myself; those hands that had pulled me back from an untimely end were living, strong and human. Looking up at the hovering face, disembodied momentarily by trailing clouds of fog, I did not find the thought entirely comforting.

The mist cleared a little; the face was, I noticed — almost with relief, I might add — attached to a perfectly ordinary jacket, collarless shirt, and trousers.

A Maori elder, I thought. Though scarce, fully tattooed faces were still to be seen here and there among elderly Maori men. Was he Tamati's grandfather? I wondered . . . and why had they been arguing on the edge of a mist-bound cliff at midnight?

"You must go from here."

His voice was deep, almost guttural but not quite and the words were accentless and spoken slowly as if brought up laboriously from a well of memory long disused. If trees could speak, I think now, they would have that voice.

"Thank you for . . . for helping me." I thought of the void into which I had almost tumbled and shuddered.

My elbow was taken and I was led haltingly — my injured ankle giving me some trouble — back onto the River Walk and pointed upward toward the house.

"You must go from here."

"Yes. Yes, I suppose I must. It was foolish of me, in any case, to come out at this time of night. Thank you again!"

My elbow was taken again and I was swung around to look at the tattooed face. Elderly, this man might be, but considerable strength was still in him. His words when they came, were hurried, urgent. "No. You must go from here — from this house,

162

from this land. You must go to your own country.

"But, why?"

"Because. . . ." In the light of the moon, the intricate coiled patterns of the tattoo stood out like ridges on a wooden carving. Only the eyes remained alive; deep, dark wells.

After a sigh, the slow words continued. "Because you bring trouble . . . you bring sorrow—as all in your family have brought trouble, sorrow. You must go, I say. You must go!"

Without waiting for an answer, he turned from me to slip back down the River Walk, silently disappearing through the mist.

I found myself shaking; there had been a totally convincing note in the old man's words that chilled me to my bones . . . but what on earth could he mean?

Though my ankle ached still, so immersed was I in my thoughts, that I found that I had arrived back at the side of the house almost without realizing it.

The study windows were dark as was to be expected but to my surprise, there was a glow from the library windows alongside. I remembered, then, the one lamp I had seen left on the rosewood table in the hall. Was Clinton still up? I wondered. Though I felt foolish with my part in the events of the evening, I felt the need for human company even more. I would slip in through the side door, I thought, and see who was in the library. But if it were not Clinton, what then?

In the end, I decided to peek through the library windows—providing, of course, there was a chink in the curtains. If Clinton was not there, I told myself, I would simply enter quietly through the side door and make my way to my lamp where I had left it in the hall.

I thought longingly for a moment of my bedchamber and the invitingly turned-down quilt on my comfortable four-poster. I thought of the damped-down fire in the grate nearby, all ready—I hoped—to be revived . . . and almost gave in; but not quite. Clinton might know the identity of the elderly Maori, which might perhaps help to explain his surprising and rather frightening words.

So I crept up to the library windows and tried to peer through the curtains.

There was slight noise behind me and a feeling that someone else was there. Before I could spin around, an iron arm encircled my waist and a hand was clamped firmly over my mouth.

"Spying, Miss Raven?" a well-known American voice whispered huskily into my ear.

I immediately lashed out with my feet, hoping to catch him on the shin. Unfortunately my ankle gave a twinge, putting me off my course. Missing my target, I struck nothing but air. To my embarrassed fury, I felt myself being lifted — or should I say, ignominiously shunted? — under one huge arm. Before I knew what was happening, I was carried in through the side door, up the dark passage with the door to the study on one side and through the opposite door to the library. There I was solicitously deposited upon a chair across from the fireside.

He stood before me, grinning. "Now, Miss Raven, you may scream, if you wish! But there is really no need — the door, as you see, is ajar . . . and you may leave at anytime. In the meantime, may I suggest a little brandy against all the cold and fog you have been through? There is a cabinet here, I have discovered, that holds all the amenities — very civilized, I must say!"

With lightning rapidity, my brain shifted through all possible replies. I elected for dignity.

"Sir, I have no idea why you felt fit to manhandle me the way you did just now, but I assure you that a little whiskey would not make up for all the indignities to which you have subjected me!"

He gave me an admiring look. "You British! Such a command for language that you have. However, I believe I suggested brandy — for medicinal purposes, obviously!"

Before I could deliver a withering reply, he seized up a poker.

Despite myself, I cowered back against the cushions of the chair.

"But if you will not take brandy, you must at least take comfort from the fire — though I am afraid that during my wanderings it has died down. Never mind, I shall stoke it up again! Then perhaps you might like to sit on the sofa here, where you will benefit from the warmth."

Wielding the poker, he advanced upon the fireplace and rearranged the coals, encouraging new flames which he built back into a blaze by the addition of a log or two of wood.

Sitting back on his heels, he looked back at me, beaming happily.

"There now, we shall soon be cozy!"

It was true; already I could feel the heat from the fire and this, combined with the closeness of the room — the more noticeable after my recent exposure to the outside air — made me feel as if I were suffocating. I struggled with the fastenings of my boat cloak, careful, of course to maintain its folds about me, only too aware that beneath my cloak only my woolen shawl and flannel nightdress separated me from impropriety.

Once comfortable I sat bolt upright in my chair and fixed my opponent with a deadly look. "Perhaps," I asked, coldly polite, "you could explain your actions just now?"

"Perhaps, Miss Raven, you could explain yours!"

I took a deep breath. "Mister Fordyke, you have just clamped your hand about my mouth and . . . and picked me up against my will . . . and brought me in here. . . ."

"Ah! But as I said, the door is ajar and you are free to go, if you wish!"

Impasse!

That I was truly free to leave, I did not, of course, believe for an instant. Looking about the room, I noticed a large, ornate — and heavy — candlestick on a low table between my chair and the door. If I moved quickly, I ought to be able to take my adversary by surprise. I would pretend to walk over to the window, I decided, but at the last minute I would duck around behind my chair and pick up the candlestick on my way to the door. If the American did indeed catch up with me, one blow delivered to his head, I thought with satisfaction, should suffice!

Wrapping the folds of my cloak about me, I rose with great dignity, intent on putting my plan into operation immediately. What excuse, I wondered, could I give for going over to the window?

A brilliant thought occurred to me. Perhaps I could maneuver my opponent into going over to the window. While his back was turned I could then beat my retreat! I swayed a little and looked helplessly toward my captor, who, I noted with some surprise, was regarding me with an amused grin.

I staggered realistically. "I believe I need some fresh air! I am feeling a little faint . . . perhaps you could open the window a little?"

"Certainly, Miss Raven!"

A true gentleman would at least have looked concerned. Not Devlin Fordyke! The grin was still on his face as he rose from the hearth rug and sauntered past me on his way to fulfill my request.

At least my ruse had worked; I congratulated myself on my cunning! As soon as his back was turned and he was engaged with the window, I would make my bid for escape!

He reached the window and pulled aside the curtains. He then turned to me, smiling politely. "I believe, Miss Raven, that I am about to turn my back. You may then run to the door, picking up the candlestick on your way—but I do assure you, that you will have no need to use it; as a weapon, that is. Please believe me, I do not intend any further assaults upon your person!"

What could I do but make a dignified exit!

Gathering up my cloak, I raised my head high and turned to go. Unfortunately, I turned so quickly that my injured ankle gave way again, causing such pain that I was hard put not to cry out. As it was, I was obliged to grasp the back of the chair to prevent my falling over.

"Miss Raven! You are hurt! Have I . . . did I? Surely I could not have . . ."

I felt myself seized yet again by powerful arms. Gently I was deposited on the sofa by the fire.

"Now what is it?"

I struggled to sit up, unsuccessfully trying to catch at the edges of my shawl—my cloak had fallen off and now lay in a crumpled heap by the chair. I felt a complete fool. "I assure you, Mister Fordyke, it is nothing! My ankle only; I hurt it when . . ."

"Your ankle? Which one?"

Despite my protests, first my boots and then my bed socks were speedily removed. "Ah, yes, I see; your right ankle! You twisted it, didn't you, in the fog, out on the cliff when you almost fell over . . . I should have realized! In fact, I did wonder, but I didn't want to . . ."

He took my ankle in both hands and gently manipulated it. "However, not a bad sprain, I think . . . a cold compress, I believe . . ."

A movement behind us caught our attention. In the doorway stood Norah Hackett, her pale gaze encompassing my nightdress-clad figure and my bare foot held tenderly by Devlin Fordyke.

"Why, Miss Raven! I do believe I have compromised you!" Mr. Fordyke grinned at me wickedly. "If you wish to save your reputation, I believe you will now have to marry me, whether you want to or not!"

Twenty-one

At last, a night with no nightmares! Despite my disturbing experiences, when I finally reached my bed at one-thirty in the morning, I fell into a deep, untroubled sleep — so deep, in fact, that I did not wake up until nine o'clock, well past the breakfast hour. Even then, I probably would not have awakened if it had not been for Mrs. Hodges.

"Miss Raven! You missed your breakfast and so I thought perhaps . . . Miss Raven?"

I stirred lazily and then came to with a start.

Mrs. Hodges, complete with breakfast tray, was hovering over me, every bit the ministering angel.

"Why, Mrs. Hodges! How very kind . . . but you really did not need . . ." I blinked and yawned and somehow geared my mind back into action.

"It's no trouble, miss, I'm sure! And besides, I've a message for you." She placed the breakfast tray on the cedar chest and helping me sit up, plumped the pillows behind my back.

"There now!" She took the tray up again and set it over my lap. "As good a breakfast as ever I did see!"

I looked at the breakfast set out before me and barely restrained myself from shuddering.

"How very kind of you, Mrs. Hodges. And how very tasty! Deviled kidneys, I do declare, with grilled bacon and sausage and a fried egg . . . and . . . can this be — a black pudding?"

"The very same, miss! A true English breakfast, if I say so myself!" She bridled happily. "There's a butcher makes it in

Wanganui—from pig's blood, I understand—and I sent Hodges in to fetch some, thinking your Canadian relations would like it."

I affected a surprised disapproval. "And didn't they?"

"That's not for me to say, miss." She looked at me darkly. "All I can say is that most of it was left and that Alfred found some of it caught in the camelia bushes under the dining-room windows. It was mold, he thought, which is why he brought it to my attention, poor little creature!"

I didn't know whether to laugh or throw up.

"But tell me, Mrs. Hodges, you say you have a message for me?"

A blush and a kindly smile. "Yes, miss. From your intended!"

Fully awake at last, I shot up, very nearly sending the breakfast tray onto the floor. *"My intended?"*

She beamed at me. "It's all right, miss; you don't have to pretend with me. Mister Fordyke saw me this morning after he brought his daughter over. She sometimes spends the day with Master Bertram, sharing his lessons and that, and she always stays the night at Ravensfall if Mister Fordyke is going to be away."

She paused a moment. "Now, where was I? Oh, yes, about Mister Fordyke and you. So romantic! He explained to me all about last night."

I restrained an impulse to scream. "He did?"

"Oh yes, miss! How you went for a walk because you couldn't sleep—so wound up as you were with coming back to Ravensfall and all—and how he saw you leave the house and fearing you would come to harm in the mist, followed you and then . . ."

She paused, her expression rapt.

"And then?"

"Why, you caught your foot, miss, on a tree root or some such and Mister Fordyke swept you up in his arms and brought you to the library."

I looked at her fascinated. "Why did he bring me to the library?"

She shot a reproving look. "Miss Raven, you should know

169

better! A young, *unmarried* lady and at such an hour of night! And in her *nightclothes!* Where else should Mister Fordyke bring you indeed? Hardly to your room! And as he had already left a lamp alight in the library—having worked there most of the evening on one of his articles—this, of course, seemed to him the most sensible of choices! As he explained to me, his next step would have been to go to the kitchen to summon me on the special bell to the housekeeper's quarters—however, Miss Hackett arrived. . . ."

She paused and for the first time an element of doubt crept into her speech.

"Aha!"

"Beg pardon, miss?"

"Nothing, Mrs. Hodges. I just wondered what Miss Hackett, *an unmarried lady*—and in her *nightclothes*—was doing wandering about the house at such a time of night?"

I had, of course, no particular recollection of Norah's attire—except, it seemed to me on reflection, that she had been wearing a rather sturdy dressing gown. But pure wickedness made me speak out.

"Oh, yes! Well, Miss Hackett is, of course, officially in charge of Master Bertram.

I thought of my poor little cousin for a moment and of his dislike of Norah Hackett. "Indeed. So she is. No doubt, Bertram was having a nightmare and she came down to the library to find a storybook to soothe him?"

Mrs. Hodges looked at me with surprised respect. "Just so, miss! Well almost . . . Master Bertram had a stomach upset rather than a nightmare, but Miss Hackett did indeed come down to the library for a book; though it was one of those medical encyclopedias she was looking for, rather than a storybook!"

I opened my mouth to speak but could find no words.

"There, miss, let me pour you a cup of tea before I go . . . but oh, dear me, what about your poor ankle, you must let me take a look at it!"

"Thank you, Mrs. Hodges, that won't be necessary!"

I smiled at her gratefully and then lied through my teeth. "My ankle is quite recovered, I assure you!"

She fixed me with a gimlet eye. "That, miss, remains to be

seen! You must ring for me as soon as you have finished break-fast and I shall bring up bandages and some of my special sooth-ing lotion; a cold compress is, I daresay, what your ankle needs! I shall go right now and . . ."

Pausing, she turned toward me, clapping a hand to her mouth. "But—oh, my goodness me, I had quite forgot—the message from your intended; Mister Fordyke, that is!"

I took a deep breath and spoke slowly and evenly, my voice well modulated. "I assure you, Mrs. Hodges, that Mister Fordyke and I are not engaged to be married."

She flashed a shocked look. "Of course not, miss! Not until you have both written to your papa! As Mister Fordyke told me, although you are over the age of consent, the conventions must still be observed!"

She nodded approvingly. "I must say that for an American gentleman, Mister Fordyke seems quite cultivated!"

She patted me on the back as I had a sudden fit of coughing. "There, miss—did something catch in your throat? Take a sip of tea!"

She beamed at me as she handed me my teacup. "As I was saying, miss, Mister Fordyke seems quite suitable—and even though he is employed by a newspaper, quite respectable! In any event, I understand he has private means . . . although, I must admit . . ."

She paused a moment, looking down at me wistfully. "I had hoped that perhaps . . . after all, you are not *close* cousins! And Mister Raven is such a handsome and distinguished gentle-man!" She clasped her hands together over the black sateen of her blouse. "So romantic to weld two branches of your family together; I am sure your father would approve! And if you should change your mind . . ."

"Mrs. Hodges!"

A blush and an embarrassed laugh. "You are quite right, my dear! Hodges is always at me about my matchmaking, telling me I should mind my own business! But I can't seem to help myself. . . . After all, what's the harm, bringing two suitable people together? If I say so myself, I've arranged a few good matches in my time!"

"I am sure you have!" I took another deep breath and tried

again. "Mrs. Hodges — really and truly, Mister Fordyke and I do not have an understanding!"

A finger was wagged before my face. "Now, now, miss! No need to be coy with me! As I told Mister Fordyke, I won't tell a soul until you have heard from your father and everything is official! But what am I thinking of; the message — I swear, I'll forget my name, next! Mister Fordyke has sent a message to ask if you would be so kind, miss, to meet him in the stable yard at half-past ten and I am to send your answer back right away with young Alfred, who is waiting in the hall. So, perhaps, miss, if after I have tended to your ankle, you feel up to a short walk?"

She clasped her hands again. "So romantic . . . I understand he is catching the steamer to Wanganui this afternoon. Perhaps he is going to look for a ring! In any event, I daresay he wants to meet you in secret to discuss arrangements! So what shall I tell Alfred, miss?"

I gave up.

The thick mist of the night before had not yet cleared; a condition I remembered from my childhood, when sometimes heavy fog would surround us day after day — wet blanket days, Reggie would call them. In those days, he and I would play a kind of "hide-and-seek" in the bush around the house, concealing ourselves behind mist-disguised trees and bushes; frightening each other half to death when leaping forward with wild banshee yells from our hiding places.

Unable to bear the thought of more of Mrs. Hodges's ministrations, I had managed to dress and slip out of the house without being seen. I stood now — on one foot only, to rest my aching ankle — at the top of the stone steps clutching my ulster close about me and tugging at the long woolen scarf I had twisted about my head and neck. It was not so much cold, I decided, as damp and uncomfortable; Reggie had been right: it was like being surrounded by a thick wet blanket, making it difficult almost to breathe.

Why had Mr. Fordyke asked me to meet him in the stable yard on such a day? He must have known very well that the track through the bush would be largely concealed by the mist.

For that matter, why had he asked to see me at all, especially as he knew I might have trouble with my ankle?

That he really wanted to marry me, I knew, was a pure tarra-diddle on his part or perhaps, Mrs. Hodges with her overactive, wishful imagination had misinterpreted his words.

In any event, *I* had no intention of marrying *him!*

I thought of the night before with an embarrassed shudder, remembering Norah's pale gaze and sly smile as she had studied us from the library doorway.

What had she thought — and what had she told and to whom?

Immediately after she had left us, I remembered, I had wrenched my foot from his hands and struggled up from the sofa.

I delivered an icy glare. "I am returning to my room, Mister Fordyke."

"Yes, Miss Raven, so I see. Allow me to fetch your cloak!"

Before I knew what had happened, my cloak was brought and draped around my shoulders — my shawl arranged first, tidily underneath.

"Your bed socks, Miss Raven, and your boots!"

From my seat on the sofa, I looked up at him, furious.

Though his tone was serious, his face was not. In fact, I detected a distinct quivering about his long, mobile lips.

"You may hand me my bed socks and my boots, Mister Fordyke, and then you may go!"

He tightened his lips, as if to repress laughter. My boots and bed socks were handed to me.

"Miss Raven, I should be delighted to help you. I am, after all, well acquainted with your naked feet!"

Despite myself, I could hardly forebear to laugh. Luckily, I restrained myself in time. "Thank you, Mister Fordyke, I believe I am capable of putting on my own bed socks!"

"And how will you manage the stairs, Miss Raven?"

"The way I usually do: I shall walk up them!"

He looked approvingly. "Quite right: it is not, after all, a serious sprain. In my experience, continuing to walk as normally as possible, usually speeds rather than hinders the healing!"

I looked at him in irritation. A true gentleman, I told myself, would have insisted — *at the least* — on helping me up the stairs!

He rose to go, bowing his head politely and giving me an urbane smile. "I believe a stout staff might be helpful; there are several walking sticks in the cloakroom. Would you like me to bring you one?"

I assumed my most dignified air. "I don't believe that will be necessary, thank you!"

He looked at me admiringly. "Such an independent young lady! In that case, I shall take my leave!"

I had to stop myself from throwing a cushion at him as he went out the door.

It was only afterward, after I had struggled up the stairs and then with great relief had sunk into my cozy bed, that I remembered his rough treatment outside the library window.

Why had he seized me in such a way, and why had he clamped his hand over my mouth? Had he been afraid that I should disturb someone? If so, who? And from what?

Standing at the top of the steps, resting my ankle before plunging down onto the mist-enshrouded lawn, I asked myself the same questions. Who really was Devlin Fordyke? What was he up to? I shivered as I felt an increasing reluctance to leaving the house.

I took myself in hand. Surely, if he had meant to harm me, he would have done so last night—he had had ample opportunity! Besides, I had to find out precisely what he had said to Mrs. Hodges. This marriage idea was really the outside of enough!

Tentatively, I put a foot forward down to the first step—and winced at a sudden pain. Perhaps, I thought reluctantly, Mister Fordyke had been right about a walking stick. My walk up the rough bush track would certainly be made easier with one. I decided to go back to the cloakroom and find one.

I did not have far to go, the cloakroom being next door to the library. Devlin Fordyke had been right: there were several stout walking sticks awaiting my choice. Having selected a strong cherrywood affair with a silver handle, I was prepared to leave, when I heard a door open and close far down the passage outside—from the study, I thought—and then, voices murmuring as their owners walked toward the hall.

Not wishing to meet up with any of the household at that moment, I stayed quietly behind the door, waiting for them to go.

". . . tomorrow?"

"No, the day after tomorrow . . . I'll catch the *Waiwere* upriver to Pipiriki—I've already booked rooms at the hotel."

"What about the fans?"

"Don't worry that's all organized—I got Georges onto it . . . and you know how he is. . . ."

"Yes, but . . . you are *sure* they will be ready in time for the house party?"

"Yes, of course!"

"But what about . . ."

The voices faded as the footsteps, muffled by the turkey carpet, made their way up the passage into the hall.

The voices, I realized, belonged to my cousin Clinton and to Paul Lucas—Paul, apparently being the one to travel to the Pipiriki Hotel.

Fans, I thought. What fans? Were Clinton and Paul organizing some kind of a fan-waving, fancy dress ball for the house party that Lucy had suggested?

I wish now that I had paid more attention at the time to what I had unwittingly overheard—but though it intrigued me, I had so much to worry about that it was not until much later that I realized the significance of that conversation.

And then, of course, it was too late!

Instead, with the help of my newly acquired cherrywood walking stick, I edged up into the hall and then—despite my awkward ankle—quick as ninepence, I was out through the front door onto the lawn and from there into the surrounding bush.

I rested a moment, leaning against the thick trunk of an ancient totara tree, somehow finding comfort in the rough touch of its bark against my cheek. I remembered, smiling at the memory, Harriet's nature walks and how Reggie and I, when her back was turned, would peel off strips of loose bark and throw them at each other.

I took a deep breath, drawing in pungent scents of drenched fern and moss and sodden, rotting leaves and then, planting my walking stick firmly before me, I started to pick my way through the ribs of ancient roots that rose above the mud of the narrow pathway.

Though the mist was thick, it was at least daylight and through pale opalescence, tree trunks gradually emerged; at first, indeterminate, blurred shadows before sharply coalescing into definite, masted shapes.

Surprisingly, sounds were not as muted as the shapes. I seemed to hear the crack of the minutest twig, the scurry of the least animal — and at the same time, a swishing sound as of a skirt keeping time with mine.

I was not sure when I had first heard it. Shortly after I had left the totara tree, perhaps? I had stopped a moment, to disentangle my skirts; at once there had been a corresponding rustle of another skirt, catching in the undergrowth as mine had.

I had to be imagining it, I told myself, but whenever I stopped, so did the swishing of the corresponding skirt. Perhaps the thick mist had somehow or other produced conditions conducive to an echo.

A low giggle sounded — bell-like, melodious — proving I was wrong.

Ishbel, I thought at once; it was just the kind of trick she would play!

But there were no ghosts, I told myself furiously, clenching my hands so tightly, my nails bit into my palms. And Ishbel was dead. Wasn't she? *Wasn't she?*

With awful clarity, I remembered the family graveyard I had visited just the day before. There had been no grave for Ishbel.

But she had died — I knew she had. Had I not watched from the window of the second-floor landing as she and Harriet had fought on the riverbank, Harriet finally twisting away and Ishbel, the long skirts of her riding habit billowing about her, sinking down into the river?

I tried to peer through the suffocating whiteness and shuddered.

This was a nightmare come alive.

Ishbel *was* dead, I assured myself.

If so, a little voice niggled at my brain, then where was her grave?

Had she really died? the same little voice asked. After all,

Reggie and I had not been present at the funeral, having been sent away to stay with friends of our father's far away, up north.

Had Ishbel actually survived? And then—perhaps to save the family further disgrace—been smuggled to an asylum, from which she had later escaped?

Was Ishbel still alive!

As if in answer, another low, musical laugh sounded from the bush nearby.

Momentarily I froze and then panicked. Clutching my walking stick as if it were a lifeline, I plunged off up the rough track to the stables, inevitably tripping over exposed roots, slipping in patches of mud, and colliding with tangled bushes and trees.

My walking stick flew from my hands as finally, almost reaching the stable yard, I made heavy impact against one huge trunk.

The trunk moved.

Too late, I discovered that my hands were clawing at a rough tweed jacket. I hardly dared raise my eyes. Would I see yet another disembodied, tattooed face hovering in the mist above me?

A pair of strong arms wrapped themselves about me and I found myself gently lifted out through the bush into the stable yard.

There was the distant rumbling of a volcanic laugh about to erupt. "Miss Raven, what are you about?" I was set gently on my feet.

I stood, swaying, resisting the urge to grab at the reality of his waistcoat. "What am I about?" I stood glaring up at him, blinking back the tears. "Should you not know what I am about, sir! Did you not ask me to meet you here?"

A pause. The face above me was solemn suddenly, all amusement gone. "I asked you to meet me, here?"

I choked back a sob. "Indeed, you did—that is, Mrs. Hodges said you did . . . that you had sent a message to me and that Alfred was waiting in the hall, ready to take back my answer."

"Alfred, you say? But I sent no message by Alfred nor any other . . ."

"Then what are you doing here?"

177

"I came out to tend Beau Brummell, that is all."

There was a sudden stirring in the bush, directly behind me.

"Ishbel!" The name escaped my lips before I could help it. Wrenching myself away from Devlin Fordyke, I stumbled into the stable yard, slid across a patch of muddy grass and fell flat upon my face.

Two warm, furry bodies twisted and turned about my shoulders and outflung arms: two damp, inquiring noses sniffed at my hair and face.

"Miss Raven!"

A concerned Devlin Fordyke loomed over me. I felt myself lifted solicitously to my feet.

"It was only the cats, you know, that frightened you—I daresay their shooting out of the bush like that . . . and in all this mist. . . ."

His voice ended on a doubtful note.

I battened down hysteria. "Bubble and Squeak!"

"Bubble and Squeak?"

I felt wild laughter surging: somehow, I managed to control it. "The n-n-names of the c-c-cats!"

A grunt of a laugh. "Of course! When I was in London on busin . . . on an assignment, I should say, a Cockney friend of mine told me all about refried potatoes and cabbage. I must say it sounds horrible! However . . ."

"It's n-not bad: in f-fact, it's quite . . . quite . . ." I wanted to say that the dish was quite tasty but somehow the words would not come.

I felt an arm firmly placed about my shoulders. "You are in shock. Something has frightened—has *terrified* you."

The arm tightened. "Come along, now!"

Before I could say yea or nay, I was whisked up the path past the stables and then, turning left, down the track leading to the former workmen's cottages, overlooking the path winding down to the river.

We stopped before the first cottage.

"Welcome to my abode, Miss Raven!"

Swept up into powerful arms, I was carried over the threshold and dumped onto the lopsided cushions of an ancient armchair, my injured foot carefully propped

178

up on a moth-eaten footstool.

"A cup of tea, Miss Raven!"

The words were a command, rather than a polite inquiry as to my wishes.

Before I could answer, the huge man busied himself about the tiny room, turning up the fire in the banked-down range beside which I was seated and setting a filled kettle on the hob.

"You need have no qualms, my mother is Irish, so despite being an American, I do know how to make tea!" From the mantelpiece, he lifted down a tin tea caddy and an earthenware teapot. "There we are: first warm the teapot and then a spoonful of tea leaves for each of us plus one for the pot."

He suited his words with his actions and grinned at me. "And now we'll wait for the water to boil — that's the trick of it, isn't it? Or so my mother always insists; that the water must be boiling and then the tea left to brew for five minutes or so. . . . Now, if you'll excuse me for a minute or two, I believe I'll fetch some more wood for the range."

He had, I realized, been chatting with deliberate casualness as if to give me time to collect myself. Furthermore, his method seemed to be working. My shivering had almost stopped and I no longer had a wild desire to laugh.

I looked about with interest. I was in a typical wooden whare, or cottage, of the kind built by the early settlers: two tiny rooms below and occasionally — as in this case — with a steep, ladder-like staircase leading up to two corresponding rooms above. I supposed the rooms were small to conserve the heat but how crowded they must have been! The room where I was sitting apparently did duty as kitchen, dining room, and living room and yet it was scarcely big enough to hold dining table and chairs and the big Morris chair I was sitting in!

Though small, the room was cheerful enough; enlivened by a red plush tablecloth and brightly colored curtains and cushions. There were colorful prints on the wooden walls, also — mainly of flowers, with one or two scenic views of rivers or lakes and mountains. One print caught my attention in particular; I struggled up from my chair and hobbled over to take a closer look.

To my surprise, it was not a print at all but a pen-and-ink

179

sketch, washed over with watercolor of a huge, straight-sided, flat-bottomed valley. The artist had apparently been situated somewhere on the valley floor for the walls — a study in mustards, oranges, and yellows — rose steep and gaunt to a breathtaking height. "Grand Canyon, Arizona," I read printed along the bottom with the artist's name — a D. Francis — neatly written in small letters across the left-hand corner.

From outside came a series of thuds, followed by the heavy sound of wood being chopped. I peered out the tiny window but could see only the mist still heavy among the trees of the bush-surrounded clearing. I started shivering again and quickly withdrew my gaze.

Below the window, on the small dining table were scattered writing materials, a pile of letters, a bound notebook that appeared to be a daily journal, and several old copies of the *New York Times*.

As the sound of another log being split rent the air, I took the newspapers back to my chair. Perhaps I would find some of Mister Fordyke's travel articles, I thought, settling back against the molting feather cushions in an attempt to find a comfortable position.

The papers were dated several months previously, the latest being an early March edition. It was already open at an inside page; one article, I noted — in fact, I could scarcely miss it, outlined as it was in red pencil — caught my attention immediately: FOLLOW-UP TO PARK AVENUE THEFT, I read, but before I could continue reading, there was a sound behind me.

Devlin Fordyke filled the doorway, his ugly face beaming cheerfully over a great stack of logs. "Good, you've made yourself at home, I see, Miss Raven!"

"Yes . . . The *New York Times*, I hope you don't mind — I thought I might find one of your articles. . . ."

"Not at all . . . you'll find them a little out of date, I fear, it takes about six to eight weeks for a consignment to arrive. But this at least is the latest shipment: a friend of mine sent them out to me — he knew I should be in New Zealand by now."

He began to wind his way through the cramped space between my chair and the dining-room table and then, apparently catching his foot on the hooked rug, lurched to one side, sending the logs he was carrying in a wooden cascade toward the range.

Quickly he recovered himself, clutching the remaining logs to his chest. "Please excuse me! You are not hurt, I hope?"

"Not at all!" It was true, the logs had fallen well clear of me to the other side of the range. Casting the newspaper aside, I struggled from my chair, down onto the floor, intent upon helping with the gathering up of the wood.

"Please, Miss Raven, do not trouble yourself!"

The logs were quickly picked up and in the process, the *New York Times*. "Now then, you wanted to read an article of mine? Let me find you one and you can look at it while you sip your tea and I attend to the fire."

The logs were added to the pile by the range and the newspaper replaced on the table. "Ah, now let me see! Perhaps my account of some Incan tombs recently discovered in Peru?" More newspapers were quickly ruffled through and I was presented with another March edition opened at a page toward the end.

Sure enough, beside some pen-and-ink sketches of a sheer, mountainous landscape was the heading ANCIENT PERUVIAN TOMBS REVEAL PRICELESS ARTIFACTS. The byline, D. FORDYKE, was prominently displayed below.

Mr. Fordyke, I was informed, *was at the actual archaeological site and would be sending in further revelations as they occurred.*"

"Milk and sugar, Miss Raven?"

"Just a little milk, thank you; no sugar."

A steaming cup and saucer were placed on the wide wooden arm of my Morris chair.

"A biscuit, Miss Raven?"

A plate of Afghans, gingersnaps, and wine biscuits was wafted beneath my nose.

I selected a gingersnap and absentmindedly dipped it into my tea as I perused the article. It was, of course, fascinating: an account of the remains, apparently of chieftains entombed with ornaments, jewelry, and figurines—mainly of gold.

One thing puzzled me: the dates mentioned. According to the newspaper—dated the second week of March—Mr. D. Fordyke was engaged on a series of articles sent directly from the archaeological site in Peru. In the next few weeks, readers were urged to look for new and revealing details.

I looked at the huge figure stacking the wood by the range.

New and revealing details, I thought; a series of articles from Peru — some yet to come — and here was the writer of them, at least six weeks' journey away across the Pacific, in Wanganui, New Zealand!

Then obviously I was right, I told myself; had indeed been right from the beginning: this man was not who he said he was. And if he was not who he claimed to be, then who was he — and, more importantly, why was he here and why was he so concerned with my identity and my movements?

I tried to prevent my fingers from trembling, but despite my best efforts, the newspaper I was holding quivered like an elm in a gale.

"There is something troubling you, Miss Raven?"

Warily, I glanced over the edge of the paper. The wood neatly stacked, Devlin was now standing, his back to the range, holding his own steaming cup of tea balanced in its saucer.

Carefully I folded the newspaper at his article and resting it in my lap, took up my teacup and nibbled on my gingersnap.

"Not at all, Mister Fordyke! Nothing troubles me. Why should it? In fact, this is a really interesting article; and very well written, I might add! And I notice it is a series. . . ." I smiled brilliantly and replaced my cup and saucer on the arm of my chair.

After taking another sip of tea, he placed his cup and saucer on the mantelpiece and then turning toward me, directed an understanding smile. "Ah, yes, a series! How very quick, you are, Miss Raven! No doubt, you are wondering how I am able to be in two places at once?"

I tried not to choke on the last crumbs of the gingersnap and reached wildly for my cup.

To my chagrin, my teacup was seized from the arm of my chair and held steadily beneath my lips. "Sip slowly, now! You are all right? Good!"

"Please excuse me; I suppose I must have swallowed the wrong way!"

"Yes, I suppose you must have! But we were talking

about my series — about my being in two places at once."

Recovering myself, I dabbed at my lips with my handkerchief. "Yes, so we were. Naturally, you have a perfectly reasonable explanation!" Despite myself, I was unable to keep the sarcastic tone from my voice.

He grinned down at me cheerfully. "Naturally! However, I must warn you that my explanation will destroy your faith in newspapers forever!"

"Indeed?" What was he up to now, I wondered.

"Indeed! You see, I wrote the articles ahead of time but to keep up the interest of our readers, my editor decided to release each account as if it were sent by cable each week. This way, the tension, the suspense would be maintained, our readers perpetually wondering from one week to the next what new discoveries had been made!"

He grinned again and shrugged his huge shoulders, spreading his hands wide. He did not wait for my answer but moved the short distance over to the table under the window. "An item of journalistic fudge, I'm afraid!" Carefully, he settled his bulk onto a straight-backed chair — which to my astonishment did not give way.

Brilliant! I did not, of course, believe a word; the explanation — and the delivery of it — was too slick and the narrowed, hazel eyes, as they studied my reactions, too watchful. I should have to be careful, I decided; I must not let him see my doubt.

I gave a deliberately light laugh. "I should have known! How stupid I am!"

The chair creaked uneasily as my huge companion leaned forward. "Stupid? You? Oh, no, you are very quick, as I remarked before. Inexperienced, of course, and perhaps . . . misled?"

He studied me a moment and I was again aware of how very big he was, his head and broad shoulders mostly obscuring the tiny window behind him, his looming presence seeming totally to fill the small room.

His head nodded decisively. "Yes, very definitely misled; but stupid? No! Which is why, when you came bursting out of the bush just now, I knew that it was not just hysterics at some imagined fright but that something had truly terrified you."

Despite all my efforts, I found myself shaking and my fingers twisting together.

"Come — now that you have had a cup of tea and a chance to relax, won't you tell me what — or who — it is, that is frightening you?"

The hazel eyes were concerned; the mocking gleam of only a few minutes ago completely vanished.

I took a deep breath and tried to laugh. "It . . . it's nothing really. It's just that the afternoon I arrived I heard the service bells ringing in the kitchen. . . ."

"I see. You heard bells? And then?"

I shivered, remembering that dark afternoon. "Although the bells rang, there seemed to be no one there . . . and then I . . . I heard a laugh. . . ."

"And again, there appeared to be no one there? Did you hear this laugh again?"

"Yes, later that night . . . and then . . . and then, in the bush just now; not just that but . . . I thought I heard the swish of a skirt. . . ."

"And, of course, you thought it was your sister, Ishbel?"

"How d-did you know?"

A comforting smile. "You called out her name after the cats had frightened you! Remember?"

He studied my face a moment and then rose and gathered up my cup and saucer in one swift movement. "I believe another cup of tea is called for!"

He poured my tea and stood again with his back against the range, waiting until I had managed to swallow a few sips and had replaced my cup and saucer on the arm of my chair.

"But your sister is dead, is she not? And from our conversation yesterday, I gather that you don't believe in ghosts . . . or is it . . ." He paused a moment studying me thoughtfully. "Of course, that's it!" His eyes gleamed with sudden understanding. "You believe your sister to be still alive!"

I shuddered and could not bring myself to speak.

"But you saw her die, did you not?"

I shook my head. "I . . . I s-saw her fall into the river — but directly afterward, I ran off to find Reggie."

"Surely you went to her funeral?"

184

"No. My brother and I were sent away to my father's friends up north — and we did not return until after Harriet's trial."

"But her grave? Surely you have visited it?"

"No. That's it, y-you see. Yesterday, I realized that there is . . . there is no grave for her in the family burial ground. . . ."

For a moment, we looked at each other in silence; Devlin looking thoughtful and myself huddled in my chair, clasping and unclasping my fingers.

"I know you must think me an idiot . . . but . . ."

He frowned quickly and then smiled. "Stop that at once! As I have mentioned before, you are very far from being an idiot! There is, however, a possibility you evidently have not thought of."

"A possibility? A possibility of what?"

He frowned again; but this time the frown was not for me. "Have you not thought that someone who knows your story — and most people in this area do — may be trying to frighten you?"

I looked at him in astonishment. "But why should anyone want to do that?"

He studied me quietly for a moment and then sighed deeply as if he were reluctant to continue. "Perhaps, Miss Raven, there is someone who does not want you at Ravensfall?"

"But what nonsense! Why should anyone not want me at Ravensfall?"

He smiled but the smile did not reach his eyes. "Forgive me . . . but the reputation of your family? Your great uncle's exploits, your half-sister's madness, and, of course, Callum Douglas. I understand that he had rediscovered your great uncle's still and that one of the charges against him stated that he had corrupted the local Maori youths by paying them to help him produce and transport illegal whiskey.

"But . . . but . . . all that is in the past!"

"Is it, Miss Raven? Is it indeed?"

Behind him, the kettle sighed on the hob: otherwise, total silence. Beyond the window, the fog still pressed down, a wet blanket trapping us in a nightmare world.

Twenty-two

Mr. Fordyke's suggestion caused me considerable surprise — but in a strange way, it also brought a small measure of comfort. After all, if someone else were trying to frighten me, this implied that Ishbel was truly dead and existed only in my nightmares.

Back at Ravensfall at last, having been delivered, despite my objections, directly to the edge of the bush around the still misty lawn, I gazed up again at the wooden façade of the house.

What mysteries did it hold? I asked myself.

As if in answer to my question, the front door flew open, revealing a ghostly, shawl-wrapped figure that crept slowly onto the veranda and stood looking out into the fog, before suddenly straightening and advancing staunchly down the steps onto the mist-wreathed lawn as if about to set out through untold horrors on an expedition of unbelievable daring.

Betty, I thought. No one could possibly mistake the determined set of those straight shoulders.

I started off across the lawn and was rewarded with a shriek.

"Lor', miss! You scared me proper! That, I don't deny! But whatever are you h'a-doing of out 'ere, in the middle of all this fog? The old duck were right worried: you slipping away like that with your bad h'ankle n'all! Then when it were nigh on luncheon and you weren't back, she sent me to fetch you. . . ."

I could not prevent a sigh of irritation. "Mrs. Hodges knows perfectly well where I've been; and even if she did not, there would be absolutely no need for her to make a fuss!"

She giggled understandingly. "Gets to you, don't it! Still, she means well, I daresay."

As we talked, we had made our way back across the lawn onto the veranda and into the hall.

I rested my ankle for a moment, leaning on my walking stick—kindly retrieved by Devlin Fordyke—looking down at the rosewood table by the drawing-room doors. Beside the lamps, already set out for the evening, was a pile of letters.

Betty followed the direction of my gaze. "Letters, miss, for the steamer. 'odges or Tamati will take them down to the landing this afternoon. If you 'ave h'any letters, I'd be glad to bring them downstairs for you."

"Thank you; how kind of you . . . and how guilty I feel! I had intended to write straightaway, but have not yet done so."

All of a sudden, as well as guilty, I felt immeasurably tired and unable to face up to the usual polite conversation over luncheon—the more especially as I had no idea as to what—if anything—Norah Hackett had revealed about my escapade of the night before.

"I wonder, if it's not too much trouble, if perhaps I could have a light luncheon in my room? I had a late breakfast and I am really not very hungry!"

She cast a shrewd look. "But you're tired, I can tell. No trouble at all, miss. You relax by your fire—it's all set ready—and write your letters; and I'll bring you h'up a nice luncheon—and a cold compress for your h'ankle."

Smiling at me cheerfully, Betty left my side and vanished behind the green baize door.

I was about to venture up the stairs when a door opened down the library passage. There was a swishing of skirts followed by the creaking sounds that usually signaled the approach of Bertram.

I had no wish to meet any of the household but decided to stand my ground with dignity, realizing that my damaged ankle would prevent a quick escape. Before we had left the cottage, Mr. Fordyke assured me that he had talked with Mrs. Hodges about our "understanding" solely to protect my reputation. Therefore, whatever stories Norah might tell, would have no substance as Mrs. Hodges would counteract any rumors with her undoubtedly romantic account of a secret engagement!

"So, my dear Miss Raven, you may tell—or not tell—any story you choose. And then after a suitable interval, if you so wish, you may inform Mrs. Hodges that either you did not receive your father's blessing or that you have changed your mind. Though, I must admit"—Devlin Fordyke had beamed down at me—"that I find your reluctance to marry me, distinctly unflattering!"

Though I could not help but smile at the memory, I was still in considerable doubt about the intentions of Devlin Fordyke. Though he had undoubtedly helped me that morning, how much of that help was disinterested? Again, I asked myself what he wanted with me.

Before I could ask myself more questions, the creaking that had attracted my attention from the library corridor turned out to be caused by Bertram—as I had correctly supposed. The swishing, however, belonged to the long skirts of Norah Hackett and the somewhat shorter ones of Miranda Fordyke.

They advanced now, all three of them, silently across the hall: Norah first, her bony hands clasped in front of her, Bertram next, and Miranda, flashing her catlike smile, last.

Norah, of course, said nothing, but inclined her flaxen head slightly, her colorless eyes glancing up at me slyly from under her pale lashes. Miranda also passed me in silence but her smile widened mockingly as she looked me over. Had Norah talked to the children about last night? I wondered in sudden panic. Surely not!

To my relief, as the other two passed into the drawing room, Bertram stopped a moment, his deep brown eyes studying me through the thick lenses of his spectacles, taking in my ulster and walking stick. "Good afternoon, Miss Raven! I see you have been for a walk. How brave of you in all this fog. I wanted to go out, too, you know, but they wouldn't let me. . . ."

He stopped a moment, looking wistfully toward the door. "That woman, you see, tells them all I have a weak chest, which I don't." He looked up at me, his narrow face tense and angry. "Weak legs, yes; weak chest, no! She just wants to show how powerful she is!"

"That woman?"

He jerked his head toward the drawing room. "Horrible Hackett, that's what Miranda and I call her. She likes secrets: she watches and listens and then, when she's learned something, she . . . makes you pay. . . ."

"Makes you pay?"

"It's hard to explain — but, fr instance, this morning, when I said, I'd go out anyway, even though she'd taken away my crutches, she told me that if I didn't behave, she'd tell my . . . my . . . uncle that I'd been up in the studio, where none of us are supposed to go. . . ."

I thought of all those stairs and looked at him in awe. "You mean, you climbed all those stairs!" I looked at his crutches and blinked. "Oh, I'm sorry, I did not mean, that is . . ."

The dark eyes were angry suddenly. "Don't patronize me!" There was something instantly familiar about the angry turn of the head, something, I thought, that had happened to me fairly recently.

Before I could quite place the memory, the angry look was replaced by an apologetic smile that brightened up his whole face. "I'm sorry, it's just that I don't like — don't *need* sympathy."

I wanted to cry but managed to keep my voice steady. "I understand. But all those stairs, did you manage them by yourself?"

A shake of the head, accompanied by a rueful grin. "Not that time — but I shall one day! No, Alfred and Miranda helped me. Miranda wanted to see inside, too, you see."

He stopped a moment, cocking his head to one side as he gazed up at my face. "Miranda doesn't like you, you know, but I expect it will pass, once she finds out what you are really like!"

"I . . . I see! Why does she not like me?"

"Oh, I expect it's because her father . . ."

"Bertram!"

We both jumped.

Just within the drawing room doorway stood Norah Hackett, her bony hands still clasped before her, her face completely expressionless.

How long had she been there? I wondered. What had she overheard?

189

Without uttering another word, she shot a glance at Bertram from under her lashes and then turning swiftly, glided away.

Bertram, casting an apologetic look up at me, steadied himself on his crutches and hobbled away. "I'm sorry, Miss Raven, I have to practice before lunch."

Suddenly tired again, I leaned heavily on my walking stick as I crossed the hall. What was going on? As I began to climb the stairs, I heard the first few notes played on the piano. It was Rachmaninoff's Funeral March.

Back in my cozy room—someone had already lit the fire—I could hardly wait to shed my ulster and walking boots. Gratefully, I sank down in the chintz-cushioned, fireside chair and stretched my stockinged feet toward the grate.

My ankle was swollen, but not much. It ached somewhat with the exertion of climbing up the stairs, but there was no sharp pain. Perhaps Devlin really was right, that the best thing was to exercise it!

Outside my door sounded a rattle and a clink and then a soft knock.

I was expecting Betty or Helena—I hoped *not* Mrs. Hodges!—with my lunch; I was surprised to find suddenly how hungry I was.

The small skinny figure bearing the tray was not, however, any of the three.

"Of course!" I exclaimed, on looking at the straight dark brows and huge, black-lashed gray eyes, so like Helena's, "You must be Alfred!"

The eyes regarded me blankly and then the tray was set carefully down on the low table by my chair.

"Thank you, Alfred."

The eyes remained blank before the small figure straightened up. It was as if his mind was directed by a spirit situated on a remote hilltop, several miles away.

I tried again. "Are you Helena's brother?"

A long pause and then a nod.

"And you come from the orphanage?"

Another pause; another nod.

190

"Did you like the orphanage?"

A pause and then a shake of the head.

Progress, I thought!

"Would you rather be here than in the orphanage?"

This time, no pause: a vigorous series of nods.

All of a sudden, I realized that I was being observed. There was a quiet glow from his gray eyes, as if, somewhere within his head, someone had turned up a lamp. Alfred had returned.

"There's fish!" a quiet, husky voice informed me. "And you can have this."

An apple, rosy, rounded, and polished, was brought out from a pocket and held up for my inspection.

"Why, thank you, Alfred; how very good of . . ."

Before I could finish my sentence, the apple was set beside the tray and he had turned and slipped back through the door, closing it carefully behind him.

So that was Alfred. Or was it? Like the door he had shut behind him, Alfred remained impenetrable.

Cautiously I removed the silver cover from the main dish. Fish, as Alfred had so succinctly informed me: something firm, white, and deboned, steamed in milk, with the requisite slice of lemon and tartar sauce. I looked about the rest of the tray: thin slices of thickly buttered bread, a saucer-size, nutmeg-dusted custard tart, decorated with a swirl of freshly whipped cream, and a silver teapot with its accompanying hot water jug.

Thirty minutes later, my emptied tray pushed aside, I found myself nodding beside the glowing embers in my fireside grate.

". . . coals, miss?"

I came to with a start!

"I did knock, miss, but when you didn't reply . . . I thought perhaps you'd gone downstairs and then when I came in, I saw that your fire had gone down and I thought perhaps you needed . . ."

"More coal?" I smiled sleepily at an embarrassed Helena. "Not really. I fell asleep, that's all and let the fire die down — but what have you there?"

On the tray she carried sat a bowl, a neat pile of linen, and a huge, square-shouldered glass bottle filled with a thick pink lotion.

"Mrs. Hodges's special lotion, miss, for sprained muscles."
She told me, particular, that I was to massage it gently into the
skin before binding your ankle up!"

I groaned in exasperation, but knowing it was useless, stripped off my stocking and allowed Helena to perform her ministrations.

Though I should have hated to admit it, the pink lotion *was*
soothing!

I flexed my firmly bandaged foot and felt not a twinge.
"Good as new! Helena, you're a marvel!"

"Not me, miss! Mrs. Hodges's lotion!" She swept up bowl,
bottle, and remaining bandages and piled everything onto my
discarded luncheon tray. "Anything else, miss?"

"Oh, no, thank you! You have done more than enough!" I
paused but could not help adding wickedly, "However, in case
Mrs. Hodges should ask, I believe I am about to spend the remainder of the afternoon writing letters!"

A smile in return and that glow of understanding that had so
distinguished her brother's dark gray eyes.

"Your brother," I said, without thinking, "brought up my
luncheon tray, you know; how alike you both are! Tell me, is he
. . . is he . . . always . . ."

There was a smile at the back of the gray eyes. "In and out,
miss? Yes, always. That's why Pa had us swear to look after him
. . . because . . . because, people don't always understand, do
they? Not like Mrs. Hodges!"

I suddenly felt very humble and bit my lip with shame at the
thought of my earlier irritation. "Yes, she's a good woman."

"She is indeed, miss!"

Picking up her tray, Helena left my room, leaving me to my
own devices.

Letters, I thought to myself. Enough of this sloth! I heaved
myself out of my chair and stretched out my foot, tentatively
trying out my ankle. To my delight, it held up and I felt no
twinge as I crossed the room to the writing desk under the window.

My writing case—a splendid, tooled leather affair, given to
me by my father before my departure—was where I had left it
the night before, between my journal and Edward's miniature.

Before I opened it, I looked guiltily at my journal. I had promised faithfully to Ariadne and Mark that I should record my experiences for them to read upon my return — and so I had, until I reached Wanganui!

I would tackle my journal next, I told myself. I reached for my writing case, my eye alighting on Edward's likeness as I did so. How remote, he seemed all of a sudden. He had had the miniature painted for me before he had left for South Africa. "You must look at it every day, old thing," he had told me, "as I shall look at yours." Despite his brusque common sense, Edward could be astonishingly romantic! And in the early days after his death, I had formed a habit of talking to him in my mind — having the fancy that his direct gaze possessed understanding. Now, however, his protuberant eyes gazed at me blankly, no more than small patches of blue paint.

I experienced a sense of loss, but unexpectedly, I also felt a sudden freedom. I could not understand myself.

Frowning, I undid the catch of my writing case. Though I had written home immediately upon my arrival in Wellington, I had little to describe then, other than my shipboard experiences. The family would all be waiting eagerly for my impressions of Wanganui and Ravensfall, I knew. I should write first to the family in general, and then a personal note to Harriet.

But what should I tell them?

Surely, if I related all that had happened to me since my arrival at Ravensfall — the bells, the laugh, the strange attitude of my cousins toward me — they would certainly be worried out of their minds; or imagine that I was going out of mine!

For that matter, perhaps I was. Could my mind — so much affected by my nightmares — when faced by the dark, empty house, have possibly imagined the bells and that chilling laugh? As for my cousins' doubtful attitude toward me, I had always . . . as Edward would persist in telling me . . . been oversensitive.

I cast my mind back to the night of my arrival: Clinton Raven's gray eyes gazing up at me from the gloom and wet of the doorway and Devlin Fordyke holding his glowing lamp, descending the stairs behind me.

That was it, of course! I could not possibly have imagined

Devlin's treatment of me—the struggle in Clinton's sitting room and again last night outside the library window!

What had I been about, to have allowed myself to be so easily lulled by him in his cottage that morning? Of course, I had been in a state of shock after my considerable fright and strangely, there had been a soothing quality about the huge man that had calmed my shattered nerves. But that was no excuse, no excuse at all for my stupidity!

Not only had he not given me any explanation for his actions, but there was the matter of that doubtful trip to Peru and his too slick explanation. And what about . . . there was something else, I thought now, something niggling me at the back of my mind. Of course, I remembered at last, the copy of the *New York Times* I had been reading when he had come back with the firewood. He had tripped—surely, an odd thing to do, for a man usually so light on his feet—and in gathering up the firewood, he had also taken the newspaper. He had placed the paper on the table and given me another. Why had he done that? Surely, the correct action for a gentleman would have been to return the paper I had obviously been reading.

I thought back to the paper I had been reading. Of course, I remembered now, there had been an article outlined in red. Was it something that Devlin did not want me to see? Why? The article had concerned a theft, something about a cover-up. Why should Devlin Fordyke want to conceal from me an article about a theft?

I had a sudden thought and shivered. Could he possibly have been concerned in the theft himself? I remembered his arrival in Clinton's sitting room—where Clinton had told me the key to the studio was kept. Had Devlin, knowing that nearly everyone was away, thought to use the opportunity to take the key? Perhaps to make a wax impression? Was he planning to steal the valuable paintings stored in the attic?

I stared blindly out my window at the still thick mist outside. On the other hand, I thought, Paul Lucas had been in the studio that night because Devlin had used that as his reason for coming over to Ravensfall. But had Paul really been in the studio? I had not actually seen him that night, I remembered. Had the huge American known that Paul was actually elsewhere?

And not just the paintings in the attic, I thought, remembering the antiques that Clinton had told me were stored by Georges Duvall. Where were they kept? I wondered. Perhaps the key to that room was also kept in Clinton's sitting room and Devlin, knowing Paul was safely in the studio, had taken advantage of an otherwise empty house.

My thoughts in a whirl, I rose from the desk. I could not possibly write letters, I decided. I crossed over to the fire and relieved some of my nervous energy by poking up the coals.

I gazed thoughtfully down into the flames. Devlin Fordyke certainly seemed to have the run of the house. Last night, for instance, at such a late hour, writing an article — or so Mrs. Hodges had said — in the library. Evidently, he had won the trust of my cousins. How much did they know about him? I wondered.

I thought back to the events of the night before. Why had Devlin seized me in such a manner? Why had he clamped his hand over my mouth?

The answer was staring me in the face. He must have heard me in the bushes before I had crept onto the veranda and then, under cover of darkness, he had come out the side door and slipped behind me. Perhaps he had thought I really was spying and he had tried to silence me before someone in the household had been alerted and had come downstairs to see what was going on.

What had he been doing in the library that he did not want discovered?

Puzzled, I recalled the scene in the library where Devlin had finally set me down. There was nothing untoward — no pulled-out books hastily set aside, no papers hurriedly stuffed behind a cushion — as far as I could remember.

What had he been afraid of?

I thought about the library, the cushioned chairs about the fireplace, the rows and rows of leather-bound books and above them all, the pictures of the sailing ships — whalers, I had always supposed they were — interspersed with scenes of Maori life.

What had he been afraid of? I asked myself again? What had he been trying to hide?

A sharp crack from the fireplace claimed my attention. I watched a coal disintegrating into ashes and was filled with a sudden, blazing anger. Whatever Devlin Fordyke's part in all of this, someone — perhaps Devlin himself, perhaps not — was engaged in trying to terrify me.

Who?

Why?

Somehow or other, I would solve this mystery and bring the person responsible to account.

And the first place I would investigate, I thought grimly as I slipped my feet into comfortable slippers and seized up a shawl to guard against the cold, would be the library!

The stairs proved dank, unfriendly; the hall, unwelcoming, its dark corners seething with half-formed shadows as if the invading mist gradually seeping in from outside was engaged upon a wholesale conquest.

I stood listening for a moment, my hand lightly resting on the carved raven of the newel post. No sound; no sound at all except for my own breathing.

It was then that the front door silently swung open to reveal a long, lean figure — a large box balanced upon one shoulder — straddle-legged on the fog-enshrouded top step.

It was familiar — terrifyingly familiar.

I found myself clutching at the wooden raven. It could not be; it just could not be!

My mind flew back over the years to another such scene: another rangy figure looming out of the fog — but he was dead, the police had insisted he was dead . . . or was my mind, indeed, demented!

"We'll take them straight up, Tamati."

The voice, a baritone, gutturally accented — the 'r's produced deep in the throat in the French manner — shattered the illusion. Weak with relief, I leaned back against the newel post.

Of course, I thought, the tall man who had greeted me in the corridor at Foster's hotel. That is why, I mentally chided my overactive imagination, he had seemed so familiar to me just now.

I watched as he swooped to pick up a valise before stepping over the threshold, a laden Tamati following close behind.

Still shaking slightly from the shock, I moved away from the newel post, intending to step down into the dim hall.

There was a gasp and a crash as Tamati let loose one of his boxes.

"Get a hold of yourself, Tamati! This is not one of your spirits!" The tall figure in front had stiffened slightly, but the voice though sharp, was calm. "I sincerely hope there is nothing breakable in that box!"

I found my voice at last. "I am very sorry; I'm afraid I startled you. . . ."

"Yes, I'm afraid you did!" The rough tones were sarcastic rather than irritable. "But I do believe we have met before?"

"Yes, the other evening, at Foster's Hotel in Wanganui."

"Ah, yes, of course. At Foster's." To my surprise, there was the hint of a laugh behind the words, though what could possibly be amusing, I had no idea.

"Yes. I am Malvina Raven."

"Of course. Miss Raven: Miss Malvina Raven." Again, that hint of inexplicable amusement. "I am Georges Duvall, agent to Clinton Raven and Paul Lucas. If you will excuse us, Tamati and I have some boxes to place in the storeroom. No doubt we shall meet again later."

As I stood to one side to allow them to take their boxes up the stairs, the green baize door opened to reveal Mrs. Hodges.

"Ah, there you are, Mister Duvall! I trust you have had a pleasant journey. Will you be needing any more help with your things?"

"No thank you, Mrs. Hodges. Your husband is bringing up the remainder with the mailbag. Tamati and I will just take these up to the second floor and then perhaps . . . Is it time yet, I wonder, for afternoon tea?"

She looked pleased. "It is indeed, sir!" Then she shot a startled glance in my direction. "Why, Miss Raven, I hardly saw you standing there . . . it's about time the lamps were lit! Now then, how is your ankle? And you will be joining the others for afternoon tea, of course, in the drawing room. . . ."

I was rescued by Hodges who plodded in through the doorway, carrying more boxes and a mail bag which he deposited by the rosewood table.

In the ensuing commotion, I made my escape to the library.

It was dark, damp and freezing cold but the fire, set ready, blazed up at once, after I had lit it with a Lucifer from the box on the mantel. After lighting two of the lamps, I crossed the room to draw the heavy curtains against the fog-bound windows.

I had always loved the library; with the fire lit and the curtains drawn, it was a cozy place. In the old days, I had often escaped there to curl up unseen from the doorway in one of the huge leather armchairs.

The chairs were still there, I noted with a smile, but tall as I had become, I could hardly conceal myself in any of them!

I strolled over to the book-lined shelves, remembering that my favorites had been on some low shelves in a corner; a collection of picture books of nursery stories, placed low, as if on purpose for children to find.

They were still there and I looked with pleasure at the still brightly colored pages of mid-Victorian children disporting themselves in luxuriant gardens filled with hollyhocks, roses, and elderberry trees or — rosy faces shining — seated around a table in a richly caparisoned parlor, apparently listening enrapt as a gentle, pretty mother read from a huge brass-bound Bible.

I smiled a little as I remembered my stolen hours with the books; it was not just the bright colors that had attracted me, but the companionship of the children in the pictures. I used to make up stories about them in my head and gradually they had become for me a sort of family that I could call upon in my many lonely moments.

I leafed through one of the books, pausing now and again at some remembered picture. Who had the books belonged to? I asked myself now. Idly, I turned to the flyleaf of one of them — *To Alice,* I read, *on the occasion of her sixth birthday, January the second, 1860, from her loving Mama and Papa.*

Alice. I wondered who she had been and what had happened to her — and why her book should have ended up in the library of a crusty old whaler.

I looked through the other books but could find no further clues.

I brought myself back to earth with difficulty. I was there, I reminded myself sternly, to find out why Devlin Fordyke had been in the library the previous night.

I fixed my pince-nez more firmly upon my nose and looked about helplessly. Where should I start? For that matter, what was I looking for?

I cast my mind back to the previous night. The room had been bathed in lamplight, and as far as I could recall nothing had been out of place.

Of course, that was it! Surely, if Devlin had truly been writing an article and using the library for research, there would have been books open, papers scattered about the table, an inkwell and pen in evident use.

I wandered over to the mahogany table that served as a writing desk. There was, indeed, a standish there, the inkwell, by the looks of it, freshly filled and a new nib on the pen. There was, however, no sign that either had been recently used.

If Devlin had not been writing an article, then what had he been doing — at one o'clock in the morning. Just reading, perhaps? If so, what? I did not remember seeing any books lying open about the room; and in any case, why should he, at that time of night, take a notion to read in the library at Ravensfall? Why had he not collected any books he wanted earlier in the day, when he had come over to deliver Miranda and to speak with Mrs. Hodges and taken them to read in comfort in his own quarters?

I shook my head, gazing about the book-lined walls; there was only one answer possible, I decided. Devlin Fordyke must have been looking for something — but what?

I thought about the theory I had formed earlier in the evening, that perhaps he had been associated with a theft. Was there something in the library that was valuable? I studied the paintings arranged on the walls above the bookcases and thought about the information Clinton had given me, regarding the increasing value of colonial paintings. Could one of those treatments of Maori life be the work of Heaphy or Kinder or perhaps of an apparently less significant master, whose potential was yet to be recognized?

On an impulse, I seized a straight-backed chair and scrambled up to view the paintings firsthand.

The first three were of sailing vessels and the second two of life in a Maori Pa on the Wanganui River. They were all dusty and cobweb-grimed except for the second one of life in a Maori Pa.

I looked at it suspiciously. Why should one picture be dusted off and not the others? Had one of the maids started to dust the picture frames and then been called away before she could complete her task? But if that were the case, why had she selected a picture in the middle of a row? Surely she would have started at the beginning?

Reaching up, I unhooked the frame from the wall. The picture, with the signature W. T. Power, was a sketch depicting the steep banks of the Wanganui River; two Maori canoes floated in the foreground, while on the far bank, the roofs of some whares were outlined against the trees.

Turning the picture over, I found that the back was also dust-free. Hearing voices in the hall beyond the door I had left partly open, I hurriedly replaced the picture and scrambled down from the chair, unfortunately in my haste, dislodging a large box from one of the lower shelves.

Luckily, the box, which was made of wood, came to no harm on the thick turkey carpet and although it had landed upside down, its poker-worked lid remained securely fastened. I wondered what was inside and carried it over to the table. Before I could open it, there was a rustling out in the hall and the door was pushed open to reveal Clinton and Georges Duvall.

"Good evening, Malvina! Where have you been hiding — we haven't seen you all day!" Clinton's voice was jocular but his eyes were coolly alert, seeming to take in every detail of the scene. I was suddenly very much aware of my hands, grimy from the dust of the bookcases. To my dismay, I found there was also a streak of dust down the front of my gown.

"Miss Raven has been climbing, it would seem!" Georges

Duvall stepped into the room. It was the first time I had seen him in any sort of light. His hair and beard were a rich nut brown, as were his thick eyebrows. The color of his eyes I could not discern; they were turned away from me in the direction of the bookcases. The chair I had used was still in front and the picture that I had rehung with such haste was crooked.

To my annoyance, I felt my cheeks burn. After all, why shouldn't I examine a picture if I felt like it; this was my father's house! I found my voice at last. "Yes, the picture up there intrigued me and I must admit, I climbed up to take a closer look."

Both men strolled over to the bookcase and peered up at the picture.

"Is it the artist or his subject that intrigues you, Miss Raven?" Georges Duvall's guttural tones as usual held a hint of amusement.

"Neither really: It just seemed odd to me that of all the pictures in the row, that one should be the only one to be free of dust."

The eyes were turned full force on me. They seemed to be greenish in color, although under those thick brows and in the soft glow of the lamps, I could not be certain. "How very observant you are, Miss Raven."

The words were not so much a statement as a question. How, he was obviously wondering, had I noticed such a detail in the lamplight.

Let him think what he wanted, I thought to myself. I could hardly explain how I had come to notice the picture without also mentioning my suspicions of Devlin Fordyke and this I was not yet prepared to do.

A glance passed between the two men. What had they come into the library for? I wondered. As if in answer to my unspoken question, Clinton nodded toward a bookcase in the shadowy, far end of the room, beyond the connecting door to the library.

"I wanted Georges to look at a greenstone ornament, Malvina—in the glass-fronted bookcase over there. Do you know anything about it, I wonder?"

He picked up a lamp and led the way.

The cabinet contained a number of curios of bone, wood, or

New Zealand jade or greenstone as it is called here, all apparently Maori in origin. The object Clinton had referred to was short and flat with a sharp, rounded outer edge.

"That's not an ornament, Cousin Clinton: it's a greenstone *mere*, a hand weapon used in warfare. I daresay, Great Uncle Josiah obtained it through trade. Papa always told us that he was a great collector."

"So I see." it was Georges Duvall who spoke. In the lamplight, his bearded face was reflected ghostlike in the glass of the cabinet door.

Again, I had that sense of ominous déjà vu and could hardly prevent myself from shivering.

"Do you think your father could be persuaded to part with any of them, Miss Raven? I have a collector who would, I know, be most interested — especially in the mere; weapons are his specialty."

I forced my gaze away from the shadowy face in the cabinet and made myself speak without stuttering. "I don't know, Mister Duvall. I don't believe my father holds the objects in any particular esteem — he left them here, after all. However, I should be glad to ask him when I write again."

"You are shivering, Cousin! Come, let us return to the fireside."

After leading us back to the fireplace, Clinton replaced the lamp on the table and then stood looking at me for a moment, his gaze thoughtful. "So you have written to your father already, Malvina?"

"Yes, of course. I wrote as soon as we landed in Wellington. . . ."

"But you have not written since? You have not given him your impressions of Ravensfall revisited — and your newfound cousins?"

His tone was playful but his eyes were not.

What was troubling him? I wondered.

He smiled as if to reassure me, his eyes lighting up his face. "I ask only to make sure that you understand our mailing arrangements here: If you have a letter waiting upstairs, for instance, you should have placed it on the hall table for Hodges to take it down to the steamer. . . . I'm sorry, I should have explained all of this before, but I only just thought of it!"

"It's all right; Betty explained it all to me — and no doubt, you will think me very lazy, but I have not as yet written home."

"That's all right, then!" He paused a moment looking at the box I had placed on the table. "Then we shall leave you to your explorations . . . we shall be seeing you soon at afternoon tea, though?"

I shuddered dramatically. "I don't think so! I am sure it will be delicious, but I don't think I have stopped eating since I arrived. . . . Perhaps I shall come down to dinner."

An understanding smile from Clinton and a lilting laugh from Georges — a laugh that in my still nervous state tugged at my memory.

"At dinner, then" — Clinton's voice brought me back to earth — "if you can escape from Mrs. Hodges until then! At least join us for a glass of sherry beforehand."

Nodding at me politely, Clinton escorted Georges from the room.

Out in the hall, Georges laughed again, the sound again pulling at my memory. "Pull yourself together, Malvina Raven," I whispered to myself furiously.

It was all the things that had happened to me over the last few days, I assured myself, that had stimulated my already oversensitive imagination, leading me to my present nervous state.

I gave myself an angry shake and reached for the box on the table. I would see what was inside; perhaps that would take my mind off my other problems.

Once open, the box revealed within a yellowing, carefully folded square of linen an interesting selection of objects: a baby's coral and silver rattle, a linen handkerchief embroidered with lazy daisies and the word "Papa" slanted in slightly straggling stitches over one corner, and three locks of hair — two fair and one darker — twisted together in the form of a brooch. Beneath them all, folded protectively in a sheet of paper, was a faded daguerreotype of a bonneted, crinolined young woman holding a well-wrapped baby, seated on a garden chair, a fairhaired little girl standing beside her.

Behind the little group stood a tall, sober-suited gentleman. Though his beard was darker and not as thick, I recognized the hawk nose immediately from his portrait on the landing: Great Uncle Josiah.

I looked at the pathetic locks of hair and could barely restrain a tear: they must have been put together of course, to form a mourning brooch. Tentatively, I put forward one finger and gently touched each soft lock in turn. This was a box of memories, of grief. What had happened to the serious young woman, her baby, and the little girl? Had they died in one of the cholera epidemics. Had the little girl been the "Alice" who owned the picture book?

Suddenly I realized the significance of the two small graves up on the bluff. So Great Uncle Josiah had been married after all and for a little while had enjoyed a family — perhaps the grave in the enclosure, with its weather-eroded lettering, was actually a double grave, containing the remains not only of Great Uncle Josiah but of his wife also. That did not, of course, explain the headstone inscribed "Ihaira."

Who had been Ihaira?

If only I had known the answer to that question then, I tell myself now, perhaps — just perhaps — I might have gone about things differently . . . and perhaps a life might have been saved.

As it was, the answer was staring me in the face, but so wrapped up was I in my own affairs, I did not have the wit to see it.

Carefully, I refolded the linen and closed the box. I would replace it where I had found it and then I would make my way upstairs again. All of a sudden, my interest in the possible goings-on of Devlin Fordyke had ceased to exist.

I placed the guard in front of the fire, turned the lamps low, and made my way out into the corridor.

After the warmth of the library, the corridor seemed cold and damp, indeed. However, a lamp had been lit in the main hall and its beams had managed — if only faintly — to penetrate the gloom at least as far as the library door.

As I approached the hall, a rattling of teacups sounded beyond the dining room doors and very softly, I heard the tinkling of a piano. It did not sound like Bertram's style and I wondered who could be playing.

204

I should have liked a cup of tea but decided I could not face an hour of polite conversation, the more especially as I should have been obliged to explain my untidy appearance to a curious Lucy.

There was also the matter of my relationship with Devlin. Clinton, I thought with relief, had not glanced at me untoward; so perhaps Norah had not told any stories. However, I could not be sure that she had told no one else and after my pathetic discovery in the library, all I wanted was to withdraw and be by myself for a while.

I turned up one of the lamps on the table but before I could pick it up, the light of another lamp lit up the first-floor landing. Someone was standing up there, his back toward the hall, his silhouette outlined against the light.

Curiously I mounted the stairs to find Tamati, his sharp profile with its high-bridged, chiseled nose etched against the light, as he studied Great Uncle Josiah's portrait.

He must have heard me coming but he did not turn around even when I reached his side.

"Devilish, old fellow, Josiah Raven, wasn't he?"

"Yes. Yes, I suppose he was!"

He turned at last to look at me, his dark eyes unfathomable. "He was a whaler, my father told me and a gunrunner. He feared no man."

"Yes. So I have been told, but of course . . ." I hesitated a moment. ". . . stories can be exaggerated, you know!"

His face lit up with the sudden flash of a white grin. "Of course — but he ended up with all this, didn't he?"

A wide gesture of his arm encompassed the hall where we were standing, the whole house.

I thought of the pathetic box I had left in the library. "But was he happy?" I asked.

"Happy?" For the first time, his voice was puzzled.

Before I could explain, below us, the drawing room door flew open to reveal the long, lean figure of Georges Duvall sharp against the light.

"Tamati, where are you?" He paused, looked up and then laughed. "Oh, there you are!"

I could not see his face in the gloom but his baritone

205

was redolent with amusement.

What was it about this man that filled me so with distaste — and fear?

Tamati looked at me then, long and deep and I believe would have spoken, but down in the shadows of the hall, Georges shuffled impatiently and then called up, "The boxes, man, have you delivered all of them? Are they all bestowed?"

"Yes."

No "Yes, Mister Duvall." No "Yes, sir." Just plainly, "Yes."

There was a sign — was it of exasperation? "Well then, if you will go into the kitchen, Mrs. Hodges will give you a cup of tea!"

The doors clicked as Georges returned to the drawing room and across Tamati's features a glance of pure amusement danced.

Before I could say a word, he executed a bow of great finesse, worthy of a participant in any famous European salon, and then backed down the stairs, giving one final, fantastic flourish before opening the front door and vanishing neatly behind it.

A giggle caught my attention and the creak that signified the presence of Bertram. I shone my lamp down the corridor: there, sure enough, out of the darkness glinted the thick lenses of Bertram's pebble spectacles. Behind him was a giggling Miranda; for once sheer, gleeful mischief lighting up her face, the mocking quality gone.

As I watched, she danced out into the middle of the corridor and still giggling, swept me an exaggerated bow, every bit as fine as Tamati's.

"Shush, Miranda, she'll hear us!" Bertram, himself trying not to laugh, directed his glance to me. "Horrible Hacket," he explained. "She's been trying to find us: I'm supposed to play for them in the drawing room — but I don't want to!"

As he spoke, there was a soft click from somewhere above and then the quiet rustle of a skirt moving over the carpet.

"Quick, Miranda, she's coming!"

Turning with surprising dexterity on his crutches, Bertram hobbled to one of the rooms opposite Clinton's sitting room — the very room, in fact, where I had sought refuge on my first night at Ravensfall.

Miranda shot a questioning glance at me, then darted after him.

To my surprise, she did not enter the room immediately; instead, she scurried up the hall to another door which she opened and carefully left ajar. I watched fascinated as she then took out a crumpled handkerchief and deliberately dropped it on the floor just in front of the opening, before hurrying back to the other room, the door of which she left wide open.

She was just in time; as she vanished into the room, a light glowed from the stairs above. As Norah descended, I retreated along the landing and holding my lamp high, pretended to be studying Great Uncle Josiah's portrait.

"Good evening, Norah!"

A silent stare was her only response, followed by a brief nod.

Taking up her skirts with one hand, to make her approach the more silent, as I supposed, she slipped without a sound into the corridor.

Still pretending to study the portrait, I watched, intrigued from the corner of my eye, as she first paused, shining her lamp into the room where Bertram and Miranda were hiding, and then, apparently seeing the handkerchief farther up the corridor, she glided swiftly toward the other room.

As she disappeared, so appeared Miranda, from a hiding place apparently just behind the door.

She signaled to me, a questioning look, her hands spread wide, as if to ask, "All clear?"

At my affirmative nod, she darted behind the door and came out again hauling a grinning Bertram piggyback.

How had they managed it so quietly and so quickly? I wondered. I watched with great respect as Miranda slipped out of the corridor and started back up the stairs to the second floor.

I shone my lamp up the stairs to help them but thinking I might somehow deter Norah if she should reappear before they had made their escape, I stayed on the second-floor landing until they reached the top of the stairs. After such an effort, I decided, they did not deserve to be caught!

Luckily, Norah did not come out into the corridor until the children had vanished into the darkness of the second floor. It was impossible to tell from her usual lack of expression, what she was thinking, but the pale gaze she directed at me, as she passed by, seemed to me — perhaps because of my guilty conscience! — to be particularly assessing.

I watched, as with her usual silent glide she descended the stairs into the hall. What a peculiar person she was. Was she a particular friend of Cousin Lucy's, or had she been engaged formally for the position, perhaps through an employment bureau? With her evident lack of affinity for children, it was strange to think that anyone would . . .

Stop it, Malvina! I told myself, you are as usual reading too much into a situation — and in any event, it is none of your business!

So I told myself at the time, little realizing just how much of my business the matter would become!

Twenty-three

A bright, clear morning, the sun rising over the bush-clad hills and no sign of fog. One of the things I love best about New Zealand is the changeable weather: from day to day, one is never quite sure what it will be like! I stood at my open window taking deep breaths of cool, balmy air, looking down at the River Walk. All of a sudden, just as on my first morning, there was a flutter of wings as a cloud of silver eyes rose chirruping from the tree ferns and I experienced yet again the eerie sensation of someone watching me.

Irritated, I glared down. Sure enough, I detected movement beneath the hanging fronds. Perhaps I could flush whomever it was out into the open.

"Good morning!" I made myself sound polite.

"Good morning, Miss Raven!"

Out from under the trees slipped Miranda; for once, with what appeared to be a genuine smile on her face. She stood a moment clad again in her woodland green frock, looking up at me, the early sunlight glinting on her copper hair.

I looked at the clock on the mantel; it still lacked five minutes to seven.

"You're an early bird!"

No answer to this, just a long, thoughtful look followed at last by a quick smile.

Suddenly, with a flick of her skirts, she slipped back under the trees.

"Miranda?"

No response. It was as if she had never been.

From somewhere above, a rasping noise as of a protesting window slid shut.

I waited a minute or two but Miranda did not reappear. What had frightened her? I wondered.

Had Norah appeared at one of the windows, scowling down on one of her pupils?

It was impossible to tell!

Dismissing the matter from my mind, I turned back into the room. I would eat an early breakfast, I decided, and because it was such a beautiful day and my ankle felt so much better, I would venture outside for a walk and perhaps take some flowers up to the family burial plot.

Breakfast, at first, proved a secluded affair until I was joined by Paul Lucas.

He breezed in as usual, his leonine head tilted to one side, the nostrils of his large, roman nose twitching delightedly.

"Good morning, Malvina! Tell me, is that the scent of *kippers* I detect? Bless Mrs. Hodges—how did she manage it, I have not tasted kippers since we were all in London!"

Kippers, indeed it was, the fried smoked herrings lying side by side on the sizzling silver platter kept warm below by a spirit lamp.

I watched in awe as Paul selected three and with practiced ease, disposed elegantly of the many fine bones with the edge of his fork.

Since "they were all in London," I thought, puzzled. Surely, I remembered Clinton telling me that because of Georges, they had never been to England? I opened my mouth to comment but before I did so, was addressed jovially.

"So, what do you propose to do with yourself today?"

I found myself regarded by bright blue eyes.

Before I could answer, Norah entered in her usual silence.

Nodding in response to my greeting, she glided over to the sideboard.

Porridge, I noted in some surprise and no milk and sugar, only the traditional salt.

I wrenched my eyes away and addressed myself to Paul. "I'm

sorry, you were asking what I was doing today? Nothing much, I'm afraid — just writing letters and reexploring the place . . . I thought perhaps that I might go for a walk. . . ."

There was a long pause; I found myself regarded thoughtfully by two pairs of eyes. What, I wondered, was so sensational about my going for a walk?

Paul dabbed at a corner of his mouth with his napkin. "And a beautiful day for it! I expect you have old memories to recall. . . . Will you be going far, do you think?"

Another thoughtful glance from both pairs of eyes.

"I shouldn't think so, just round about . . . perhaps down to the landing and back."

"Down to the landing and back? Ah, yes, a pretty walk indeed! Would you like some company, I wonder?"

He glanced at Norah who replied with a quick nod.

"How thoughtful of you! Perhaps when I have finished my letters. . . ." I smiled politely and secretly crossed my fingers. I had no intention of being accompanied by anyone, but especially by Norah Hackett.

Quickly, I finished my toast and ginger marmalade before folding my table napkin and rolling it to replace it in its silver ring.

"If you will excuse me?"

Hurriedly, I made my escape.

Out in the hall, the morning light filtering through St. George and the Damsel in Distress dispersed as if through a prism, a series of soft, delicately colored rainbows.

"Malvina?"

In the glowing half light, the drawing room doors had opened and between them stood Clinton.

I could not distinguish the expression on his face, but his voice was ragged.

"Malvina, there is something I must say to you!"

Even in that light, his eyes — usually clear as water — were dark, impenetrable.

Before I quite knew what had happened, I had advanced into the hall and met him halfway.

I found my shoulders clasped by one strong arm—a decidedly pleasant sensation—my chin uptilted and my hair smoothed by a delicate, caring hand.

"Malvina, you must know that I . . ."

Behind us, a door clicked.

Horrible Hackett, I thought, in resignation.

I was wrong.

"Clint, old fellow! Oh, I say, do pray excuse me! I had no idea that . . ."

Behind us loomed Paul Lucas. About my shoulders, I felt Clinton's arm slacken as he quickly straightened up.

"Paul, trust you to choose the devil of a time to make your presence known. . . . There was something particular I wished to say to Malvina!"

He cast an arch look. "So that's the way of it, is it? I thought as much—well, well at least let me be the first to wish you happy!"

I found my tongue at last. "Happy about what? I do not believe that Cousin Clinton and I have come to any kind of an agreement!"

He chuckled deeply. "You'll have to watch this one, Clinton, got a mind of her own. You'll have to keep *her* on a short rein!"

"I was not aware, sir, that I was any kind of a horse! If you will excuse me, I believe I have some business to attend to!"

Sidestepping swiftly, I detached myself from Clinton's arm and headed out through the front door onto the veranda.

From behind me, a deep-throated male laugh billowed. How was it, I wondered furiously, that I had managed, totally without planning—nor indeed without any *wish*, on my part—to engage myself to two gentlemen at once?

Twenty-four

Outside, the faint warmth from the rising sun softened the chill of early morning. In the stone urns beside the bottom of the steps, some early freezias bloomed, their piquant scent mingling with the odor of grass and leaves still damp from the retreated fog.

I took a long, deep breath and stepped down onto the lawn. Paul had, of course, been teasing me, I told myself; but what about Clinton? I thought back over the scene in the hall: Clinton had held me tenderly, but from the troubled expression in his eyes and his tentative tone of voice, I could have sworn that what he had been about to say was a warning rather than a declaration. But a warning against what?

A light brush of feathers against my cheek brought me out of my revery. A group of fantails hovered nearby, no doubt after the tiny insects in the air that I had stirred up as I moved about. What a delight; they were the first I had seen since my arrival. I held up my hands as I had done when I was a child, but as usual the little brown birds though tantalizingly close remained, except for an occasional brush from their long tail feathers, completely out of reach.

What memories they brought back! Harriet had loved the little birds, and had wondered if they could be tamed but old Moana had soon put such an idea out of her head. A fantail in the house, she had told us, meant death!

I shrugged my shoulders, chasing away morbid thoughts. I would gather some flowers, I decided, and take a brisk walk through the bush up to the burial plot.

Beau Brummell snickered softly in greeting as I entered the stable yard and a sleepy Bubble stretched languorously as she rose, purring, to meet me. The door to Tamati's whare was wide open and somewhere inside I could hear quick running footsteps as if small children were about. Intrigued, I wandered over. As I did so, there was a heavy crash as of a chair or table falling over, followed closely by a child's shrill wail.

Ordinarily, I would not, of course, have thought of interfering but as no adults seemed to be about and as the wailing continued, I gathered up my courage and stepped inside.

The room I found myself in was used as an office and with its wooden shelves of dingy ledgers, deal table, and straight-backed chairs, did not seem to have changed since I had last seen it in the days of Callum Douglas. The wailing, however— now punctuated with another childish voice shrieking apparently futile commands — was issuing from what I supposed to be the kitchen area through the closed door behind.

I opened the door and found that I had been correct. Facing me was the back door situated by a kitchen sink and a window framed on the outside by trailing passion fruit vines. On the left side of the door I had just opened, a flight of steep stairs led up to the floor above and to my right was a huge fireplace containing a kitchen range, a fragrant stew simmering on its hob.

Along the remaining wall was a large table piled high with boxes. A heavy, plush tablecloth partly covering the boxes had — from the direction of its folds — been half pulled off, the culprit apparently being a small, wailing child now wedged by a fallen chair in a corner by the fireplace. Another child, not much larger, stood nearby, pulling ineffectually at the chair.

Instant silence as two startled little faces turned toward me.

"I'm sorry: don't be frightened . . . I thought perhaps someone had been hurt . . . and so I came in, to see if I could help. . . ."

I paused, feeling infinitely foolish — but what after all could one say to two small children in a fix?

The larger of the two — by her long, glossy dark locks, evidently a girl — frowned up at me and then gave a tentative

214

smile. She pointed toward the smaller child. "He's stuck!"

"So he is! Did he hurt himself?" Swiftly, I dropped the flowers I was carrying onto the table, then tugged out the chair before picking up the child who, his face turning purple, immediately began to wail again. No bones, however, seemed to be broken and accustomed as I was with the antics of my little sisters, I decided that there was nothing much wrong—except, perhaps, a bruised psyche.

"I looked at the disarranged cloth and fallen chair. "Naughty boy—did he try to climb up onto the table, then?"

"Naughty!" agreed his sister. "Naughty, naughty! Daddy said 'No.'"

I looked at the partly revealed boxes. They appeared to be stuffed with newspaper-wrapped objects—one of them having become undone, revealed a *mere* carved from New Zealand greenstone.

Of course, I thought, remembering Clinton's explanation, Georges Duvall was acquiring objects for an American collector—although it was strange that they were stored here; I had thought that all the items were placed in a room on the second floor of Ravensfall.

I smiled down at the little girl. "What is your name, sweetheart?"

A giggle and a shy smile was my reward.

I smiled back. "Come now, what is your name?"

"Huia." The reply, spoken in a clear baritone came from behind me.

Startled, I turned to find a coldly angry Tamati standing in the doorway. "My daughter's name is Huia, Miss Raven. I trust that satisfies your curiosity!"

I was aware suddenly of how it must look to him, the privacy of his home invaded, myself holding his son while questioning his daughter, the artifacts garnered for his employer laid out on the table beside me.

"I'm sorry . . . I didn't mean. That is, I heard a crash and then a child crying—but he does not seem to be hurt!" Hurriedly I pushed the still protesting child back into his father's arms.

Embarrassed but angry, I exited the house at once, gather-

215

ing up my flowers on my way to the front door.

Once out of the house, I headed immediately for the stables, intent on pushing the embarrassing scene out of my head. I was going to need water, I told myself, and a jar for Miss Inglewood's flowers. I wasn't concerned with the other graves, which had been provided with jars by their benefactor — whoever he or she could be. Out of hand I dismissed Lucy and Clinton and their entourage.

I grabbed up a jar from a shed beside Beau Brummel's stable and filled it from a tap outside. I carried extra water in an ancient watering can I had discovered at the same source.

Up on the bluff, my shattered nerves were soothed a little as I was struck anew by the quietness, the serenity of the setting.

Thoughtfully, I arranged my flowers under Miss Inglewood's memorial, wondering yet again why the person who had tended the other graves had neglected hers. Perhaps because it was only a memorial and not a true grave, I speculated. But in any event, who was it who had shown such care for the others? Mrs. Hodges, perhaps? Her housekeeping conscience moving her to care for the dead?

The flowers on the other mounds were still fresh. I filled the jars with water, wondering again if one of the little graves indeed contained the remains of the Alice who had once possessed my favorite storybook and if the other little grave was that of her brother or sister.

I thought again of the pathetic box I had found in the library and decided that I was right. But what of Ihaira? Who had she been? Had Great Uncle Josiah married twice, I wondered, the second time to a Maori? And if so, what had happened to her?

The library! Surely there must be papers kept there, a record of some sort — if only a list of names and dates in an old family Bible? On my return, I would explore the library at once.

My decision made and my task completed, I sat back on my heels and surveyed the scene below.

The mists evaporated, the river deep in its gorge, sparkled a glowing blue-green, its steep, vine-draped cliffs gleaming in the early sun.

How calm and peaceful everything seemed from this vantage point; no petty misunderstandings, no unsolved mysteries — or if there were, no worries about them! How different from the atmosphere at Ravensfall.

I sighed, thinking about my situation here. This was only my third morning, and yet in that time, I seemed to have uncovered . . . uncovered what?

That, of course, was the problem: there was absolutely nothing tangible that I could put my finger on — just little glimpses of things not quite right and the feeling hanging over me like a dense cloud that something was terribly wrong.

I shook my head and struggled to my feet. Really, I told myself, my imagination was more than enough . . . and yet . . .

Picking up the empty watering can, I turned slowly toward the gate. Perhaps if I could list all the things that bothered me, I could somehow make an entire picture. If I could not do so, I told myself, then obviously the whole thing was a mere phantasm worked up by my overactive imagination.

Closing the gate behind me, I set off down the path through the bush. As I walked, I made a list in my head of all the things that had bothered me since my arrival: the seeming disbelief on the part of so many people that I was who I said I was — and perhaps because of this, the feeling I had of being perpetually observed and my actions evaluated — and my cousins themselves, so surprisingly different from what I had been led to expect, and their odd companions. Just who exactly *was* Norah Hackett, and why had my cousins engaged such an obviously unsuitable person to look after Bertram?

I paused to disentangle my hair from an overhanging fern frond. And Cousin Clinton, I thought, what an enigma — cold, hard, his cool gray eyes perpetually appraising and yet . . . I remembered our meeting in his studio . . . so sensitive . . . and so desperately unhappy! Of course, most artists were perfectionists. No doubt his portrait of Cousin Lucy would turn out to be much better than he had thought. After all, if his paintings were in such demand — as indicated by the activities of his agent — then his work must be good.

Georges Duvall, I thought next, barely restraining myself from shuddering as I called up in my mind his bearded face and mocking, greenish eyes. Why did I feel such a repulsion toward this man?

217

After all, I had met him only four times: twice at Ravensfall and twice at Foster's Hotel. Of course, I thought suddenly; at least one mystery cleared.

I thought back to my first night in Wanganui, the dim passage behind the hotel stairs, the glimpse through a half-ajar door at a baize-covered table and the whispers mentioning Ravensfall and somsething about the Maoris. Of course, Georges must have been making arrangements for the Maori artifacts he was collecting.

There now, I told myself, a perfectly simple explanation for something that had seemed mysterious at the time. No doubt, there was just such a sensible answer for all the other questions I had been asking myself.

Except, I thought, for Devlin Fordyke! For had he not appeared at the foot of the stairs, seemingly out of nowhere, just when I had thought to make my escape? With embarrassment, I remembered ploughing into his broad chest.

Devlin Fordyke! In my agitation, I snatched at a meandering vine of supplejack to prevent my tripping over an exposed root.

Devlin Fordyke. Of course! It always led back to him! Devlin Fordyke at Foster's Hotel, Devlin Fordyke mysteriously presented at my first evening at Ravensfall, Devlin Fordyke seizing me outside the library . . . Devlin Fordyke whose Irish-American blarney had somehow smoothed over all inconsistencies leading me almost to believe that after all . . .

All of a sudden, I was furiously angry.

I found myself at the junction of the path leading on my left to the stable yard and eventually back to Ravensfall and on my right, the path that led to the former workmen's whares, Devlin Fordyke's rented cottage among them.

Miranda, I knew, was staying at Ravensfall until the return of her father and according to Mrs. Hodges, Devlin Fordyke had left on the *Waiwere*.

The cottage would therefore be empty.

The copy of the *New York Times* with its articles outlined in red, that Devlin had carefully whisked from my view, should therefore be available.

I took a deep breath.

I had never contemplated such a thing before.
I had never been so angry before.
Swinging determinedly on my heel, I turned to my right.

In the sunlight, Devlin's cottage presented quite a different prospect from my visit of the morning before. Now, free from an enshrouding mist, its vine-draped, wooden walls rising from a wild tangle of undergrowth — the remains, no doubt of a garden planted by some early, homesick settler — it appeared peaceful, charming even; somewhat like an illustration from a children's book of fairy stories.

To my annoyance, I found myself hesitating, all the taboos instilled into me from my early childhood preventing me from intruding on another's property.

This was ridiculous, I told myself furiously. Again I thought over all of Devlin's offenses since I had first met him. Gathering up my courage, I stepped firmly forward up the garden path.

Even to my shaking hand, the knob of the front door — unlocked, of course, as with most houses in New Zealand — turned easily.

Once inside, I stood a moment, absorbing the atmosphere. On the wall opposite, in the fireplace, the kitchen range stood cold but with a stack of firewood piled ready with a basketful of kindling and scrunched newspapers nearby, ready to ignite a fire. In front sat the ragged Morris chair Devlin had dumped me in and to the left, sunlight streamed through the tiny window onto the table beneath.

For a moment I lost my breath; no newspapers were on the table.

Setting down the empty watering can I was still carrying, onto the vacant table, I told myself to keep calm; the newspapers could still be somewhere in the room. I was right — the scrunched-up newspapers, of course, by the fireplace. In the end, however, I did not need to go through them; as I crossed the room, I found the paper I wanted — turned to the outlined article — on the seat of the chair.

Now that I had found it, I could hardly bear to pick it up. Telling myself not to be an idiot, I finally brought myself to put forth a shaking hand.

Carrying the newspaper over to the window — to keep watch in case Miranda should suddenly return — I quickly read through the article. I had been right, the story concerned the follow-up of a theft of valuable paintings from a Park Avenue mansion. However, in the course of the burglary, the thieves had been disturbed by the younger son of the house who — my eyes widened in shock as I read the phrase — *had been most foully murdered*.

I hardly remembered my journey back from the cottage; so many thoughts were whirling in my mind. Investigations concerned with the crime, according to the newspaper, had revealed that the thieves may have been associated with an international gang and that some members of the ring actually specialized in making several copies of the paintings they stole, thus, as the newspaper put it, *allowing them to double, even quadruple, their ill-gotten gains by selling forgeries of the originals to unsuspecting art connoisseurs*.

The article then went on to decry the greed of the collectors, who often suspecting that a work of art had been stolen nonetheless asked no questions — *such was their avid desire to add to their treasures!*

Theft, forgery — murder! Could Devlin Fordyke possibly be involved with such dreadful crimes? And yet, out of all the articles in the newspaper, why had he outlined that particular one and saved it? And why had he been so determined that I should not see it?

Could it be because of the mention made of the progress of the police investigations? The article had stated that a promising lead had been established — a member of the underworld, once swindled by the gang, having come forward, suggested that the chief instigator of the gang activities had managed to escape the authorities by fleeing to Mexico.

". . . Miss Raven. . . ."

With a start, I awakened from the nightmare of my thoughts to find myself back in the stable yard, an anxious Tamati facing me. The boxes I had last seen on his kitchen table were now stacked outside his front door. Apparently, I had interrupted him as he transferred the boxes onto a small cart.

"I'm sorry, Tamati, my mind was elsewhere! In fact . . ." I looked around, still half in a daze, at the peaceful, sunlit scene, ". . . how I got here, I'm not quite sure!"

A long look from the dark eyes. "Something has frightened you."

I laughed nervously. "Frightened me? Don't be silly; what could possibly frighten me here? I'm just out of breath that's all, from my walk and then, you startled me. . . ."

Another long look. "I'm sorry. . . ."

"No need to be; I was deep in thought, that's all! But you wanted to speak to me?"

"Yes." A dull flush glowed along his high cheekbones. "When I found you in my house, I thought — I don't know what I thought, but I spoke too strongly. . . ."

"It's all right . . . I understand."

A brief glimmer of amusement. "I doubt it. That *mere* that you saw and the other objects in these boxes are worth a fortune to me; I'm hoping to sell them to Mister Duvall . . . you see. . . ."

If he could have spoken then . . . I think now, but he was prevented by his children spilling out of the whare and running to greet him.

Swiftly, he caught them up. "Huia! Ihaira! Gently, now!"

"Ihaira? But I thought your youngest child was a boy!"

A thoughtful look followed by a mocking grin. "So he is: he's named after my father."

"Ihaira." My mind flashed back to the grave I had just left. So both Reggie and I had been wrong — it was a man who lay there, but who could it be? Why should a man named Ihaira lie in our family burial plot?

Before I could think further, the little Ihaira crooked an engaging grin at me and belched.

"And your wife?"

The dark gaze clouded. "She died — which is why you find me here. Tuberculosis, the doctor said it was."

He paused to ruffle Ihaira's hair before setting him down. "I thought I'd bring them back here — some sort of a family, I suppose, to leave them with, while I . . ."

Before he could continue, a stirring from the bush walk proclaimed a new arrival. A Maori woman, plump and motherly, emerged into the stable yard.

"My cousin Ngaire, Miss Raven — who has kindly agreed to look after my children while I am away — but there is no need to introduce you, is there? I understand that Ngaire was parlor maid at Ravensfall when you were still a child!"

Ngaire, I thought. Ngaire — a true face out of the past at last! Ngaire, who would cuddle Reggie and me when we were down and slip us goodies from the kitchen whenever she could.

She grinned at me as only Ngaire could, broad, loving, including the whole world in her smile. "You've grown," she said, and opened her arms.

After much hugging, I reluctantly detached myself. "Oh, Ngaire, how good it is to see you!"

"And you, too, Mallie. . . ." The deep brown eyes regarding me were thoughtful beneath their warmth. "I'd heard you were back but I didn't believe it at first!" She gave me another quick hug. "But — now listen — you must leave Ravensfall as soon as you can; there's danger. . . ." She placed her lips close to my ear but as she whispered, there was another disturbance from the bush behind us.

From out of the trees stepped the old Maori gentleman I had encountered on my excursion through the bush on my second night at Ravensfall.

He stood for a moment, gazing at me silently, his eyes dark pools in his tattooed face. At length, he nodded slowly and sighed heavily as if coming to a conclusion of great sadness, eventually turning from me and looking toward the door of Tamati's whare.

Following the direction of his gaze, I could not prevent a gasp.

Within the entrance of the whare a fantail fluttered.

Twenty-five

After such a morning, my mind, to say the least, was in state of turmoil. Try as I might to maintain an outer calm appearance, I could hardly prevent my hands from shaking as I made myself ready before going down to luncheon.

What had Ngaire meant by her warning, whispered so urgently into my ear? Unfortunately, with the appearance of the ancient Maori gentleman, she had been diverted by a quarrel that had developed between him and Tamati.

Tamati had ranged himself in front of the boxes he was loading onto his cart and an argument in Maori had ensued the only word of which, I recognized—repeated over and over again—was *tapu,* the Maori for forbidden or sacred.

At the sound of that word, Ngaire, with a last look of warning at me, left my side and protectively gathering up the children, had disappeared down the bush walk.

What had Ngaire tried to warn me against? Had she suspicions also about Devlin Fordyke? And if so, what? And in any event, supposing I . . . and presumably, Ngaire . . . was correct, that Fordyke was a villain, why should that mean any particular danger to me?

The trouble was, that despite Devlin's high-handed behavior and all that I had found out—notably, the article he had evidently wished to keep from me—there was something about the man that I found intriguing. Though I hated to admit it, when he had lifted me out of the misty bush and then again over the threshold of the front door of his cottage, I had felt a warmth, a certain sense of security, a feeling of coming home.

Perhaps it was because he was so enormous, I told myself in an attempt to rationalize my feelings; I was unused to gentlemen being so much taller than myself and the sensation of being as light as thistledown as I was picked up was, I had to admit, delightful!

Peering in the mirror, I gave myself a shake as I tried to tidy my hair. You must not let your feelings run away with you, Malvina, I told myself irritably. What would Edward have said about this situation? I had a sudden mental image of a short, red-faced Edward determinedly trying to pick me up and was unable to stop myself from giggling helplessly.

It was sheer hysteria, I realized, brought on by my badly frayed nerves. Taking a deep breath I managed to calm myself down.

Try to think objectively, I adjured myself. Think over what you have observed: Fordyke's unexplained comings and goings, the newspaper article, my suspicion that he was not who he said he was. Should I tell Clinton of my fears? I wondered.

I thought of Clinton's cool, gray gaze and the discerning question he was bound to put to me: "so you have these feelings, Malvina, and you have found a newspaper article which you say backs them up? An article that, by the by, you discovered after you had illegally entered Fordyke's cottage. . . ."

I shriveled. I could not go to Clinton yet. Even if I told of Devlin's manhandling me outside the library, there was nothing I could do to prove it: my word against his.

But what about Ngaire's warning that there was danger—that I must leave Ravensfall? Was there some element that I had missed? Perhaps her warning had not been about Devlin Fordyke at all—but if not, then what?

Gathering up my shawl I decided that my appearance—dressed as I was in my white piqué shirtwaist and black serge skirt—was respectable enough to grace luncheon at Ravensfall.

With some amusement, I gazed at myself in the glass. The very proper Miss Raven, the epitome of respectability, armed in her sober, respectable clothes against a world of doubt and mystery.

Luncheon proved quiet, neither Clinton nor Paul being present. They were up in their studio, Lucy informed me, with Duvall, readying their collection for the guests invited to the house party. Perhaps, she suggested, I would like to assist with the writing of the remaining invitations in the library after lunch; she was hoping to catch the afternoon steamer on its way back down to Wanganui.

Absent-mindedly, I agreed.

With quick little bites, Norah was attacking the lamb cutlets that was the main course of our luncheon.

"You are inviting a great many guests, Cousin Lucy?"

She shrugged her plump shoulders and politely concealed a yawn behind a lethargic hand. "Not a great many, I don't suppose — just enough to ensure a sufficiently interesting company."

And of course to show off the work of Paul and Clinton, I thought.

As if she had read my mind, she added, "Mrs. Smythe, the lady who lent Clinton the Heaphy he discovered, will no doubt be particularly interested in seeing Paul and Clinton's paintings. . . . I believe she had indicated an interest in purchasing at least one of them."

I thought of the attic studio with its treasure trove of art. "Perhaps she might also want to purchase the other Heaphy?"

Lucy looked at me thoughtfully until the silence was broken by Norah dropping her fork with a clatter against the rim of her plate.

"Oh, yes of course, the other Heaphy. No doubt, Clinton showed it to you. . . . He and Paul have quite a collection, have they not?"

"Indeed, yes . . . and not just of New Zealand work but — I remembered the canvasses stacked along the studio walls — of European artists, also. Cousin Clinton told me that some of the early settlers sometimes brought such works out with them and that the present owners do not always realize the value. Apparently, he and Paul have been helping Mister Duvall by tracking them down. . . ."

I paused embarrassed, wondering if I had said too much.

Perhaps, I thought, too late, I should not have referred to Clinton's business affairs in front of Norah. In fact, now I came to think of it, Lucy herself, might not be aware of the situation her brother had found himself in. On the other hand, she had been present that evening in the drawing room when Clinton had told me the reason for his and Paul's bondage to Georges Duvall. I felt my cheeks blush as the memory of his kiss on the tip of my nose being observed by a suddenly wakeful Lucy on the sofa opposite.

Lucy now was regarding me with the same thoughtful look, while Norah, her lamb cutlets devoured at last, glanced at me slyly, her colorless eyes gleaming from under her pale lashes.

I coughed to cover my embarrassment and plunged into a change of subject. "How clever of Cousin Clinton to find the Heaphy! How did he manage it? I wonder."

"Quite by accident, I assure you," Lucy answered at last, yawning again. "We were at Mrs. Smythe's for dinner and the conversation having veered to art, someone told how a relative of theirs had discovered a Vermeer among a pile of old paintings, stuck behind some discarded furniture in an ancient house they had inherited in — let me think — Cornwall, was it? Another of your English counties?"

She paused, looking doubtfully at the egg custard and whipped cream Helena had placed before her, before finally taking up her spoon and delicately trying a morsel.

The concoction apparently to her satisfaction, she continued to talk in between mouthfuls. "And Mrs. Smythe said that such a thing was hardly likely to happen in New Zealand, the country having been settled only during the last sixty years or so and that's when Clinton said that one never knew, some of the early settlers had brought all their belongings with them and old paintings might be among them."

"And that's when he made his offer to explore Mrs. Smythe's attic?" I asked intrigued, as Lucy fell into silence again.

She nodded over another spoonful of egg custard and gently dabbed at the corner of her mouth with her napkin. "Yes. Of course, Mrs. Smythe was very doubtful. The house itself is really quite modern, having been built in the late eighties after she and her late husband arrived from England, however . . ."

"However?" I found myself leaning forward, more and more interested in the developing story.

Two spoonsful of custard later, Lucy continued. "However, Mrs. Smythe did admit that she had recently inherited the contents of a deceased cousin's house and that not knowing what else to do with them—not at all her taste, you know—she had stored them in her attic."

"And so?"

Lucy spooned up the last of her custard and looked at me thoughtfully. "And so, that was when Clinton made his offer to explore the attics and see what he could find!"

I looked at the Heaphy where it hung on the wall above us. Why did it seem so familiar to me? I wondered yet again. Surely not just for the upriver scene it depicted as I had informed Paul, casting my mind back to the morning after my arrival, but for the painting itself. I had seen the painting *somewhere* before, I was sure of it, but where? How could I have seen a painting stored for so many years in Mrs. Smythe's attic?

I came back to myself to find Lucy and Norah studying me curiously.

I laughed self-consciously. "I'm sorry, my mind was elsewhere! I was thinking of Mrs. Smythe's good fortune. How pleased she must have been—and how grateful to your brother!"

Lucy folded up her napkin, looking at me with—to my surprise—what appeared to be a gleam of amusement. "Yes. Yes, she was. Grateful. Of course, the Heaphy is not really valuable, you know—at least, not yet—though Clinton says that sometime in the future it will be. . . ."

Resting her napkin beside her plate, she rose slowly and stood looking down at me, the gleam of amusement still in her dark eyes. On the other side of the table, Norah tittered.

Twenty-six

A restless night but one in which my usual nightmares chased themselves about in a whirlwind of uneasiness against a murky, fog-bound background, rather than manifesting themselves into the usual, specific, vividly colored scenes I normally had to endure.

Except for one episode: in it, I seemed to be within the painting in the dining room. Painted trees were everywhere, seemingly solid but as I approached and reached out they would dissolve. I could hear Ishbel's laughter in the distance and I could see her faintly through the trees but when I turned, it was Callum I saw close beside me—a grinning, cruel Callum who reached out at me, a painter's palette knife somehow transformed into a dagger, clutched in his long-hooked fingers.

I woke screaming.

"Miss Raven! Miss Raven?"

My door had opened and in the light of a fluttering candle, Miranda's face appeared.

I managed to swallow another scream and jerked myself upward in my bed.

"So stupid, don't you think, to practice such economies! Candles are all very well in their way but lamps are so much more efficient!"

The candlestick thudded down on my bedside table and somehow my lamp was lighted from it.

"There now. That's better . . . 'all the better to see you

with!', as the wolf said to Little Red Riding Hood—although, I must admit, a not very pleasant comparison, just at   the moment . . . !" Giggling, she perched herself on the end of my bed.

I managed to pull myself together. "You're no wolf!"

A sudden serious look. "Am I not? No, perhaps not, perhaps rather a . . ." The mischief gleamed again in her amber eyes. "But you don't want to hear about that just at the minute. . . . Tell me, are you feeling better now?"

"Thank you, much better!" As I spoke, the final scene from my nightmare flashed into my mind and I could hardly repress a shudder.

"No you're not. The nightmare is still in your head, isn't it? I know all about nightmares, you see!"

"Really? Do you have them, too?"

"Oh, no, I'm much too wicked. You only have nightmares if you have a conscience and I'm totally without one—my teachers always say so! I know about nightmares because of Mary Jane Schuyler at the last school I was at. . . . We shared a room and sometimes she would cry out in the middle of the night. . . . It was always connected with something she'd done during the day: something I'd led her in to, usually!"

She grinned at me again, the look on her little elfin face reflecting pure wickedness. "That's what I mean: Mary Jane has a conscience and I don't!"

A sudden thought occurred to me. "You were at boarding school, then? I suppose your father must have decided to give you a holiday. . . ."

An amused twinkle. "Not a bit of it—I was expelled as usual! And this time, Papa gave up!"

I looked at her in wonder. "You mean, you get yourself expelled on purpose?"

"Of course! Education for females is so unutterably boring—always, 'Don't do this! Don't do that! Wear your hat *and* your gloves.' There's only so much of it I can stand—and then I break out!"

"Your poor father!"

"Not really. He shouldn't listen always to Grandmother, should he? She's the one who always insists that I go to boarding school."

She paused a moment and then after a naughty look, proceeded to imitate someone, raising her head and looking down her nose in cold disdain. " 'The establishment of a single gentleman—even a widower—is not a proper place for the rearing of a young lady: if you cannot find yourself another suitable wife—and goodness knows, I have introduced you to any number of presentable females—at least send the child off to boarding school!' "

I laughed, I could not help it. "But how did you manage to persuade your father to bring you with him to New Zealand?"

For the first time, a vague look. "Oh, he needs me, you know, in his present situation and besides . . ."

The vagueness disappeared abruptly, leaving me to wonder if it had existed at all. The amber eyes looking at me glowed with pure mischief.

"Besides?"

Another giggle. "Oh, I threatened all sorts of things and—especially after Loathsome Lydia—he knows I mean it!"

"Loathsome Lydia?"

A dark look. "My stepmother—he married her in a fit of idiocy. Grandmother's fault, of course; she was quite unsuitable for him, all clinging ivy and perpetual headaches!"

I gulped. "Your stepmother, the one you . . . er . . ."

"The one I killed? Yes."

I hesitated a moment. "What an odd conversation we seem to be having here, in the middle of the night!"

"Yes, we are, aren't we! That's why I've decided to like you. You listen to people and you don't preach . . . and in any event, you helped Bertie and me with Horrible Hackett!"

"So I did. But tell me, you can't possibly mean that you actually killed your stepmother!"

I had a dreadful inner vision of a string tied at the top of a steep staircase or perhaps a sudden push at the side of a road busy with traffic.

With a musical laugh that made me sit upright, so familiar it seemed, she proclaimed, "Oh yes I did! The death wish, you know!"

"Excuse me!"

She looked at me pityingly. "Death wish. You put ideas into a person's head and every time you see or indeed think about him or her, you concentrate on death. I read about it in a book I found, about the practices of some African tribal witch doctors. . . . In fact, that was why I was expelled the last time—unladylike reading material found among my books and . . ."

Pure mischief again lit up her amber eyes, before, with evident enjoyment she continued. "And my consequent subversion of the innocent, young minds of my fellow pupils!"

"I . . . I see!"

She giggled. "No, you don't! You think you do, but you don't . . . but still, that's not entirely your fault, is it, confused as you are with so much going on. . . ."

I looked at her, puzzled. "So much going on?"

Another musical laugh that jerked again at my memory strings. "Yes, of course! Haven't you twigged it yet?"

"Twigged what?"

Another laugh was my reply as she jumped off my bed and stood looking at me for a moment, her head cocked to one side. "Never mind . . . don't worry about it for the moment, at least your nightmares are now at bay!"

To my surprise, I found that she was right. Callum and his palette knife had faded into the mists.

"So, you should be able to sleep now without worries?" Surprisingly, she dug into the deep pocket of her dressing gown and produced a rosy apple and a small, napkin-wrapped parcel. "You are welcome to these; I stole them from the kitchen pantry—a piece of rabbit pie and some cheese left over from our midnight feast!"

I blinked at her. "Midnight feast?"

"Yes, of course—that's how I knew you were in trouble. I was on my way back to my room when I heard you screaming. And just as well I did—Horrible Hackett is just down the hall and I don't think you would have liked her to have found you!"

I shuddered. "No!" I looked at her, intrigued. "But you said a midnight feast?"

"Yes. For Bertram. He never has any fun, you know. He's made to practice for hours on end and for the rest of the time, he's forced to study in his room."

I thought of the little boy bravely . . . always bravely . . . struggling on his crutches—and was horrified. "But why should he be made to work so hard?"

A toss of the copper curls. "Oh, the money I expect when they return to Europe: concerts and so forth—you know, 'Child Prodigy Performs Brilliantly.' That sort of thing!"

"But surely Lucy . . . surely his mother would not want her son to have to . . ."

A peal of sarcastic laughter. "But Lucy is not his mother . . . haven't you realized that yet?"

I looked at her in shock. "Lucy not his mother . . . but why should you think such a thing!"

She could not be serious, I thought as I watched her pick up her candle before crossing to my bedroom door.

She turned at last but her smile this time was not so much mischievous as sad. "Have you not noted the complete lack of interest she displays in him?—and in any event, Bertram told me so!"

I had one last thought as she whisked around my door. "How did your stepmother die, Miranda?"

She looked back at me, her expression one of pure disgust. "The doctors *said* it was of typhoid fever; but they would have to say something like that, wouldn't they!"

Twenty-seven

Despite all the questions Miranda's visit had raised in my head, and after a bite or two of the rabbit pie she had left behind, I fell into a deep, dreamless sleep.

The next morning beamed just as bright as if — I thought, leaning out my window — fog and mist had never been heard of!

Far over to the west, Mount Egmont raised his graceful, snowcapped cone and many miles farther to the northeast, above miles upon miles of tangled, deep-green bush, Mount Ruapehu towered snow-clad against a brilliant sky.

It was a beautiful day; time for clearing out all the cobwebs of my mind and starting anew. No doubt all the stories I had heard — half heard? — and all the conclusions I had reached would prove to be mistaken — mere figments of my over-indulged imagination.

I was wrong.

The day started propitiously enough: breakfast attended by all the adult members of the clan — except for Lucy, of course — all seemingly in an affable mood. And luncheon also, a very civilized affair — plus an inevitably sleepy Lucy — all of us exclaiming over the vagaries of the weather and how pleasing it was that it might be fine for the house party.

Though I had dismissed Miranda's remarks about Bertram's parentage as preposterous, throughout the day I could not help discreetly studying Lucy in an attempt to ob-

233

serve any likeness between her and Bertram.

They were both dark, of course—black hair and deep brown eyes—but otherwise, the relationship was not discernable: but, of course, it might simply be that Bertram strongly resembled his late father.

Miranda, full of mischief as she obviously was with all her stories—no doubt exaggerated, in a perhaps kindly attempt to divert me from my nightmare—must simply have made the whole thing up!

What if she had not? What if she was right?

Who then was Bertram?

I gave myself a shake. The answer was surely staring me in the face. Obviously, if Bertram was not actually Lucy's son, then he must be adopted!

Another apparent mystery, I told myself smugly, with a perfectly simple answer! So much for Miranda and her mischief-making. And no doubt her assertions that Bertram was overworked with the intention of making a fortune out of his genius, were equally ill founded.

Miranda, I thought, as I started on my promised walk down to the river in the late afternoon, as much as her father, was an equally mysterious person.

"Miss Raven!"

Speak of the devil.

Devlin rounded the bend before me, a portmanteau in one hand and a mailbag dangling from the other.

I had, of course, heard the hoot from the steamer's siren deep down in the gorge but had paid no particular attention and so intent had I been on my thoughts that I had heard no footsteps ascending the River Walk.

"Miss Raven!" The crooked smile on the craggy face above me was, I could have sworn, genuine. "How delighted I am to have caught you alone . . . there is something of a particular nature that I wish to show you in private, after I have delivered the mail and collected my daughter. Perhaps you could spare me a little of your time in the garden?"

* * *

Needless to say it was not as simple as that. No sooner had the mailbag been placed on the rosewood table, than the baize door flew open to reveal Mrs. Hodges in all her righteous hospitality.

"My dear Mister Fordyke, how kind of you to bring up the post! And how fortuitous that I should catch you before you go—you must stay for afternoon tea, of course! And your dear little daughter—I am sure she is all ready to be collected—must participate, also!"

The "dear little daughter" in the act of descending the stairs behind the unknowing Mrs. Hodges, raised her eyes to the roof and made such an engagingly monkey face, I found it hard put not to collapse into giggles.

Willy-nilly, we were escorted into the drawing room where we received a lethargic welcome from an already ensconced Lucy.

"Ah, Mister Fordyke! Mrs. Hodges is quite right, you must stay for afternoon tea and . . . er . . ." The brown eyes looked blankly toward Miranda, as if seeing her for the first time. Your daughter, also! But do pray have a chocolate! Mister Duvall brought them specially from France . . . and you, too, dearest Malvina—I believe you will find these cream and cherry liqueurs particularly delicious!"

She was right. With difficulty, I staved off her offer of a second chocolate. Fortunately, afternoon tea arrived at that moment, followed by Clinton who explained that Paul had decided to stay up in the studio.

To my surprise, Norah did not appear, either. Her absence was not commented on, but remembering Miranda's remarks of the night before I had a sudden vision of a "Horrible Hackett" brow-beating an overworked Bertram somewhere in an isolated room.

"Malvina!" Lucy, doing the honors behind a silver teapot, recalled me to my senses.

Sternly I forced myself back to reality by accepting a cup of tea politely passed on to me by an amused Devlin Fordyke.

"I'm sorry, my thoughts were elsewhere. . . ."

What was it this man had to show me, I wondered—and

why in private?

He smiled at me blandly, as if guessing my thoughts and passed me a cucumber sandwich.

In the background his daughter munched steadily, her slanting, amber eyes considering me from under their long, dark lashes.

I could have killed them both!

My murderous thoughts were put aside, however, by the late appearance of Georges Duvall. He lounged for a moment in the doorway, his beetling brown brows frowning thoughtfully as he looked us over and then rising—apparently in friendly recognition—as he spied Devlin Fordyke.

"So how was Pipiriki? Was it all you expected?"

"Yes, thank you! It will make a very good article, my readers will be most interested. . . . I even managed to make a sketch or two: my paper always likes illustrations."

Pipiriki, I thought, but had not Mrs. Hodges told me he was going to Wanganui?

As if sensing my surprise, the huge American glanced down at me with a kindly smile. "Mister Duvall was kind enough to suggest I write an article about Pipiriki, Miss Raven. Not only is it situated in surroundings of scenic beauty but the hotel—only recently rebuilt, after an unfortunate fire—is totally modern with—would you believe—electricity, which is worked by its own generators, of course, and therefore highly appealing to my countrymen."

His enthusiasm was totally unlike his usual quiet, tongue-in-cheek style and as he paused, I waited with bated breath to hear what he would say next. He was beginning to sound more and more like a travel pamphlet, I thought.

Sure enough, he exulted further. "And somewhere in the bush behind the hotel is a thermal pool, I believe . . . although, of course, I did not have time, this trip, to visit it as I had to go back down to Wanganui on the returning steamer—to keep my appointment with the editor of the *Herald.*"

"The *Herald?*" It was Clinton who spoke, his gray eyes

236

coolly interested.

"Yes, indeed, sir! He had heard through a mutual acquaintance of my arrival and was most eager to hear all about the workings of such a great newspaper as my own. He was also kind enough to propose that on my return to New York, I should send him some articles about life in the United States. . . ."

After taking a sip or two of tea, he continued, but I found it difficult to concentrate on his words. Was it the mesmeric quality of his voice that made me so sleepy? With difficulty, I restrained a yawn and tried to pay attention.

". . . Cousin Malvina. . . ."

I found myself the center of attention for a circle of amused faces.

I was overcome with embarrassment. "I do beg your pardon. I really don't know what came over me!"

"Perhaps the warmth from the fire?" suggested a concerned Clinton. "Or perhaps your travels have caught up with you at last . . . this, after all, is only your fourth day here. You have been doing too much, I fear!"

I shook my head and then wished I had not: across from my chair, the flames in the fireplace seemed to unite as one quivering rainbow. With difficulty, I made myself stand up. I tried to smile nonchalantly. "N-nonsense! All I need is some fresh air!"

"Allow me, Miss Raven! Perhaps a short stroll in the garden?"

I found myself firmly escorted to the door by Devlin Fordyke.

Outside at last, in the waning light, I looked questioningly up at my huge companion.

"I really don't know what came over me!" I swayed a little as I took a lungful of fresh air. Thankfully, the remaining dizziness I felt departed

"How do you feel now?"

I took another deep breath, drawing in the scent of the

237

freezias and the woodland fragrance of the bush from across the lawn. "Much better, thank you! But you have something to show me, I believe!"

He chuckled amusedly. "So I do!"

I felt my face grow hot. "That was *not* the reason I left the drawing room just now!"

"Of course not!"

I looked up at him suspiciously but could perceive nothing on his face but bland, good humor.

"However, if you are sure you are all right, I must fetch something from my portmanteau in the hall."

He returned with a manila envelope, which he handed to me with a smile. "Despite what I said to Mister Duvall just now, this was the main reason for my journey to Wanganui."

I looked at him mystified, before opening the envelope and removing a sheet of thick, white drawing paper. On one side of the paper was a pen-and-ink sketch washed over with watercolor in a style that, for a moment, seemed faintly familiar; the sense of familiarity, however, faded to secondary importance as I realized the subject depicted.

"Oh, Ishbel!"

I could not help the exclamation nor the sob that followed it. The picture showed the side of a church wall and a grave under a weeping willow. On the plain gravestone were carved the words: ISOBEL WILHELMINA MCCLEOD followed by the dates, 1875-1892 and lastly, the phrase, FORGIVE US OUR TRESPASSES.

I found Devlin's strong arm about my shoulders and could hardly forbear turning to press my tear-streaked face into his broad, comforting chest.

"I am sorry. I should have prepared you before you opened the envelope but — I realized that it would be a shock, of course, but I did not realize how much — I thought after our conversation of the other morning that you would be relieved to see a picture of Ishbel's grave — to know that she is really and truly dead; and in this life, exists only in your dreams."

I searched fruitlessly for my pocket handkerchief only to find a large, white linen square, faintly redolent of sunlit herbs, presented to me.

"Thank you." Surreptitiously, I dabbed away my tears. "I'm sorry. . . ."

"There is no need to be sorry—*you* have done nothing wrong."

"No. It's just . . . it's just that, now that I know she is really dead, all that I can think of is, what a beautiful, *glowing* person she could be when . . . when she was not . . . was not . . . troubled."

I looked at the picture again, at the narrow, lonely grave and at the words carved on the tombstone FORGIVE US OUR TRESPASSES.

"You are prepared to forgive her, then, for the deaths of your mother and governess and the untold horrors to which she subjected you and your brother?"

I looked again at the picture of the lonely grave.

"Yes."

He sighed deeply, his arm tightening around me. "So then, you are free of her. When you dream of her tonight or the next night, perhaps you will turn and face her and send her on her way with a blessing. . . ."

Just then, a low, rippling laugh erupted from the hall behind us.

I froze.

Twenty-eight

"Miranda!"

Devlin Fordyke's American tones rang out strong and true.

"Papa?"

In the front doorway, Miranda stood poised, as if about to take flight, the glow from the just lighted lamps behind her, outlining her slender, delicately boned figure.

From somewhere in the background sounded the creaks and squeaks that proclaimed the arrival of Bertram.

Quickly, I removed myself from the shelter of the strong arm that still enfolded me. Slipping the watercolor back into its envelope, I wandered over to the edge of the veranda and made a pretense of gazing up into the sky as if trying to discover the Southern Cross.

"Miranda, you have been terrorizing Miss Raven!"

"Yes, Sir, but not entirely. Especially not since . . . not since . . ."

"Not since when, Miranda?"

A long pause.

"Come now, remember our bargain!"

"Yes, Papa . . . that I would tell you when I really disliked someone . . . and that in the meantime I would keep myself out of mischief!"

He uttered a deep sigh. "Then you have broken our bargain, have you not?" Another sigh. "So, therefore, what did we agree?"

"Oh, Papa, please! Don't send me back . . . I couldn't pos-

240

sibly live with Grandmother! I really did try, you know: I really did! It's just that . . . well, for a while I was bored . . . and then, you were away and I couldn't talk with you. Give me another chance—*please!* I promise I shall try harder. And in any event, could *you* live with Grandmother?"

Before her father could make his reply, however, a door clicked open behind Miranda and voices sounded as if the hall were about to be invaded.

Miranda jumped back as if on cue and Devlin reappeared at my side as if by magic.

"Miss Raven, I must apologize for my daughter . . . all the laughter you have heard . . . those bells . . . I should have known!"

Before he could continue, a long, lean shadow, dreadfully familiar, detached itself from one side of the doorway. With an effort, I managed to keep myself from clutching at Devlin though I could not prevent a gasp.

"Miss Raven, what is it?"

I recovered myself with an effort. "Nothing . . . how stupid of me . . . it's only Mister Duvall. He gave me a start, that's all . . . and after all our talk about Ishbel . . ."

"I'm sorry, Miss Raven. I am afraid I gave you a fright!" The guttural, French-Canadian accent was apologetic but in the half light, the greenish eyes were mocking as they looked first at my face and then at the envelope clutched in my hands.

How long had he been there? I wondered. Had he followed us out of the drawing room and been in the shadows ever since?

Why did I feel such a loathing for this man?

"You are quite recovered then from your indisposition, Miss Raven?"

"Thank you, yes. A little fresh air was all I needed."

I was regarded with doubt. "Perhaps—but I think that Clinton was probably right. . . . After all, you have been with us only four days . . . perhaps you need to take a little time to refresh yourself before you fully enter into the activities of the household."

I looked at him in disbelief. Activities of the household, indeed!

Support for Georges Duvall came from an unexpected source. "My dear Miss Raven, Mister Duvall is quite right . . . you must not overtax yourself!"

Devlin patted my arm and gazed down at me anxiously. "The female constitution, so delicate as it is . . . and my own dear daughter, loathe that I am to admit it . . . so very excitable, bless her heart. . . . No, no, Mister Duvall and Mister Raven are quite right, my dear, you must take to your chamber, for a while at least, and allow yourself to be refreshed!"

He bowed awkwardly, quite without his usual aplomb and bumbled off back into the house from whence he emerged again almost immediately with both his portmanteau and his daughter.

I gazed after them in astonishment as they crossed the lawn.

I turned to speak to Duvall but found, to my relief, that he had gone.

In his place was Bertram.

He peered at me through the lengthening dusk, his eyes behind the pebble lenses of his spectacles, impenetrable. "Mister Duvall and Mister Fordyke are quite right, you know, Miss Raven, you should proceed at a slower pace!"

I looked down at the little old man imprisoned behind a ten-year-old face. "Do you think so?"

"Oh, yes! You should relax in your room, and write letters or . . . or . . . sew?"

"Sew?"

A doubtful look. "Yes; is that not what females do?"

I tried not to laugh. "Why, is that what your mother does?"

A blank look. "My mother? Oh, of course . . . no, no, she doesn't sew, at least, not as a general rule—though I did see her once embroidering a waistcoat."

His words of wisdom delivered, Bertram turned and hobbled away.

Shaking my head, I reentered the house and stood for a moment in the hall. I still held the envelope and could feel the crisp drawing paper through its fold. What a man of contradictions Devlin Fordyke seemed, but his reaction to Georges Duvall out on the veranda really had me completely puzzled. . . . . It was almost as if he had been acting out a part in a play.

On the rosewood table, one lamp glowed, the others standing by, ready. Perhaps, I thought, I would follow Bertram's advice and go up to my room and write letters.

Letters!

I had forgotten all about the mailbag, kindly brought up by Devlin.

Without any real hope that there would be a letter for me, I approached the table. Most of the post had been collected, of course, by the various members of the household—although there were two letters remaining, one addressed to Miss Helena Saxonham and the other, an official-looking affair in beige with an embossed coat of arms, for a Mr. T. Raven.

T. Raven; who was T. Raven? Did Clinton have a middle name? I wondered.

Puzzled, I walked over to the stairs; then, remembering my decision earlier that day, changed my mind and turned down the library corridor instead. I would see if there were any old family papers stored somewhere on the shelves, and at least solve the mystery of Ihaira, once and for all!

The library was cozy from the light of a lamp and the glow of a newly lit fire. I was pleased to find no one else there; I did not want to have to explain my search to anyone.

Unfortunately, my search, thorough though it was, did not turn up any papers whatsoever; nor was there any sign of a family Bible.

In some disgust, shaking the dust from my hands, I gave up and stood away from the shelves. As I looked one more time over the books, my glance took in the paintings lining the wall above the bookcases. With everything that had happened to me, my odd discovery of the previous evening had completely left my head. The arrival of Clinton and Duvall had interrupted my examination of the other paintings.

I looked at the clock on the mantelpiece. There was still plenty of time before I had to change for dinner. I would finish looking at the other paintings, and see if any of the rest of them had been treated the same way.

To my surprise, as I held up the lamp to examine them, I saw that *all* the paintings had been dusted. Had Clinton told Mrs. Hodges about all the dust? How odd, he did not seem the kind of person to pay much attention to household affairs.

I walked slowly around the library, shining the lamp on the pictures of old sailing ships interspersed with scenes from Maori and early colonial life, and here and there by a portrait or two. One portrait in particular caught my attention and I dragged over a chair and climbed up to study it more closely.

It was a watercolor of a Maori woman holding a baby. Underneath in spiky, yellowed writing was the inscription, *Moana and Child, 1862.*

Moana? Could this possibly be a portrait of old Moana in her younger days. It was hard to tell, but the woman looking out at me seemed to be in her thirties or early forties. The Moana I remembered had a face deeply etched with lines; but like Moana, this woman also had a tattooed chin. Was it the same pattern as old Moana's? I could not remember. And if this portrait was a younger version of old Moana, who was the child?

I climbed down from my chair and dragged it back to the table. Really, I thought, not without irritation, it would seem that at Ravensfall, one mystery was perpetually superseded by another! I decided to return to my room.

The library passage was dark; I was grateful for the faint glimmer from the lamp in the hall. The light, however, dimmed a moment as I reached the end of the corridor. Stepping out into the hall, I found Tamati, the boxes from his whare piled beside him, standing by the lamp and holding a letter close to its glow, in an effort to read more easily. On the rosewood table rested the discarded envelope, the official-looking one that had been addressed to a Mr. T. Raven.

He glanced up at that moment, turning his head sharply. Of course, I thought, looking at the arrogant hawk-nosed face so like that of Josiah Raven—so like, indeed to that of my own father's; no wonder he had seemed familiar to me. How could I have been so stupid!

All of a sudden, everything fell into place, the picture of Moana in the library and her child—Tamati's father? And the name, of course. Ihaira. Had not Tamati said his son was named after his father?

I thought, with embarrassment, of the Maori lesson I had given Devlin Fordyke up at the burial plot: how I had explained to him the key for translating Maori names: Ihaira must, of course, be Maori for Josiah!

"Cousin Malvina!"

I came to myself to find Tamati Raven looking at me, amusement glinting in the depths of his deep, brown eyes. "So, you have guessed?"

"Yes. Yes, I suppose I have." We looked at each other for a long moment.

"You have questions?"

"Not really. Just the in-between parts: Who? Why? What happened? That sort of thing. . . ."

With a bitter laugh, which he swiftly held in check, he asked, "Who? Why? What happened? What easy questions to answer!"

Grinning sarcastically, Tamati ticked off each question and answer, one by one, on his finger tips.

"Who?"

"Your Great Uncle Josiah and my grandmother, Moana." They became . . . let us say . . . close friends."

"Why?"

The death of Josiah Raven's first wife and children in a cholera epidemic.

"What happened?"

For a moment Tamati discontinued his question-and-answer recitation and directed an especially wicked grin toward me. "Need you ask?"

I felt myself blushing. "You mean that . . . that . . . Moana . . . and Great Uncle Josiah?"

I looked at him in disbelief, thinking of the portrait of the straight-lipped, gray-bearded man at the top of the stairs and of the ancient crone Reggie and I had always been so afraid of.

There was an amused but understanding gleam in the deep brown eyes. "They were younger once, you know . . . although, Moana did have a grown family at the time. . . ."

His eyes darkened suddenly. "Or would have had a grown family, if it had not been for one of your whiteman's diseases—the cholera. As it was, only my Uncle Hemi survived . . . and Rangi, of course, for a time, until . . ."

Rangi, I thought. Rangi, who had been Moana's favorite grandson and had been a Hau-hau and had died at the hands of the British.

As if reading my thoughts, Tamati nodded slowly. "But, of course, by that time, old Josiah had married her because of the child to be born . . . the child, Ihaira, who became my father."

"And so, what happened? I mean . . ." I thought of the plain headstone up on the lonely bluff.

"What happened to Ihaira? What happened to my father?" Tamati paused a moment, before answering. "Before he was six years old, he was sent away."

I looked at him in shock. "Sent away? You cannot mean it!"

"Can't I?" Bitterness again clouded his eyes. "Moana, remember, after seeing most of her family die, had to suffer the death of Rangi at the Battle of Moutoa—and Ihaira, a son who was half Pakeha, she found it hard to tolerate—especially as Josiah had, of course, been helping Bully Hayes with his gunrunning during the land wars."

"Yes, I suppose I can understand that perhaps for a time

246

but surely . . . even if she—surely Great Uncle Josiah would have looked after his son. . . ."

For the first time, there was a hesitation, although only a minor one. "Well, he did—in a way."

"In a way?"

"He sent him to friends up north, with instructions that he be raised and educated as a Pakeha—eventually to take over Ravensfall."

"I see."

"No, you don't." The eyes studying me were grim. "You see, my father—Ihaira—met and married a woman like himself who was neither fully Pakeha nor fully Maori and old Josiah did not approve. . . . And it was on a visit to Ravensfall, to come to terms with the old gentleman, that my father fell ill and died."

I looked at him, puzzled. "Then Ravensfall belongs to you."

"Does it?"

"You mean that Great Uncle Josiah . . ."

"Willed it to your father, instead? Yes."

"But, that's not fair!"

"Isn't it? Surely Ravensfall was his to do with as he liked. In any event, I shall be leaving here shortly to make my own fortune." He looked about the hall appreciatively. "One day, I shall have a place far better than this!" He indicated the letter in his hand and then the boxes by his feet. "I have just sold some shares left me by my grandfather and when I have sold these artifacts to Mister Duvall, I should be able to buy some land for myself."

I looked with interest at the boxes, remembering when I had last seen them outside the front door of his whare. "How busy you must have been collecting all these objects; where on earth did you get them all from?"

For the first time, he flashed a look of guilt. "Oh, around and about the place."

Not exactly lying, I thought, but prevaricating. All of a sudden I remembered the old, tattooed gentleman and his anger with Tamati . . . *"Tapu! Tapu! Tapu!"* was the

247

word I had heard over and over.

"But the old gentleman." I queried, "why was he so upse
with you?"

"You mean old Tauhu?" Tamati shrugged his shoulders
"Just because he's my great uncle doesn't mean he can tell m
what to do!"

"Your great uncle?"

"Yes. Moana's brother."

Grinning at my surprise, Tamati folded his letter an
stashed it away in his jacket pocket. "And now, *Cousi*
Malvina, I must get these boxes up to the storeroom on th
second floor, ready for the estimable Mister Georges Duvall'
inspection!"

Loading himself up with the boxes, he paused a momen
before starting up the stairs. "Georges Duvall, Malvina . .
he is not all he seems, is he?" He lowered his voice befor
speaking again. "Be wary of him . . . Cousin!"

I looked after him, troubled. There was something he wa
not telling me, something vital.

Try as I might, I could not rid my mind of a presentimen
of doom.

Back in my room, I could not shake off the gloom tha
seemed to have overtaken me. What was wrong, I asked my
self irritably — had not three mysteries been solved? An
mysteries to which the answers were really very simple: th
ghostly bells and laughter, the identity of Ihaira and o
course, the location of Ishbel's grave.

Settling down in my fireside chair, I slipped the sketch ou
of the envelope and studied once more the lonely grave. Why
was it that the scene seemed so familiar? Then, suddenly, jus
as with the Heaphy in the dining room, I realized that it wa
not the *scene* that was familiar but the *style* of the artist.

Somewhere, recently, I had seen just such decisive stroke
of pen and ink, just such delicate hints of color conveyed by
the washed-over watercolor. Where? I looked down to where
Devlin Fordyke had made his signature, plain and neat,

slanting across the lower left-hand corner: his initials, only —
D.F.

I sat up in shock. Of course, I remembered then the picture of the Grand Canyon on a wall in his cottage, executed in just such a style . . . and the signature, D. Francis.

Twenty-nine

That night, for the first time in my dreams, I met Ishbel face to face without fear. She was standing on the edge of the cliff above the *taniwha* pool and as Devlin had suggested I do, I raised my hand in farewell to dismiss her with my blessing.

She had smiled at me then — not her terrible smile, but gentler — her great aquamarine eyes filled with such sadness, I found myself weeping.

Gradually she had faded through the trees but before she had disappeared entirely, she pointed behind me, as if in warning. But when I turned there was nothing there, just a great dark vastness with the sound of rushing waters.

I woke suddenly in the darkness of my chamber.

What had disturbed me?

I struggled up and listened.

Nothing.

Behind the guard, the remaining red-gold embers of my fire still glowed faintly.

I forced myself out of bed and lighting a spill from the special holder placed beside the fireplace, managed with it to light first the candles on my mantelpiece and then the lamp beside my bed.

Rejoicing in the light, I crouched on my fireside chair, rocking myself to and fro.

Ishbel had gone, I knew that.

Gone.

Unexpectedly, I felt also a great loss.

"Let her go," Devlin had said — and so I had. And she had gone. Truly gone.

Why then did I still feel such unease?

I rose and restlessly roamed about the room, finally taking up the picture of Ishbel's grave again, remembering my conclusions of the evening before. Did the initial, F. really stand for, Francis? And if so, what did the D. stand for?

Was Devlin Fordyke really D. Francis? And if so, what did this mean?

I thought about the newspaper article I had read, with its references to burglary, forgery, and murder and tried not to shiver. After all, what actual facts did I have . . . what did I really know about this man? Nothing really, except what he or his daughter had told me or implied.

He had never satisfactorily explained — or attempted to explain — his high-handed actions with my person. On the other hand, he had been there when I had seemed to need him most — rescuing me from the fog-bound bush, furnishing me with proof of Ishbel's demise.

I looked down at the sketch I still held in my hand. But was this actual proof? Was this really a picture of Ishbel's grave . . . or one that Devlin Fordyke/Francis had conjured up in his imagination? And as for him appearing out of the mist that day . . . had he known all along that I would be there? Had he, indeed, also known all along about Miranda and her tricks — perhaps even encouraged them?

But why should he do such a thing?

The answer, of course, was staring me in the face and had been all along, but — heaven help me! — I had not wanted to admit it.

Obviously, the huge American, suspecting my doubts about him, was attempting to gain my confidence, just as he had apparently gained the confidence of my cousins!

Why should he do this?

Keeping the *New York Times* article well in mind, and considering Fordyke's obsequious behavior toward Georges Duvall and my cousins, I forced myself to look objectively at the situation.

Could the huge American actually be the leader of the gang referred to in the article? To further elude his captors, could he have fled from Mexico to New Zealand? Once in New Zealand, had he looked about for a means of supporting himself by finding new victims to rob?

Was Devlin Fordyke actually gaining the confidence of my cousins, only to make it easier to rob them later? The article, I remembered with a shiver, reported that some of the paintings were copied and the forgeries later sold as originals. . . . I looked down at the little sketch and remembered the watercolor of the Grand Canyon: if Devlin Fordyke was not a great artist, he was certainly talented.

Slowly, I slipped the picture back into its envelope. What was I to do? Again all I had were mere suppositions.

I was going to have to find proof.

How?

I shuddered as I remembered the remaining fact in the article that I had kept at the back of my mind

The younger son of the house had been killed in the process of the robbery.

I was going to have to be careful.

Though I made myself return to bed, I spent the remainder of the night tossing fitfully. No wonder then, that the morning's early light found me heavy-eyed and listless.

At breakfast, I was relieved to find myself, apart from Helena, the only one present: I did not think I could stand the usual morning's polite conversation! Out in the hall, however, I could hear the sounds of some activity going on.

"They're bringing the paintings down, miss, and some of the antiques. They have to decide where to put them before the guests arrive," Helena answered in return to my look of inquiry.

"Guests? Oh, yes, of course, the house party. How many will there be, do you think?"

"I don't know but" — her little face lit up — "I had a letter from my sister, Victoria, and she is coming with them. Mrs. Smythe, you know — her benefactress — is ever so kind. She said that as Victoria has formed an attachment it is only right that she should help in every way!"

"An attachment? Oh, yes of course, the other evening you told me that Victoria — the pretty one? — had met a 'certain someone' as I recall. But how will her coming here help her?"

She smiled shyly and blushed. "Because Ravensfall is just over the river from the Turners' place, miss, and Mister Turner—my sister's intended—has told her that while she's here, he'll persuade his parents to invite the household here over for an evening's entertainment!"

I looked at her, puzzled. "I see."

She grinned. "No, you don't, miss! You see, Victoria wouldn't meet Mister Turner's parents in the ordinary way and he can't very well go to them and tell them he wants to marry a penniless orphan, now can he?"

"I don't see why not!"

Helena shook her head at me reprovingly. "Because he's the heir, isn't he . . . he wouldn't want to be cut off, now would he?"

She paused, as she poured me another cup of tea. "But once they've seen her, Mister Turner says, everything will be all right because of course, she's as pretty as a picture!"

"I see. Her face is her fortune!" A sudden thought struck me. "Tell me, which Mister Turner is Victoria's . . . er . . . intended? Surely not Mister Jonathan Turner?"

"The very same, miss. Of course, he's a good deal older than Victoria but they should suit very well just the same!"

Jonathan Turner, I thought, the once determined suitor of my sister Ishbel and who after her death, had accused Harriet of her murder! Would wonders never cease!

Out in the hall I paused to watch Hodges, Betty, and Alfred stacking paintings against the walls and the side of the stairs.

I looked at them in surprise. "Are you going to display them out here?"

Oh, no, miss. Too dark and h'anyways with the light from the stained-glass windows, the colors would be all funny, wouldn't they?"

It was Betty who spoke while Hodges nodded approvingly at the drawing room doors.

"Of course. I suppose you'll have to put them in the drawing room and library." I walked over as I spoke and paused to examine an oil of a country scene depicting in a style that seemed hauntingly familiar, a cottage situated beneath enormous leafy trees. I was looking for the signature, when I was interrupted by what could only be described as a snort from Betty.

"Really, miss! Of course, artists are . . . well, that's to say . . . me mam told me they's h'always painting naked women, but that I thought that lot" — she nodded up the stairs — "being your relations would be more — well, respectable!"

She had taken up a picture of a nude woman who, back turned, was reclining on a blue chaise longue. With one hand, she was reaching out to a small table beside the chaise longue while with the other, she was holding back her long flaxen hair. Again, I experienced a sense of recognition but I could not imagine why. Was it the style? Really, Malvina, I chided myself in my mind, you are becoming a great deal oversensitive!

"Ah, Miss Raven!" Georges Duvall had materialized from the library passage. "I see you have discovered our Matisse! Beautiful, is it not? I persuaded him to part with it when I was last in Paris. He is not so well known, yet, but he will be . . . and I don't think he will be completely wasted on the people of Wanganui. I understand that a Mister Henry Sargeant, who has a fine collection himself, is proposing to start up an art gallery here."

As he spoke, he took the painting gently from my hands and held it up to the light.

Betty was right. The light through the stained glass completely transformed the painting, the chaise longue no longer seemed blue and the hair of the lounging woman appeared to be green!

"I had wondered about that," I admitted.

There was a mocking look from the green eyes. "Had you indeed? You were wondering doubtless, why I should be bringing such treasures around the world with me to, of all places, New Zealand?"

"Well, yes."

"My dear Malvina — I may call you Malvina, may I not? — you have much to learn about the world of agents! Whether in New York, Wanganui or Reykjavik, we always have to be on the alert for interested buyers — or indeed talented artists who might be capable of producing world-class material that may supply some future demand!"

He bent to replace the oil with the others stacked beside the stairs. "But to be honest with you, I should never have bothered with Wanganui, if it had not been for Clinton's problem."

"Clinton's problem? Oh, you mean his having to be here because of Cousin Lucy's convalescence?"

Duvall straightened up slowly and stood for a moment as if thinking. "Cousin Lucy's convalescence?" He gave me an amused look. "Yes, I suppose so!"

Which only backed up the idea that tragic though the accident had been that had removed her husband, that Cousin Lucy herself was a mere hypochondriac!

As if in answer to my thought, Cousin Lucy, herself, invited me to the library late that afternoon to finalize plans for the house party—the first guests, she told me, would be arriving the next afternoon.

She was lounging back on the sofa by the fire, the inevitable box of chocolates beside her. At the table sat Norah watching Bertram busily copying out of a book.

"I thought perhaps that we might organize some parlor games, Malvina . . . something that does not require too much preparation. I myself am not in the best of health and dear Norah occupied as she is with my darling Bertram . . ."

At that moment, darling Bertram looked up and catching my eye, poked out his tongue at Norah Hackett whose pale attention had been taken momentarily by Lucy.

Hurriedly I restrained a laugh, disguising it into a cough.

I found myself regarded thoughtfully by Lucy, her huge dark eyes limpid. "And as for you, dearest Malvina . . . incommoded as you were yesterday by your sudden dizziness! And today at luncheon, I could not help noticing how peaky you looked—now I hear you coughing!"

"Not really coughing, dearest Lucy, merely something caught in my throat."

Over at the table, Bertram winked at me.

I restrained myself with difficulty.

Lucy picked up a paper from a pile of letters on an occasional table by her side. "Fortunately, I have received an invitation from the Turners over the river . . . you know who they are, of course? We met them at Mrs. Smythe's. Apparently, they are holding a dance in their . . . wool shed?" The delicate brows were raised in askance as she glanced from the invitation to me.

"A common practice, Cousin Lucy, of farmers hereabouts. The wool shed is actually a huge room — something like a barn, I suppose — where sheep are sheared during the season and wool is stored. On festive occasions, the building is cleared, cleaned, and decorated and . . . and . . . it's tremendous fun!"

I paused, remembering nostalgically the few occasions when Reggie and I had actually enjoyed ourselves.

"I see — if you say so. . . ." Lucy looked at me doubtfully before replacing the invitation on the pile and selecting a chocolate. "But where are my manners?" The box was held out to me. "I believe you will find those hazel nut creams quite delicious. . . ."

She was right.

"So, that is one day and night taken care of," I remarked, absent-mindedly accepting another chocolate."

"Sorry?"

"One day and night: the preparations, you know, for the dance . . . and, of course, they will want you for refreshments beforehand; and more than likely the entertainment will go on into the early morning hours — which will take care of the next morning. . . ."

With difficulty, I refused another chocolate. In the hall beyond the door, a rattle signified the arrival of the afternoon tea trolley.

As the door opened, I thought of something that had been puzzling me. "By the by, Cousin Lucy, you have mentioned more than once meeting Mrs. Smythe and being invited to dinner. Where did you meet her?"

She shot an amused glance. "Why, in Wanganui, dearest Malvina. Your father's solicitor — Mister Glenby? — was pleased to open up your family town house in Wicksteed Street for us. In fact, while we were staying there, he introduced us to Mrs. Smythe when we met in your parish church in Victoria

Avenue—Christchurch?—the very week we arrived, in fact! So good of him! Because of his kindness, we have been able to make all manner of acquaintances!"

Of course, I thought; our town house, which we used to visit every month to take Holy Communion at Christchurch. Before I had left England, Papa had suggested that instead of going all the way to Ravensfall, I might like to stay in our town house, instead. But, of course, I had declined.

I watched as Helena pushed in the tea trolley and placed the silver tea things close to Lucy.

Absently, Lucy placed a napkin over her lap before preparing to pour tea. "Which reminds me, dearest Malvina, did you not say that you had brought letters for Mister Glenby—and for us, too—from your dear father?"

Letters! In all the excitement of the last few days, I had completely forgotten the disappearance of my letters.

I was almost grateful to hear the American tones of a familiar voice from the doorway behind me.

"Good afternoon, Mrs. Wilkinson! I am sorry to intrude, but I have some books to return; I wonder if I might leave them with you.

I did not need to turn. From where I sat, I could almost feel the overpowering presence of Devlin Fordyke.

Devlin Fordyke or Devlin Francis, I wondered sarcastically as at Lucy's invitation, he settled his bulk into one of the leather chairs near me.

"Miss Raven?"

I found myself staring down at a cup of tea handed to him by Lucy and then politely handed on to me.

"Thank you!"

A plate of finger sandwiches was offered to me by Helena whose wide, gray eyes, I noted, flickered constantly between me and Devlin.

Bother Mrs. Hodges, I thought, yawning, she must have at least given out a hint of what *she* thought was the true state of affairs. I selected an anemic affair which turned out to be spread with fish paste.

"A sausage roll, Miss Raven?"

This time the dish was held by Fordyke.

Bother the man, I thought sleepily, why couldn't he leave me alone? Why, for that matter, could they not *all* of them leave me alone? All I wanted, after all . . . all I wanted . . . I couldn't remember what I wanted—nor did I care. . . .

"Miss Raven, I believe you are unwell! Perhaps a little fresh air?"

I found myself raised unceremoniously to my feet and helped to the door.

From the veranda I took a deep breath of the damp, leaf-scented evening air—sporadic raindrops spotting my upturned face—and whether I wanted to or not, was forced to rest my head against the broad, unyielding bulk of Devlin Fordyke.

To my disgust, my arms were seized and I was forced down the steps and made to march up and down the lawn in a steadily increasing rain.

"Better now?"

I fought down a strong urge to gag and nodded.

"Now then, listen; you must go to your room and *stay there*. Do you understand?"

I did not understand in the least, but—raindrops streaking down my face—nodded anyway, in the hope that he would stop bothering me.

He emitted a deep sigh. "No, of course, you don't understand—and why should you? But you do have a devil of a way of getting into things that do not concern you!"

A twittering figure emerged on the veranda.

I found myself seized yet again, this time hoisted up into strong arms. "My dear Miss Raven, this is becoming quite a habit, but as your intended, I suppose I am well within the bounds of propriety, even if I do carry you up to your bedroom!"

I heard a long sigh from the veranda and a clasping of hands over a black bombazine bosom as I was carried past.

Thirty

I awoke to a splattering of raindrops against my window-pane. In the dim lamplight I found an anxious Helena ineffec-tually dabbing at my temples, droplets from her eau de cologne-soaked handkerchief running uselessly down my cheeks.

"Oh, Miss Raven!"

"It's all right, Helena. . . ." With great effort, I raised a slug-gish hand to my dully aching head. "I believe I am still alive . . . although," I added, as I tried sitting up, "only just!"

Everything seemed in a haze. I reached down for my pince-nez and found only the front of my flannel nightdress. Helena handed me my spare spectacles from my bedside table. "Mrs. Hodges and I undressed you, miss — I hope you don't mind."

With difficulty, I forced my seemingly thick tongue into more words. "Of course not; but whatever came over me?"

"I dunno, miss. Mrs. Hodges said you were taken quite pe-culiar-like on the front lawn and that . . ." Helena paused as she gazed at me soulfully. "Mister Fordyke swept you up into his arms as if you were as light as thistledown . . . and then bore you as gently as if you were as fragile as . . . as . . . a precious jewel, up the stairs to this room."

Somehow, I held myself in check — I knew that if I so much as giggled, my head would break. Besides, I still felt decidedly groggy.

A thought occurred to me. I shaped the words carefully, forc-ing my reluctant tongue to enunciate every syllable. "How long ago was this?"

"Oh, hours ago, miss . . . but now that you are awake, I expect that you might like a nice cup of tea. Mrs. Hodges said to ring as soon as you stirred."

My eyes finally focused on the clock on the mantelpiece and with difficulty, I wrapped my tongue about the appropriate words. "But . . . it's . . . after midnight . . . can't expect you to . . ."

A quarter of an hour later, after a visit from an extramotherly Mrs. Hodges armed, needless to say, with beef tea, bread and butter fingers, and a softly boiled egg, I fell once more into a deep sleep.

A sleep gradually invaded by disturbing dreams.

First, a voice softly calling my name and then the flutter of a light, as of a candle, held in my doorway and slowly, the approach of the candle to the foot of my bed and then — oh, horror of horrors — above the candle's flame, shielded by skeletal fingers, spread wide and half obscured in the swirling darkness of my dreams, a well-remembered pair of green eyes.

"Call . . . Callum . . . ?"

I cowered back against my pillows.

"Mallie."

A soft whisper, the lilting syllables floating delicately as leaves on the trickling waters of a highland burn.

"Mallie."

I tried to open my mouth and could not.

The candle flame fluttered closer, the green eyes above it, all-compelling.

"Mallie. Ye maung go . . . maung go . . ."

"Must go. Yes. Yes. I must go, but . . ." I tried to struggle out of the dream. "I must go but where and why?"

No answer.

Total silence: then, at last, the soft corner of a smile.

"Questions. Ye hav'na changed . . . but, ye maung go. There's danger here . . . danger here . . . danger. . . ."

Gradually the light fluttered back across the room, disappearing into darkness.

"Danger. . . ."

A turmoil of swirling, twisting shapes, myself caught up in the vast reaches of a storm-filled firmament.

"Miss Raven! Miss Raven!"

Anxious hands pulled at my bed sheets, only to find their palpitating way to my face.

Under lightly patting fingers, I found myself gazing up at liquid brown eyes, magnified by thick pebble spectacles.

Was I awake or asleep?

I found my voice at last.

"Bertram?"

There was a long sigh, followed closely by another. "Oh, Miss Raven — you are all right!" He sighed again and I found my hands taken up and held close to a throbbing temple.

I tried to gather my wits. "Yes. Yes . . . of course, I'm all right. . . ."

He pulled urgently at my hands. "Miss Raven, there's danger — you must be careful; you must stay here in your room until . . ."

"Bertram!"

We both froze in shock.

Norah Hackett loomed in the doorway.

Thirty-one

I awoke at last to a light shower pattering on the roof of the veranda canopy below my room and a swishing of my closed curtains swaying together in a rising breeze billowing through my partly opened window.

Not a good day for riding out on the moors. I thought sleepily: perhaps I would carry out my promise to my little sisters and take them some chesnuts that we would all roast along the grate of the nursery fire.

I smiled at the thought of their eager little faces and then stiffened as slowly returning to consciousness, I gradually remembered where I was.

The Yorkshire moors were thousands of miles away, I reminded myself. Outside my bedroom window were wild, tangled ferns and trees with strange, unpronounceable names and a legendary river flowing swiftly through its steep-sided gorge.

I stretched experimentally, then sat up slowly and carefully, finding to my relief that my headache had disappeared. Apart from a slight grogginess, I seemed to be all right.

Carefully, I reached out for my spectacles and then slowly swung my legs over the side of the bed. Through the curtains, dim light seeped. Early morning, I guessed, staggering across to the window.

I was wrong. Though the light struggling through layers of lowering pewter clouds was indeed dim, it was no early morning light I observed. I turned toward the clock on the mantel. Sure enough. It lacked a quarter of two — in the afternoon!

How could I have slept so long, I wondered — and then remembered my nightmare of Callum, so vivid still, it was more like a waking dream . . . and Bertram's visit and his removal by Norah Hackett. Had that been a dream also?

Though it was chilly, I threw my window wide open and stood a moment taking deep breaths of the cool, fresh air. What had happened? Though I had suffered the usual childhood ailments, I had always kept good health. Had it been something I had eaten?

I thought back, reviewing what I had eaten and when. Both times the dizziness had overcome me at afternoon tea. Finger sandwiches, scones, and sausage rolls. I had eaten the same as everyone else. Why then was I the only one to have been affected?

I studied the scene in my mind's eye—the cozy library and the laiden tea trolley: Lucy presiding at the teapot, Devlin Fordyke handing me my cup and saucer.

Devlin Fordyke!

Devlin handing me my cup and saucer on *both* occasions. . . .

Devlin . . . could he possibly have? . . . surely not . . . but then . . . ?

I shivered. In my mind, I saw again the huge man, his back turned for a moment after receiving the cup and saucer from a Lucy already intent upon pouring the next cup.

Could he possibly have?

Yes.

I remembered how Ishbel had slipped laudanum into our mother's medicine. With everyone's attention on their plates, it would have been simple enough for Devlin to have slipped a dose of laudanum into my tea—and if the dose was small enough, I would not have tasted it, especially after eating a fish paste sandwich!

Why? Why should he want to do such a thing?

The answer came crystal clear as if a voice spoke in my mind. Because, Malvina Raven, he must have guessed that you doubt his identity.

It was sheer nonsense. I tried to giggle and failed as I remembered the valuable paintings in the house. Had Devlin Fordyke realized that I suspected him? Was he planning to keep me moribund until he managed to pull off a theft of all my cousins' works of art?

263

I remembered, shuddering, that my second attack had been far worse than the first. Perhaps to avoid suspicion he intended to make my "illness" seem natural. Did he plan to increase each dose in strength until I was safely out of the way, confined all day and night to my room?

What was I to do? I still had no proof.

What would Harriet have done? I wondered, thinking with longing of my practical little stepmother — and then I laughed in truth. Harriet would hardly stand in a flimsy nightgown before a wide-open window on a damp, cold winter's day!

Reaching up, I pulled the window down. I would get dressed at once and then make my way downstairs. Perhaps a little action would dispel my fears, dissolve that horrible knot of fear I tried to ignore in the pit of my stomach.

Before I had finished dressing, however, I was visited by an anxious Betty "to look in on me" as she said. Grinning with delight at my apparent recovery, she disappeared only to reappear a short time later with a laden tray of buttered toast, scrambled eggs, and ham.

All in all it was not until more than an hour later that I found myself making my way down the stairs.

The hall was dim and an intermittent rain against the darkened stained-glass windows was the only sound I heard.

As I was halfway down the flight, the front door bell pealed with a consequent flying open of the green baize door before Betty erupted across the hall.

Had she been lying in wait directly below the kitchen bells? I wondered in amusement.

Flinging open the door, she bobbed politely. "Good evening," she announced in careful tones, obviously carefully coached. "Please to come in!"

Three behatted, heavily cloaked figures entered, followed closely by Cousin Clinton and a weighed-down Hodges bearing carpetbags and other items of luggage.

Clinton glanced up the stairs and spied me on my descent. "Cousin Malvina, by all that's capital! You're just in time to greet our first guests — Mrs. Smythe with her companion, Miss Victoria Saxonham and Mrs. Smythe's friend, Mrs. Trillingham-Bean."

I could not help a start of a not totally pleasant surprise as I looked down at the dumpy figure in the process of handing her cloak and hat to Betty. Mrs. Trillingham-Bean, that mysterious presence at Foster's Hotel, who had not chosen to reveal herself to me on our trip upriver on the *Waiwere*. What was she doing at Ravensfall?

I forced myself to smile politely as I continued my descent.

"How delightful! We meet again, my dear Miss Raven! But how pale you look—have you been ill?"

"My dear Malvina!" I found myself scrutinized by Clinton's clear gray eyes. "Should you be up? Lucy told me all about your sudden turn yesterday." He turned toward his guests. "I'm afraid, ladies, that my cousin was taken with an attack of dizziness yesterday afternoon . . . the second attack in two days, so I understand!"

"I assure you that I am quite well now, Cousin!"—and intend to remain so, I added under my breath! I forced another smile at Mrs. Trillingham-Bean and nodded toward her companion. "How do you do? How pleasant to make your acquaintance at last! I understand that you are the lady responsible for the Heaphy in the dining room."

Mrs. Smythe, to my surprise a woman even taller than myself and twice my size, nodded down at me graciously, her puce-complexioned face contrasting with the startling white of her intricately curled coiffure. "How d'ye do, Miss Raven." Her voice like a foghorn nearly blew me away. While I was recovering, she gave what can only be described as a coy smile toward Clinton. "But, no, you are quite wrong! Your dear cousin is responsible for the Heaphy, for it was he who discovered it in my attic!"

I looked suitably impressed. "Yes, of course; so I had heard!"

"Sheer good fortune, I assure you . . . but come and warm yourselves by the fire; you must be chilled after such a journey." With a deprecating smile, Clinton waved us into the drawing room.

The lamps were already lit and across the windows, the portieres were half drawn against the gloom of the late afternoon. Lolling on her sofa, Lucy greeted us with a sleepy smile and wafted a plump, long-fingered hand in greeting.

"So honored, Mrs. Smythe, that you have assented to visit us! And your friends. . . ."

The stentorian voice roared out. "My house guest, Mrs. Trillingham-Bean, on a world tour with her son Gervase — unfortunately, he is of a delicate constitution and is obliged at the moment to be taking the waters in Rotorua — and . . ." The voice softened as the puce face turned toward the young woman at her side "My protégée, Miss Victoria Saxonham."

Of course, I thought, taking in the large gray eyes under delicate, feathery black brows, the long eyelashes fluttering invitingly on either side of a short, straight nose, this was Helena's oldest sister, Victoria — 'the pretty one' — and pretty she was, I had to admit.

Before I could say a word, a rattle outside the door announced the arrival of the tea trolley.

Mrs. Hodges entered with all but a fanfare of trumpets.

"Tea is served, madam!" she announced, gazing sternly at Lucy.

Lucy waved a helpless hand.

Mrs. Hodges advanced majestically, her minions behind her — Betty wheeling the trolley with Helena last as usual bearing the silver tray with its complement of silver teapot and hot-water jug, sugar bowl, and milk jug.

As Helena approached, she and Victoria exchanged a quick, surreptitious glance of affection and then studiously ignored each other. Noting my glance, Helena looked toward Mrs. Smythe and then gave me a minuscule shake of the head.

So that was the way of it; the sisters must have decided that Victoria's success might be hindered if it were known that her sister was a servant. Mrs. Smythe, I thought, must be a snob; or perhaps they were worried about Jonathan Turner's parents. I winked at Helena and gave her a reassuring smile. It would be interesting to see how it all turned out. Jonathan Turner — from the little I remembered of him — had been a bit domineering but Victoria, I noticed, had a strong, little chin. . . .

". . . doctor . . . Malvina, are you all right?"

I came to with a start to find myself the focal point of a concerned circle of eyes. Clinton, sitting next to me, leaned over and gently took my hand. "My dear, I was suggesting that we send for a doctor or even better, I should be glad to escort you to your father's town house in Wanganui where a doctor could attend to you more readily. We could catch the steamer tomorrow on its way back to town and Norah would be pleased to come along to look after you until you are better."

His grasp on my hand tightened and his glance was all tender concern. From out the corner of my eye, I saw Mrs. Smythe and Mrs. Trillingham-Bean exchange knowing looks.

With difficulty I dragged my eyes away from his mesmeric gaze.

"Thank you, but I believe I am quite recovered." Gently, I removed my hand and then lied through my teeth. "I was merely daydreaming just now, thinking what fun the house party will be when the other guests have arrived. It must be an age since Ravensfall entertained so many; how pleased Great Uncle Josiah would be! And what about tomorrow? Did you not say that we are all going over to the Turners? I certainly would not wish to miss that!"

"But my dearest Malvina." A throaty warning from Lucy. "Surely such hectic entertainment will be too much for you in your present state. . . ."

Almost in unison, the heads of Mrs. Smythe and Mrs. Trillingham-Bean nodded. Mrs. Hodges, as befitted her place as supervisor, remained firmly rivetted by Lucy's sofa, her steel gaze quietly encompassing the scene and finally coming to rest in silent reproval — on me.

I took a deep breath and was careful to keep my voice level. "I believe that I should be the best one to know how I feel, Cousin Lucy. Believe me, if I say I am all right. I really am all right!"

Lucy began pouring the tea and smiled prettily at Mrs. Smythe. "How stubborn our dearest Malvina is! Well, we shall just have to see! Do you take sugar, Mrs. Smythe? Yes? One lump or two?"

Somehow I survived the polite conversation that followed and the occasional surreptitious glances cast my way by our guests.

Finally, it was decided that the ladies would retire to their rooms to refresh themselves and that we should all meet in the drawing room at six o' clock for sherry.

"Dinner will not be served until eight," Lucy informed us, "to give you time to view the paintings we have hung in the dining room."

Mrs. Smythe handed her empty cup and saucer to Betty. "I am all agog, my dear Mrs. Wilkinson! What an honor to be the first to see your collection . . . which I hope will also contain some of the paintings of Mister Lucas and Mister Raven?"

She threw another coy smile at Clinton and glanced up girlishly from beneath her lashes.

Clinton responded with a bow. "You honor us, Mrs. Smythe! I am very much afraid that beside the masters that Mister Duvall has acquired on his travels that our poor attempts will seem trivial indeed!" He glanced politely at the other guests. "And you, Miss Saxonham, Mrs. Trillingham-Bean? Do you have a fondness for art, also?"

Victoria smiled and blushed prettily, leaving the field to Mrs. Trillingham-Bean who — small brown eyes gleaming — took over nicely. "Not so much a fondness as an admiration, dear Gervase and I on our travels make it a point to visit each and every gallery in whatever city we find ourselves. Of course, unlike myself, my darling Gervase, having had the best of tutors, is quite an expert. In fact, there are times when he quite despairs of me!"

How very like a pigeon she was, with her short, plump figure and shelflike bosom. She did not so much sit on her chair as roost! I was obliged to turn a sudden spurt of giggles into a coughing fit. Hurriedly, I excused myself, well aware of the raised eyebrows on concerned faces as I left the room.

Five o'clock on a dark, wet evening I dressed in rose-pink velvet, an amethyst and sapphire necklace — my father's twenty-first birthday gift — about my neck, complemented by my stepmother's gift of seed pearl and amethyst earrings.

There was a knock at the door.

Helena.

"If you please, miss . . . ooh, Miss Raven! You do look beautiful; if you'll just let me get at that hair!"

Within five seconds I was seated at the dressing table and an animated Helena, a pair of scissors produced magically from her apron pocket, had clipped a feathery fringe about my forehead and feathery tendrils over each ear. The rest was piled in a gleaming topknot encircled by a lace-edged, rose-pink taffeta ribbon which was sufficiently loose to allow tendrils of my fine hair to drift naturally down to my shoulders.

I looked in the glass. "Oh, Helena . . . how ever did you manage it?"

Total incomprehension. "I dunno, I really don't — it's just that once the scissors are in my hands, they seem to have a life of their own!"

I started to laugh then stopped as an idea occurred to me. "You know, Helena, you really have a gift — and you could make your fortune with it! Perhaps not in Wanganui, but in some larger city. . . ."

"Do you really think so, miss?" The little face gazing into the glass was rapt. "But whatever am I thinking, miss! I had quite forgot — Mrs. Wilkinson told me to ask you if you would go down to the drawing room a few minutes early as she has something particular to say to you. . . . Oh, dear, I do hope . . ."

I glanced at the clock. "Don't worry, there's still plenty of time.

On my way downstairs, the strains of a Beethoven sonata wafted up to me through the partly opened doors of the drawing room. Bertram, I thought — and remembered his nighttime visit. Or had the whole thing been a dream, just like the nightmare preceding it?

I paused a moment, my hand tightening on the banister. How real that had seemed, that nightmare interview with Callum, his green eyes mocking me above the candle flame and then immediately afterward, Bertram's brown eyes pleading wih me at my bedside — and they had both warned of danger. "Ye maung go," Callum had murmured and then Bertram's urgent whisper. "There's danger . . . danger. . . ."

What was real? What was not real?

The two dreams seemed indissolubly tied together.

It was because of them, I told myself, that the foreboding I had sensed all evening seemed to build in force.

"Don't be ridiculous!" I told myself out loud. Seizing the banister firmly, I sailed down the staircase, crossed the hall, and entered the drawing room.

The music stopped as I entered and the usual creaking sounded as Bertram struggled down from the daïs. Lucy, lounging on her sofa by the fireside, a box of chocolates inevitably by her side, greeted me with a thoughtful stare. "How very charming you look, Malvina, your hair is particularly becoming! However, you still look a trifle pale: I really think it would be wise for you to see a doctor."

"Is that what you wanted to talk to me about, Cousin Lucy?"

"Well, yes; I thought perhaps it was a matter of pride."

"Pride?"

"That you did not want to admit to a weakness in front of our guests. I thought that if I saw you alone, you would feel free to confide in me . . . that perhaps I could persuade you . . . Clinton and I are both very concerned about you, you know. . . ."

At that moment, lulled by the golden light of that lamplit room and basking in the warmth from the fire, I very nearly told her my fears about Devlin Fordyke. What, I wonder now, would have happened if I had?

Before I could begin, however, Bertram, who had finally managed to negotiate the steps from the daïs, hobbled up to the sofa.

A look of distaste passed over Lucy's features before she addressed her son. "If you are not going to practice, Bertram, you had better go to your room . . . and now, Malvina, you were about to say?"

Relapsing into her usual somnolence, she settled back against the cushions and selected a chocolate with lethargic fingers before absentmindedly passing the box to me. "Do try one of these cherry liqueurs . . . they are delicious."

"Thank you." Perhaps, I thought, now was the time to find out just what my cousins actually knew about Devlin Fordyke and how he had conned them into trusting him . . . and then perhaps, I could reveal my anxieties. I would wait though until Bertram was safely out of the room.

Raising the chocolate to my lips, I took a small bite. As usual, she was right; it was delicious. I smiled at her, "You certainly are a connoisseur of chocolates, Lucy!"

I raised the rest of the chocolate to my lips but before I could bite into it, there was a thud and a crash. Bertram, making his way past Lucy's sofa, had somehow tripped, one of his crutches missing his mother by a fraction of an inch, the other swooping down on the chocolate box between us sending its contents out over the carpet.

Several events then happened at once: Lucy shrieked, the remains of my own chocolate flew out my fingers as I struggled up to help Bertram, and the drawing-room door opened to reveal Devlin Fordyke.

Never have I seen such a large man move so quickly. Almost instantly, it seemed to me, Bertram was set upright — his bones were examined for possible hurts — then sent on his way; Lucy was restored with a glass of sherry from one of the decanters already set out for the evening; and I was rewarded with an ironic smile.

"We meet again, Miss Raven! And in yet another moment of crisis!"

I adjusted my pince-nez and gazed coolly up. "So we do, Mister Fordyke, but certainly not in circumstances of my choosing."

He barely restrained a laugh. "Not of your choosing. No, not precisely. . . ."

I curbed an impulse to kick him in the shins and retained my cool exterior. "What then, do you suggest, Mister Fordyke?"

He flashed a positive grin of delight. "What do I suggest, Miss Raven? Why nothing more than a glass of sherry! Please allow me?" Bowing, he gestured invitingly toward the sherry decanter.

I thought of the cups of tea passed to me by him and barely repressed a shudder. "No, thank you."

At that moment the door opened again to admit my cousin Clinton shepherding Mrs. Smythe, Victoria Saxonham, and Mrs. Trillingham-Bean, all accompanied by a benignly smiling Paul Lucas and a silent Norah Hackett.

Introductions were performed and sherry served; Devlin Fordyke raised an amused eyebrow as I accepted a glass from the silver tray held by Betty. He and Mrs. Trillingham-Bean, I noted with interest, greeted each other as if they had never met before. Absent-mindedly, I sipped at my sherry, remembering my first evening at Foster's Hotel; Mrs. Trillingham-Bean's reaction when Fordyke had entered the dining room and her watchful presence afterward, as I had parted from the huge American at the foot of the stairs.

With a little shiver, I remembered the newspaper article; was it possible that Mrs. Trillingham-Bean was another member of the gang? Were she and Devlin Fordyke planning a robbery this weekend . . . or was she here simply to size up the situation? Either way, I decided, no matter how foolish I might sound, it was my duty to let my cousins know my misgivings. I made up my mind to corner Clinton by himself after dinner.

Nervous though I still was, I felt relieved that at last I had made a decision. I looked toward Devlin Fordyke chatting politely with a blushing Victoria Saxonham.

"Such a gentleman, even though he is an American," hissed Mrs. Smythe beside me in a discreet whisper loud enough to be heard out in the hall. "I daresay his family is descended from the Essex Fordykes — a very distinguished branch, don't you know!"

It was on the tip of my tongue to say that they were probably smugglers, when I was saved from indiscretion by Lucy suggesting that we all go to the dining room to view the pictures kindly arranged by Mr. Duvall, who, unfortunately, having urgent business, could not be present. But no doubt the ladies had met him as he had boarded the steamer they were leaving?

The ladies admitted that they had.

"Such a distinguished-looking gentleman!" Mrs. Trillingham-Bean agreed as we all moved toward the door. "And I understand from Mister Raven, very well known in the art world! I am looking forward to speaking with him on his return!"

"So exciting, my dear Miss Raven, to be the very first to view the paintings!" Mrs. Smythe's foghorn voice blasted my ear. "Mrs. Wilkinson arranged it on purpose, don't you know, telling me to come two days earlier than the other guests, so that I could have first choice — so very kind!" She squeezed my arm delightedly as we left the drawing room.

Rubbing my smarting arm, I nodded my assent.

Before I could prevent it, she grabbed my arm again. "How fortunate you are, Miss Raven, to have such distinguished relatives! But then an artistic streak runs in your family, does it not? I understand that the late Josiah Raven was quite a collector of early colonial art. Just the other day, Mister Sargeant — Mister Henry Sargeant, you know, of the Wanganui Arts and Crafts Society — was telling me that you have some splendid early watercolors in the library here and also in your town house. I was telling him about my Heaphy, don't you know, that your clever cousin found for me and he said — Mister Sargeant, that is — that he had heard there are one or two fine Heaphys in your town house and also a splendid Kinder! Mister Sargeant would like the city to have an art museum, don't you know, and he was wondering if perhaps . . . oh!"

The flow of words was interrupted by the opening of the dining room door and the sight beyond.

The dining room, usually a trifle gloomy, was ablaze with light; freshly lit candles in the chandeliers and candelabrum and it seemed to me that every lamp in the house had been put to use. Against the dark paneling of the walls, the paintings were arranged in splendid display.

We all stood for a moment, dazzled. No wonder, I thought, that Mrs. Smythe had suddenly been bereft of words!

With soft exclamations of delight, we made our way around the room, stopping now and then to gaze raptly at a particularly fine work of art. I recognized many of the oils I had seen stacked aagainst the walls in the attic studio and the watercolors Clinton had shown me, were all there, but Mrs. Smythe's Heaphy still hung in pride of place above the dining room table.

What was it about this picture, I asked myself yet again that rang such a bell of recognition in my head? I gazed up at it for so long, I felt my head swimming.

"Malvina, my dear, are you quite all right?"

My arm was gently taken and I found myself looking up at a concerned Clinton.

"Quite all right," I assured him, though it seemed to me that his face kept shifting out of focus. I blinked my eyes and disengaging myself, moved away. Oh, please God, I prayed in my mind, not dizziness again! I forced myself to stand still and under the pretense of gazing at an oil, took a deep breath and blinked rapidly.

It was no use; the picture before me seemed to move in the dazzling light and I felt the all too familiar fuzziness inside my head.

Mind over matter, I told myself firmly! The attack at least was not as bad as the other two I had suffered, not nearly. Keep calm, I told myself, think logically.

On the other side of the room, Devlin Fordyke's back seemed

to sway slightly as he studied a watercolor. How had he done it? I wondered. I had refused the sherry he had offered and the glass I had finally accepted, had been one of many I had watched Betty pouring from the same decanter. And I had neither drank nor eaten anything else, except of course, the chocolate Lucy had offered me — and not, remembering the debacle Bertram had caused, much of that!

I moved onto the next picture; it was the Matisse I had noticed in the hall the day before of a flaxen-haired nude stretched out on a many cushioned, blue chaise longue. Again, I experienced a sense of recognition. What was wrong with me, besides the dizziness? Was I also now imagining things?

I blinked again and forced my eyes to focus on the picture. The nude, back turned, her long flaxen hair half obscuring her profile, was reaching out to a small dish on a nearby side table. The cushions upon which she was reclining were in shades varying from orange to purple. The carpet beneath the chaise longue was rose pink and in Matisse's usual detailed, colorful style, patterned with garlands of roses and what appeared to be carnations.

The carpet; I had seen it before — and the chaise longue with its cushions, that despite the diversity of their coloring, seemed to blend into the scene as a whole. Yes. I had studied this scene before — in Clinton's and Paul's studio.

I took a deep breath and told myself that I must have misheard or misunderstood Georges Duvall — unless in the unlikely event my cousins had entertained Matisse recently, obviously, this could not be a painting of his! I bent forward to examine the signature, expecting to see that of Paul or Clinton.

The small, neatly brushed signature across the lower right-hand corner was that of Henri Matisse.

The picture had to be a forgery, a brilliant forgery; but if indeed it had been painted up in the attic studio, who had been the model?

I turned. Across the room, next to Devlin Fordyke stood flaxen-haired Norah Hackett.

How could I have been so deluded?

I had worried about Fordyke's diabolical plans when all this time he and the others must have been laughing at me — no wonder he had "won their confidence"; quite obviously, they were all in the plot together!

I looked toward a delighted Mrs. Smythe, exclaiming over the Kinder—if it was indeed a Kinder—Clinton had shown me in the attic. With Victoria in tow, she turned to look at the next picture quite unaware that she was the focal point of several pairs of observant eyes. Poor Mrs. Smythe, I thought, her snobbery making her so vulnerable to a clever confidence trick. I remembered my sarcastic thoughts concerning Mrs. Trillingham-Bean and the way she had seemed to roost pigeonlike upon her chair. How wrong I had been—it was Mrs. Smythe who was the pigeon; a rich pigeon, all ready to be plucked!

As I watched, she paused beneath her Heaphy.

The Heaphy. Of course! What had Mrs. Smythe told me about the Heaphys and the Kinder in our town house? No wonder the watercolor had seemed to be familiar! I remembered now, the paintings where they had hung in my father's study. Had Clinton taken it and placed it in Mrs. Smythe's attic in order to win her confidence? Or was it perhaps a copy? What had the article said? That the thieves would make copies of the paintings they stole and sell them as originals to gullible collectors? Sometimes, in fact, to prevent discovery of the theft, they would hang a copy in the place of the original they had stolen.

I looked back at the supposed Matisse. Either make copies of originals, I thought, or paint brilliantly in the *style* of the artist, which in a way made more sense, as with this method they were saved the danger of having first to steal!

I looked at all the paintings. Were they all forgeries? What a fortune—even if an illicit one—was repesented here! No wonder they had been giving me laudanum. Sooner or later, they must have thought, I would have realized what was going on.

My head was aching from my whirling thoughts and I knew from the burning of my cheeks that my face was flushed. Whatever was I to do?

Fortunately, although I still felt a certain fuzziness, it had grown no worse: with effort I could focus my eyes. The main thing, I realized, was to prevent myself from falling asleep and to do that I had to keep moving—preferably in fresh, outside air.

That I was indeed, no worse, puzzled me.

The chocolates, I thought suddenly! Of course, what a fool I had been! Lucy and her chocolates. It was the chocolate that had contained the laudanum and I was no worse, simply because I had not eaten all of it. I remembered my waking dream of Bertram and his warning of danger. Had it then, after all, not been a dream? Did Bertram, in fact, know what was going on and had he tripped deliberately with the intent of spilling the chocolates, thus saving me?

Had Lucy seen the chocolate flying from my fingers? I did not think so. She had shrieked and thrown up her hands to ward off one of Bertram's crutches.

Despite myself, I could not keep from shaking. They all thought that I had taken the laudanum and would soon succumb.

What was I to do? What would they do if they discovered that I knew all about their dreadful business? I remembered with a shiver that a young man had been killed during their last robbery.

A brilliant thought occurred to me. I would do what they expected. I would pretend to have a dizzy turn and thus manage to escape to my room where I could restore myself at my open window before deciding what to do.

"Dinner is about to be served, madam," announced Hodges, just as I staggered and collapsed artistically onto the floor.

Thirty-two

It was half-past six on a dark, dismal morning, with rain pounding against my window pane. Despite my best intentions of the night before to stay awake, once my head rested on the pillow and a clucking Mrs. Hodges accompanied by a concerned Betty had left my room, I had fallen fast asleep.

So deep had been my sleep that I remembered no nightmares, but it seemed to me that sometime during the night I had sensed a presence in my room. Exhaustion, probably even more than the laudanum, had kept me from stirring—and there had been a familiar, soothing quality about the rough-skinned hands I dimly remembered lightly touching my forehead and smoothing back my hair, totally chasing away my fears.

I struggled up against my pillows and found to my relief that that there was no hint of headache or grogginess, but the memory flooding back of the previous night's events brought with it a chilling numbness; the ice-cold numbness of fear.

What was I to do?

Was there anyone I could trust?

Mrs. Hodges? Betty? Helena?

Would they believe me, if I told them? Or would they go straight to Lucy or Clinton concerned that my illness had unhinged my mind?

The same was true of Mrs. Smythe, if I tried to warn her. Clinton and Lucy had done their work well, making me appear so ill.

I could trust Bertram, of course—but poor little mite, how

could he help me? Further, heaven knew what they would do to him, if they suspected! In fact, the same was true regarding the domestic staff, if I persuaded any of them to help me. I thought of the young man they had killed and shuddered: these people would stop at nothing.

Perhaps, I thought with grim humor, I was fortunate that so far they had done nothing more to me than ply me with laudanum . . . if, indeed, it *was* laudanum!

I thought of Clinton's offer to escort me to our town house. No doubt this was a tactic to get me out of the way. Did he hope to have me half drugged before we started, to show the world how sick I was . . . so that any stories I might try to tell would be discredited? And once in Wanganui, would he really fetch a doctor or would he leave me under lock and key in the charge of Norah Hackett?

What I needed, I told myself, was *proof* — one of the forgeries, perhaps? — that I could show the police. But how would I manage to obtain the painting and to leave with it, undetected? And once in Wanganui, how would I prove that it was indeed a forgery? By the time experts had been called in to back up my story, the thieves would be gone — and Mrs. Smythe's money . . . and no doubt the money of the other guests . . . with them.

Proof, I thought. There must be something incriminating besides the paintings themselves. With a start, I remembered the letters I had seen on the night of my arrival in Clinton's sitting room and the accounts I had noted on the table in the studio. There had to be something I could use among all those papers . . . but how was I going to get hold of them?

Of course! They were all going over to the Turners later in the day and as was usual on these occasions, the servants with them.

There would be no surprise at my continued "illness." All I had to do was to breathe stertorously and feign extreme dizziness if roused. In such a condition, they could hardly put me on the steamer. Instead, I would be left in peace in my room. I would have the house to myself. No doubt someone would be left to look after me, but I would cope with that problem when it arose!

My ruse worked.

Well after the time the *Waiwere* would have called in on her way back to Wanganui, I "awoke" sufficiently to assure an anxious Mrs. Hodges that I was indeed well enough for her to go with the others and that Helena was perfectly capable of looking after me for an afternoon.

"For we shall be back, miss, Hodges and me, directly after dinner!"

I made my voice sound suitably sleepy. "Oh, please, Mrs. Hodges, not on my account, I beg you! Surely you will want to stay for the dance in the wool shed?"

She glanced wistfully. "No. Hodges doesn't dance. And anyway, we're beyond all that. I just want to see my sister, who's housekeeper to the Turners.

I nodded, remembering my first evening at the deserted Ravensfall. "Your sister, yes; naturally."

"Yes, miss. As I said, I just want to see her—at her age—though, of course, she's much younger than I am, being rightfully only my youngest half-sister—and in her condition?"

"Her condition? Oh!"

A blush. "Yes, miss. Of course, Hodges and I had always hoped that we . . . but there was only the one—and then . . .excuse me, I shouldn't be mentioning such things to a young, unmarried lady!"

"Why ever not, Mrs. Hodges? I assure you that Harriet—that is, my stepmother—has always been quite frank about these things!"

A ruffling of the black-bombazined bosom. "Well that's as maybe, miss. But I'll say no more about it. Now, if you are quite sure you are feeling a little better, I'll take my leave . . . the family has left already and Hodges and I and the rest will go when the dinghy comes back for us." She turned toward the window. "Thank goodness the rain has let up! Hodges tells me the river's been rising; a real worry-wart is Hodges. . . ."

In the end, of course, Mrs. Hodges was wrong and Hodges was right. The rain started up again with a vengeance and the river already swollen with its accumulated burden of the past few days, rose swiftly into flood.

Helena stood excitedly at my bedside. "Ooh, miss, you should see it! Great branches of trees floating down and I saw the carcass of a sheep, poor creature . . . ooh, miss!"

Pausing, she gazed at me, her gray eyes wide. "Mrs. Hodges and them and your cousins . . . they'll never get back across the river—they'll all have to stay with the Turners until the rain stops and the flood goes down—and that could take days! Whatever are we going to do?"

I could hardly conceal my elation. "Do? Why the best we can! We have plenty of supplies and you can cook—and so can I, for that matter. We should do well enough! Oh, Helena, I feel so much better!"

"It must have been Mrs. Hodges's special posset, miss!"

I crossed my fingers and lied. "Indeed it must!" Unknown to Helena, I had carefully tipped the posset out the window to be washed away by the rain. I trusted Mrs. Hodges but not Norah Hackett who had delivered the posset and who—thankfully— had left the drink by my bed, when, not responding to her urgent tugs and pulls, I had pretended to be in a deep sleep.

I smiled at Helena, a plan formulating in my mind. "You know, I feel so much better, I am actually hungry. Do you think you could prepare me some poached eggs on toast? With perhaps a slice of Mrs. Hodges's ham? I believe I shall get up for a while; perhaps I could have a tray by the library fire?"

As soon as Helena had shut the door, I eased myself out of bed and crossed to the window. One of these days, I thought, I would find some way of thanking Bertram for his help: if it had not been for his "accident" that I was sure he had carefully staged, I was well aware that I would have been totally disabled. I thought of my state of the morning before and shuddered.

I threw open the window and immediately closed it before pounding rain had the chance to drench my hair and nightdress.

As I closed the window, my glance fell upon my writing case

280

where I had left it, still unopened, on the desk beside Edward's miniature. Perhaps, I thought—just in case—I should write down some of my worries and suspicions and leave them in a sealed envelope with Helena.

I pulled the case toward me and opened it. On the top reposed Papa's letters to his solicitor and to Cousin Clinton.

I gazed at them unbelievingly. I *knew* I had not put them there. But if I had not put them there, who had—and why? And why had they taken them in the first place?

It is time, Malvina Raven that you took some action!

Half an hour later, warmly dressed, my woolen skirts concealing my sturdy riding boots—my boat cloak and carpetbag hidden behind a chair—I sat beside the library fire, the promised tray on a small table in front of me.

Helena, I was relieved to see, had done her best to impress me. Besides the poached eggs on toast and the inevitable teapot, there were several slices of ham, extra toast, a plate of buttered date scones, and a selection of apples and pears.

As soon as Helena left, I quickly made sandwiches with the ham and extra toast, wrapping these with the scones in my napkin, placing the resulting package with the apples and pears in my carpetbag.

I then devoured the poached eggs and sank back as if drowsy, into the chair cushions as I heard Helena's approach down the passage.

"Oh, miss! You really must have been hungry!"

The look on Helena's face as she looked down at the denuded tray was comical. Despite the nervousness that ate at my nerves, it was hard to refrain from laughing.

I affected a drowsy surprise. "Yes. Yes, I suppose I was! Perhaps that is why I feel so sleepy!" I yawned. "Perhaps I shall stay here for a while. Doze and then read a little . . . please don't worry about me, Helena, I really am much better and would like to be left alone for a while. You must have things to attend to?"

"Well, yes, miss! If you're *sure* you're all right? Mrs. Hodges said as how I was to sort the laundry, mend some bed linen, and clean the silver."

281

Thank God, I thought, looking at the closed door after Helena had left, at least an hour of freedom!

I sprang into action.

While eating my poached eggs, I had finalized the plans I had made while I was dressing. I would conceal my cloak and carpetbag in the cloakroom off the hall and then make my way to Clinton's sitting room on the first floor. If my search revealed nothing incriminating, I would find the key to the studio and climb up to the attics. There must be something, surely, that I could use — and after I had found it?

That, of course, was the tricky part.

The flood that kept my enemies over the river also prevented me from making my way down to Wanganui. The *Waiwere* would not, of course, sail in such circumstances and I had no knowledge of the time-honored tracks leading through the bush down to the coast.

I should have to go in the opposite direction, upriver rather than down. When we were children, Reggie and I had often ridden with Ishbel and Miss Inglewood through the bush to visit the vineyard on the other side of the bluff. Ishbel had taken piano lessons there, from Hélène DuPrès, the wife of the owner. Of course, as I had found out from Clinton on my first evening at Ravensfall, the DuPrès were no longer there. The question was, were the new people friends of Lucy and Clinton, or not? Were they part of the gang?

I should have to take my chances; there was nothing else to do. Perhaps, after sounding them out, I found I distrusted them, I would make some excuse to leave and hide out in the bush until the flood had subsided and the *Waiwere* was sailing again.

Seizing up my cloak and carpetbag, I put the first part of my plan into action.

In the late afternoon light, Clinton's sitting room was damp, dark, and cold, and yielded no clues. Thoughtfully, I drew the curtains over the rain-drenched windows before lighting the lamp on his writing table.

Still nothing.

Of the letters I had noted earlier, there was no sign.

The key, then. Nothing for it, but a visit to the studio, much as I disliked the idea of making my way up those dark, lonely stairs.

Finally, I found the key secreted in an ornamental urn on the mantelpiece.

I turned off the lamp and drew back the curtains. All must appear as usual, I decided, in case — somehow or other — Clinton managed to return.

The attic stairs were as dark and lonely as I had expected and the studio, once I had reached it, almost as dim, lit only by the last pale light seeping through the rain-pounded, westward-facing dormer windows.

The deal table, however, was still piled with papers, I was relieved to see and — surprisingly — Clinton's portrait of Lucy was still on its easel. I looked about for a lamp to dispel the dimness and was shockingly rewarded as I glanced back through the door behind me, by a soft glow seemingly emanating from somewhere down the attic stairs.

As I watched, the light quickly grew in intensity.

Please God, let it be Helena, I prayed. On finding the library empty, she had probably set out to find me — but just in case, I looked about for a hiding place, finally in the short time left to me, settling behind the japanned screen beside the chaise longue, my eye peering frantically through the gaps above the fastenings securing the panels.

It was not Helena.

The enormous, ranging shadow, magnified even more by the roving light that seemed to explore every corner and crevice of the studio, belonged to Devlin Fordyke.

I drew a deep breath and stood paralyzed as the huge American rested his lamp on the table and sorted through the piles of papers. Finally, carefully folding some of the papers and placing them in an inner pocket of his jacket, he turned toward some low cupboards under the windows that on my last visit had been obscured by rows of canvasses, which I supposed were now on display in the dining room.

Taking a key from his pocket, he unlocked the doors to the cupboards and after rummaging, took out several rolls of what looked like canvass, which he unrolled and brought over to the light. After carefully examining them he stood still a moment, his head bowed. At last, giving himself a shake, he carefully re-rolled the canvasses and returned them to the cupboard, which he locked.

I waited fearfully as he shone his lamp once more about the studio and then — to my intense relief — finally left.

I crept out from behind the screen and watched from the head of the stairs until the glow from his lamp died away. What had he been about? I wondered.

There was just enough light left for me to see the outlines of the studio furniture: the deal table with its pile of papers, the chaise longue with its accompanying japanned screen and side tables, the two easels and in the shadows at the back, the smaller table where I had seen the folder containing the watercolors. It was on this smaller table that I finally spied a lamp.

Did I dare light it?

I decided to take the chance.

I lit the lamp from the box of Lucifers I found nearby and held it up. The light fell at once upon the easel holding Lucy's portrait.

The one portrait, I thought ironically, that had to be original!

Curious, I wandered over.

From her straight-backed chair, the japanned screen behind her, Lucy's dark eyes gazed out at me. A very good likeness as I had assured Clinton — but the languor, the lethargy that at the same time conveyed an insolent contempt; in other words, the innate Lucy was missing.

I remembered Clinton's agony when he had showed me the portrait and compared it with the one by Bonnard he had thrown up on the other easel. "An excellent copyist, am I not?" he had asked, his eyes filled with despair.

Was this then why he forged paintings; seeking, always seeking to make other men's skills his own?

I leaned forward, examining the portrait more closely.

Across the lower left-hand corner was painted neatly, the signature in careful hooks and whirls — Aaron Blunt.

Aaron Blunt?

Where had I seen that name before? Of course! I remembered my arrival — only, what was it, three, four nights ago? — and the letters floating down from the table in Clinton's sitting room, one of them, as I remembered, addressed to Aaron Blunt. In my ignorance, I had thought my cousin must have been writing to someone named Aaron Blunt — but in actual fact, the letter was to him.

My cousin?

If Clinton Raven in actual fact was Aaron Blunt, then he was not my cousin. And if he was not my cousin then who was he and how did he — and all the others — come to be at Ravensfall?

In a daze, I wandered over to the deal-topped table and riffled through the papers. Sure enough, most of them were addressed to Aaron Blunt and appeared to be agreements of some kind with Jacques Pascal.

What was I to do?

There was more — much more — to this whole situation than I had thought. And what would happen if they found out how much I knew? I thought of my close brush with Devlin Fordyke and shuddered.

Quickly, I seized two of the letters at random — but proof or no proof, I decided, it was time that I was gone!

Downstairs at last. To my surprise the long clock in the hall showed a mere five o'clock — hardly a half hour had passed since my excursion to the attics.

Swathed in my boat cloak and carrying my carpetbag, I opened the front door a fraction and peered out into the still teeming rain. It was still light outside, though barely.

I would make my way to the stable yard, and hide in one of the empty stalls — and at first light, I would saddle one of the chestnuts and set off for the old DuPrès vineyard.

What about Helena? I could hardly leave her!

Five minutes later, accompanied by a protesting, frightened

Helena—I would explain everything later, I had told her—I made my way along the track to the stables.

A light glowed through the open door of Tamati's whare; otherwise the yard was wrapped in gloom. Beau Brumell's stall was empty, I noted, surprised but pleased. Where Devlin Fordyke could have gone on such a night and in such circumstances, I had no idea; but the thought that he was not around made me sigh with relief; my one fear had been that we might have met up with him before we could hide ourselves in the empty stall.

We reached the stall at last and settled ourselves on some straw. I was about to explain everything to Helena, when reaching into my pocket for a handkerchief to stifle a sneeze, I felt the cold iron of the key to the attic studio. I had been in such a panic I had completely forgotten to return it to Clinton's sitting room.

What if the man calling himself Clinton Raven came back to find that not only myself but also the key was missing? He would know at once that I had discovered his identity. Surely, this would give him even more reason to search for me—and if he returned before we reached the vineyard . . .

I shivered. The key would have to be returned.

After all, I told myself, there should be no danger. The house was empty. My so-called cousins could not possibly return that night—and Devlin Fordyke had evidently ridden off.

The rain had eased at last and in a rising moon's weak light revealed by parting, storm-tossed clouds, Ravensfall stood out, dark, ominous.

I was not afraid, I lied firmly to myself. The house was empty; all I had to do was walk firmly up the steps into the hall, light a lamp, climb the stairs and put back the key into the urn on the sitting room mantelpiece.

Wishing all at once that I had brought Helena with me instead of making her stay behind, I forced myself across the lawn and up the steps onto the veranda.

The door swung open at my touch and I stood a moment, listening—no sound except for an occasional creaking expected from an old building made of wood.

The house was empty, I reassured myself. Why then did I have that inexplicable feeling of a presence other than my own?

You have too much imagination, Malvina Raven. Firmly I stepped across the threshold into the hall, comforted by the thought of the lamps on the rosewood table. I struck a light and as I did so, a faint glow appeared at the top of the stairs.

I stood in shock, the flickering Lucifer between my fingers, as onto the first-floor landing stepped the long, dark figure of a man. He was holding the lamp at such an angle, only the top half of his head was fully illumined; green eyes staring from a pale face.

The Lucifer flared, searing my fingers and then dropped unheeded onto the floor.

This was no nightmare, this was no ghost; this, in truth, was Callum Douglas.

Thirty-three

Callum Douglas. Subconsciously, I must have known the truth from the beginning — that feeling of familiarity I had experienced when we had met that first evening at Foster's Hotel; and then, of course, my sharp sense of recognition as his rangy, long-legged figure emerged out of the mist on that fog-bound night of his arrival at Ravensfall.

Why had I not trusted my senses? I asked myself. Why had I allowed myself to be fooled — even after twelve years — by dyed hair, a bushy beard, and a guttural, French-Canadian accent?

Because I had been told he was dead? Or, more importantly, because I desperately had wanted to believe this? In other words, had I been more accepting of the nightmare than the reality?

The lamp Callum held shone down the stairs, enveloping me in a pool of light.

On the rosewood table, clear for him to see, lay the iron key to the studio that I had put down while searching for the Lucifers to light the lamps.

The door creaked in a rising breeze, exaggerating the silence. At last he spoke, the tone regretful, the French-Canadian accent abandoned.

"I tried to warn you, Mallie. . . . Why did ye not go, when ye had the chance?" His highland accent was soft, compelling. "Clinton would not have harmed ye?"

Looking up at those cool green eyes, I knew it useless to dissimulate, to pretend I did not know who he was. "Clinton, perhaps not — but Norah Hackett?"

288

A soft chuckle as he began to descend the stairs. "Aye, ye have me there. But see ye here, even Norah Hackett would be preferable to what must happen now."

He stepped down another stair. "I'm sorry, Mallie, I really am . . . ye've grown into better than I expected, puling brat that ye were. But ye see the necessity for it?"

Behind me, the front door still yawned open onto the moonlit lawn but I did not dare turn my head. Humor him, I told myself and when you see your chance, pick up your skirts and run.

He flashed an engaging smile. "Ye wish to humor me? To distract my attention — and then run through yon doorway? Ye can try it but . . ."

He descended another two steps.

"It wouldna work. . . ."

Another step. "Malvina, lassie, it's the *taniwha* for you."

He was enjoying this, I suddenly realized, in the manner of a huge cat stalking its prey.

"Aye, it's the *taniwha* for you, just as Ishbel would have wanted."

Three more steps were descended as the smile turned cold. "You think you are a superior race, you Ravens. . . . How will you like it, I wonder, when you meet with Ishbel in the river — the river, where, because of you and your kind, she ended her young life. . . ."

The last few remaining stairs were bounded down.

Quickly, I seized up the lamp I had decided upon as a weapon, but before I could use it, from somewhere down the passage leading to the library trilled a low, bell-like laugh.

For an ice-cold moment, total silence, then two things happened at once with great speed: Callum Douglas rushed off down the library passage and I fled across the hall, hurtled through the doorway and — leaping down the steps from the veranda — twisted my still weak ankle as I fell into a heap on the moonlit lawn.

Somehow, I struggled up.

To the stables, I told myself, right away.

Unfortunately, as I limped toward the bush track, a familiar figure broke out of it.

Tamati, I thought in fright, in league with Callum Douglas.

Panic-stricken, I turned and ran haltingly back over the lawn, paying no attention to Tamati's shouts. Trying to ignore the shooting pains from my ankle, I at last stumbled around the side of the house and past the library window.

Sobbing for breath, I paused a moment. Where, I wondered, could I hide? Perhaps somewhere at the back of the house?

Not to be. Paying little attention, in my frantic haste as to where I put my feet, I tripped over the roots of the ancient pohutakawa tree outside the study window, again wrenching my ankle as I fell.

Somewhere behind me, a door burst open and footsteps thudded to where I lay, desperately trying to untangle myself from my twisted skirts. I felt myself seized and dragged up. Above me loomed the pale face of Callum Douglas; even in the moonlight, I could see the cold fury of his green eyes.

My struggles availed me nothing, hampered as I was by my skirts and wrecked ankle. Though I twisted and turned and raked the face above me with my nails, I felt myself hoisted up, thrown over a shoulder, and then carried swiftly over the lawn down to the River Walk.

The river, I thought in terror; even from the top of the cliff, I could hear its flooded waters rushing in the gorge below.

"The *taniwha*, Malvina Raven; go join your sister and tell her . . ."

There was a sudden lurch as abruptly his words stopped in midsentence and I found myself falling to the ground.

Tamati Raven had come to rescue me. As I looked up he and Callum Douglas began their death struggle.

Thirty-four

I felt a tugging at my arms and shoulders. "Malvina! Malvina Raven!"

In the moonlight, a pale triangular face gazed down at me; slanting, tawny eyes sparking authority.

Miranda Fordyke.

"Come along, do! They'll be at it at least another twenty minutes — if we're lucky, half an hour — they're well-matched . . . Tamati is young but Callum Douglas knows all the dirty tricks!"

She panted as she spoke, tugging again at my arms until, at last, I managed to make it to my feet.

I gritted my teeth, trying to ignore the agonizing pain from my ankle. "The stables. . . ."

"No. Too far . . . and anyway, that's the first place he'll look; there and in the bush. . . . We'll go back to the house. . . ."

"To the house?"

"Yes — but not to your room. . . ."

Somehow, with Miranda's help, I struggled up to the house, in through the side door and up the stairs to the third floor, reaching at last the governess's room that Harriet had once had and before her, Miss Inglewood.

"This is the room that is given me when I stay at Ravensfall." She spoke scarcely above a whisper and in the darkness — we had not dared to light a lamp or candle — I could hardly see her face.

We felt our way over to the window which Miranda raised cautiously while I collapsed on the cushioned window seat. Outside, the moon, almost losing its battle with the clouds, cast

291

forth but little light. Nothing could be seen — worse still, above the tumult of the flooding river, nothing else could be heard.

Was the fight over?

If so, who had won?

What had happened to the one who had lost?

Beside me, Miranda stirred. "I'm going now. Lock the door behind me and I'll lock all the other doors just to confuse him!

"Him?"

An exasperated sigh. "Callum Douglas, of course!"

"You mean, you know that Mister Duvall is actually . . ."

A moonbeam escaped a cloud, lighting up her scornful, amber eyes. "Of course I do — and so should you have done, earlier than this!" A wicked smile. "Although, to be honest, I should not have known, if I had not spied upon Papa!"

"Papa," I thought, Miranda's father — Devlin Fordyke. . . . Could I trust her or was this another part of the plot? Were they planning that I should lock myself in my own prison to wait there until . . .

My shoulders were seized and I was given a brisk shake. "For goodness, sake, Malvina, haven't you realized yet who my papa is?"

In the moonlight, her face glowed with pure amusement. "It was obvious, of course, that after you had read the *New York Times* article, you jumped to all the wrong conclusions! But I should have thought that by *now* you would have twigged!"

I tried to look innocent. "Whatever are you talking about, Miranda? What article?"

A delighted giggle. "How hopeless you are! The article you read, of course, the day you visited our cottage — and left a watering can on the dining table."

I felt my face burn, remembering my secret visit to the cottage, still carrying the watering can I had used to tend the flowers in the family graveyard.

"Of course," Miranda continued with revolting cheerfulness, "we realized at once, what had happened. . . . Who else would have used a watering can? Can you imagine Lucy Wilkinson bestirring herself — or even Horrible Hackett? And as for the men . . ."

She grinned and shrugged her shoulders.

I admitted defeat. "No, I suppose . . . but what made you think I had read the article?"

"You didn't put it back in quite the same way."

I took a deep breath. "Miranda, you seem to be on my side . . . that is, I *think* so. . . . What is this all about — I mean, apart from the art forgeries and the gulling of Mrs. Smythe and her friends?"

She cast a long, thoughtful look. "You mean the part played by my papa in all of this?" A sudden twinkle. "Yes, I thought — hoped, actually — that, that was the way of it?"

"*What?*"

She grinned. "Never mind, you'll find out soon enough, when Papa comes back. He's ridden up along the bush track, to Pipiriki. He intends to use the steamer company's pigeon post to send a message for the police in Wanganui."

The pigeon post, I thought, was used mainly to send the upper river soundings back to Hatrick's Wharf. The message would get through, of course — but how long would it take for help to arrive? And in the meantime?

Miranda read my thoughts. "And in the meantime, you must stay here, until either the police or my papa arrive."

"And why should I stay until your father arrives? Just who exactly *is* your father — and what part *does* he play in this?"

A sigh half between exasperation and amusement. "My father, Miss Raven, is Mister Devlin Fordyke of the *New York Times*."

"But . . ."

"And his part in this, is to find the murderer of my Uncle Dennis."

"But . . ."

At last the moon sailed freely from behind the clouds; in its light, Miranda's face appeared pale, strained, all amusement gone.

"Come now, Miranda. What is it — tell me. . . ."

She shook back her head, daring the tears to come. "I liked my Uncle Dennis, you see; he was kind to me. When I was little — after my mother died — he'd bring me sugar plums when my governess had put me in the corner or Grandmama had been especially stern. . . . Of course he was only twelve years older than I am. . . ."

She paused a moment and smiled a little at my puzzled face. "Grandmama married twice, you see; first to Grandpapa Fordyke and then after his death, to Mister Wellingford Francis."

"I . . . I see. . . ."

"No, you don't! What I'm trying to tell you is that my Uncle Dennis is — was — Papa's half-brother, and that he was the young man you read about in the news article — the young man who surprised the thieves and was killed."

Through the open window, the dull roar from the swollen waters rushing in the gorge far below, increased in intensity before, at last, she continued. "Papa told Grandmama that no matter what, he would find out who killed Uncle Dennis and bring him to justice!"

I thought of the watercolor I had seen in Devlin Fordyke's cottage. "Of course, D. Francis!"

"Sorry?"

"That picture I saw in your cottage, of the Grand Canyon, signed D. Francis — your uncle painted it?"

She sighed. "Yes; two summers ago. Papa took him along on one of his trips and taught him how to paint with watercolors. . . ."

"That accounts for it, then — the similarity of styles — I thought your father had painted the picture. But tell me, how did Mister Fordyke manage to trace the criminals to New Zealand — and to Wanganui, of all places?"

"His colleagues on the *Times* and Pinkerton's, of course."

"Pinkerton's?"

"The detective agency — the woman who calls herself Mrs. Trillingham-Bean and her so-called son, are agents of theirs."

I could not prevent a gasp of surprise, as into my mind flashed a picture of Mrs. Trillingham-Bean and her sharp, always-watchful, pigeon eyes.

There was an undertone of laughter in Miranda's voice as she continued. "Mrs. T-B and 'Gervase' were sent to New Zealand as soon as Pinkerton's learned that Jacques Pascall as

Callum Douglas called himself in the States, had gone there—after that it was easy."

Jacques Pascal, I thought, remembering the name on the accounts on the studio table. I recovered my voice. "Easy?"

"Yes, to find Pascall/Duvall and the others. Pinkerton's figured that once escaped from the United States, they would set up another forgery enterprise and New Zealand is such a small place, you see, that it was easy for Mrs. T-B. and Gervase to learn of it. All they had to do was to travel from town to town, making inquiries about new arrivals, painting exhibitions being held, and so forth—and that's how they heard of Clinton Raven and his tragically widowed sister, newly arrived from Canada and settled at the long-empty Ravensfall . . . and the surprising find, all Wanganui was talking about, of the Heaphy in Mrs. Smythe's attic."

The moon retreated behind the clouds again and the rain, light at first, pattered against the windowpane. In the darkness, I could hardly make out Miranda's face—but I could certainly hear her sigh of deep satisfaction before she continued. "And that was where Callum Douglas made his big mistake . . . and gave away his true identity. You see, only he could have known about Ravensfall and your family situation. But, of course, Papa didn't know all this for sure until the other day in Wanganui, when he received a cable from the *Times*, confirming that the real Clinton Raven and his sister are indeed living in Vancouver, Canada. He reported his suspicions to the police, of course, but he needed more proof. . . ."

The rain increased in momentum, pounding against the window, as Miranda began to feel her way over to the door. "You should be safe enough in here—just make sure you lock the door after I leave."

I hobbled over, clutching at chairs and table to support me. "No, Miranda—you can't—you must stay here! Callum probably saw you helping me, he might . . . !"

She laughed softly. "Oh, I shall be all right; I'm used to slipping in and out of this place—besides, I shall be very careful. But I must go back to wait for Papa and to tell Helena you are all right."

"Helena. I had forgotten all about her!"

"Luckily for you, I saw her in the stable yard as I was on my way over to Ravensfall. Papa thought you were still suffering from the effects of the laudanum and had told me to check on you. He thought the house was empty, you see, he would never have left you, else . . . Callum Douglas and Tamati must have returned from Pipiriki shortly before Papa left. . . ."

"Pipiriki!" Despite the circumstances — or perhaps, because of them — I could not prevent a note of exasperation. "What Is so compelling about Pipiriki? Mrs. Trillingham-Bean went there — and tried to hide herself from me on the steamer — your father went there just — when was it — two days ago? And now you say, Callum Douglas and Tamati have just returned from there. Just what is in Pipiriki?"

She smothered a giggle in the darkness. "Electricity!"

"What?"

"Electricity. The hotel generates its own. Oil paintings take a long time to dry, my dear Malvina, and if you are going to forge one, electric fans will speed up the process."

Fans, I thought, and remembered the conversation I had overheard between my so-called cousin and Paul Lucas — if indeed, that was his real name — when I had concealed myself in the cloakroom, the evening after my arrival. They had been worried about the fans being organized in time for the house party. In my ignorance, I had thought they were organizing some kind of fancy-dress entertainment.

A sudden, unwelcome thought occurred to me. "Tamati. You said he had returned with Callum Douglas. Is Tamati aware of what is going on?"

A soft sigh. "I fear so . . . and not only that, but some of the artifacts he is selling to Callum Douglas, he steals from the old burial caves up the river.

Tamati Raven, I thought, locking my door after Miranda's departure. Tamati, that embittered, newfound cousin of mine who had wanted so much to build a rival Ravensfall that he had defied the traditions of his Maori ancestry by selling forbidden Maori artifacts, thus inviting the consequences of *tapu*. I shuddered, as I remembered the fantail hovering in the doorway of the whare and afterward, Tamati's confrontation with his great uncle.

Tamati Raven, I thought again, my embittered, profiteering cousin who, nonetheless, had cast all thoughts of fortune aside when he had come to my rescue.

Struggling over to the window, I collapsed again onto the window seat and gazed out. The rain had eased again and again a pale moon fought its way through swirling clouds, casting its uncertain light over steaming mist rising from the tumultuous river flooding its gorge far below.

Tamati, I thought, trying to make out the River Walk and the cliff beyond. What had happened to him?

"You are accursed, you and your family . . ."

It was as though the words were spoken, so clear were they and in my mind, I saw again the ancient tattooed face of old Moana's brother — Tamati's great uncle.

"You must go from here . . ." he had told me, ". . . as all in your family bring trouble, sorrow. . . ."

He had warned me, I thought, and I had taken no heed. The moonlight grew stronger. From the River Walk below, a pale face gazed up — and although from that distance, I could not see each detail, I remembered from my nightmares, the green blaze of the eyes.

Callum Douglas.

Thirty-five

The day draws to a close and still Tamati's uncle stands on the riverbank opposite, his implacable gaze directed toward my window.

The rain has eased but down in the gorge, the swollen waters still rage in their mad rush to the sea. A wind is rising and the old house creaks and shudders and from the hall, a cold breeze whistles under my door.

Callum Douglas.

I think of his pale face in the moonlight of the night before. Is he out there somewhere in the sodden bush, searching for me through the dripping trees and ferns? Or is he already in the house, searching through the cold, dark rooms — perhaps even now creeping up the stairs? What is that soft scuffling I hear above the moaning wind? Is it Callum Douglas, slipping relentlessly along the hall, scenting me out?

Does the old man over the river know this? Is this what he is waiting for?

Why should he blame me?

What could I have done to prevent Tamati's death?

You should have left, I tell myself now, after you had been warned.

All those warnings of which I had taken no heed; the old man approaching me in the mist, Callum Douglas himself, pretending to be an apparition in a laudanum-caused nightmare, Bertram's anxious words and warning glances — even Nellie Possett, I remember, on the *Waiwere*, uttering her veiled warnings from beneath the fluttering ribbons of her hat.

Most of all, I think of myself, Malvina Raven.

Despite all the warnings, despite my own innate feelings from the beginning that something was badly wrong, I had continued on my headstrong course.

If I had left Ravensfall, would Tamati Raven still have perished?

The house shudders in a sudden burst of wind and the rain, heavy again, dashes against my window. In the hall beyond my door, the floor creaks and the scuffling grows louder then stops.

As I watch, horrified, the doorknob turns.

Will my nightmare at last meet up with reality?

A well-known voice utters my name. "Malvina Raven, open up this door before I break it down!"

Epilogue

New York
December 31, 1904

Outside, snow falls softly onto a broad, busy street bordered by massive stone buildings. How different this place is from New Zealand and how far away Ravensfall seems. Will I be happy here? I wonder.

I look down at the ruby on my finger and think about the huge man who has given it to me — of his strength and warmth when he takes me in his arms, of the surprisingly gentle touch of his large, rough fingers brushing back my hair.

I think back to that last day of terror at Ravensfall, of Devlin Fordyke striding through my doorway, catching me up, and hugging me against his broad chest.

"This is becoming a habit, Miss Raven! Tell me, is it a particular practice of yours to inveigle gentlemen into picking you up?"

I sighed, snuggling into the rough tweed of his jacket. "Only, sir, if the gentleman is sufficiently large!"

Inside his chest, the volcano rumbled, finally erupting into a joyful laugh. "In that case, Miss Raven, you had better stay with me, don't you agree?"

I looked up at him, savoring the ugly, crooked nose, the lines of humor about his hazel eyes and long, curving mouth. How could I ever have doubted this man?

I smiled sweetly. "I shall give the matter some thought!"

Somehow my chin was tipped up and a kiss, gentle at first,

but swiftly rising in intensity, was planted firmly on my lips.

"Perhaps that will help you to make up your mind?"

Being breathless, I could only nod.

He grinned and buried his face in my hair. "How could I ever have doubted you, Miss H.?"

I glared up at him in indignation. Doubted me? *You* doubted *me!*

"Of course we did! When you first arrived, Mrs. Trillingham-Bean and I both thought you had been recruited by Callum Douglas . . . we even warned your lawyers. We had been expecting something of the kind, you see!"

I thought then of my missing letters. "So, it was you who took my letters?"

"Not me; Mrs. Trillingham-Bean—after you left for Ravensfall, she took them to your lawyers to have the handwriting checked with other letters written by your father.

Another hug accompanied by a rumbling laugh. "It was soon obvious to me that your abilities—though considerable—are not suitable for forgery . . . or spying!"

He grinned wickedly. "What member of a criminal gang would leave a watering can as evidence of her visit!"

I smile now at the memories of more kisses before I was carried carefully down the stairs.

I look down again at the ruby ring he gave me, and then across the room at the mass of white tulle and satin that is my wedding dress.

Of course I shall be happy . . . no doubt there will be times when I may want to box his ears and there may be times when he will be tempted to box mine; but happy we shall be—I know that.

Through my partly opened door, a bell-like laugh hovers on the air. The sound no longer frightens me. Miranda, I think fondly, arraying herself in all her bridesmaid's glory.

"One of the things I most love about you," said Devlin, as he slipped his ruby ring on my finger, "is that way you have with the young."

"What way?"

He shrugged his huge shoulders. "Oh, I don't know, but it's obvious you really like them and you are the only person

Miranda has ever opened up to. . . . You must be wondering why I took her with me to New Zealand. . . ."

"Compassion for her grandmama?"

He grinned. "Yes. I never intended to take her to Ravensfall, you understand — at least, while that thieves' crew was there. In fact, I boarded her at the Wanganui Girls' College, but I'm afraid . . ."

"She was expelled."

A rumbling of the volcano finally erupting into a cataclysmic laugh. "Of course!"

"And afterward, you could not contain her?"

"No. Could you?"

"Probably not!"

We exchanged understanding grins.

Down the hall, Miranda's laugh sounds again and with it, the creaking, signaling the arrival of Bertram.

"I shall not marry you, Devlin Fordyke," I remember saying, "unless you agree that we adopt Bertram."

Miranda, of course — as in so many things — had been right. Callum Douglas, well aware of Bertram's potential worth, had spirited him away from an orphanage, to play the part of Lucy's son.

And Lucy and Paul Lucas and Horrible Hackett, I think now, all arrested and waiting to stand trial. What would happen to them?

And Clinton Raven — I cannot bring myself to think of him as Aaron Blunt — what of him?

In my mind, I see again the attic studio at Ravensfall and Clinton's gray eyes despairingly studying his inadequate portrait of Lucy — who was, of course, not his sister, but his mistress. It was Clinton, Devlin informed me, who had killed Dennis Francis. Though the killing had been accidental rather than intentional — the young man hitting his head against a marble statue when in the heat of the moment, Clinton had knocked him down — it was enough to put Clinton in the power of Callum Douglas, who had become an increasingly hard taskmaster, threatening him with exposure when he tried to leave the forgery ring.

Callum Douglas, I think now, with a shiver, remembering

that stormy night and his pale face gazing up from the moonlit River Walk. What had happened to him?

"He is gone, Malvina," Devlin had assured me, taking me in his arms. "Slipped away in the bush somewhere, no doubt; banish him from your thoughts, my darling, and from your dreams. You will always be safe with me."

I give myself a brisk shake and move over to my wedding dress. Soon Harriet and my sisters will come up to help me dress and Devlin's mother — too frail to make a winter journey for an English wedding — will come by to give me her blessing.

I raise the ruby ring to my lips, dismissing Ishbel and Callum Douglas forever from my mind. Soon I shall be starting a new life in a new land, safe for always in the arms of Devlin Fordyke.